LITTLE HAVEN

FIVE NOVELS BY

MEREDITH O'REILLY, ADALINE RAINE, ALEX REYNOLDS, SUMMER GRAYSTONE, AND NORMANDIE ALLEMAN

Published by Stormy Night Publications and Design, LLC.
www.StormyNightPublications.com

O'Reilly, Meredith

Raine, Adaline

Reynolds, Alex

Graystone, Summer

Alleman, Normandie

Little Haven

Cover Design by Korey Mae Johnson

Images by Bigstock/Julenochek, Bigstock/Alex Staroseltsev, and Bigstock/Karamysh

ISBN-13: 978-1512305838

ISBN-10: 1512305839

FOR AUDIENCES 18+ ONLY

This book is intended for adults only. Spanking and other sexual activities represented in this book are fantasies only, intended for adults.

Daddy's Little Angela

Alex Reynolds

CHAPTER ONE

Angela Locke lay on the carpet in her living room, idly flipping through one of Charlie's design magazines. She didn't really bother to read any of the articles, but she liked to look at the pictures of the houses and imagine what kind of people lived there. She turned to an image of a sleek, modern house that was obviously located somewhere warm, given the landscape of succulents that surrounded it. She started to think about who might want to live there and what kind of life they lived when she heard the sound of the dishwasher clicking shut come from the kitchen.

Angela pretended that she didn't notice this, or the sound of Charlie walking across the tile kitchen floor, his footsteps becoming softer as he crossed over onto the carpet, approaching her. She hoped she was giving off an air of nonchalance, but in reality, her heart was beating quickly in her chest.

Charlie stopped walking and stood a few feet away from Angela. She knew he was waiting for her to notice him, but she intentionally pretended that she didn't. After a moment of uncomfortable silence, Charlie finally spoke.

"Angela, I know you know what time it is," he told her. His voice sounded stern and serious, and it made Angela want to squirm a little.

She put the magazine down and sat up, glancing at her watch. "Oh," she muttered. "I guess it is getting kind of late."

She looked up at her husband. He was standing with his arms crossed, and a serious expression on his face. Despite the nervousness growing in the pit of her stomach, she couldn't help but mentally note how handsome he looked as he stood there. She shivered a little bit.

"It's 11:05," Charlie said. "that means it's past your bedtime already. Get upstairs, get undressed, and wait for me."

Wait for me had a very specific meaning for Angela, and she couldn't shake the words from her mind as she put her husband's magazine away on the coffee table and silently headed upstairs. She found herself fidgeting as she walked up the stairs, and she twirled the ends of her blond hair around her finger, taking comfort in the softness.

Angela walked into their bedroom and flopped down on the bed. She lay there on her stomach for a moment, sulking. She was in trouble again. *It seems like this always happens,* she thought with a deep sigh. *I can never get it right.*

Angela and Charlie had moved into their comfy, cottage-style house about two years ago. Twenty-six-year-old Angela was a California native, and as much as she liked their house and as glad that she was that Charlie had gotten such a wonderful job at a very respected firm, she found the cold, whipping wind of the Midwestern winter impossible to deal with. She had been so excited the first time she had watched snow blanket the town, but that excitement had turned to dread as she had realized just how long the winter was.

Now, in the middle of her second one here, she had found herself getting grumpy easily. She dreaded getting up in the morning and feeling the cold air hit her as she exited the nest of blankets. She felt less patience, like every little thing wore down on her and made her irritable.

The sound of her husband walking up the stairs made her bolt upright, ripped right out of her thoughts. She was instantly on her feet, her hand instinctively going for the button on her jeans. She started to shimmy out of them, trying her best to quickly get the tight material over her round bottom and down her legs. She was hopping on one foot, doing her best to shake the jeans off when the bedroom door opened.

Charlie was standing in front of her with a small, wooden paddle in his hands and a look of bemused disapproval on his face.

"Having trouble, baby?" he asked, his words sounding sweet and loving.

Charlie's gentle tone made Angela melt inside a little bit. A moment ago, she had felt frustrated and grumpy, but when Charlie spoke to her that way, she felt like a very young girl who knew her daddy would take care of her. Her worries and her crankiness washed away.

She looked down at the puddle of her half-removed jeans and nodded, biting her lip. "Can you help me, daddy?" she asked.

Charlie set the paddle down on the bed and steadied Angela, letting her slip her legs out of her jeans. He reached down and picked them up, then folded them neatly and set them aside.

"Arms up," he then instructed, and Angela immediately lifted her arms above her head. Charlie grasped her light blue sweater and pulled it over her head, revealing a pale pink undershirt beneath. The ritual of being undressed this way made her feel secure, even though she knew exactly what was coming next.

Charlie removed Angela's undershirt, revealing her breasts; she wasn't wearing a bra. Although they kept the house fairly warm, the air still made her nipples perk up, and the feeling of them hardening gave her a rush of arousal.

Now that she was only wearing a pair of soft, light pink panties, Angela

felt the desire to cover herself, although she did her best to keep her hands at her sides. It seemed silly to her that she felt embarrassed to be stripped in front of her husband, who saw her naked on a regular basis, and who knew her body more intimately than anyone else ever had, but she couldn't help herself. In the context of being punished, her nudity always made her blush a little.

"If I send you to your room, what are you supposed to do, Angela?" Charlie asked her, placing his hands steadily on her hips.

Angela looked down, biting her lip. "I'm supposed to get undressed, sit on the bed, and wait for you," she said. She took a deep sigh, then added, "And think about why I'm going to be punished."

"What were you doing instead?" Charlie wanted to know, his voice still loving, but with an undercurrent of sternness. This wasn't play time.

"I was just thinking about things," Angela mumbled back, her hand toying with the edge of her panties.

"What things were you thinking about?" her husband asked.

"I guess just the reasons why I've been out of sorts recently," she admitted.

Charlie sat down on the bed, leading Angela over to him, then he positioned her so that she was standing in front of him. "Are you going to share those reasons, little girl?"

"I guess, I've just been cold," was the best way that Angela could come up with to describe what she had been thinking.

Charlie's face looked entertained by this. "You've been cold? I can certainly help warm you up," he teased.

Angela pouted. "I'm serious, though. I just want better weather. When I wake up in the morning, and I know it's going to be ice cold out there, I don't want to get out of bed! And when I have to, then I get grumpy and that's why…" She trailed off, looking down at the floor.

"That's why you're rude to people in our community?" Charlie asked. For the first time in the conversation, his voice had lost its affectionate edge. It sounded firm and foreboding. Angela felt a shiver that certainly wasn't from the temperature.

"Daddy, I didn't mean to be rude," she protested, squirming a little bit as she thought about her situation. She was standing in front of him wearing nothing but a small pair of panties and he had a paddle next to him on the bed. His tone said that she was in serious trouble. Despite all this, she could feel the gusset of her panties growing wet as he spoke to her, and her nipples hardening even more than they already were.

Charlie shook his head. "Honey, I don't see how you could have thought that your behavior today was anything but rude."

"I was just teasing her, that's what girls do to each other! I thought it was funny," she insisted. She knew that she wasn't fully telling the truth here; she

had been aware while she was in the store that she wasn't exactly being nice.

She had run into Morgan, a girl who lived a couple of blocks away from her, while she was in the shopping center just outside of the community where she and her husband lived. While there was a small store within the gates of Little Haven, Angela almost always shopped in what she thought of as 'the outside world.'

Angela and Charlie lived in what looked like, from the street, a normal, gated community. It had rows of houses, all with their own charm but within a unified style, and it had its own little parks and community center, but Little Haven was different than the other developments that dotted the Minnesota landscape. Unlike 'The Oaks' or 'Waterford Village,' those who were interested in dwelling in Little Haven had to complete a complicated application. Specifically, they had to describe the ways in which they participated in age play: it was a community designed around giving a safe space for those who shared this interest to fully embrace their lifestyle.

Angela and Charlie had decided to apply to live in Little Haven after Charlie had gotten hired at the firm where he now worked. They had gone to a convention for age players back in California, where they had heard about the community. Angela would never have wanted to leave her home state, but the chance for her husband to grow his career this much had been worth the move.

It had taken a lot of adjusting to get used to having to call her husband 'daddy' not only in the privacy of her own home, but in public, too, and to lose privacy about other things as well. She remembered how much she had cringed the first time she was threatened with a spanking while they were out in public! But as Angela got to know the people in her little town, and she made friends with other 'girls her age' who identified as teenagers, although their real-life ages varied quite a bit, she sometimes felt a little bit too comfortable.

By venturing out into 'the outside world' for errands, Angela brought a little bit of the thrill back into age playing. So, when she had seen Morgan in the store, she had figured that it would be fun and exciting to poke at her a little bit.

"Would you say that Morgan is your friend?" her daddy asked her.

Angela knew the answer to this, but didn't want to admit it. "Kinda?" she tried.

"I would say she is not," Charlie told her. "Actually," he corrected, "I would say that you are not her friend. I think that Morgan would be happy to spend time playing with you *if only you were nicer to her.*" Charlie emphasized the last few words very sternly.

Angela felt a little bit ashamed when she was told this. She didn't feel the exciting tingly feeling of being about to be spanked that she had been focusing on earlier; that had been replaced with a truly bad feeling in her

tummy because she knew that her daddy was right.

"What did you say to Morgan?" Charlie asked, using one finger to lift her head and force her to make eye contact.

Angela wished that she could escape his disappointed gaze, but she couldn't. She looked deep into his dark eyes as her heart pounded against her chest.

"I just asked if she was allowed out of the house without a babysitter," Angela whispered.

Charlie nodded. "And then you laughed at her," he added.

Angela gave her own nervous little nod.

"You know that you weren't just playing around. You know what your tone was. You were making fun of her, weren't you?" Charlie scolded, carefully articulating each word.

Angela felt like she was about to cry, but she sucked it in. She was going to be a big girl about this. "Yes, sir," she managed to get out.

And with that, her daddy reached forward and pulled her over his lap. He positioned her so that she was supported by the bed. His efforts to make sure they were both relatively comfortable while he spanked her meant one thing—that her punishment wasn't going to be quick. She grabbed one of the gray cushions from the head of the bed and clutched it to her chest.

Charlie responded by reaching to the other side of the bed to grab Angela's stuffed tiger and handing it to her. Angela squeezed her plush companion close to her with gratitude.

"You think you're such a big girl, but here you are, over your daddy's lap, cuddling your little stuffie as you're about to get your bottom spanked. Do you feel so grown up now, Angela?" Charlie chastised.

Angela hid her face. "No, sir," she whispered.

"My little girl is going to get spanked now," her daddy announced, tugging her panties down to her knees.

Angela did her best not to squirm as Charlie raised his hand and brought it down hard on her bottom. No matter how many times she had been spanked, the first smack always startled her, as if she had forgotten just how much a spanking hurt. It even happened if she had just been spanked the day before. After a moment, obviously to let it sink in, Charlie gave her another swat, this one even harder. Angela gasped.

He gave her a few more well-placed, carefully timed smacks like this, and Angela grunted and whined after each one. They were hard and slow, and each one stood out from the one before it and after it, not letting her fall into the rhythm of the spanking.

Soon, though, Charlie began to pick up the pace and was peppering her bottom with smacks. Angela felt the heat growing and building and she began to struggle a little bit, twisting her hips away from the punishing swats and tightening her grip on her tiger.

"Don't fight me, young lady," Charlie scolded. "You know that you were a naughty little girl, and that in this household, misbehaving girls end up with very sore, red bottoms."

Charlie's words were punctuated by a series of hard slaps, and Angela tried her best to be still. She couldn't help but cry out, though, as her daddy's strong hand visited her bottom again and again, with no end in sight.

"I'm sorry!" Angela finally cried out, unable to keep quiet and wanting something to do with her voice besides just shriek and wail.

"I hope you are," Charlie said. "I hope you're sorry that you hurt someone's feelings. I hope you're sorry that you embarrassed me with the way you behaved today. I hope you're thinking about how to be a truly well-behaved girl in the future."

The words stung more than the hard smacks and Angela sniffled. "I promise I'm going to be good! I'll be nice and polite and friendly!" she howled.

At first, Charlie's only response was to continue with the steady rhythm of the spanking, but after a moment, he stopped.

Angela felt a mixture of relief that she wasn't being spanked at that moment and a deep, tingling fear—she knew that the paddle was sitting within her daddy's reach. She took a couple of deep breaths.

"Angela, I'm tired of you acting like you're better than the other girls here. We moved here to be part of a community, and you do that by making friends and getting along with others, not by holding your nose in the air and acting snooty. It doesn't make people think well of you."

"Yes, daddy," was all that Angela could whimper.

"I won't have any more of this, for any reason. If I ever hear about you acting this way again, I will go out and buy a cane."

Angela gasped, her body going rigid as if she had just been given a particularly powerful smack. She knew that some girls in the community got the cane every now and then, but it had never even occurred to her that she would be in for it! She certainly was able to take a fairly hard spanking, but the mystery surrounding an implement that she was unfamiliar with, and one that was rumored to be one of the most severe, left Angela without any feeling of bravery.

"Daddy, no!" she cried. "Please don't!"

"If you make me, I'll get a cane and I'll punish you with it. And don't think that will be all that I'll do to you. I'm warning you now, Angela, you need to be on your best behavior."

Charlie's mysterious threat left room for Angela's mind to wander. Would he plug up her bottom? Give her an enema? Spank her pussy? She ran through a list of as many humiliating and painful punishments as she could think of. As much as she dreaded the idea of being in big trouble and needing to be punished so thoroughly that her daddy thought it would be necessary

to buy a cane just for the occasion, Angela felt herself growing wet between her legs, and she had to try hard to keep from grinding against Charlie's knee.

"I promise, I'm going to be good!" she insisted.

Charlie responded by reaching behind him again. Angela knew what he was grabbing, and she braced herself, tightening her muscles to prepare for the impact.

"Relax," Charlie ordered.

Angela took a deep breath and willed herself to untighten.

"Good girl," her daddy praised her.

Angela beamed: those words made her whole body feel warm, in a good way.

She didn't get to bask in the feeling long, though. Charlie lifted the paddle and brought it down hard against her bare, defenseless bottom with a resounding crack.

Angela yelped. "Owwwwwwwww!" The small paddle was dense and carried a lot of weight, and the small size made all the pain concentrate in one spot. Angela could feel the smacked area pulsing hotter than the rest of her bottom, and she imagined that it had to look like a raised welt based on how it felt. It stung and bit and burned.

There was another swat. Angela bucked forward, starting to kick her feet, as if her rapid movement would make the pain dissipate.

"Daaaaaadddddyyyy, I'm going to be good! I'm sorry!" she wailed.

Charlie's only response was another hard smack, followed immediately by another, and then another.

Angela couldn't help herself anymore: the pulsing, burning heat in her bottom made her twist around and, letting go of her tiger for a moment, she threw her hand back, hoping that she would be able to rub some of the sting away.

Charlie caught Angela's stray hand before it even landed, though. He grabbed it by the wrist and held it against the small of her back, using his elbow to keep her whole upper body pushed down.

"That's not being good," he scolded her. He punctuated his words with a pair of sharp swats to her sit spots.

Angela secretly loved it when her daddy pinned her arm like this. It made her feel like her last fragments of control had been taken away from her and she was truly helpless. She was strong and athletic, but under her daddy's firm grip, she found herself feeling weak and powerless, and the feeling made her pussy throb with arousal.

"I belong to you, don't I?" Angela whispered, breaking the flow of Charlie's harsh scolding.

It didn't stop him from spanking her, or slow his pace. "Of course you do," he reminded her, "you're my little girl."

Angela felt her pussy tighten with arousal.

"That's why I have to discipline you, isn't it?" he asked.

"Yes, daddy," she moaned. Angela felt overwhelmed with the combination of the soreness in her bottom and the wetness in her pussy. Her daddy's scolding no longer felt harsh, and Angela no longer felt ashamed. Instead, despite the hard, punishing swats that Charlie continued to rain down, Angela writhed over his lap.

"Alright, little girl," Charlie finally said. "I think you've been spanked almost enough."

Angela wasn't sure if she felt relieved or disappointed at this point, but she nodded her head vigorously anyway.

"I'm going to give you twelve more with the paddle, and then your punishment will be complete," her daddy told her.

Angela braced herself; she knew that the last few swats were always the hardest. And she was right. The first of the twelve bit into her with such a searing heat that she cried out desperately. The second stroke was no softer, and she reached for the cushion again, worrying that she was squeezing too hard and might damage her precious tiger. The third and fourth came in quick succession, and she bit the pillow to keep herself from crying out.

Eventually, she stopped being able to focus on counting and just trusted that Charlie would stop when he was supposed to, as each additional stroke of the paddle overloaded her senses. Then, finally, he did stop.

Angela felt Charlie's hand return to her bottom, this time rubbing gentle circles on her burning skin. Angela took a moment to catch her breath and to enjoy the glowing feeling that came when a spanking was over.

"Come here, baby," Charlie coaxed, pulling his little girl up into his lap.

Angela did as she was told and climbed up into his arms, resting her head on his shoulder and leaning back so her weight wasn't on her bottom. Charlie continued to stroke her sore, bright red bottom as he cradled her in his arms.

"I hope you know that I meant everything I said, little one," Charlie reminded her. "This behavior is going to stop."

Angela nodded, only giving half of her attention to her husband's words. Instead, she was focused on the feeling of warmth that flooded both her bottom and her pussy. She reached between her legs and could feel the wetness there with just a light touch.

Charlie obviously noticed her doing this. "Are your pretty little girl parts all wet, honey?" he asked, half teasing.

Angela blushed. "Yes, daddy," she told him, looking away while she said it. That babyish language for talking about her sex made her feel squirmingly embarrassed, but it also made her wetness problem even worse.

"Don't be embarrassed, sweetie," Charlie told her, "it's quite normal for little girls to get aroused when they're punished."

Charlie had told Angela this hundreds of times, but every time he did, it sparked something that made her desperately horny. The idea that she was

just one little girl of many who were punished this way, and that her spankings and accompanying need for sexual attention were normal, almost par for the course, made her oldest fantasies feel real.

That was a big part of why she loved Little Haven: what she was imagining was true. Surely she was not the only girl in the town who had found herself bare bottomed over her daddy's strong lap getting her round little bottom turned bright red. And surely she was not the only who had ended her punishment with a soaking wet pussy and a desperate desire to be fucked.

"Daddy," Angela begged, "won't you touch me there and make me feel nice?"

"You want me to make you come?" Charlie asked.

Angela nodded.

"You know that my doing this doesn't mean that the punishment wasn't serious, don't you?" Charlie confirmed.

Angela was disinterested by this. "Yes, of course I know, daddy," she told him.

Charlie frowned just a little, but then lifted his little girl off his lap and set her down on the bed.

Angela let out a little moan as her punished bottom touched the sheets, reminding her just how much it still stung. She leaned back on the bed, wantonly spreading her legs and showing off her pussy, which was pink with desire.

Charlie leaned close to her and gently placed his hand where she wanted it to be.

Angela let out a coo as he did, and found herself starting to grind against him. She was relieved when Charlie's fingers found her clit and began to rub it in little circles.

First, his touch was gentle and teasing, but it soon became stronger and faster, and Angela found herself starting to let out a long, continuous moan, her voice trembling when his touch was exactly what she wanted.

Charlie smiled and slipped a finger from his other hand into her pussy. Her muscles tightened around it as he continued to fondle her clit. Soon, he slipped a second in, then began to work both of them back and forth.

Angela's body was blown away by pleasure, and she convulsed and writhed, continuing to moan and whimper.

"Oh, please, please," she mouthed, her body growing hot from her horniness, beads of sweat starting to form on her forehead.

She thought about the spanking she had just had, about Charlie catching her arm and holding it firmly behind her back, and about the soreness the paddle had brought. She thought about his threat to punish her more severely in the future. She imagined the feeling of the cane leaving stripes against her bottom, of touching the welts afterwards and how they would feel.

It was with that thought that she felt the little spasms in her legs that told

CHAPTER TWO

Charlie looked at Angela as she lay on the bed, naked and exhausted from the orgasm he had just given her and the spanking that had come before it. Her tan skin glistened with sweat, making Charlie smile to himself. *Not too cold anymore,* he thought. Her blond hair, which was usually carefully styled, now lay as a mess. Charlie thought that she looked just as pretty this way, with her makeup smearing on her face and her hair disheveled. He sometimes wished that she could see that it wasn't all her careful grooming that made her pretty: it was just her.

Even though he had been truly unhappy to hear of Angela's behavior today, he certainly would be lying if he said that he hadn't looked forward to punishing his little girl tonight. It had been a while since he'd had her across his lap, or at least it felt that way.

"Turn over," he commanded her, and Angela did exactly as he said. She rolled onto her belly, showing off her bottom, which was still glowing bright red. Charlie reached out and grabbed one of her cheeks, pinching it and squeezing it between his fingers.

"Owwww!" she whined as he did. "That makes it hurt more."

"I know," he told her, a wicked smile crossing his face. "It makes me want to spank you again," he admitted.

Angela pouted. "No more spanking, daddy!" she whined.

Charlie chuckled. "I'll spank you again if I want to, young lady. You know perfectly well who makes the rules in this household. But luckily for you, I have other thoughts on my mind right now."

He wasn't kidding. He had been hard since the spanking started, and as he was fingering her he had felt her slippery wetness. He wanted his cock in her, now.

So, he stood up and unzipped his pants. He thought about just pulling his cock out and shoving it into her tight, pink pussy, but he controlled himself long enough to start unbuttoning his shirt. He knew Angela liked the intimacy of skin on skin, and that she enjoyed the shape of his muscular, naked form

16

as much as he liked looking at every inch of her body.

He quickly undressed, not wanting to wait any longer, then climbed back up onto the bed. "What do you think is going to happen now, my darling?" he growled into Angela's ear.

"I dunno," Angela replied teasingly.

"I think you do know," he told her, gripping her by the waist and pulling her to all fours. He put a hand on her shoulders to push her upper body down, leaving her with her face against the bed and her red bottom high in the air. Charlie took a second to enjoy this view, stroking his hard cock, which was already dripping with pre-cum.

"You're gonna fuck me, daddy?" Angela asked, although it wasn't really a question.

Charlie's answer was to tap his cock against her pussy, which was shimmering with wetness from her earlier orgasm. He felt Angela's body twitch, the way he knew she did when she was excited.

"I'm going to fuck you right now, my darling," he told her, and then he entered her. He couldn't stifle the moan as he slipped into her, feeling how warm and soaking wet she was. She pushed her bottom back, driving his cock deeper into her body, then she gave a little shimmy back and forth.

"Oh, Angela," he whispered. "I've been wanting to fuck you all evening. I love having my cock in you."

"I do, too, daddy," she told him. "Please fuck me hard."

Charlie took her words seriously, and he pulled back and then quickly thrust into her. Just like he had spanked her, he started with a few slow, hard thrusts and enjoyed the sound of her moaning and whimpering with pleasure. Then he began to thrust more quickly, ramming his cock into her over and over again. He reached forward and grabbed her hair, lacing it between his fingers and giving her a firm tug. He loved to do this. He loved holding Angela in any way that signified his ownership over her, and despite her feisty attitude, he knew that she loved to feel herself under his command.

Angela wasn't being passive as she was taken, and she continued to work her hips back and forth, grinding and gyrating against his cock, which greatly increased his pleasure. He breathed deeply, every nerve in his body standing at attention as he listened to her sounds of enjoyment and looked down on her lovely little body.

Charlie let go of Angela's hair and grasped her thighs, guiding her back and forth as he penetrated her. By shoving her body backwards onto his cock, he was able to truly bury himself in her and make her take him all the way. As soon as he started doing this, her moans and whimpers started to once again turn to howls of pleasure, and he thought to himself that this was one of the advantages of where they lived: he didn't really mind if they woke the neighbors.

"Is my sweet little princess going to come for me again?" Charlie asked,

his own words making his cock throb and pulse. He knew that he wasn't far behind her.

"Yes, yes, yes, yes, yes," she repeated, as if the arousal had made her brain stick in a loop. "Yes, I'm going to come now," she finally managed to say.

Charlie grabbed her tighter, leaning down to whisper in her ear, "Think about who owns your body as you do, Angela."

As he continued to thrust hard and deep, he felt her muscles tense tighter and tighter, preparing for the release of orgasm. Then her breathing got faster and faster, until suddenly her quick little breaths exploded into a yelp of pleasure.

"Ohhhhh, daaaaaaaaaaaaaaaaaddddddyyyyyyyyy!" she practically yelled.

Charlie could feel her coming and could feel her shaking under his control. It aroused him so much that he could give her that kind of pleasure and make her scream that way. It only took a few more thrusts before he felt himself reaching a similar tipping point, his body preparing for the release he had been craving.

Angela began to move her hips in a circular motion as she rode the tail end of her orgasm, and that little change made everything feel that much better to Charlie. He groaned with satisfaction.

"Oh, baby," he growled, gritting his teeth as he felt himself about to come. He let go and collapsed onto her back, breathing heavily as he shot his load deep into her pussy. He stayed that was for a moment afterwards, panting.

Finally, he slipped out of her, enjoying the sight of his seed dripping out of her as he did. He got up from the bed for a moment to take a better look at what was in front of him.

His beautiful wife was still posed with her head down and her bottom up, and her bottom was still almost as red as it had been when he had finished punishing her, but her face wore an expression of blissful contentment and satisfaction. Her pussy looked swollen from all the attention, and it was soaked with the evidence of their mutual enjoyment.

Charlie had a hard time keeping himself from smiling smugly. He wasn't sure why he deserved to be so lucky.

CHAPTER THREE

Angela woke up the next morning feeling unsure why she still felt so tired. She was reminded quite quickly when she rolled over, and her still sore bottom made contact with the sheets. It wasn't bad enough to make her jump or yelp, but she felt a dull, achy pain when she put weight on her bottom.

Although she thought about the cold that was waiting for her outside of the cocoon of covers that she had made, she took a deep breath and climbed out. She found that, when she was standing in the middle of the room fully naked, it was not so cold. Maybe the weather was warming. She silently hoped this was the case, and hopped off to take a shower.

Charlie had already left for work by the time that Angela woke up, as was usual. He had a bit of a commute to the city from Little Haven, and had to leave fairly early. Angela was between jobs at the moment. She had studied graphic design in school and had previously worked for a studio not far from where she lived, but the whole company had gone out of business, leaving Angela unemployed. Charlie's job earned more than enough money to pay for their expenses, but Angela often felt stressed by her unemployment. She wanted to prove herself as a 'real adult' because of the lifestyle that she lived, and not having a job to take pride in really affected her ability to do that.

After drying herself off and doing the rest of her personal care routine in the bathroom, she padded back down the hallway to her bedroom to get dressed. She put on a pair of conservatively cut, white cotton panties and a push-up bra, giving herself the illusion of cleavage. She paused before pulling on some jeans to twist around in front of the full-length mirror: she wanted to take a peek at her butt.

It was a faint pink color this morning; the scarlet hue that she had been wearing last night had vanished overnight. Angela still thought that the pink flush looked cute peeking out from under her panties. They were what her daddy called 'good girl panties.' The kind of underwear that a good, modest young girl would wear, instead of the slightly racy things she sometimes liked to push the line with. She had a feeling that she needed to be a good girl

19

today. She was still sore, after all.

She added an undershirt and a sweater and headed downstairs for a quick bite to eat before settling in front of her computer. She started the tedious, daily task of looking for jobs to apply to, sifting through listing after listing and leaving the promising ones open in a series of tabs.

She got bored and frustrated pretty shortly, so she signed into her instant messaging program under her age play screen name: *brattyteenangela*. She had several Internet friends who had originally been the only people she could talk to about these things. Now that she lived in the community, she also added her local friends to this account, so they would know when she was in the mood to talk to them as her younger self.

Honestly, Angela found that she felt like a teen more often than she didn't. Instead of the feeling that she was play-acting that she had the first time they had role-played daddy and little girl, she felt more like she was putting on a face when she went into the outside world as an adult. She felt like a fourteen-year-old girl who was overly capable at certain things. Perhaps that was why she always got stuck babysitting, she thought, as she saw Claire's screen name sign onto the messaging system. She snickered to herself for a moment, wondering how a little as young as Claire even managed to use the Internet. *Girls that age aren't allowed on the computer without supervision*, she thought to herself with a wicked smile.

Claire was another girl who lived in Little Haven. Angela didn't really know her; they had met a couple of times, but she wasn't one of her friends. Claire was so shy and withdrawn, and while Angela didn't know much about her as an age player, she could tell that she played at a particularly young age, especially compared to Angela and her friends. Her daddy and Charlie were planning to go out tonight and had decided that it would be fun for Angela to babysit Claire.

Angela sometimes did babysit the other girls in the community. It could be fun sometimes, especially in the summer when they could run around in the yard. Besides, she liked having some authority once in a while. She even sometimes fantasized about spanking the girls that she looked after herself, lifting the skirts of their babyish little dresses and pulling down their Barbie-doll panties before turning them over her lap for a good, hard punishment, but Charlie had made it clear long ago that this was forbidden. Especially with his threat hanging in the air, she didn't want to take any risks, so she abandoned that train of thought.

Angela didn't feel like chatting with Claire, so she started a conversation with Liz, a friend who lived in Texas. She had gotten to know her over an age play forum and had never actually met her in person, but she was a trusted confidante.

Angela typed, the words appearing on the screen in pink font on a baby blue background.

Hey, how are things?

Having custom fonts online had stopped being cool ages ago, but Angela clung to things that she remembered from her teenage years, or her 'first teenage years' as she liked to think of them.

Liz replied almost instantly.

Life is good. Staying out of trouble?

Angela quickly typed back.

Nah, never. I'm sitting on a sore bottom as we speak.

Angela began to tell Liz about everything which had happened last night, and Liz had asked lots of questions about the spanking Angela had received, although she got quite giggly when Angela started to talk about the sexy parts.

Right when they were getting to the best part of the story, another tab on the messaging program started to flash, signifying the start of a new conversation. It was with Charlie.

Shit, Angela thought before she even clicked on it to read it. *I forgot to go on invisible.*

The plain black font seemed to emphasize the sternness of Charlie's words:

Angela, you know perfectly well that you are strictly forbidden from using messenger when you're supposed to be working on applying for jobs. You can chat once your work is done, not during.

Sorrrrryyyyyy, daddy. I'll sign out now and get back to work.

I think you need something to focus your mind on what you should be doing. I would have thought that a sore bottom would be enough, but it apparently isn't. Let's see if having something in your bottom hole does the trick.

Angela's face grew ashen as she read the words and her heart rate sped up. Anal play was something that had been newly introduced, and Angela found it far too embarrassing to cope with. The feeling of her daddy spreading her cheeks and then inserting one lubed finger into her bottom hole made her face burn with humiliation, and the stretching feeling of fullness that the plug that followed caused was truly uncomfortable, at least at first.

The idea that she would have to insert the plug herself was mortifying.

She wasn't sure she could even do it. She squirmed in her seat uncomfortably, unsure of what to do.

Finally, she typed back, adding an emoticon in an attempt to signify her displeasure at the idea:

Yes, daddy >_<

Go upstairs and get your purple plug and the lube and then come back and wait for my instructions.

Angela considered disobeying, but she didn't want to get caught not following through with a punishment, even though she wasn't sure how he was going to find out whether or not she did what she was told. Still, her daddy could be tricky sometimes, and she knew it was best to just obey.

Yes, sir.

She typed '*brb*' in her other conversation window and then headed upstairs.

In her bedroom, Angela opened the top drawer of Charlie's dresser, where most of the toys were kept. The drawer was a strange mix of things. There were things that Angela loved and constantly desired to have used, like the fuzzy glove used to rub her bottom after a spanking and, of course, her vibrators. There were also plenty of things that made Angela's body tighten with nervousness, like the butt plug that she had been sent for. She found it and the lubricant, and then shut the drawer and hurried downstairs.

I have them, daddy.

Good girl. Tell your friends that you're chatting to that you're going to have to go because you're being punished for being a naughty girl and disobeying your daddy, and that you aren't supposed to be online during the day.

With no one present to prevent her from doing so, Angela stomped her foot. She didn't want to tell Liz that she was in trouble *again*. Liz could be even feistier than Angela, and she thought that she might get teased.

Angela typed a quick message to Liz:

Ugh. I have to go because I got in trouble by my daddy for being online during the day when I'm supposed to be applying for jobs.

Liz's message came moments later:

Sucks to suck. You probably deserve it, always breaking all the rules.

Angela wrote back quickly, then closed the window:

You're one to talk! Bye for now!

Then she typed to her daddy:

Ok, I told her.

Good. Now stand up and pull down your pants and panties.

Angela slowly stood up and did as she was told, butterflies growing in her stomach as she did.

Ok, I did.

Charlie's message appeared in moments:

Now set the plug in front of you and think about where it's going to go, and the fact that you're going to put it there. If you can disobey me when I'm not around, you can be punished when I'm not, either.

Heat grew on Angela's face as she set the purple butt plug on the table in front of her. Even if she hadn't been instructed to think about it and contemplate what was going to happen next, she wouldn't have been able to do anything else. It looked so big, the widest part seeming so flared to her, even though she knew it was one of the smaller plugs that was available at the store where they purchased it.

Once, when she had gone over to her friend Becca's house on the other side of Little Haven, she had opened up their medicine cabinet in search of dental floss. There, she had seen a couple of Becca's butt plugs, all lined up and waiting until they had to be used next. She had been so taken aback by seeing them, but also by how much bigger they were than the ones that Charlie had purchased for her. They still weren't huge, but Angela found it somehow even more embarrassing to know that her friend could take a much bigger plug than she could. She didn't like feeling inexperienced.

A message from Charlie showed up in the conversation window:

Have you been thinking about it?

Yes, daddy.

I'm glad. Now I want you to go get your phone. Text me when you have it.

Angela panicked a little bit. What was he going to do? Was he going to call her and walk her through putting the plug in, so he could hear her whimpers and sighs? He was at work, though. Surely he couldn't do that.

Still, Angela went and found her phone, which was covered in a pale lilac case with white polka dots. She sat down on the chair at her computer desk and texted him that she was ready for whatever he wanted her to do next.

Within a few seconds, her phone vibrated again.

Get the phone stand.

Not sure why, Angela rummaged through her desk drawer until she found the small stand that she used to prop up her phone when she was using it to video-call someone. Then she texted Charlie, her thumb moving quickly across the screen.

Ok, I have it.

He wrote back a moment later:

Set your phone on it and put the camera on self-timer, then spread your cheeks and take a photo of where that plug is going to go and send it to me.

Angela felt the butterflies in her stomach increasing, and looked around to see if anyone could see her out the window. No one was around, of course, but the snow was softly falling outside again, and that little motion gave her the feeling of being watched, so she got up and closed the blinds. She opened her phone's camera and set it up like she had been told to, then, taking a deep breath to gather courage, she posed herself in front of it.

Charlie sometimes asked Angela to take naughty photos for him, especially when he had to go to a convention or when Angela was visiting her family in California. He also sometimes embarrassed her by ordering her into the pose she was about to adopt, with her cheeks spread and her most private area on full display. She had never been photographed this way before, though, and she had certainly never taken the picture herself.

It took another few seconds to build up the courage to set the self-timer and then get into the humiliating pose, grabbing her fleshy cheeks and pulling them to the sides. Even though no one was watching, her face burned as she stood there on display.

The worst part was when she had finished taking the picture and had to send it to her daddy, though: this meant that she had to look at it. Angela rarely ever saw herself when she was in such a humiliating position, and the

24

image on the screen showed a part of her body that most people would never see. She had done a good job of spreading her cheeks apart, and her tight, puffy bottom hole was well displayed. Looking at it for just a moment made Angela want to cover her face with her hands, but she managed to send the snapshot to Charlie.

After a moment, he wrote back:

Well done. Now set it for a longer timer, lube up your finger, and warm yourself up. Make sure you get a good clear shot of your finger in your tight little hole.

Angela knew that her bottom hole needed to get used to being filled before it could fit the plug, but she hadn't really thought about how that was going to happen. Her daddy always did this process for her, and it hadn't ever occurred to her just how humiliating it was to have to finger her own bottom. She obviously masturbated, and not infrequently, but she had always left anal play up to her partner, and the change made it somehow feel more shameful to her.

Please, daddy, can't you just do this when you get home?

No, darling. I told you before: if you disobey me when I'm not there to watch you, you can be punished that way, too.

Angela pouted for a moment, but accepted that her fate was inevitable. No matter how much it embarrassed her, she was going to have to take these photos for Charlie. She set the camera up with the timer waiting for a minute, then bent over the back of her chair. Just being in this position, with her bottom high and vulnerable and her legs apart made her blush, usually, and presenting herself to the camera made it really feel like a punishment.

As was always the case in these situations, Angela felt herself growing wet between her legs. She wished she could be slipping her finger into that hole instead of what she was about to do. Still, she grabbed the lubricant anyway, and applied a generous amount to her finger. Spreading her cheeks with her free hand, she rubbed a dab of it onto the outside of her hole, just like her daddy would have done if he was there. The lube always felt so cold, and the wet, slippery texture signaled to her what, exactly, was going to happen next. Then, taking a deep breath in first, she started to tease her finger against the tight entry.

"Relax," she said aloud to herself, doing some deep breathing. She did, and she carefully worked her finger in. She began to work it back and forth, just like Charlie would have done to prepare her for the plug. The feeling was not unpleasant, and she felt herself growing more aroused as she did it, but when she heard the timer on the camera start to count down to the shutter,

her muscles involuntarily tightened around her finger with shame.

Click, went the shutter. Angela continued to move her finger in her tight hole to loosen it up and get it ready for the plug, helping herself to relax by reaching her other hand around to stroke her clit while she did so. It was effective, and as she grew wetter and wetter, she was able to move the finger in her bottom hole more comfortably. It felt slick and glossy. She knew she was ready for the plug.

Angela slipped her finger out and quickly wiped her hands off with a paper towel from her desk before sending the photo to Charlie.

I'm ready for the plug, daddy.

Charlie's response came moments later:

That's a very good little girl. Put it all the way in and take a photo. You'll wear it until I get home, and any time that I ask for one, you'll send me another picture, understood?

Angela groaned at these instructions, but typed her agreement to them. As Charlie had probably figured out, Angela sometimes cheated at her punishments if she had any control over them, so by asking for photos like this he was guaranteeing that she was going to continue to have the uncomfortable little plug in her bottom until he returned.

Angela again set the camera up, then lubed the plug up well. As she stroked the soft surface of it, she thought nervously about how wide the biggest part was. She knew exactly how it felt as her bottom hole stretched to take it, and she shuddered a little.

Finally, she bent over and pressed the pointed end of the plug against her tight opening. With all the lube and preparation, it only took a moment for her to start sliding it in. The first bit went in easily, but as it began to flare out, Angela had to concentrate on relaxing. It was so much harder to push it in herself than to feel the helpless sensation of her daddy sliding the intruder up her little shaft. She managed to get closer to the biggest part, and, once again, in order to relax herself, began to stroke her clit.

Angela claimed that she hated the feeling of having the plug in, especially when it stretched like this and made her feel so full, but when she truly admitted it to herself, it made her incredibly aroused. She couldn't wait until she had the plug fully inserted so she could masturbate properly.

As she pushed the plug further, she felt things start to feel particularly uncomfortable, but her arousal allowed her to keep going, letting it work its way further and further into her bottom. Finally, the stretching, full feeling reached its apex, and Angela let out a little yelp before her final push cleared the widest part, allowing her muscles to clamp down on the neck.

Feeling well stuffed with the plug, she carefully finished pushing it in, so that the base was pressed right against the outside of her anus. The base was a little bit wide, and it kept her cheeks just slightly apart. She knew, though, that the camera would start counting down soon, so after taking a second to catch her breath, she reached back and spread herself again, so that in the photo the full insertion of the butt plug would be visible. Doing this made her muscles twitch again, contracting against the neck and giving her another wave of arousal.

After the camera clicked its shutter, Angela got up. She found it hard to walk with the butt plug in; each motion made it slip and slide a little bit inside her, and made it very obvious that it was there. She gently shuffled across the room to the bathroom, where she washed the lube off her hands before she went back to send the final, disgraceful picture to her daddy.

Charlie was obviously pleased with her work, and reminded her that she was to leave the plug in her bottom no matter what she was doing for the rest of the day.

Angela knew that she was supposed to be getting back to work now, but the process of inserting this herself had made her so horny that she decided that she could get away with taking a couple of minutes of 'alone time,' as Charlie called it when she touched herself.

She lay back on the sofa, letting her weight press down on the plug. She felt it push itself back into position, having wiggled a bit when she was walking, and the fullness was delightful this time. Angela gently inserted one of her fingers into her very wet pussy, enjoying the feeling of having both of her holes filled at once.

She wondered how it would feel to be fucked while wearing the plug, the feeling of Charlie's stiff cock on the other side of the silicone toy. She imagined this as she began to pull her fingers back and forth, swirling them around a bit to try to stimulate the feeling of the plug a bit.

The idea of her daddy fucking her while she wore the plug brought another idea into her head, one that both sparked passion and terrified Angela. She imagined how it would feel if Charlie was to fuck her in the ass. She thought about how he would go through the same process that she had just done, warming her little hole up for his cock, and how embarrassed she would feel knowing what was going to happen next. She thought about how it would feel as his hard member gently probed at her entrance, and then the slick, sudden, filling feeling of his insertion into her.

She imagined how helpless she would feel as he held her tightly in place to fuck her this way, every part of her body truly owned by him as he penetrated her, hard. She imagined how it would make her wail and cry out, how it would surely hurt, and how he wouldn't stop, and would go hard and deep to really drive his point home: she belonged to him and he was totally and entirely entitled to her body.

She had begun to circle her clit with her fingers, going faster and faster as the thoughts of her fantasy got more and more clear. Suddenly, and a bit without warning, she found the perfect rhythm and felt her body grow warmer, her muscles tightening, blood rushing to her head, her face growing hot. Then orgasm ripped through her body, making her clench hard against the plug. This sudden reminder of its presence made her orgasm continue, blending into another, and then another as she wailed and cried on the sofa, her legs sticking straight out.

CHAPTER FOUR

Charlie arrived home from work a little bit early that day. He hadn't been having a particularly productive day in the office, as he was rather distracted by providing long-distance discipline to his naughty little girl. Four times throughout the rest of the day he had stopped work to request an updated photographic record of her disgraceful chastisement. Each time he had received a new picture of her spread, bare bottom with the purple plug penetrating her, he had grown instantly rock hard. It was difficult to concentrate on designing a strip mall after that.

So, he had decided to skip out on his last hour and head home, which meant that he got an early enough start to miss most of the traffic coming out of the city. The drive to Little Haven wasn't bad once you got out of the metropolitan area. The fields and the rest of the countryside were the prettiest in the spring, when Charlie appreciated how beautiful the greenery was, but he also enjoyed how everything looked blanketed in snow.

As he pulled into the gates of the community, he thought about the fact that his little girl was waiting for him at home after having spent the afternoon being punished, and he grew hard again, the desire for relief becoming almost painful. He parked the car in the driveway and walked to the house carefully, since more snow had fallen since he had shoveled this morning while Angela was still slumbering.

Entering the house, he found Angela at work on her computer like she was meant to be. Her desk was tucked away in an alcove in the living room near a window, and it provided her with a bright place to work that was both open but free of distraction. He noticed that she had shut the blinds and snickered to himself for a moment.

"Hi, princess," he said to her, tousling her hair. "Been a good girl since the last time I checked?"

Angela sprung to her feet, turning around to hug him with a bright smile on her face. "Daddy!" she practically sang.

Charlie gently stroked her face with his hand and smoothed her soft blond hair back down.

"Yes, I've been good! I got everything done that I wanted to and then some!" she bragged.

"Good girl!" Charlie praised. "That's really great. See what you can do when you have something to focus your mind?"

Angela smiled widely, beaming, then she stood up on her tiptoes so she could whisper in Charlie's ear. "Daddy," she asked, her voice hushed and shy, "can I have the plug out of my bottom now?"

Charlie grinned a wicked grin. "Not yet, my little princess. First, there's something that you need to do for daddy."

Angela blushed and looked away, twirling her hair around one finger. Charlie suspected that she could guess what he was about to say,

"Little angel, how did you feel today when I punished you? How did it make you feel to have to take those embarrassing photos?"

Angela looked at the floor. "Humiliated," she answered.

"What else?" asked Charlie.

"Well… like I wanted to be a good girl."

"That's all?" he insisted.

"It made my little girl parts wet," she finally whispered, her voice barely audible.

"I see," said Charlie. "I expected as much. Never be ashamed if it makes you wet to be punished. Did you do anything about that tingly, wet feeling between your cute little legs?" he asked.

Angela was growing redder and redder in the face, her adorable features accentuated by the bright blush. She didn't say anything.

"I won't be mad if you did. Like I always tell you, it's quite a normal reaction," he consoled.

Finally, Angela opened her mouth to speak. "Yes, daddy, I sat on the couch and made myself come with my fingers, like how you do it," she admitted.

"You were so horny from being punished that you just had to touch yourself, didn't you?" Charlie asked.

Angela nodded, her big eyes looking up at her daddy with a sense of innocence and coyness.

"Well, it made me horny to punish you this way, little girl. It made me so hard to see your pictures. I loved seeing you spread your cheeks and show off your bottom hole to me. And I loved knowing just how embarrassed it must have made you. I loved imagining you squirming in your chair all day with the plug in your bottom, reminding you to behave yourself."

Charlie had to struggle not to grip his cock as he said these words. It was pressing hard against his pants, hard as a rock and already wet with pre-cum.

"But I was working today, wasn't I? When I'm at my job, I can't just pull my cock out and make myself come, no matter how much my sexy little girl makes me want to. So I've been waiting all day. What do you think I want now?" he asked.

Angela slowly raised her head to look Charlie in the eyes. "You probably want me to..." Her voice lowered to be much quieter. "You probably want me to suck your cock now, don't you, daddy?" she murmured.

"That's right, Angela. I want my little girl to take my cock in her mouth and make me come. Then, if you're a good girl and do as you're told, *then* you can have your butt plug out."

Angela silently dropped to her knees in front of Charlie. He looked down and watched as his demure, obedient wife unbuckled his belt, then unfastened and unzipped his fly without saying another word. The feeling of her reaching out to grab his cock sent a shockwave of pleasure through his body. Having been aroused but unable to do anything about it all day had been torture.

Angela opened her mouth wide at first, like she was going to put his whole cock down her throat immediately, but then seemed to change her mind and began to lick the head teasingly. He gasped a bit at the sensation.

"This isn't going to take long," he told her with a smile. "I'm so hard for you."

Angela smiled, then licked down the length of his shaft, caressing every inch of him with her tongue. She ran her soft, baby-smooth lips over it, too, each move sending Charlie into a new wave of pleasure. It occurred to him that Angela was teasing him a little bit now, that she was probably enjoying just how horny and desperate she could make her husband, but he didn't mind. He knew that he still had all the power in the situation.

To demonstrate this, Charlie gripped Angela by a handful of her golden hair, then gently tapped on her cheek, signaling her to open her mouth nice and wide. She did as he instructed, and then he thrust his cock into her mouth.

Charlie had taught Angela what to do when he was guiding her head like this: she obediently placed her hands behind her back, grabbing each wrist. Charlie found it incredibly erotic to see her posed like this, especially without the need for a verbal command. She was willingly giving herself up to be used by him.

He began to fuck his wife's mouth, not too hard, but hard enough. She did her best to use her tongue when she could, but otherwise simply let him thrust in and out and decide just how quickly and how far he wanted to put his cock down her throat. Angela was well practiced at this, and though her eyes watered and her makeup ran as he continued, she never coughed or choked. Whenever he looked down at her, her expression was always blissful and serene.

31

"You're such a good girl, Angela. You really are my little angel," he moaned as he rocked his cock back and forth. "You're such a good little slut for me, aren't you?" he asked.

Angela normally would have looked away and blushed when he said that to her, but here, she was in her element and she just nodded, the corners of her open mouth raising into a smile.

Charlie started to thrust harder and more quickly, feeling the pleasure of her throat and mouth overwhelm him. Angela was starting to whimper a bit, but he didn't slow; he knew she could take it. And then, suddenly, his muscles went tight and his breathing got shallow as everything felt just too good to bear.

His cock started to spasm, shooting hot semen down his little girl's throat. He shoved her head so far down his shaft that her face almost touched his body and held her there as he groaned and grunted, continuing to ejaculate after having needed to for so long. Finally, he finished, and with a gasp he gently released Angela from his grip, easing her off his cock. He shuddered a little at the motion, then sighed contentedly.

"You're a very, very good girl," he told her.

Angela smiled, her face a mess of makeup but her expression genuinely pleased. "Thank you, daddy," she said.

CHAPTER FIVE

Angela was in a pretty good mood by the time that she arrived at Claire's house to babysit her. It always pleased her when her daddy ordered her to suck his cock; she knew that she was good at it, and it always earned her a lot of praise. Despite how horny she had been about it earlier, she was very glad to have her butt plug out, too.

After her body had gotten used to having the plug in it for so long, it had been a little bit painful to take it out. Some plugs just slipped right out of Angela's bottom, but this one required more effort to be pulled past the flare before the base. Fortunately, Charlie had done it quickly, and much like ripping off a Band-Aid, it had hurt for a second and then been over with.

Charlie was going to eat dinner with Jensen, Claire's daddy, while Angela was babysitting, so she had just made herself a salad and eaten it while chatting to her daddy about their days. Then, it was time to go get ready to leave the house, since her face and hair were an unpresentable mess after having been face-fucked.

Angela and Charlie had taken a shower together, during which Charlie had gotten only a little bit handsy with his little girl. Angela had giggled and leaned away from him.

"Daddy! Don't touch me there!" she kidded, as Charlie used 'helping her wash' as an excuse to spend a while fondling her breasts in the hot, steamy water.

"I can touch you anywhere I please," Charlie insisted.

Angela was glad for the running water in the shower, since it didn't make it obvious how soaking wet those words had made her.

While Charlie went to get dressed, Angela started the process of getting ready to go out. She was a perfectionist about this, and always had to make sure that everything looked perfect. She added a few products to her hair before blow-drying it, then carefully flat-ironed it before arranging it into the perfect ponytail. She applied concealer, foundation, highlighter, powder, and blush, and was halfway through doing her eyeliner when Charlie came into

window instead of finishing her sentence.

"If I did what?" Charlie insisted.

"If you maybe wanted to fuck me there one day, that's all." She felt beet red.

"You want me to fuck you in the ass?" Charlie asked, sounding entertained by her shyness on the subject.

"Well, it's scary, but I like the idea, I think," Angela confided.

"This is something we can work on, baby," Charlie said. "Of course I'd love to shove my cock up your tight little bottom hole. But the first time is really going to hurt. So, I want you to practice with your plugs more, to get your hole ready for me and my cock."

Angela continued to blush, but felt happy that Charlie had accepted the idea. She wasn't sure what she had thought he would say to it.

"We'll start working on it soon," he told her. "You might not like all of your training, though," he warned.

"I'm a big girl!" Angela insisted.

"So, you're not going to make a fuss when it's time to have a bigger plug in your little bottom hole?" he inquired.

Angela nodded. "I'll do my best not to," she told him.

"This is a big shift," he said with a grin. "I thought you hated having your bottom plugged."

"I dunno, I just felt so horny when I had it in today, and it made me start thinking," was all Angela could tell him.

They soon pulled up to Jensen and Claire's house. Charlie stopped the car, but before they got out he turned to Angela.

"Sweet girl, remember to be on your absolute best behavior tonight, alright?" he reminded her.

Angela nodded. "I know, daddy. I have to be a good girl."

"You'll have fun, won't you?" asked Charlie.

"Yes, I'm sure it will be fine."

The walk up to the front door was freezing, even though they had parked close by. Angela shivered as they waited to be let into the house. It only took a moment for her to start to get too cold, and she began to hop up and down.

Then Jensen opened the door and invited them in. There were introductions all around. Although Angela and Claire had talked online and seen each other a few times in town, they had never formally met before, and though Charlie and Jensen were friends, they had never met one another's partners.

After both girls promised their respective daddies that they were going to be well behaved for the night, the two men were off.

Angela wasn't sure what to do now, since Claire had seemed so shy. Claire had practically hidden behind Jensen when they first came in. Her weakness bothered Angela a little bit. She didn't know how to interact with a person

like that.

Of course, Angela felt afraid and timid often, too. The difference was, she did her best never to let it show. She couldn't understand inviting people to see your weaknesses like that. The same with playing at such a young age, and doing it publicly: how could Claire, and the other girls who did it, be so vulnerable? Out in public?

Instead of marveling at this behavior, Angela dismissed it. She turned to Claire and asked her what she wanted to do for the evening. Claire wasn't sure, maybe unable to make choices for herself, either, so Angela decided to turn the TV on.

She sat on the couch watching a reality show about cos players that was filmed in Los Angeles. She remembered what it had been like to be able to go outdoors in the middle of winter in just a light cardigan and sighed. She got fairly engrossed in the show, even though it was already half over, and tried to pay careful attention to the makeup artists when they were on. Maybe she could pick up a few tips.

It bothered Angela that she hadn't really heard from or seen Claire since she got there, though, so as soon as the show was over, she went upstairs to look for her. She didn't think that Claire was actually in need of supervision, but she figured that if she did something dumb and naughty, like get glitter all over the house, Angela would probably get blamed for it and end up with another spanking. She felt like she had been spanked more than enough recently, and wasn't going to let that happen.

Angela climbed the stairs, listening for sounds. She hadn't been given a tour of their house, so she guessed at which room might be the master bedroom. She found it, and opened the door just a crack, not wanting to snoop, really. She was just looking for Claire. If Claire was being naughty, Angela would rather catch her in the act. It would make her look better when she told the grownups later.

The master bedroom was empty, and it was the room of a normal adult. Angela was fairly surprised: she had expected it to be more childish, at least in part, given the fact that Claire had showed up to the door wearing a Barbie t-shirt in a way that Angela could tell was not the least bit ironic.

Down the hallway she heard a little bit of sound, and she followed it to another room. Her earlier surprise was explained as she realized that Claire had her own room for being little in: it was decked out to the max with cute, girly, childish things. Claire herself was sitting on the floor, surrounded with Barbie dolls and accessories.

Angela sighed. She didn't play with toys. Once in a while, she might color in a coloring book along with a girl who she was babysitting, and she enjoyed playing games and even watching cartoons once in a while, but there were limits for her. Spending time and money to collect a bunch of dolls and then sitting on the floor dressing them was one of them.

"What are you doing?" Angela asked her, even though she already knew what the response was going to be.

Claire looked a little bit uncomfortable. Angela wondered if Claire was afraid of her.

"I'm playing with my Barbies. Do you want to join me?" she asked, her voice sounding sweet and innocent.

Angela looked around the room for signs of mischief, but was disappointed to discover that there was no mess, no broken lamps, no glitter everywhere. Claire was being a good little girl. *What a letdown*, Angela thought.

"Thanks, but no thanks," Angela told Claire. "Barbies are for babies."

Claire's face looked hurt right away, and Angela thought that all of her emotions had to be kept pretty close to the surface.

"No, they aren't," Claire defended herself. "My daddy says that big girls play with them too. Come on, they're fun."

"I told you no. I'm the grownup here and you have to listen to me and I'm telling you that I don't want to play with your dolls like some kind of baby." Angela rolled her eyes.

"I'm not a baby," Claire insisted. She stood up, getting close to Angela. Claire was almost as tall as she was.

Something inside Angela snapped. She couldn't help it. It bothered her that some of the girls could sit on their floors being carefree and not having to worry about anything. It bothered her that even within a community for people who were deviant from society in the way that she was, Angela wasn't entirely the norm, as she was pretty sure that most of the girls in the community enjoyed younger age play than she did. It made all of her insecurities rush back to her, even though she had tried her best to let them go during her sexy times with her daddy earlier, and then paint them over with makeup and straighten them out of her hair before leaving the house.

"Yes, you are!" Angela almost yelled. "Look at this room. It has stuffed animals everywhere. There's a rocking chair in the corner. I don't know how you survive in the outside world. You work, don't you? What do you do at work? Do you sleep in here all by yourself? Do you have to wear pull-ups to bed to keep from wetting it?" she ranted.

Angela looked at Claire's innocent little face again and noticed that she was crying. Part of her felt suddenly guilty for her outburst, and like she needed to apologize right away. The other part felt even more annoyed at Claire for not being able to control herself in front of a total stranger.

Just then, she heard her daddy's voice behind her. "We're back, girls," Charlie said. He then seemed to survey the room and asked, "What's going on here?"

Angela decided that the best thing to do was to try to make it seem like nothing had happened. She had assumed that Charlie and Jensen were going to be gone much longer than this, and had intended to calm Claire down

before they returned.

"Nothing! Claire just dropped one of her Barbies and I was helping her," she lied, smiling to make things seem more believable, or so she hoped.

Jensen seemed concerned about Claire. It made sense to Angela that he would, of course, because she was standing there crying.

"Is what Angela said true, Claire?" Jensen asked.

Charlie gave Angela a stern look, as if he was trying to figure out exactly what was going on. Angela had a sinking feeling that he had a pretty good idea that she wasn't telling the truth.

Claire tried to push past Jensen, but he wouldn't move.

"Claire, I asked you a question." Jensen repeated to his little girl again, gently grabbing her by the shoulders.

"Just leave me alone, Jensen. She was fine. I just want to be left alone now," Claire blurted out as she pushed him aside and ran out of the room and down the hallway.

Angela would have felt vindicated by the fact that Claire was covering for her if she hadn't done it in the middle of an emotional outburst, making it clear that something had happened that made her really upset. Angela began to worry that Charlie would think that she had ordered Claire to lie for her.

"Claire!" Jensen called out, his face tense with worry.

"I want to be alone... as an adult!" Claire shouted without turning around. She went into the master bedroom and slammed the door.

Angela was left alone with Jensen and Charlie in Claire's little room, studying the mess of Barbie clothes on the floor.

Charlie looked to Jensen. "I'll take Angela home and have a talk with her and we'll see if we can't figure out what happened," he suggested.

Angela just looked at the floor, feeling sheepish and uncomfortable. She couldn't even try to pull off her usual attempt at teenager nonchalance in the face of a situation she didn't want to deal with. She considered apologizing to Jensen, but she didn't want to get into something more complicated here, in front of people she hardly knew.

Well, that was as bad as it could have been, she thought to herself, shrugging her shoulders with a deep sigh as Charlie led her downstairs to get her coat and shoes.

CHAPTER SIX

Charlie's heart was beating angrily in his chest as he led Angela to the car after saying goodnight to his friend. He got into the driver's side and shut the door without saying a word to his wife.

In the car, he turned on the heat and started to drive, the silence between the two of them awkward and heavy. Charlie wasn't ignoring Angela because he wanted to punish her with his silence, though; he was simply too upset with Angela's behavior, and he didn't trust himself not to blow up at her. He knew that he needed to be calm to properly address the situation, so he took deep breaths as they drove.

Charlie and Jensen had come back to Jensen and Claire's house early, since their event had ended up being cancelled because of the bad weather. As he had come up the stairs, he had heard his little girl taunting and teasing Claire about her little behavior and he had been outraged by what he was hearing. He had heard reports from others that Angela had been mean to younger girls, like the other day with Morgan, but he had never heard it for himself, and it made him furious to hear such cruel ideas coming from his little girl's mouth.

What had made things worse, though, was the fact that once he and Jensen had confronted the two girls, Angela had lied to his face. He wondered how often Angela said things that weren't true. Charlie had always assumed that his little girl was honest with him. And then there was the fact that Claire had insisted that nothing had happened so vehemently while being clearly upset.

• • • • • • •

When they arrived home, Charlie brought Angela into the house and took her coat for her.

"Sit down," he instructed, pointing to the sofa. "I want the truth and I want all of it," he demanded.

Angela took a deep breath, looking like she might burst into tears herself. "Well, Claire made me feel weird," she started.

Charlie felt the impulse to butt in and ask what exactly that meant, but he did his best to hold his tongue and not interrupt her. It was important to him not to talk over Angela, because while he wanted her to know that he was in control, he also didn't want her to think that her words and thoughts weren't important to him.

"Like, she was so shy, and she was just so much younger than me and my friends. Like, when she hid behind her daddy, you know? She couldn't even say hi to us like a normal person."

"I don't like the idea that some people in our community are normal and others aren't," Charlie said very calmly. "There isn't a right and a wrong way to express their feelings and there isn't a right and a wrong way to do age play."

Angela nodded, tears starting to escape her eyes and roll down her face, leaving marks in her previously perfect makeup.

"Go on, I want to hear the rest," Charlie said, his words somewhere between being encouraging and demanding.

"Well," Angela started, "she didn't seem to want to do something with me, like when I babysat for Wendy we just played games together and it was fun, but Claire just wanted to do her own thing, I guess. Maybe she just didn't like me, I don't know. So I watched the rest of the cos play show by myself and then I went up to see if she was okay."

Charlie's brow furrowed. It seemed strange that Angela would be hung up on the idea that Claire didn't like her, but it didn't seem manufactured to him. Her face and her big, teary eyes told him that this was truth.

"Anyway, she was playing with Barbies in her room, like you saw. She has…" Angela sniffled. "She has her own room for her to be a little girl in, I guess. And I dunno, she's just so little and babyish…"

Charlie did interrupt her this time. "That's not nice, and you know it," he scolded.

"I just don't get it. I didn't know that there were other people that wanted to act younger until I got on the Internet and I met the other girls 'my age,' the other middles! But then we came here and I feel like it's normal to be like Claire! I feel like little girls are supposed to be so little. They're supposed to be like babies!

"Maybe I'm just doing it wrong!" Angela continued. "But I don't wanna do those things! I don't want to play with dolls and have a rocking horse and wear baby onesies to bed or something. I thought if I came here I could just be me and no one would think I was weird, but I'm not the same as everyone else here, either!" Angela wailed, starting to sob.

Charlie walked over to his little girl and pulled her into his lap. He gently rubbed her back, soothing her as she cried.

"Angela, this isn't about what's right and what's wrong. There are so many different couples in Little Haven! And they're all different. You have lots of friends who like to be teen girls like you. And sometimes, when you want to be a little bit littler—because I know you do—that's alright, too. I wouldn't even say that there are more girls who play like Claire do!"

Charlie sighed. He should have known that there were a lot of complicated emotions behind Angela's behavior. He almost felt bad for assuming that she had only been being mean-spirited. Angela was a complicated girl. She came from a comfortable family life, with a pair of sweet parents who had loved her and her sister and taken good care of them growing up. Angela's mother even knew, in vague terms, about her relationship with Charlie and why they had moved to Minnesota and she didn't judge her daughter for it.

Angela had always been pretty, had always been good at athletic activities, and had even done competitive dancing in high school, and while there was no sign that she had ever been bullied or mistreated, Charlie could tell that she hadn't had many friends and hadn't felt like she was liked or normal. He knew that his wife's long-kept secret that she wanted to be treated like a little girl and spanked hard on her bare bottom had made her feel different from others before they had moved here, but he had hoped that over the past couple of years she had gained confidence and accepted herself.

"Angela," Charlie started again, "everyone feels insecure sometimes. I bet you that every little girl in this town cries to her daddy because she isn't sure that she's doing things right, or she thinks that no one here likes her, or she's scared of being judged. You just have to let that all go. The only thing that's going to make people dislike you is if you're mean to them."

Angela started to cry harder. "I didn't mean to be mean!" she insisted. "It just happened."

Charlie held her tight and gently stroked her hair until she calmed down.

"I understand why you acted this way now, Angie," he told her, "but that doesn't make it okay. You're going to get a serious punishment for this behavior. I think you need it. I think you need to let go of all your feelings about this subject, and I think you need to realize just how much you upset and embarrass other girls when you take your insecurities out on them."

Angela nodded slightly, "Yes, daddy," she whispered.

"For now, though, it's time for my little girl to go to bed. You've had a big day."

Charlie helped Angela to her feet and led her up the stairs. He waited at the doorway while she washed all the makeup off her face and moisturized it, then took her hair down and brushed her teeth. He led her to the bedroom, then he undressed her and slipped a nightie over her head. He then pulled back the covers on the bed and helped Angela in. He got up on the bed and sat down next to her, continuing to gently stroke her hair and back.

"No matter what you do to act up and be a naughty little girl, I still love you so much. You're my little princess and you are my whole world," he whispered to her. "I'm going to punish you harshly tomorrow, but only because I adore you and I want you to be your best self. I know you understand, and I know you know that you need it, don't you?" he asked.

Angela nodded, seeming suddenly very tired out, even though it was nowhere near her bedtime. "I love you, too, daddy," she said.

"Get some sleep, my love," he said, kissing her on the cheek and turning the light out as he left the room.

Charlie then went downstairs to make a couple of phone calls before it got too late. There were people he needed to connect with before tomorrow.

CHAPTER SEVEN

Angela woke up the next morning to find Charlie standing next to her, already dressed. She rubbed her eyes, remembering that it was Saturday. Then she remembered everything that had happened the night before and Charlie's promise of big trouble the next day and her heart sank.

"Good morning, little girl," Charlie said to Angela. "I thought long and hard about this, and I decided that the best way for me to teach you how much you humiliate other girls when you're mean to them the way you were mean to Claire last night is to give you a punishment that emulates that humiliation."

Charlie smiled a sort of wry smile. "So, for this weekend, you're going to be treated as a very little girl, in addition to the other punishments that you have coming. I'm hoping that this brings the message home. Being treated like a very young girl is the punishment that I referred to before, the special one that was reserved particularly for this situation."

Angela groaned and sank back down in bed, hiding her face under the covers. Surely Charlie wasn't being serious, was he?

"So, come on, get up! I'm going to give you a bath before I dress you," he demanded.

"Daddy, I'm too old for baths! I can take my own shower," Angela tried to complain.

"Not today you can't. Today you're my little girl, and little girls have to be helped in the bath. Let's go," he said matter-of-factly, taking Angela by the hand and practically pulling her out of bed. He marched her down the hallway to the bathroom, where he knelt by the tub and started to run the tap.

"I have to make sure the water isn't too hot for my little one," he explained as he checked the temperature.

"Don't make it cold!" Angela whined, worrying that the water wouldn't compare to her usual hot morning shower.

"Don't worry, daddy will take care of you," he cooed.

Angela looked at the floor, feeling overcome with shame and

embarrassment.

Once Charlie seemed content that the water was the right temperature for Angela, he turned back to her. "It's time to get undressed. Put your arms up."

Being undressed by Charlie was fairly normal to Angela, so she wasn't so embarrassed as she lifted her arms for him to pull her flimsy nightie over her head. He then rolled her panties down her legs and ordered her to step out, then left her in the bathroom while he walked into the hallway to throw them in the hamper.

Angela wasn't sure what was going to happen next, as the tub still needed to fill quite a bit, but Charlie had a plan. He turned the sink on and got Angela's toothbrush from the holder. He wet it, then opened the cabinet door to pull out a small tube of 'Little Bear'-themed toothpaste.

"Where did this come from?" Angela whined. "I don't want baby toothpaste!"

Charlie gave her a swift smack on her bare bottom. "Hush," he said. "No more complaining. I went to the store outside the community before you woke up and picked up some things that I'm going to need to discipline you today. There are still a few things missing, but we'll go to the store here in town together and get those later," he explained.

Charlie squeezed toothpaste onto the toothbrush and handed it to Angela.

"Go ahead and brush. But make sure you do a good job, because daddy's gonna check," he told her.

Angela groaned, but stuck the toothbrush in her mouth. She made a face; the toothpaste tasted like bubblegum, and had a strong, artificially sweet taste.

Charlie snickered at her reaction, which only made Angela pout more.

She began to brush her teeth, feeling a bit self-conscious to have Charlie watching her. When she was finished, she spit out the rest of the toothpaste in the sink and went to rinse her toothbrush, but Charlie stopped her.

"Let me check and see if you did a good job," he told her. "Open wide!"

With her cheeks flushing red, Angela forced her mouth open. Charlie peeked inside and declared that she had, indeed, done a good job. He let Angela rinse her mouth, but rinsed her toothbrush himself and put it back in the holder.

"Now," he said, "it's time for your bath."

Angela sighed deeply as Charlie helped her into the tub. To her surprise, the water was exactly the right temperature, and the soothing warmth of it relaxed her muscles. She couldn't remember the last time she had taken a bath, and she had forgotten how nice it could feel.

Charlie grabbed a washcloth, then knelt down next to Angela, rinsing the cloth in the warm bathwater. He then reached over and grabbed Angela's face wash, which was resting on the edge of the tub. He squirted a little bit of it onto the cloth and rubbed it until it foamed.

"Time to wash your face, little girl," he said. "Close your eyes and mouth

tight!"

Angela couldn't believe how every simple part of her morning routine could be made into something so humiliating and punishing. She didn't feel like arguing again, though, so she shut her eyes and mouth as tightly as she could. It felt strange to have someone else washing her face, especially when he cleaned behind her ears.

When he had finished, she cupped her hands to splash water on her face, but once again, her daddy stopped her.

"Let daddy do it," Charlie chided. He rinsed the washcloth out in the bathwater, then used it to sponge away all the cleanser from her face. He then repeated the action, to make sure she was really clean.

Angela had a feeling she knew what was coming next, and her suspicions were confirmed when Charlie reached for the body wash and began to do the same thing, working some into a thick foam on the washcloth. He then started to scrub her, washing her chest, stomach, and back before instructing her to raise one arm, which he then scrubbed. He washed her armpit, too, and then told her to switch arms. He repeated this with the other arm. Then he told her to sit back and put her legs out of the water so he could wash those.

Once her legs were washed, Charlie ordered Angela to get up on all fours. The water was not too deep, and she did this with ease. Charlie then began to wash her between her legs, which made her blush deeply. It was a strange thing, she thought, how she could find no embarrassment in being touched there for pleasure, but his clinical, parental touch made her ears burn. It was even worse when he began to wash her between her bottom cheeks in the same way.

When Charlie had finished cleaning every part of his little girl, he instructed her to rinse off in the water, then to lean back and get her hair wet. He washed her hair, rinsed it for her, and then did her conditioner and rinsed that as well.

By the time bath time was finished, Angela didn't even try to dry herself; she had realized that she was going to have to just stand still and wait for her daddy to do it for her. He toweled her off with the same kind of distanced touch: it wasn't a sensual caress, it was just a towel being used to dry her, even when he ordered her to spread her legs.

Certain parts of the bathroom proceedings almost felt nice, like when Charlie blow-dried her hair for her and did a surprisingly alright job at it, or when he gently applied her moisturizer to her face, but she never forgot that he wasn't doing it to pamper her, but instead to make her feel helpless and embarrassed.

"I need to do my own makeup," Angela insisted when this was done, "and flat-iron my hair."

Charlie shook his head. "No, no, no. Do you know any little girls who are

allowed to wear big grownup makeup? That's far too grown up for you today."

Angela wanted to stamp her foot. It was so unfair. She tried her best to contain her emotions, though.

"Besides, I want you to think about something else today. I want you to think about the fact that you're beautiful without makeup." Charlie directed Angela's eyes to the mirror. "See your bare face? It's still gorgeous. Every part of you is gorgeous."

Angela felt a warm, glowing feeling inside, and the sudden shyness that came over her was not caused by embarrassment.

CHAPTER EIGHT

"Go stand in the corner and think about what you did to earn this punishment. Think about being courteous to others, about not taking your problems out on them, and about being a nice and polite little girl. I'm going to go pick out your clothes for the day, and then before I dress you, I'm going to give you your first spanking of the day," Charlie told his temporarily much littler little girl.

Angela looked back at him with very wide eyes. Obviously it hadn't occurred to her just how many spankings she should expect for the day.

Charlie figured that Angela would protest at this announcement, but was pleased to see her compliantly turn to face the corner. She posed herself with her hands on top of her head, exactly the way that he had taught her to stand when she was being punished.

"Good girl," he praised, then added, "Don't move."

He left the bedroom to go downstairs and get a bag that he had picked up this morning when he had gone shopping. Wendy, the other girl who Angela often babysat for, was a particularly young little. She age played at about four years old. She also happened to be about the same size as Angela. Charlie had called her husband last night and explained the situation and he had been more than happy to let Charlie borrow a bag of Wendy's clothes.

Charlie came upstairs and spread out the clothing on the bed. Today, Angela would be wearing a pale purple romper suit with legs that puffed out like bloomers before cinching in just above the knees, a big bow on the front, and a sailor collar. Charlie found a pair of Angela's own tights for her to wear when she went outside later, in order to keep her legs warm in the bitter Midwestern winter, and set those aside. For now, he completed her outfit with a pair of Hello Kitty panties and a pair of ruffly, pink ankle socks, along with Angela's plainest white tennis shoes. Above those items, he set a big, oversized bow on a headband, which he had also borrowed from Wendy.

"Alright, Angie," he called after he had finished assembling the outfit for her. "It's time to get your spanking before I dress you for the day."

Angela came out of the corner, looking very sheepish indeed. "Daddy?" she asked.

"Yes, my darling?" Charlie responded.

"Do I really have to get a lot of spankings today?" she wanted to know, nervously wringing her hands.

"Oh, yes, sweetie. You're going to spend more time over my lap today than you usually do in a month, I suspect. You are going to have a sore, stinging bottom every moment of the day today and tomorrow. And you'll be getting other punishments this weekend, too."

Angela's face fell, and she bit her lip nervously.

"I meant it when I said that I would punish you severely if you did this again. You had every chance to avoid this. But instead of talking to me about how you felt, you chose to use your emotions to be mean and hurtful, so now you're going to get a serious punishment," Charlie explained.

He beckoned the nervous girl over to his side, and she slowly walked to meet him. He then gripped her by the arm, pulled her over his lap, and took a moment to inspect her bottom. Although she had been spanked only a couple of days ago, her bottom was in perfect condition: it didn't even have the slightest pinkness left to it. *Time to change that,* he thought with a slight smile.

Charlie raised his hand high and then applied it strongly to Angela's pert little bottom. She let out a yelp. He followed it with another swat, keeping his pace slow but his hand heavy. Angela bucked forward on his lap a little after each swat. Once her bottom was glowing a very pale pink color, he began to spank her more quickly, finding a rhythm that worked for him. Angela kicked her feet just slightly as the spanking got faster.

"I hope that when all this is said and done, you've truly learned a lesson, Angie," Charlie scolded. "I expect this to be the final stop for this behavior, do I make myself clear?"

"Yessssss, daddddyyyyyy!" Angela wailed, her feet starting to kick more vigorously.

"Good," Charlie said, and then continued to spank at the exact same pace, without giving Angela a moment of respite. Her bottom was turning a bright pink color, but that wasn't enough for Angela's daddy. He was waiting on a strawberry red. He wanted the sting to last at least a little while.

"You're only getting my hand right now, but if my little girl acts up today or tries to do any big girl things at all without daddy's help, I won't hesitate to get the hairbrush, or a paddle, or to take my belt off."

Angela nodded that she understood. Charlie could feel her chest rising and falling and hear the sound of gentle sniffling; she was already starting to cry.

"I know I'm not spanking you hard enough to make you cry. Are you crying because you're a humiliated little girl? Or because you let me down so

badly and you regret your behavior?" Charlie asked her.

"Both!" was Angela's sniffly answer.

She sounded so pathetic and cute when she said that that Charlie couldn't help but smile. He continued to spank her for a few minutes anyway, just to drive the lesson home. Then he continued to spank her for a few minutes more, just because he was enjoying the lovely red color of her bottom.

By the time Charlie finished, Angela was crying hard. "There, there," he said gently to her. "I know my little girl is learning, aren't you?" he asked.

Angela nodded pathetically, using the back of her hand to wipe at her face.

Her gestures seemed younger than she usually would behave after a spanking, which made Charlie smile. He pulled Angela up onto his lap and cradled her in his arms, reminding her how much he loved her and that this was the reason why he had to punish his little girl. Then it was time to show her what she was going to be dressed in for the day.

CHAPTER NINE

After her spanking, Charlie led Angela to the bed, where he had laid out her clothes for the day. Angela took one look at the outfit and began to cry again.

"You can't be serious, daddy!" she wailed. "I don't want to wear this!"

"No protesting," Charlie said sternly, "or you'll go right back over my knee. I mean that."

Angela bit her lip and pouted hard.

"Come here," Charlie instructed. "Let me get you into your panties."

The tights and Hello Kitty panties that Charlie was holding up for her were the only clothes on the bed that belonged to her. The rest, she wasn't sure where they had come from. He held them open by the waistband for her and helped her to step in one foot at a time. Then he pulled them up her legs and onto her now red bottom.

"If your bottom stops feeling sore, let me know," Charlie said. "If I check and your bottom isn't at least a little pink, you'll be getting a much harder spanking."

The idea of having to have a freshly spanked bottom all day was overwhelming to Angela, just like the humiliation that she felt when Charlie instructed her to sit on the bed so he could put her tights on her because they were going to go out of the house on an errand first thing.

"I can't go out of the house like this, daddy," she moaned. "People will see me!"

"That's the point, my little one. A humiliation punishment isn't complete if no one sees you in your humiliating condition, now is it?" Charlie knelt down in front of Angela and bunched up one leg of her white tights to help her get into them. Angela knew that it would be much easier for her to just put them on herself, but she also knew that Charlie wasn't going to permit that.

Eventually, Charlie got Angela into her tights and then he helped her step into the purple jumpsuit. It looked like it was designed for a toddler, with the

bloomer-shaped legs giving it an extremely babyish effect. Angela hadn't noticed the bow that Charlie had set on the bed before, though, so when he pulled it out she gasped.

"That's huge!" she complained.

"Yep. And you're gonna wear it," Charlie said matter-of-factly, popping the headband onto her head. "Let's go look in the mirror."

Angela had trouble looking at herself at first. It was horrible how easily she had been transformed into a tiny little girl. Her teenage middle persona seemed incredibly mature compared to what she was being forced into.

Upon closer inspection, though, Angela did notice that her makeup-free face wasn't as bad as she thought it would be. In fact, aside from a few stray zits and the dark circles under her eyes, she felt like she looked pretty cute without makeup. It was an interesting revelation for her, since she usually avoided leaving the house without makeup for any reason, and only even really looked at herself this way when she was in the process of applying it.

"We're going out, little one," Charlie told Angela. "Of course, you can wear your big girl coat since I couldn't get you a little girl one and I would never want you to be cold, but as soon as we get indoors you are to take it off and hand it to me, do you understand?"

Angela nodded glumly. She had been hoping that she would be allowed to leave her coat on. Although it didn't cover the puffy legs of her jumpsuit, which were arguably the most embarrassing part, it at least covered the sailor collar and the big bow on the front.

Charlie led Angela to the car, but instead of getting in the driver's side like he usually did, he kept holding her hand and walked her to the back door. "Little girls aren't allowed to sit in the front seat," he explained. "You're lucky that we don't have a booster seat for you," he said as he buckled her seatbelt for her.

Each little humiliation was starting to pile up for Angela, and she was realizing that she couldn't exactly fight the feelings that were overtaking her. She was going to have to just give up and let whatever happened next happen, she thought, as Charlie got in the front seat and started to drive.

"Where are we going?" Angela asked, more out of curiosity than anything else.

"There are two things we need to buy for this weekend that I couldn't get in the big store, so we are going to the Little Haven Shop," Charlie explained. "I called Mr. Larson last night to see if they had the things we need and he said that they do."

Mr. Larson was a man in his early fifties who ran the store in Little Haven. He was one of the only people in the community who wasn't married, but he was a kind and gentle man who all the littles loved. He often gave the girls treats when they came into the shop to get supplies. Angela particularly liked Mr. Larson, and felt similarly toward him as a middle-schooler might feel

toward a teacher who they had a crush on. She always wanted his praise and grew shy around him.

"I don't want Mr. Larson to see me in this outfit!" Angela insisted, sounding a little panicked. "What will he think of me?!"

Charlie smiled. "Relax, little girl. I already explained the situation. Mr. Larson agreed with me that this was a most effective punishment for naughty girls, and even gave me a few suggestions on how to make it more effective. He's looking forward to seeing what a cute little, little girl you make."

Angela looked out the window with a serious pout. For once, she was grateful for the falling snow; at least she got to have her coat and tights for now. She couldn't imagine what it would have been like if she had undergone this treatment in the summer and had been marched right down the street dressed like this, with nothing to cover up with.

When they arrived at the Little Haven Shop, Charlie warned Angela not to unbuckle her seatbelt until he told her that she could. Angela sat compliantly until her daddy came around and opened the door and undid her seatbelt, then helped her out of the car. They walked into the store, making the bell on the door ring cheerfully.

"Coat off," Charlie instructed.

Angela sighed and pulled her jacket off, handing it to her daddy. She looked around the store anxiously, hoping that no one she knew was around. She shrank back behind a counter full of sweets in hopes of camouflaging her bright colors there.

"Tom?" Charlie called as they walked in. Mr. Larson wasn't at the front counter like he usually was.

"Hi, Charlie," Mr. Larson called from the back of the store. "I'm just back here unboxing some stuff that came in yesterday. I'll be right up."

Mr. Larson appeared from beyond the displays of basic food and household supplies on the far aisle of the store. Besides everyday convenience items, the store also sold things that would be especially important for an age play community, like toys and accessories for littles and a wide variety of spanking implements. There was a rack of hairbrushes near the front of the store with a small bench next to it, much like what one would see in a shoe store, only instead of sitting on the bench to try on shoes, one was invited to sit there and pull your little across your lap to try out a hairbrush before you bought it. Angela felt quite certain that whatever they were there for today was from that part of the store, not from the sweets and treats area where she was currently hiding.

Mr. Larson strode over to Charlie and shook his hand. The older man was about the same height as Angela's daddy but not as strongly built, and his once dark hair was primarily salt and pepper. Although Angela often thought of her daddy as looking distinguished, he looked young and fresh-faced next to Mr. Larson.

"Hi, Charlie," Mr. Larson said again. "Where's your little?"

"Angela?" Charlie called, looking around the store himself.

Angela slowly peeked out from behind the candy display, hoping that the other two people shopping in the store wouldn't notice her if she didn't move too quickly.

Mr. Larson smiled as he saw her poking her head out from behind the stand. "Don't you look cute today, Angela," he said. His voice wasn't teasing. He seemed to really think so.

Angela blushed furiously anyway. She wondered if there were any medical side effects caused by spending so much of one's day embarrassed. Could it be bad for her circulation if all her blood was constantly rushing to her face?

"Let Mr. Larson see you up close," Charlie suggested.

Angela came forward and stood by Charlie's side. To her surprise, she found herself wanting to hide behind her daddy, just like she had made fun of Claire for doing the night before. She felt a sudden rush of shame as she thought about her behavior then, and she reminded herself that she really did deserve this punishment.

"Do a turn so that we can see your full look," Charlie instructed.

Angela awkwardly spun around, twirling on the toe of her tennis shoe.

"Slower," Charlie ordered.

Angela understood what her daddy wanted her to do now, and though it made her wince, she turned in a slow circle so that Charlie and Mr. Larson (and the other shoppers, if they happened to be looking) could see her shameful attire from every angle.

"Well," Mr. Larson said, "this looks like the start of a lesson well learned." His smile was still as kindly as ever, which made Angela feel a little bit less nervous around him. "What else do you need, Charlie?"

"Well," Angela's daddy started. "I promised Angela that if she ever made fun of another girl in this community again, I was going to go out and buy a particular implement to use for her punishment. Angie, do you remember what I said?"

Angela's heart began to pound quickly against her ribcage. She honestly hadn't remembered this threat until now; she had buried it deep in her brain and had been focusing on the other aspects of her punishment. She bit her finger nervously.

"You said you were going to buy… a cane," she whispered, her voice very small and vulnerable.

"A cane is quite a fearsome implement for a little girl like you!" Mr. Larson said, maintaining his smile.

"But it's not too severe for my teen girl, is it?" asked Charlie, the question being obviously hypothetical.

"No, not at all. The cane is ideal for punishing a naughty young lady of Angela's usual age," he said. "A few good, hard, welting strokes will drive

home any lesson she needs to learn."

The descriptive language that Mr. Larson used made Angela squirm.

"You see, Angela," Charlie said. "The cane is going to be the final part of this punishment. Once you've learned your lesson and you're ready to be my big girl again, you'll get your big girl thrashing on your bare bottom. And then, after that, the cane will always be in the house, so if you ever think of this sort of behavior again, I'll have a very effective deterrent."

Angela was sure that she was as white as a sheet.

"That sounds like an excellent plan to me," Mr. Larson told Angela's daddy. "Let me show you where the canes are."

The three of them walked into the part of the store that featured implements and toward a rarely used back shelf. There were a variety of canes there, but Mr. Larson took down a straight rattan cane that was about a foot and a half long. It was just a little less wide than Angela's pointer finger and had a wrapped leather handle and a string to hang it by.

"This one would work well for your purposes, I think," he suggested to Charlie.

Charlie took the cane from Mr. Larson and flexed it between his hands. To Angela's surprise, it bent quite a bit, forming a shallow arch for a moment before Charlie released it. Then he took a step back from where the other two were standing and sliced it through the air. It made a loud whooshing sound as it made its descent. Angela jumped back, startled by the sudden and frightening noise.

"Yes," Charlie said, "this will do nicely."

"What else did you need?" Mr. Larson asked Charlie, gesturing that he would carry the cane he had selected while they were shopping.

"For part of Angela's punishment today and tomorrow, I've decided that I want her to wear diapers," he announced. "So, we're going to need a couple of days' supply of those, as well as some powder and wipes."

"*Daddy!*" Angela nearly shrieked. She felt so humiliated that she might cry. There was nothing in the world that was more embarrassing than having to wear a diaper. Surely there could be nothing worse.

Charlie flexed the cane menacingly again, and Angela took a step back, hanging her head. She knew she deserved this punishment, but she wished it could have been anything but what it was.

"If Angela is going to keep acting this way," Mr. Larson suggested as he led them over to the area of the store that housed equipment for the littlest of littles, "you might want to get both proper diapers and some pull-ups. The advantage of pull-ups, of course, is really more in the 'pull-down' part of it than the pull-up part," he said with a wink.

"I see your point," Charlie said. "Angela is in for quite a few spankings over the next two days, so I think I'll take both."

Mr. Larson reached up onto a shelf and pulled down a package of thick-

looking, bright pink diapers. The front of the packet showed a grownup baby girl with pigtails wearing only a t-shirt and a diaper. It looked particularly thick and padded and had teddy bears printed on the front.

"I recommend these in terms of diapers," he told Charlie, the conversation on the normal level for a shopkeeper and a customer, despite the fact that Angela was squirming in the background from the sheer disgrace of her situation.

The shopkeeper then reached up and grabbed a different packet. This one was full of what looked like more diapers, but they were white with an assortment of colorful zoo animals outlined on them. "These should be able to withstand coming up and down quite often," he told Charlie.

"Sold!" Charlie said.

Angela buried her face in her hands as one of the other shoppers walked by. It was a little who she didn't know, just out to buy normal groceries and looking much more grownup than Angela was at the moment. She could hear a faint snicker from the other customer, and Angela had to choke back tears.

"Do you see how it feels when people laugh at you in the store?" Charlie whispered to his little girl.

Angela nodded miserably. It had never occurred to her just how cruel her teasing of the other littles had been, but now that she knew, she was never going to forget it.

Mr. Larson took down a packet of baby wipes and a bottle of baby powder and handed them to Angela. "Could you carry these for us while we're shopping?" he asked.

Angela clutched them to her chest, not sure which she would rather hide: the embarrassing evidence that she was soon to be diapered, or the humiliating clothing that she was decked out in.

Charlie looked at the things on the wall in that area and thought for a moment, then he picked up a pink pacifier. "I think we'll get this, too," he said.

Angela groaned as quietly as she could. Here she was, feeling like a teenager, but about to be taken home and forced into a diaper and made to suck on a pacifier.

"Well, Charlie, is there anything else I can help you with?" Mr. Larson asked.

Charlie thought for a moment. "Actually," he said, "I do remember one other thing. I've realized that the plug that I've been using to punish Angela's little bottom hole isn't quite as effective of a discipline tool as it should be anymore. She seems to be enjoying it a bit too much. Do you have some bigger plugs here?"

"Of course," Mr. Larson said with a smile, "and I have a little trick to make them more effective for naughty bottoms." Mr. Larson gathered up all the items that Charlie had picked out so far and set them prominently on the

front counter, the cane balancing on top of the stack of diapers. He then led the couple over to another small corner of the store that housed sex toys.

Angela looked around to make sure that no one was looking as she walked back there. Much to her chagrin, the other little who she had spotted before was waiting at the counter to check out and giggling to herself as she viewed the items that they were about to purchase. Angela wished that the floor would swallow her up.

"So, how big is the plug you're using now?" Mr. Larson asked Charlie.

Charlie pointed to a similar one in a package on the wall. "This one is like the one I had been using as a punishment plug," he explained.

"Well," Mr. Larson said, "if that's no longer effective for punishment, you can make that her daily plug."

"Daily?!" asked Angela, sounding shocked.

"Oh, yes," Mr. Larson explained. "Aren't you getting anal training every day?" he then asked.

Angela shook her head, her eyes wide.

"We were planning on starting some before Angela got herself into trouble like this," Charlie explained.

"Many girls in this community get anal training," Mr. Larson said, as if that was meant to be comforting. "I fully recommend that every little girl spend at least an hour with a plug in her bottom hole every day. It doesn't just make her bottom more ready for other sorts of play, but it keeps her humble and polite."

"We'll definitely start doing that, then," Charlie said. "I so appreciate all the advice you have to offer, Mr. Larson. You're really an asset to this community."

Mr. Larson winked at Angela, then thanked Charlie for the compliment. "Really, I've just been learning for others over the years. None of my knowledge is anything new," he added.

Then he pulled a package off one of the shelves that contained three more butt plugs, each of increasing size. They had wide flares, thin necks, and big, round bases. The writing on it read 'Punishment Plugs for Naughty Bottoms.'

"These punishment plugs really should do the job for when you want something bigger and less comfortable for Angela's bottom hole," he explained. "The three sizes increase depending on how much she's misbehaved, and the shape of them helps them to stay well in place."

"Those look too big," Angela whimpered.

"They'll certainly feel big, and they won't be comfortable, but they're not too big," Mr. Larson assured her. "You might have to warm up to the biggest one at first, though."

Angela couldn't imagine ever taking the biggest plug. It was the size of the plug that she had marveled at when she had seen it in her friend's cabinet. Her bottom hole clenched unintentionally at just the thought of it.

"Now, to make anal punishments more effective," Mr. Larson began.

Angela was really beginning to wish that he would be less helpful.

Mr. Larson handed Angela the package of butt plugs, which she held with great shame. He then led them over to another display.

"Ginger is, in my opinion, the most effective punisher of bottom holes," he explained, "but it can be a bit much for a little girl, and it can be a lot of work to prepare. What I generally recommend is this." He held up a small container of all-natural vapor rub. "Instead of rubbing this on your chest when you have a cold, you can put a small amount on a butt plug after you lube it up to really make it burn inside her." He handed the jar to Charlie for him to look at. "It's perfectly safe, though."

Charlie smiled. "Could I use this on her pussy, too?"

"Oh, yes, it's very effective for that, too. Just remember to use it sparingly: a little bit goes a long way."

Charlie grinned. "Great! I think we're ready to check out, then," he told Mr. Larson.

Angela stared at the floor as they went to the cash register to check out.

"Angela," Charlie said. "One more thing."

Angela groaned. She couldn't imagine what else there might be here that could make her impending punishment worse.

"You were very well behaved during this shopping trip, despite how humiliating I knew it was for you. You can get a piece of candy as a reward for that good behavior," he said, giving her a little kiss on the forehead.

Angela smiled a little bit. She felt reminded of the fact that no matter what happened, she was always her daddy's special girl.

CHAPTER TEN

Charlie pulled the car into the driveway of their house with a bag full of punishment equipment sitting in the front seat and his naughty little girl buckled in the back. He turned off the car and then went around to unbuckle Angela and let her out of the car. The cane hadn't fit in the bag properly, so Mr. Larson had wrapped it up in brown paper for safekeeping; he handed that parcel to Angela to carry and took the bag in one hand and held onto her hand with the other.

When they got into the house, Charlie got a blanket and set up an impromptu changing station, right in the middle of the living room floor. He organized the diapers, pull-ups, wipes, and powder. Then he opened up the package of butt plugs and looked at them up close. He couldn't help himself from growing hard as he looked at the bigger plugs; he couldn't wait to put one of them in Angela's bottom.

"Oh, look!" he said to Angela as he looked at the plugs more carefully. "The bases of these have writing on them! See?" He held them up for Angela to look at.

"This one says 'Naughty,'" he explained, showing her the smaller of the three plugs, which was bright pink and only a little bit bigger than the purple plug that she had worn all afternoon yesterday.

Next, he held up the middle size. It was yellow, and was a bit longer and thicker.

"This one says 'Bad Girl' on it."

Finally, he picked up the largest one, which was thick and long, and which Charlie knew would really help to prepare Angela to eventually take his big, hard cock up her ass.

"And this one says 'Disgraceful.'"

Charlie smiled, seeing how wide-eyed Angela looked when he held up the red plug.

"To be perfectly honest, your behavior has been disgraceful, hasn't it?" he inquired of his little girl, thoroughly enjoying her downcast eyes, as if she

didn't dare look at the big plug directly. "But I think we'll start your punishment with the pink one. That should be enough for now," he said.

He thought about sending Angela to go get the lube, but then decided against it. "Sit down on the blanket and wait for me to come back," he instructed.

He quickly climbed up the stairs and grabbed the lube off the top of the dresser where Angela had left it last night instead of properly putting it away. Then he came back down to find Angela sitting cross-legged on the blanket, exactly where she was supposed to be.

"Good girl," he told her. "Now stand up so that I can undress you."

Angela slowly rose to her feet.

Charlie reached around, found the zipper on the back of Angela's jumpsuit, and unzipped it. He helped it off her arms and then pulled it down, uncovering her Hello Kitty panties. Then he helped her step out of it and set it aside. He gently turned his little girl around to look at the back side of her.

"Angela," he scolded, "your bottom is not pink anymore. Is it still sore?"

Charlie knew that the short hand spanking he had given Angela that morning was not enough to last for the amount of time that they had spent out shopping.

Angela shook her head nervously. "But daddy," she said. "I couldn't ask for a spanking in the middle of the store."

"Why not?" Charlie asked. "Have you never seen another little girl being punished in public before?"

Angela dropped her head. Charlie could remember a few occasions where they had both seen unhappy daddies turn their little girls over their laps for impromptu, public spankings. In fact, the chance that they might happen to see that taking place was one of Charlie's favorite things about living in Little Haven.

"I'm sorry," she whimpered. "Are you going to spank me harder now?"

Charlie nodded. "You're going to get a few swats with the brush for that," he told her. "I made my instructions on this matter very clear."

Charlie rose to his feet and walked over to a magazine stand that housed some of his architectural magazines. On top of them was a wooden hairbrush that he kept tucked away there. He liked to have implements hidden around the house so one was never too far out of reach. The brush wasn't heavy, but he knew that it stung Angela's bottom fiercely. She instinctively covered her bottom as he walked toward her with it.

"Take off those panties and give them to me," he instructed. "Even though these are good little girl panties, you won't be wearing them today. You're going to be in a diaper or pull-up until your punishment is over."

Angela pulled her panties down carefully and handed them to her daddy. He looked right into her pretty, clear eyes as he took them from her. He wanted to make sure that Angela was alright; he needed to make this

punishment truly memorable and as embarrassing as possible, but he didn't want to push his little girl too far over the edge. The look she gave him back told him all the she needed to know: she needed to be spanked just as much as Charlie needed to discipline her right now.

He sat down and turned her panties inside out, inspecting the gusset of them. As he suspected, it was soaking wet with her pussy juice. As much as she had seemed to have hated their shopping trip, he wasn't surprised to see that it had made her tremendously aroused.

"Angela," he chided. "Your panties are soaking wet. Being punished is making you horny, isn't it?"

Angela nodded nervously. "A little bit, daddy," she admitted.

"This is not just a little bit," he said, pointing to the wetness in her panties. "I want to make it clear to you that you are not to touch yourself without my permission when you're being punished today. Do you understand?"

"But I didn't, daddy," Angela replied.

"I know, I haven't let you out of my sight long enough for you to get a chance to. I just want you to know that when I do, I expect you to keep your hands to yourself like a good girl you age. Masturbation is something that big girls get to do."

Angela shyly affirmed Charlie's command. The idea of leaving Angela horny and unattended to in that state all day made Charlie grow hard; he loved the way that she screamed and writhed with orgasm when she was very pent up.

"I'm going to put this plug in your bottom before your spanking," Charlie told her, picking up the pink punishment plug and the lubricant and setting them next to the hairbrush on the arm of the sofa, where he could easily reach them while having Angela over his lap. "Get in position," he instructed.

Angela draped herself over Charlie's lap and he adjusted her so that her bottom was high in the air and her head was low down, near the floor. Then he lubed up his finger and inserted it into Angela's bottom.

"Tell me how you're feeling right now," he ordered as he slowly began to work his finger back and forth. Angela's bottom hole accepted the finger easily, after having worn the plug for so long yesterday.

"I feel so embarrassed that I wanna cry," was Angela's first answer, but given a moment of silence to think about it, she added, "And I feel like I'm never going to make someone else feel ashamed of themselves again."

"Being a bully isn't nice, is it?" Charlie asked as he twirled his finger a little bit, stretching her just slightly. He could tell that the plug wouldn't feel nice to Angela, but it would be easy enough to put in.

"No, sir," Angela whimpered. "I never meant to be a bully, but I also never thought about how it made the other girls feel when I teased them."

"I think you saw how bad it made little Claire feel the other night, didn't you?" he asked, still preparing her bottom hole with his finger.

Angela agreed sadly. "I know I need all the punishments that you're going to give me," she admitted.

"I'm glad you understand that, sweetie," Charlie told her. Then he pulled his finger out of her tight little bottom and opened the lube again, putting a generous amount on the pink 'Naughty' plug.

"Relax and get ready to take this," he told Angela. Angela's weight felt limper across Charlie's lap, and he gently began to push the plug into her hole. It gave way to the tip of it easily, but it took a little bit of effort to get it to start slipping in the rest of the way.

"Daddy, it hurts!" Angela insisted.

"I know it hurts, sweetie. It's a punishment. It's not supposed to feel good. It's supposed to teach you a lesson."

Angela started to whimper, but Charlie was able to keep pushing the plug into her bottom without much resistance. He loved watching it disappear into her cute, puffy bottom hole.

"Owwwwww," Angela cried as it reached the widest point. "Daddy, it's too big!"

"This is the smallest of your new punishment plugs," Charlie reminded his little girl. "I know that this isn't too big for you." With that, he gave the plug a final push and it went far enough into her bottom hole for her muscles to clamp down around the base. He tapped on the word 'Naughty,' still visible on the base when it was firmly planted between her little cheeks.

"There!" Charlie said. "Now my little girl is ready for her spanking."

Angela whined a little, but didn't try to wiggle away.

Charlie rarely spanked Angela when she had a plug in her bottom, so he started off with less severe swats than he usually would for a warmup. Angela wiggled over his lap furiously anyway.

"Daddy, it feels weird!" she cried out. "I don't like it!"

"I don't want you to like it," Charlie reiterated, picking up the pace of the spanking until the pink color returned to Angela's pretty, round backside. "I want your bottom to be nice and sore today, and I want your bottom hole to feel the same way. Like Mr. Larson said, it will help you to focus on being humble. That's something I think you need. You should never act like you're better than your peers just because you're different from each other," Charlie lectured.

Angela had started to cry already, probably more from the plug and the shame she had endured that morning than anything else. Charlie picked up the pace once she started to tear up, pushing her into full-bodied sobs.

"I'm going to give you ten swats with the brush now, Angela," Charlie explained. "I want you to remember to let me know when you need another spanking next time, or else it will be twenty."

Angela nodded through her tears.

Charlie picked up the brush and swatted her bottom with it. He didn't use

it too hard, but it was enough to make her cry out and struggle over his lap. Each swat was a little bit harder than the last, and when he had finished all ten, Angela's bottom was back to being bright red, and she seemed worn out as she lay over his knee.

Charlie rubbed her sore, swollen cheeks gently, then, once Angela's crying had started to settle, he helped her up onto his lap. He knew that moving around with the plug in would feel strange to her, so he helped her to move slowly. Then he rocked her back and forth, kissing her forehead and smoothing her hair.

He then gave her a kiss on the mouth, passionately caressing her mouth with his. She gripped him and returned it with fervor, climbing so that she was straddling him on the couch. Catching his breath, Charlie took a look at his wife, who was naked but for the plug between her cheeks and the bow on her head. "My gosh, you look cute," he told her with a smile.

He helped Angela to her feet. "You'll look even cuter in a diaper," he said.

Angela looked at the floor. "I don't need a diaper. I'm far too grown up for that," she insisted.

"Whether you need one or not, you aren't allowed to pee in the potty today, so a diaper it will be. Using it is your only choice." Charlie thought for a moment, then added, "Besides, this way I'll know you aren't being a naughty girl and touching yourself without my permission during your nap after lunch, or trying to mess with the punishment plug that I put in you," he explained.

Angela didn't have much to say to this, and instead let Charlie lead her to the changing area, where he lay her down on the blanket. He opened the package of pink diapers and pulled one out. He moved it a little bit to listen to the crinkly noise it made. "This way I can hear where you are!" he said with a smile. Angela didn't seem to think this was funny.

Charlie grabbed her by the legs and lifted her up. In this position, he could see her red bottom, her wet little pussy, and a flash of the pink plug's base. He felt himself growing hard again.

"I can see everything when I lift you up like this," he whispered to Angela, making her squirm a little bit. "It belongs to me," he added, "every part of you does, so you can't hide from me." Charlie slid the pink diaper under Angela's bottom, then gently set her legs down.

He pulled her legs apart so that they were open. He then sprinkled her lightly with the baby powder they had purchased earlier before gently positioning the diaper between her legs and fastening it on the sides. The diaper was big and padded, and it made Angela's backside look even rounder than usual. Charlie thought this was adorable.

Once Angela had been diapered, Charlie helped her up and back into her playsuit. It bulged out in the back from the padding, and he gave her a gentle swat there.

"I didn't feel that," she said. "Maybe diapers are good for something!"

Charlie kissed Angela quickly. "Let's get some lunch and then you can take a nap, ok?" he said, leading her into the kitchen.

CHAPTER ELEVEN

Angela awoke from her nap and wanting to get out of bed, but the crinkling sound she heard when she turned over reminded her of her current condition. Getting up without permission was probably not allowed.

Next to her on her pillow sat the pink pacifier that Charlie had purchased at the store earlier; he had put it in her mouth before bedtime and told her that little girls sucked on pacifiers to fall asleep. Based on the bulge in his pants as he had finished her discipline earlier, Angela thought that maybe her daddy wanted her to suck on something else, but she wasn't sure if little girls were allowed to do that, so she hadn't brought it up.

Angela reluctantly put the pacifier back into her mouth. She felt so stupid as she sucked on it, but she couldn't help but admit that it felt comforting and calming. She just hoped that no one ever found out that she was upstairs in her house in a diaper sucking on a pacifier and waiting for her husband to come let her out of bed.

Angela rolled over onto her stomach. The motion made her realize that she desperately had to use the toilet, and it also brought her attention to just how sore her bottom hole was after having had the plug in there throughout her nap. She considered trying to get out of her diaper and then back into it, but she realized that this would only bring her more trouble than it was worth. She was going to have to just go ahead and use it.

As full as her bladder was and as badly as she wanted to pee, she couldn't bring herself to let go in the diaper. Her body felt confused by the instruction to simply pee while lying in her bed. So she gently climbed out of bed and snuck into the in-suite bathroom, making as little noise as possible. Her diaper crinkled loudly when she moved, but despite what Charlie had said earlier, it wasn't loud enough for him to hear from downstairs. She carefully sat down on the toilet, still dressed, still diapered, still plugged, and still sucking on her pacifier.

Sitting here in this familiar location, she was able to let go and wet her diaper. The feeling of the padding growing wet and warm was strange, but

not unpleasant. She had to admit it was kind of nice. She did, after all, like warm sensations.

Angela crept back into her bed and lay down on her tummy, waiting for Charlie to come and get her. She wanted to call for him, but she had been instructed not to take the pacifier out of her mouth if she could help it. The helplessness of the situation made her feel horny, though it was hard to tell if she was growing wet given the condition of her diaper. She was forbidden from touching herself, but she decided to relieve a little bit of the feeling by just straddling a pillow a little bit.

Angela knelt up on the bed and bunched a pillow up between her legs. There were so many sensations in her body at the moment: the sore, stretched feeling of her bottom hole and the fullness that the punishment plug gave her, the wetness and padding of her diaper, the rubbery taste of the pacifier in her mouth, and all the memories of her shameful humiliations throughout the day. Plus, there was the knowledge of more to come: her bottom no longer hurt, which meant that she was in for a spanking whenever her daddy finally decided to retrieve her.

Angela rocked back and forth on the pillow, biting down hard on the pacifier in her mouth. The friction between her legs felt so good, she couldn't help but let a moan escape around the rubbery nipple in her mouth. She humped the pillow more vigorously, feeling her body fill with pleasure.

"Ahem," she heard from the doorway, just as she was about to come close to orgasming. "Is this what you call staying in bed?" Charlie asked.

Angela felt sheepish, having been caught in the act. She once again remembered how silly she must look, and she was embarrassed by the crinkling sound that she heard as she self-consciously dismounted the pillow.

Charlie walked to Angela's side and pulled the pacifier out of her mouth so she could answer.

"You told me not to touch myself, and you told me not to come. I haven't done either of them," she insisted. She knew it was a loophole, but she hoped it was one that would work.

Charlie sighed. "I suppose that's technically true," he told her.

"Also, my diaper is wet and my bottom isn't sore, so I…" Angela felt her lip trembling as she prepared herself to say the next few words, "so I need to be spanked again."

"Good girl for letting me know," Charlie said, smiling at her and gently brushing her cheek. "Because you were honest, I'm going to take it easy on you this time. Let's go downstairs and get you changed," he said. He reached out to help her out of bed.

Between her full diaper and her plugged bottom, Angela found it difficult to walk, but she did her best to get downstairs. She was sure that she looked comical trying to manage.

When she arrived, Charlie instructed her to lie down on the blanket again.

She did as she was told, and Charlie unfastened her diaper and then lifted her legs again to pull it out from under her.

Angela particularly disliked this position; no other pose that Charlie put her in made her feel more exposed in a more uncomfortable way.

"Keep your legs up," Charlie commanded as he went to throw the wet diaper in the trashcan. He returned with a baby wipe, and gently cleaned her pussy and bottom with it.

It felt like he was taking longer than he really needed to, and the cold, wet sensation was strange to Angela. It made her feel helpless to have someone else cleaning her up this way, and she couldn't bring herself to think too hard about what, exactly, he was doing.

Angela was athletic and flexible, so it wasn't too much of a feat for her to stay with her legs in the air, but she could feel the air of the house circulating against her pussy and bottom, and it only reminded her of how horny she was.

Charlie returned and took a moment to eye Angela as she held her legs up. Then he reached down and gently slid his finger under the edge of the butt plug's base, coaxing it away from her body. Angela let out a hiss of relief as he gave a gentle tug to let it pop out. It hurt for a second as the flared area stretched its way out of her bottom, but it was soon over. Her bottom muscles tightened, not used to not having something to grab onto.

"Thank you, daddy," Angela whispered, her legs still pointing at the ceiling.

"You're welcome, little angel," he told her. "Now, it's time for you to be spanked again."

Angela knew this was coming, and hardly reacted to it. She got ready to get up, but she felt Charlie's hand holding her by the leg.

"Stay like this," he instructed. "This is how I'm going to spank you."

Angela thought this was a terrible idea. "Noooo, daddy, please! Haven't I been good today?" she begged.

"You had been until I caught you masturbating on my pillow," he chastised. "And I made it clear that I would accept no whining from you today."

Angela looked away so that her husband wouldn't see her pout.

"I'm going to spank you now, because you deserve it, and you're going to hold still and keep your legs up or else you'll get hairbrush swats in this position. Do I make myself clear?"

"Yes, daddy," Angela said with as little whining in her tone as she could muster.

Charlie began to spank her, using his free hand to steady her legs and keep them from kicking too much. The spanks started faster than they usually did, and Angela couldn't help but cry out right away. Her bottom felt stretched taut in this position, and every swat stung more. Plus, he was able to reach

areas that were usually not so easily accessed, like the crease where her bottom cheeks and thighs meet.

Charlie peppered her bottom with swats and Angela let out a howl, but she tried her best to be still. He focused on her sit spots, and Angela could feel the heat blossoming there. She felt like her bottom had to be swollen and bright red already. It was agonizing.

Even worse, Angela was still incredibly horny, and she was worried that there was no relief in sight. Was Charlie going to put her through this series of spankings without giving her any relief? Surely he must be longing to fuck her, too?

Her thoughts were broken by a series of four very hard swats that sent a shockwave through her body.

"Daddy!" Angela cried out. "I promise to be a good girl! I promise!"

Charlie's only response was to set her legs down and Angela immediately rolled over onto her tummy, not wanting her bottom against the floor.

"That should keep you tender for a while," her daddy told her. She found this strangely reassuring.

"Now," Charlie told her, "we need to address your horniness. I know you know it's natural for little girls to get aroused when they are punished, don't you?"

Angela nodded vigorously. She knew that her horniness did need to be addressed, and soon.

"Still, it's not appropriate behavior for little girls who wet their diapers and suck on pacifiers to masturbate, and I told you not to. I didn't tell you not to use your hands. I didn't tell you not to make yourself come. I told you not to masturbate, and that's exactly what I caught you doing, isn't it?" Charlie asked scoldingly.

This conversation was not going the way Angela wanted it to, but she did her best not to pout.

Charlie got up and grabbed the jar of vapor rub that he had purchased at the store that morning.

"I'm going to give you some relief and your discipline for this behavior all at once," he told her.

Angela watched nervously as he opened the jar. The minty scent wafted out and she took a deep breath. It reminded her of having a cold, and she tried to remember if the rub felt tingly on her skin when she had applied it last time she was sick. She couldn't muster the memory.

Charlie positioned Angela so she was lying flat on the changing blanket with her legs apart, then he dipped his forefinger into the jar. He got a dab of the rub on it.

"I'm going to make you come," he told her, "by rubbing your little clit the way I know you want me to. But I'm going to be rubbing this punishment cream into it, too, and that's going to make your little girl parts sting and

67

burn. It's going to teach you a lesson about who the area between your legs belongs to, and that naughty little girls aren't allowed to play with themselves. It's also going to remind you not to try to find loopholes in what I tell you to do. Am I clear?"

Angela swallowed hard, but she nodded. "Yes, sir," she whispered.

Charlie began to rub Angela's clit with the gel. At first, it just felt cool and wet, similar to the way that lube would feel when it was first rubbed on her bottom hole. His finger felt so good rubbing her there, though, and she raised her hips up, trying to bring herself closer to him. Then he began to rub her faster, and she felt her body react to the vapor rub. It was a cool feeling, not at all stinging or burning. It felt sort of tingly and fresh, but cool and nice. She moaned loudly.

"Not so bad?" Charlie asked.

"No, it's nice," Angela admitted.

Charlie dipped his finger back in the jar and gently spread a line of the rub down the sides of her labia majora. Then he added a little dab of it to the outside of her bottom hole. Again, they felt cool and almost comforting, especially as Charlie went back to working her clit with his fingers.

Her bottom hole began to sting a little, and after a moment, the tingling turned to a gentle burn. She couldn't help but focus on the pleasurable feelings coming from her clit, though. Her clit felt so warm and throbbing with arousal that even when the cream began to tingle there, too, she didn't mind. All the sensations mixed together into a painful pleasure, and the burning feeling only made her grow wetter. She gripped the blanket with both hands and tightened her leg muscles.

Charlie smiled down at her, his dark eyes twinkling. "Can you feel it?" he asked.

Angela nodded. "Yeah, it's… stinging and cool… feeling," she tried to get out in between gasping breaths of pleasure.

"Are you going to come for me now, my darling?" Charlie asked.

Angela nodded, her attention darting back and forth between the stinging on her bottom hole and the lovely waves of pleasure that were radiating from her clit. The more she focused on her clit, the more she could feel the tingly sensation there. It was growing, reaching a higher level of stinging just as she was reaching a higher level of intense ecstasy. She threw her head back and let out a desperate howl, writhing back and forth as orgasm took her into its hold. She wasn't sure when one orgasm ended and the next began, or if she simply came for a minute straight, but by the time she was done, she collapsed, feeling totally exhausted.

Charlie kissed her again, passionately scooping her up in his arms and holding her close to him as he did so.

It was during this post-orgasmic bliss that she really started to feel the vapor rub.

"Oh," she whimpered. "Now that you aren't touching me there, it really burns."

Charlie held Angela closer. "Owwww," she whined. "I don't like this feeling at all!"

"Are you going to obey me properly in the future?" Charlie asked sternly.

"Yes, daddy! I really am! Please make it stop," she begged.

Charlie got up to get a baby wipe to clean her off with, but while he was up, the burning in her pussy died back down to the same cool feeling she had felt at the beginning of the experience, just as quickly as the pain came on.

"That was weird, daddy," Angela whispered. "It stopped hurting and kinda feels nice again."

Charlie wiped her down with the baby wipe anyway, then slipped a pull-up onto her.

"I think this will be a good tool to add to your discipline in the future," Charlie said. "It doesn't last too long, but it seemed to teach you your lesson."

Charlie stood Angela up and helped her back into her clothes over the pull-up. "Ready to be a good girl for the rest of the night?" he asked.

"I am! I'll be so good," she replied quickly. She didn't want to get punished any more.

"If you can obey me, I won't punish you again tonight. You still will be treated like a very little girl, of course, but you won't get any more spankings or other punishments unless you earn them. I'm proud of how well you've taken your discipline so far today," he told her, giving her a kiss on the cheek.

"Thank you, daddy!" Angela said, surprised at how little she minded the residual tingle from the vapor rub, soreness in her bottom, and the soft feeling of the pull-up around it in that moment.

CHAPTER TWELVE

The next morning, Charlie woke up before Angela like he did almost every day. This time, though, instead of seeing his wife next to him sleeping in short nightgown or a pair of casual pajamas, he looked over to see her snuggled up to him in a pair of footies, her bottom heavily padded with a diaper. He couldn't help but smile at just how cute she looked.

Angela had managed to behave herself for the rest of last night, and had made Charlie proud. She hadn't even had a tantrum when he pulled out the embarrassing footie pajamas and then diapered her for bed. He hoped that this was a sign that Angela was taking the lesson to heart.

He got up and took a shower, shaved, and then got dressed. He headed downstairs to make a quick breakfast for himself and his wife: a couple of fried eggs and some toast with a side of strawberries was easy enough to make. He knew that Angela liked her eggs over hard, and made sure there was no runny yolk for his picky little girl. He couldn't imagine loving anyone else as much as he loved Angela, no matter how naughty or willful she could be sometimes.

After he had finished cooking, he went upstairs again to rouse his sleepy darling.

"Angie," he whispered, shaking her gently.

Angela stirred and muttered, "Time to get up?"

"Yes, breakfast is ready. Is your diaper dry, sweetie?" he asked.

Angela nodded. "Yes, daddy, but I have to go now."

"Well, once you've used your diaper, I'll change you into a pull-up and get you dressed for the day," he told her.

"Can't I just use the toilet?" Angela whimpered.

Charlie shot her a stern glance from the corner of his eye. "I'm going to pretend I didn't hear that, young lady," he scolded.

Angela hung her head.

"I'll go in my diaper, then," she said as she pouted.

Charlie nodded. "It's not coming off until you do," he told her, helping

her out of bed.

The two of them headed downstairs for a quiet breakfast. Angela wasn't entirely awake yet, and she rubbed at her eyes while she nibbled on her toast or took bites of her egg, which Charlie had cut up for her before she arrived at the table.

Charlie let Angela go off on her own for a little bit while he cleared the table, and as he was loading the dishwasher, she returned, her face pink with embarrassment.

"Daddy," she whispered. "I need my diaper changed. I wet myself."

"Go lie down on the blanket in the living room and wait for me to come change you," Charlie instructed, grabbing her diapered bottom to feel that it was, indeed, warm and full.

Charlie stripped Angela out of her footie pajamas and then laid her down, removing her diaper and cleaning her off with a wipe like he had done before. Then he set her legs down and told her to stand up and go over to the couch.

Angela bit her lip hesitantly, but obeyed her daddy. Charlie was pleased with her obedience.

"Bend over the arm of the sofa, bottom on display," Charlie instructed. He eyed her bottom carefully, making sure he hadn't left any marks yesterday. Once again, she had healed overnight.

"Today," he told her, "is the last day of your punishment. To start today off, I want you thinking about being kind and respectful to everyone you meet, no matter who they are or how they're different to you. I want you to hold that thought in your mind while I whip your bottom with my belt," he told her.

"Daddy! Please! Haven't I been punished enough?" she asked.

"Clearly I don't think so," Charlie said. "I promised you a set of severe consequences when I warned you about behaving this way and you still let me down."

Angela pouted, looking back at her daddy grumpily.

Charlie went and found her pacifier and stuck it in her mouth.

"Grumpy, pouty little girls need their binkies to keep them from whining," he told her, watching the red flush that he had grown used to seeing on her face return.

"Stick your bottom out more. I want to be able to see your pussy while I punish you," he ordered.

Angela responded by pushing her hips back and widening her stance a little.

"Good girl," Charlie praised.

Then he quickly pulled his belt through the loops and into his hand. Angela shivered as she heard the noise of it. She was no stranger to his belt; it was one of the implements that he used most often in her day-to-day correction.

71

Charlie measured his first stroke like he always did, being careful not to wrap or hit too high, then he swung it. It wasn't particularly hard, but without a hand spanking to warm her up, Angela gasped.

"Owwwww! Daddy, I'm sorry!" she tried to whimper, but it was obviously hard for her to talk with the pacifier in her mouth and her words came out slushed and slurred.

Charlie admired the wide, red stripe that the belt left across his little girl's perky bottom, then pulled back and swung again.

Angela cried out again, pounding her fist against the sofa.

Charlie gave her three strokes in quick succession and Angela let out one long, continuous howl.

"Pleeeeeeassssse?" she tried to whine. The effect of her trying to talk around the pacifier was comical.

"You know you deserve this," Charlie said as he delivered another set of rapid fire strokes, this time five.

Angela was starting to sniffle again, and her bottom was no longer striped, but solid red. She swayed her hips back and forth as if trying to shake the soreness out of her backside.

"Five more, baby girl," Charlie said. "Remember the lesson as each one stings your bottom."

He made each one count, increasing the intensity with each swat. Angela had tears running down her face by the time that he delivered the last stroke.

Charlie left her in position as he replaced his belt, then brought her into his arms for her customary aftercare cuddles.

When her tears had stopped, he whispered to her, "I'm going to get you dressed up for the day, and then we're going to go on another errand. After that, you can have your final punishment and get ready to be a big girl again if you're good. Do you want that?"

Angela bounced giddily when she heard this news, promising that she was definitely going to be good.

Charlie bopped her on the nose and then led her upstairs to get her dressed and into a pull-up to go out.

CHAPTER THIRTEEN

Angela sat in the car and didn't want to move. Her bottom was sore and tender from the belting that she had just received, and she worried that today's outfit was more embarrassing to be seen in than the jumpsuit that she had been wearing the day before. Charlie had dressed her in a short, pink baby-doll dress that barely covered her pull-up. The dress was as flouncy and lacy as possible, and she had to be very still to keep it from flashing her padded, sore bottom.

The errand that her daddy had referred to earlier turned out to be the last thing that Angela wanted to do: she had to go apologize to Jensen and Claire for her behavior the other day. She didn't have to tell them the myriad ways in which she had been disciplined for this outburst, but at least one of them was going to be pretty self-evident when they saw her.

Charlie came around, opened Angela's door, and then unbuckled her seatbelt. He held her hand as she walked up the icy driveway toward their porch and then rang the doorbell for them.

Jensen answered the door, looking kind and friendly. Angela still felt scared to see him, though, and she didn't know what to say to him. He invited them in and then offered to take Angela's coat.

Angela handed her coat over to him hesitantly, for taking it off fully revealed what she was wearing. Jensen made no comment on her dress, and Charlie didn't point it out. Jensen invited them into the living room and then called for Claire.

Claire came down the stairs with an anxious look on her face. Angela realized that she was scared of her, and her heart fell a little bit. She truly never wanted to hurt someone's feelings like this again.

"Well?" Charlie asked. "What do you have to say for yourself, Angela?"

Angela still didn't know what she had to say for herself, but she took a deep breath and decided to just say whatever she was thinking.

"I'm really sorry that I was mean the other day," she started. "The way I acted to Claire was really not fair, and she didn't deserve that. There's nothing

wrong with what being little means to her, and I was only acting out because I was feeling bad about myself. I know now how bad my behavior has made people feel in the past and I promise it isn't going to happen again."

Charlie put his arm around Angela. "That was really good, sweetheart," he praised. "I'm proud of you."

Both Claire and Jensen accepted Angela's apology, and Angela told Claire that she hoped that she would give her another try and that they could be friends in the future. She still seemed a little apprehensive, but Angela couldn't blame her for that.

They didn't stay at Claire and Jensen's house long, since the situation had been awkward to begin with, but Angela felt much better once they had left. They obviously didn't hate her, and deep down inside, she had been pretty convinced that they would. Her heart felt lighter as they drove home, even though she knew that it was only to face more discipline. At least the end was in sight.

CHAPTER FOURTEEN

When they got into their house, Charlie gave Angela a big hug and kiss.

"I'm so proud of you for being brave with your feelings when we went to apologize," he told her. "I know that's hard for you. You've proven to me that this punishment has been effective and that you've really learned something."

"Can I have my big girl clothes back now?" Angela asked enthusiastically. She was obviously not thrilled with the extreme laciness nor the excessive shortness of her current attire.

"Not yet, baby," he told her. "There was one more punishment that I promised you, wasn't there?" he asked. His eyes pointed to the brown paper parcel that they had brought home from Mr. Larson's shop.

"Yes, daddy," Angela said with a sigh, her hope rapidly fading.

"I'm going to give you a little break before I cane you," he said. "We can snuggle on the couch and watch some TV or something, if that sounds good to you."

"Can we watch a grownup show?" she asked.

"I think that would be okay," Charlie told her.

The two of them snuggled up on the sofa and Angela picked a program that she wanted to watch. Charlie wasn't particularly interested in it, but it felt nice to just relax for a moment. It had been a long weekend.

When the show drew to a close, Angela seemed relaxed and a little bit more bubbly than she had been since her punishment began yesterday morning. She giggled at the sillier parts of it, and chattered to Charlie about what she liked and didn't like when the show was less interesting to her.

"Angela, I love you so much," Charlie told her. Every time he said this to her, it felt like the first time. He got a rush of butterflies as he thought about how lucky he was to have found such a sweet, lovable woman with whom he could live out all of his fantasies.

"I love you, too, Charlie," she responded, and he could tell by the look in her eyes that she was thinking the same thing. "I'm so glad you're my husband

and my daddy, and I'm so glad you love me enough to correct me when I'm not a good girl."

"I always will," Charlie promised.

He turned to the TV and saw that the credits for the show were rolling and the 'Next Up banner was on the bottom of the screen.

"I think you know that it's time for a little more discipline, don't you?" he asked his wife.

Angela nodded nervously.

Charlie flipped off the TV and took Angela by the hand. He picked up the brown paper package and led her up the stairs and into the bedroom.

CHAPTER FIFTEEN

Angela had thought that she was at her most nervous when Charlie had led her to Jensen and Claire's door to apologize, but now that she was being led into her own room for her first caning, she wasn't so sure. Her heart was beating a mile a minute and her hands were sweaty. She had no idea what to expect, but the memory of the sound the cane had made when it had been sliced through the air in the store scared her.

Charlie stood her in front of him and then slowly and ceremoniously unwrapped the paper from the cane. It had a slightly yellow color to it and the finish glistened in the light.

"Take your pull-up off," Charlie instructed. "You can have big girl panties back after I'm done with you here."

Angela slowly slipped the pull-up off her legs and handed it to her daddy.

He took it and tossed it in the trashcan before returning to stand in front of Angela.

It felt good to Angela to see him throw the pull-up away. It meant that her time as a little girl was truly going to be over, and she would be able to go back to enjoying life as usual. She was so appreciative of her daily routine now that it had been interrupted, and she could not wait to dress herself, to sit in the front seat of the car, and to cut up her own food. But one more obstacle stood between her and that freedom, and it was a long, thin piece of rattan in her daddy's hands.

"I'm going to give you ten strokes," Charlie told her, his voice serious. "This is going to hurt, a lot, but I want you to stay in position until it's finished, do you understand me?"

Angela agreed with him, promising to do her best. Then Charlie instructed her to bend over the bed. She thought about how bare and vulnerable her bottom was as Charlie pulled the hem of her short dress up even higher. Then she felt a gentle tap, tap, tap of the cane against her bottom.

Suddenly, she heard the same swishing noise that had scared her in the store, but this time it was followed by a cracking sound as it collided with her

bottom. She cried out pitifully as she felt a line of fire burning into her bottom. Charlie paused and the pain continued to grow, making her twist her hips for a second, but she soon returned to her position.

"Good girl," Charlie praised. "That was one."

The second stroke arrived just below the first, and the pain felt even sharper when it was coupled with the growing agony that the first stroke had caused her. She let out a little howl.

Charlie didn't wait so long before delivering the third stroke, and it caught Angela by surprise. She yelped, jumping up and down in pain. No spanking had ever hurt so much, so quickly before.

The fourth stroke crossed the third, and all of Angela's attention was focused on that small patch of skin. It was like her universe had shrunk, and she was only able to pay attention to the hot, white sting that was biting into her.

The fifth and sixth strokes happened back to back, with no break in between, but they weren't as hard as the previous few had been. The rapid-fire feeling made adrenaline surge through Angela's body, and she knew she could endure the next four strokes.

The next stroke was the one that made Angela start to sob. She had been too shocked by the pain before to cry, but now that she was used to it, she couldn't fight it as much, and the tears started to roll down her face.

Once she crossed that threshold, the final strokes were more manageable. She gripped the blankets hard, but the last three didn't make her wail the way the others did. She had accepted her fate.

When Charlie finished, Angela's bottom felt hotter than it ever had. She reached her hand back to rub it and was surprised to discover that she could still feel each line where the cane had struck.

Charlie stood her back up and then lifted her arms for her, her face still wet with tears. He pulled her pink baby-doll dress over her head and then looked her straight in the eye.

"You took your punishment like a big girl. I'm so proud of you, sweetie."

Angela hugged him around the waist, hard. She rested her head on his strong chest and snuggled there until all her tears were gone.

As the pain started to fade away, Angela discovered that there was a second layer of soreness beneath the stinging burn that the cane had left when it first met with her tender bottom. As that began to dissipate, she was left instead with a deep ache and a feeling of heat.

"Daddy, I'm the horniest I've ever been," she admitted to her husband. "I need you to fuck me now that I'm your big girl again."

Charlie grinned from ear to ear. "I've been waiting for this, my love," he told her.

Angela hopped up onto the bed and knelt on all fours, wanting to be taken from behind like she had been the other night. Charlie left the room for a

second without saying anything, and Angela wondered what he was looking for. When he returned, she knew right away why he had left.

Instead of slipping his hard cock into her dripping wet pussy, Angela felt Charlie's lubed finger probing at her bottom hole.

"This isn't a punishment," he told her. "This is a reward. I know you've been wanting this, haven't you?" he asked.

Angela felt her juices running down her leg. Oh, God, how badly she wanted him to fuck her ass. After taking her caning, she was no longer afraid of anything and all she felt was desire.

"Please, daddy," she begged. "Please, I really want you to put it in my bottom."

"Yeah?" Charlie asked as he moved his finger quickly in and out of her hole. "Is that what you really want?"

"Yes!" Angela whimpered, reaching down to touch her clit as Charlie warmed her bottom hole up. He slipped a second finger inside and continued at the same pace, but it didn't hurt in the least. She was floating on endorphins and her whole body felt made of pleasure.

"I'm ready, daddy," she insisted. "Please put your cock in me."

Charlie responded by pulling his fingers out and quickly stripping out of his t-shirt, jeans, and briefs. Angela peered back over her shoulder to admire his muscular body, thinking about how strong he looked and how easily he could control her. She stared down at his cock as he coated it with lube: it was big and as hard as she had ever seen it, but she felt no fear of how it would feel inside of her. She simply had to know.

Charlie came back to her and returned his fingers to her bottom hole once more, moving them more roughly this time. It probably should have hurt, but if it did, she wasn't processing it. She could feel the heat and the soreness coming from the cane lines on her bottom, but all that her bottom hole told her was that it wanted to be filled with cock.

Finally, she felt Charlie prod her with the head of his member. The lube and warmup helped him to gently slide in.

"Oh, God," Angela moaned. It felt different than the plugs or fingers had; warm and big and so much more filling. He pulled back to thrust forward, and she gasped. The motions were painful, but they hurt in a way that she couldn't get enough of.

"More! Please!" she whimpered.

Charlie laughed and began to fuck her with a slow but steady pace. "You like having my cock in your bottom hole?" he asked.

Angela's answer was more of a yell. "Oh, yes! Oh, God, yes!"

"Rub your clit while I fuck you," Charlie commanded.

Angela dropped down lower, resting her head against the bed and waving her striped, sore bottom in the air as Charlie pounded into it. Her fingers worked at her clit as quickly as they could, and it wasn't long before she came

to a powerful orgasm.

As her body shook with pleasure, she felt her muscles tighten around Charlie's cock and Charlie let out a moan of his own.

He began to fuck her even more vigorously now. Even in the last waves of her orgasm, Angela could feel her bottom hole growing sore and tired from all of the attention it had received, but the pain only made her wetter.

Charlie took her hips in his hands and slammed her back and forth, forcing her to take his cock deeper and deeper into her bottom. She cried out with each pump, but begged him not to stop.

Finally, Charlie's grunts and moans combined into one long cry of pleasure and he moved more desperately, grabbing hard onto Angela as he thrust quickly and deeply. "Ahhhhhhhhh," he groaned. "Oh, Angela." Then he let out a primal sound, like some deep hunger in him was being fulfilled, and Angela felt his hot ejaculation flow out of his cock and deep into her.

When he had caught his breath, he carefully pulled out of her and she turned to face him, not caring at all what she looked like in that moment. She knew that to Charlie, she looked perfect, and that was all that mattered. She looked at her husband, as he stood there nude in front of her, trying to catch his breath from the powerful orgasm that he'd just had. His muscles glistened with sweat and his hair was disheveled. She pulled him close to her and kissed him on the mouth for a moment before they collapsed into each other's arms.

"You're such a good girl," he told her. "I love you so much."

"I promise I will be a good girl," Angela reaffirmed. "And I'll always love you."

THE END

DADDY'S LITTLE SWEETHEART

MEREDITH O'REILLY

CHAPTER ONE

"Oh! I hate that jackass!" I yelled as I walked into the living room. I tossed my briefcase a little harder than normal onto the leather couch, sat down, crossed my arms, and let out a huff.

Jensen, my darling husband, looked up from his laptop from the opposite side of the room as he sat in the leather recliner. "What did he do now?"

Seeing as I had frequently complained about Alan Smith, a.k.a 'The Jackass', Jensen knew exactly who I was talking about. Smith was one of my co-workers and he had a tendency of butting his nose in my business and then finding a way to give himself all the credit for my hard work. I had tried to stop him before, but the little sneak always found a way to take responsibility for my projects. I didn't want to complain to the partners of the company because then I would look like a tattle-tale and what boss wanted one of those on their staff?

"He took another one of my big clients and told me that I worked with the smaller clients better and should leave the big ones for him. That is total crap! He just wants a big client—a big client that I got to come to our company, yet Smith is getting the credit for bringing him there. I don't get why the partners don't realize that he does this shit. Ahh! I just want to shove a book up his ass!" I ended with a shout and a kick against the coffee table. "*Ouch!*" I yelped, as I grabbed my right foot and rubbed it to try and ease the pain.

Note to self: don't kick wooden coffee table without a shoe on, I thought as the pain started to dissipate.

Once I stopped moaning about my foot, I looked up at my husband, who had been surprisingly quiet during my rant and my moaning about my injury. Normally he would have been by my side, kissing my boo-boo to make it all better. Well, if it had been the weekend, that's what he would have been doing. Still, I was surprised that he hadn't even offered to get me some ice.

"Aren't you going to say something?" I asked, when he continued to remain silent.

"You should make the book a paperback. Hmmm… probably a cookbook, or a yellow pages book," he said with a straight face.

"What are you talking about?" I asked as I began to get irritated that he wasn't listening to me when I needed to vent about my stupid co-worker.

"I'm talking about the book that you're going to shove up Smith's ass. I'd make it a paperback, but make sure it's thick—like a yellow pages book."

I stared at my husband's straight face and then all of a sudden, I burst out laughing. I laughed deep belly-aching laughs and then noticed that my husband had joined in.

After several minutes, I calmed down to a constant giggle as I imagined actually shoving a yellow pages book up Smith's ass. Oh, that would feel good. He'd finally get what was coming to him.

"Feel better, honey?"

I nodded. I felt great. That was what I loved about my husband. I could be ready to murder someone and he could pull me back from the edge and make me laugh until I completely forgot what had made me upset in the first place.

"Come here. Why don't we have some cuddles?" he asked, putting his laptop on the small end table next to the recliner and opening his arms for me to come and sit in his lap.

"Cuddles? Honey, it's Tuesday. We don't do cuddles, except on the weekend," I said, wondering what had gotten into my husband.

Jensen and I had a semi-traditional marriage. During the week, we lived like any other regular couple. We both had our own jobs, we hung out with friends, and did normal things.

But on the weekends, things deviated from what most people would probably consider a traditional marriage. I would regress to a five-year-old little girl, and my husband would take on the role of daddy. We started doing this right after we said our marriage vows. It was a great way for me to relax and not have to worry about work, and my husband enjoyed getting to take care of me. He said that he liked the control and he liked knowing that I had so much trust in him that he could take care of basically every decision for me.

Jensen and I took our age play relationship so seriously that we had moved to a special community called Little Haven, which was a private community where couples who engaged in age play relationships could live together without any judgement. It was actually a really neat place. We had a daycare for the residents who wanted to be little twenty-four seven, and we had a pool, a park, a doctor's office, and a library. It was our own little town, where everyone could act how they wanted without worrying about what others' thought. It was perfect.

We had always agreed that we would only play on the weekends because I didn't like the idea of having a twenty-four seven relationship. I felt like if I

did, I would lose the adult side of me and Jensen would end up taking over my life. For some girls, that might sound glamorous and like a dream come true, but I liked my adult side just as much as I liked my little side. Jensen knew this, so I didn't understand why he was offering to do something that we only did on the weekends, as it was only a week night.

"I know, sweetie," he said, getting up and walking over to me. He moved my briefcase, set it on the coffee table, and sat down next to me. "I've been watching you for the past couple of weeks. You constantly come home stressed from work, and because of that you've been eating less and you haven't been sleeping as well. I want to help you, and I know that acting little helps you."

"No!" I shouted, standing up a little too quickly. The room spun for a moment and I had to put my hand on the couch to balance. Thankfully, Jensen didn't notice.

"Honey, hear me out—"

"No! I... thank you, sweetie, for thinking of me and hoping this would help, but I'll be okay."

"Claire," he said, standing up.

"Enough, Jensen!" I screamed, but once the words were out of my mouth, I knew I had made a big mistake. It didn't matter if it was a weekday or if it was during the weekend, Jensen had a firm rule about treating each other with respect, and I had just broken that rule by cutting him off.

His face visibly darkened as it always did when I had crossed a line with something I had said or done.

"Jensen... I'm sorry. I didn't mean to be rude," I said, taking a few steps back, hoping that my apology would get me out of the spanking I had just earned.

"Claire, I know that you know better than to speak to me or anyone else like that. You should always treat other people with respect and not cut them off just because you disagree with them. Now come here."

"But—" I said, stopping in my tracks as he continued.

"The only butt I want to hear of is yours coming over here—right now— and lying across my lap," Jensen said as he walked into the kitchen, pulled out a chair, and sat down.

I sighed, knowing that no matter what I did now, I wasn't going to be getting out of this spanking.

I walked over to him. He gestured for me to lie over his lap, so I did. Thankfully, he didn't prolong anything and began rapidly smacking my clothed bottom. The smacks didn't really hurt, but I knew that wouldn't last long.

He continued to spank my clothed bottom for a minute more and then he said, "I think this has to come off." He tugged at my skirt and panties, pulling them off of me, exposing my creamy rounded bottom to his gaze.

"Tell me why you're getting spanked, Claire," he said, rubbing his hands over my cool skin.

"Because I was rude to you…"

"You were, and I will not tolerate rudeness," he said, and just like that, the spanking began again.

He spanked every inch of my bottom, spreading the heat and pain. I squirmed against his thighs, trying to get away from his hand, but within seconds, he had a firm hand on my lower back, keeping me still.

"Ouch! Jensen! I'm sorry…" I cried out, hoping that my apology would make him end the spanking. But it continued anyway.

He started spanking me harder, and each slap sent a fiery pain through my cheeks. I imagined the skin on my bottom turning as red as a stop sign and I started to sob. I tried to keep still as I knew I'd have to wait until he decided that I had been properly punished.

Finally, he stopped and repositioned me so I was sitting on his lap.

"I'm really sorry…" I cried as he rocked me in his arms.

"It's okay, sweetie. You're forgiven," he said, kissing my forehead.

My bottom felt very sore, and I cried for a little while longer. I hated punishment spankings. I always avoided them, but lately, it seemed like I was getting them at least three times a week. I knew that wasn't going to help my case about how I shouldn't act little more often, and I remembered my mother always saying that children who acted out were the ones who needed attention. I hoped that Jensen didn't think that way too.

"Claire, I know that you don't like the idea of being little more often, but I think that you should try it. I hate seeing you so stressed, especially when I know that I can help you release some of that stress. Please, just try this. Let daddy help you," he said, giving me a kiss on my cheek.

I snuggled into his chest. I knew that no matter what I decided, he would respect my decision. And in a way, I wanted to act little more often, at least for a while. I knew that he was right. It would help me relax, and lately, I really had been stressed.

But I also remembered reading some age play books where the little girls were forced to be little and they soon lost all their adult freedoms. I couldn't let that happen to me. I knew that it sounded paranoid, but I was better safe than sorry.

Reaching my decision, I pulled my head back so I could look at Jensen. "No, Jensen. I'm sorry, I just… I don't want to act little more than I already do. I'm really fine. I just need to be more assertive at work."

His smiling lips fell and became a grim line. I knew that meant that he disagreed with my decision, but instead he said, "No, you aren't fine. But for now, I'll respect your decision. However, if you continue to be this stressed or get worse, I won't care what you say, you'll be acting like my little girl every night."

"But—" I tried to protest. That went against what we had agreed on when we got married. He was the one that had stressed that I was the one who would decide when I got to be little or not.

He held a finger to my lips to stop me. "It's my responsibility to take care of you, Claire. I won't let anyone—not even you—get in the way of doing that."

"But—" I tried to say my piece, but he continued.

"No buts. Unless you wish for me to spank yours again."

"No, thank you," I said, shaking my head as he pulled his finger away from my lips.

"Good girl. Now, I think it's time for someone to take a shower, and after that, we'll eat dinner," he said, then stood up and carried me bridal style upstairs.

"Jensen! You don't have to carry me! I can walk."

"I know you can, but I like taking care of you," he said as he finished climbing the stairs and headed into our bathroom.

I sighed, then placed my head on his shoulder. *I guess there are worse things a husband could like.*

CHAPTER TWO

Despite my protests, Jensen got in the shower with me and washed my body and hair with such tenderness that my heart began melting. I truly loved this man. When we finished, he dried me off, brushed my hair, and got me dressed in a fresh pair of warm, comfortable pajamas. He placed me in bed, then said, "I'm going to run downstairs and get dinner. I hope you're okay with just sandwiches tonight."

"That sounds perfect," I said, giving him a smile as he left the room.

I lay back against my pillows and thought about what he had said earlier. I loved when I was little. It was always such a relaxing time for me. I got to regress back to my five-year-old self and just color or read. I didn't have to worry about my work, what bills needed to be paid, what to make for dinner, or stupid Smith and his thieving ways. I really didn't like that guy. The partners of the firm had hired him a couple of months after me and even back then, I could tell that he was a weasel. I still didn't understand why they had hired him.

Most of the time, I caught him in the act of stealing my work and stopped him, but there were a few occasions, like tonight, when he managed to steal one of my clients and I somehow missed it. It was really unfair, but that was life.

Still, I had to figure out how Smith had stolen this last client. I knew that it was going to keep me up most of the night as I wouldn't be able to sleep until I'd figured it out. And of course, Jensen was going to love that, so I was going to have to make sure to be extra quiet. If he woke up in the middle of the night and found out that I was still awake, he'd try to make me go back to sleep. But even when I tried to be extra quiet and not wake him, he seemed to always know when I was awake and thinking during the night.

Coming home tonight and hearing Jensen's idea about being little more often had been the cherry on top of my cake. The idea was tempting, but I knew that I couldn't do it. I loved being little, but I couldn't help being afraid that if Jensen and I played more than we already did, he would start to see

me as only a little girl and then start treating me like that permanently.

I had read more than my fair share of age play books and found that to happen often. If it happened to me, I didn't know what I would do.

"You have such a serious face for someone who is supposed to be relaxing," Jensen said as he came back in with a tray full of sandwiches and drinks.

"I was just thinking about work and stuff," I said, not wanting to lie. I was a horrible liar and Jensen had a firm rule about lying. I figured if I said at least half of the truth, he wouldn't know that I had been worrying about his offer. Technically I was telling him part of the truth and then I wouldn't look like I was lying. I was just omitting the part that I knew could give him crazy ideas.

He sighed. "Claire, that's precisely why I want you to start acting little more often. If you did, then you could be coloring right now or playing with your Barbie dolls, instead of worrying about that jackass."

"Don't worry, Jensen. I have it all under control. Is this one mine?" I asked, reaching for the tuna salad sandwich and hoping that it would divert his mind from the subject.

"Yes. I know how much you like tuna salad."

"Thanks," I said, picking it up and taking a bite. As I did, my stomach let out a grumble. I'd forgotten how hungry I was. *Probably because you missed lunch today,* a little voice in my head whispered.

Jensen and I talked about our days as we continued eating. When I finished, I couldn't help yawning loudly.

"Hmm… it sounds like someone is tired. I think it's time for you to go to sleep."

"But, it's only eight o'clock!" I protested.

"I don't care. I know that you haven't been sleeping well these past few nights. I want you to brush your teeth and be back in bed by the time that I get back up here. No arguments," he said, then picked up the tray and left the bedroom.

I got up and did my nightly routine—brushing my teeth, going to the bathroom, and brushing out my long blonde hair and putting it into a braid. I hated sleeping with my hair not braided or up in some way. If I left it down, it never failed to clump up into what felt like one big knot the next morning. I couldn't wait to cut it and donate it to Locks of Love.

Once I finished all of that, I jumped back into bed. I let out another yawn as my head hit my pillow.

"All ready for bed?" Jensen asked, walking back into the room and coming over to my side of the bed.

"Yes."

"Good. Now I want you to go right to sleep. No staying up and thinking about ways that Smith got another one of your clients," he said, pushing the

covers up to my chin.

"I know. Don't worry. I'm tired enough to go to sleep now. 'Night."

"Goodnight, Claire," he said, kissing my head.

CHAPTER THREE

I woke up the next morning to the sound of Anna Kendrick singing her hit song "Cups". I couldn't stand beeping alarm clocks because they always put me in a bad mood. Who wanted to wake up to that obnoxious sound? I clicked the alarm off and rolled over to see that it was six. My eyes bugged out at that. I couldn't believe I'd slept the entire night through without waking up once. I had thought for sure that I would wake up in the middle of the night like I always do, stressing about work or about something else.

I turned my head to see that Jensen wasn't lying next to me. That was odd. He normally was always next to me when I first woke up. He always said that he wanted to be the last thing that I saw at night and the first thing I saw in the morning.

I noticed a note on his pillow and I reached for it.

Dear Claire,
I forgot to tell you that I had an early business meeting this morning. I'll be home at the same time as usual.
I'll see you tonight. Remember to not let the small things bother you today at work.
Love,
Jensen

I couldn't help being disappointed that I wasn't going to get to see him before I left for work. But, I knew that I could deal with it.

With that thought in mind, I hopped out of bed and began getting ready for the day.

• • • • • • •

I pulled my car into the garage, set it to park, then shut the engine off and leaned my head back against the headrest. Today had not gone well at all. Smith had been all too happy to gloat about how he was taking the client he

stole from me out to lunch. It took all my strength not to open my mouth and tell him what I really thought of him.

I took a deep breath and tried to reign in my emotions. I didn't want to walk into the house upset. That was the last thing I needed as it would surely give Jensen the excuse to mention me being little more often.

Taking a few deep breaths to calm myself, I got out of my car and headed inside. "Hi, honey. I'm home," I called out as I slipped off my heels and headed towards the kitchen.

"Hey. Leftover pizza for dinner tonight. Sound good?" he asked, pulling out the box in our fridge.

"Sure," I said, then sat down in my chair and let out a yawn. I was tired, which was odd because I had slept for almost twelve hours the night before.

Jensen quickly brought the pizza over and we silently ate. I just couldn't help but continue to think about my day. I needed to figure out how Smith had gotten this past client and put a stop to it. *Maybe it was my secretary*, I mused.

When I finished dinner, I quietly excused myself to go take a shower. I wanted to escape into the warm bliss of the spray.

I walked into the bathroom and then made fast work of stripping and stepping into the steamy shower. After wetting my body and hair, I reached for the shampoo, put some in my hands, and began to massage it into my scalp. My eyes were closed when two large arms wrapped around me.

I jumped, not expecting to be interrupted in the shower.

"It's just me, baby," he murmured in my ear as he kissed my neck and squeezed me closer.

A warm tingle started in my stomach, then traveled to my core as he continued to kiss my neck. My pussy was beginning to get wet—and not just from the shower.

"Jensen… my hair."

"I'll wash it, baby," he said, removing his arms from around my waist and placing them in my hair. He began to knead my scalp, and I almost melted. It felt so heavenly. I sagged against his chiseled body as I let out a moan.

"Oh gosh… the sounds you make are driving me insane. Keep your eyes closed, baby. I'm going to rinse the soap out," he said, turning me around and bending my head. The warm water washed out the soap and Jensen was soon putting the sprayer back on top of its hook. "Okay. It's safe to open your eyes."

I opened my eyes to see that he was standing there before me. His eyes had darkened and his expression was set in one of determination. It made me giggle for a second because it looked like he was a predator and had just found his prey. I glanced down to appreciate once again the sight of his slightly tanned, muscular body, and his thick cock standing at attention.

Wanting to play, I licked my lips.

I was so busy looking at him that I didn't see him make a move until I was pushed up against the shower wall. He held my hands in one of his, while the other began to play with my breasts. He pinched and pulled at my nipples, each tug sending little sparks of pleasure straight to my pussy. His cock ground into my pussy and made me moan in pure, wanton desire.

"You like this?"

"Yesss…" I moaned as he twisted my nipple extra hard. The pain turned into a bolt of pleasure within seconds.

He smirked and leaned down to kiss me. At the same time, he plunged his cock into my wet folds. My pussy walls squeezed onto him, and Jensen pulled back and let out a moan.

"You like that?" I parroted back at him.

"Funny, honey," he smiled, pulling me forward a little and giving my bottom a smack before he bent down to kiss me again.

He pumped in and out of me until we were both on the edge. Jensen finally pulled me extra close to him, his cock hitting my G-spot perfectly, and we both came, calling out each other's names.

I leaned against the bathroom wall for a few seconds to catch my breath. He was still holding my arms up above my head so I couldn't move.

"That was amazing," I breathed.

"Yes, it was. Let me wash the rest of you off and then we can get out of the shower."

He treated me with such loving affection, washing the rest of me, drying me off, and then dressing me, and brushing my hair.

"Jensen, you really don't have to do this," I said for what felt like the millionth time that night as he tucked me in to bed.

"Nonsense. I know that you're tired. It's my job to take care of you. Now, I want you to go right to sleep, missy. When I come to check on you, you better be asleep or else," he said, tapping my nose.

"Yes, sir. Goodnight," I said as he gave me a goodnight kiss on the forehead.

I snuggled under the covers and then fell sound asleep.

CHAPTER FOUR

A week had passed since Jensen had suggested that I be little more often and nothing had gotten better at work. In fact, things had become worse. I was working longer hours and had to watch my back even more when I was around Smith. I didn't get why the guy kept trying to take my clients.

On Wednesday night, I was exhausted. I hadn't eaten lunch again and I was starving after only eating a bagel for breakfast—which had been hours and hours ago.

I tossed my shoes off at the shoe mat and headed into the house. Jensen had beaten me home from work... again.

"Hi, honey. How was your day?" he called out from somewhere upstairs.

I followed his voice upstairs and walked into our bedroom, noting the bathroom light was on. I tossed my briefcase on the ground and fell face down onto the bed and groaned.

"Rough day at work?" he asked, sitting down next to me and rubbing my back.

"Yeah," I murmured, turning my head so I could face him.

"I know something that would make you feel better."

"I know what you're going to suggest, Jensen, and the answer is still no. I don't want to be little today. In fact, maybe I should be little less often. I could work more on the weekends that way." That sounded like a really good idea to me. Those forty-eight hours where I did basically nothing productive would be an excellent time to secretly go to the office to work. I would finally be able to figure out how Smith was stealing my clients without his watching eyes, plus I could get so much more work done.

However, my husband didn't agree with me.

"No way. The weekends are the only times that I see you relax. I won't let you give that up or you'll give yourself a heart attack in a matter of months."

I was about to respond when my stomach let out a very loud grumble.

"It sounds like someone's stomach is hungry."

"Yes, I haven't eaten since—" I began, but stopped before I revealed that I'd skipped lunch. If Jensen found out I had been missing meals to focus more on work, I wouldn't be able to sit down for a month. He had this weird obsession about always making sure I ate enough food.

"What were you saying? When was the last time that you ate, Claire?"

"I... at lunch," I said, trying to sound more confident than I felt while not looking at him, because I knew that my face would give me away. I was a horrible liar. He always said that it was my eyes that gave me away, so if he couldn't see my eyes, then maybe I'd be able to get away with lying this time.

"Claire, look at me and answer my question again," he said, giving my bottom a firm slap.

I met his gaze as I realized that I couldn't lie my way out of this one. Oh, he was going to be angry. A wave of disappointment washed over me. I didn't like making him angry—especially when I knew what I had done was wrong.

"The last time I ate today was at breakfast," I said shyly, casting my eyes away from his.

"I see. Is this something that keeps happening?"

"Kind of," I mumbled, finding the bedspread to be fascinating all of a sudden.

"What do you mean by kind of, young lady?" he asked in a much firmer tone, grabbing the hand that had been playing with the bedspread.

I sighed, then looked up at him again and admitted, "On weekdays. I'm too busy working to take a break and eat lunch." The look of sadness on his face had me quickly apologizing. "I'm sorry, Jensen. I promise from now on I won't miss lunch again," I said, hoping that my promise would get me out of any punishment.

He was silent for several minutes and that had me frightened. It never boded well for me when he was thinking about what was sure to be a punishment that I wouldn't like at all.

Finally, he said, "You're right, young lady. You won't be missing lunch anymore because you'll be taking off the rest of this week and all of next week."

"What! No! I can't!" I protested, sitting up in the bed and pulling my hand from his grasp. If I missed that much work then I would fall behind and Smith would take all of my clients. I couldn't let that happen, not after all the hard work that I put into getting them.

"Yes, you can. It's almost the end of the year. You are given a month's worth of vacation days and you haven't used one this entire year, despite my protests. Now you're going to, because I'm not going to watch you work yourself to death."

"But—"

"No buts! This is final, Claire Boyer. Now, I'm going to go make dinner. When I come back, you're going to have already called your boss and taken

the time off as I told you. Then you'll eat your dinner, and afterwards, we'll discuss your punishment."

"That's not fair!" I cried out.

"Yes it is, young lady. I've let this go on long enough. For the next week and a half you'll be acting little. That is final," he said, then got up and walked out of the room.

I threw myself back down on my bed, pulled my pillow close, and began to sob into it. Jensen was being *so* unfair! I knew that it was wrong of me to skip eating my lunch and to not tell him about it, but I didn't deserve having to miss almost two weeks of work and to get a spanking. But did he care that it wasn't fair? No, he didn't!

I was so upset that I just kept sobbing into my pillow—until I felt Jensen pick me up and set me in his lap. I wanted nothing to do with him at the moment and tried to fight his embrace, but his arms were like metal bands around me.

"Shhh, little girl. I know that this is hard to accept, but it's for your own good," he said, rocking back and forth a little, holding me close.

Finally, I tired myself out and stopped trying to get away from him, but I continued to cry until my voice was hoarse, my nose was running like a river, and my eyes were all swollen and puffy. When I stopped sobbing, I laid my head against his shoulder, all of my energy spent.

"Feel better, sweetie?" he asked, rubbing my nose with a tissue.

I shook my head.

"Listen, sweetheart. I know that right now this punishment seems very unfair to you, but it's for your own good. Do you think I would ever do something that wouldn't benefit you in the long run?"

I shook my head because it was the truth. I knew in my heart of hearts that he would never do something to intentionally hurt me or cause me unnecessary pain. However, that knowledge didn't make this any easier.

"I know that, Jensen… but this is still so hard for me. I don't want to miss work. If I do, then Smith could steal all of my clients and all of my hard work would have been for nothing," I said, trying to get him to see reason.

"I don't care what Smith does. What I care about is you. You're far too stressed. If you keep going the way that you're going, you'll have a heart attack. I won't allow that. If I have to tie you to this bed to keep you in it for the next week and a half, I will."

I sighed, knowing that there was no way out of this punishment and that he was right. I had been pushing myself too hard. I just got so competitive with Smith, and I wanted to be the best at my job so I would get a promotion. But no job was worth my own health.

"Okay, Jensen. I'll email my boss and let him know that I'm taking the next week and a half off."

"Good girl," he said, kissing the top of my head.

I figured that since I had agreed without a huge fight and since he was in a good mood, I should try and get out of the spanking.

"Since I'm being such a good girl and taking off work, does that mean that I won't have to get my other punishment?" I asked, hoping that he would say yes.

"Sorry, sweetie. You lied to me for weeks and you were deliberately hurting yourself by not eating lunch. You deserve a spanking, and you know it."

I dropped my head. I hated when he had to give me punishment spankings. I didn't feel like his good little girl then. It made me feel like I was naughty, and it hurt me because I knew I had disappointed him. Also, the spanks were a lot harder and he felt colder throughout the spanking.

"Okay... but can we please do it now? I don't want to have this hanging over my head as I eat." That was the truth. If I knew I had messed up and was going to get punished, I'd rather just get the punishment over with. Otherwise, I'd hardly eat because I would be worrying about what was going to happen.

"Alright. Over my lap," he said, then helped me reposition myself so the top part of my body was over the bed and my legs were dangling over his lap.

He pushed the skirt I had been wearing up over my butt and pulled my panties down, exposing my bare bottom. He gently rubbed his hand over my behind, sending goosebumps all over my body.

I took a deep breath and waited for the spanking to start. What probably was only a couple of seconds felt like an eternity.

Then he smacked my bottom hard three times. At first, the sound of his hand making contact with my flesh was worse than the sting, but I knew that the pain would heighten. It always did with a punishment spanking.

He continued spanking me, rotating between hitting each cheek in different spots and then sometimes hitting my sit spots. I soon felt my skin heat up and pain spread throughout my bottom. But it wasn't a horrible pain yet—more like a dull ache.

"Why am I punishing you, Claire?" he asked, pausing his assault on my bottom as he rubbed his hand over my heated, sensitive skin.

"Because," I sniffled, "I lied to you about eating lunch."

"Yes. Do good little girls lie to their daddies?"

"No," I admitted, knowing it was the truth and that caused me to really begin to cry. I had disappointed my daddy again, and that was the worst feeling in the world.

He began spanking me again. His smacks were harder than before, and I began to kick my legs, hoping that my movement would get him to stop. I hated being punished and it was hard for me to stay still during it.

"Claire, stop moving and take your punishment like a good girl," he said, wrapping his left arm around my back to keep me still.

He smacked the area where my thighs and bottom met, causing me to howl in pain. No matter how much I moved, he continued spanking me, until I swore that I would never be able to sit on my bottom again.

Finally, I had been reduced to a sobbing mess and the spanking ended. Jensen tried hushing me and rubbing my bottom gently, but that wasn't helping me much.

"Good girl. Stay right there. I'll go get you something to help you," he said a few moments later, moving me up the bed so my legs were no longer dangling over the bed.

I didn't really pay attention. Instead, I pulled my pillow close, hugged it, and cried, trying to breathe through the pain.

I didn't notice Jensen had come back until I felt something very cool being poured onto my fiery bottom.

"Ouch!" I said, trying to squirm away, but he had one hand on my back as the other rubbed the liquid into my heated flesh.

"Relax, baby girl. This will make you feel better in a minute."

He was right. Whatever he'd poured onto my skin was taking the sting out of my bottom and making me feel very grateful. I lay there, just trying to calm down.

By the time that he'd finished rubbing the lotion in, I was done crying. And now that my spanking was over, I felt much better. I felt forgiven, and that was the best feeling in the world.

"I'm proud of you, Claire. You took your spanking like a good little girl," he said, pulling my panties back up and moving my skirt back down.

"Thank you," I said, not moving a muscle.

"You're going to have to get up, sweetie. Dinner is waiting on the stove."

"Can you carry me?" Normally I'd never ask him for such a childish thing, but punishment spankings always made me tired, and since I'd cried so much before the spanking had even started, I was exhausted.

"Sure, sweetie," he said, lifting me up and carrying me down to the kitchen. He placed me on one of our kitchen chairs and I couldn't help but let out a groan as my sore bottom made contact with the seat.

He just smirked as he went to get dinner.

When I finished eating, he made me wait for him to clean up the kitchen before he carried me back upstairs and sat me on the toilet as he started to run a bath.

"Jensen, come on. You don't have to do this," I said, wishing that I could just take a fast shower so I could hop into bed that much sooner.

"Yes, I do. Claire, I don't know why you're so against me treating you younger during the weekdays, but I think that you need it, so I'm going to do it. That means that I give my little girl her bath. Now, please stand up. We need to get you undressed."

I sighed and stood up. I was too tired to fight him tonight, but I would

be sure to do that first thing tomorrow morning. I was not going to be forced to act little without a fight.

He quickly undressed me and helped me into the bath. At first the warm water stung my bottom, but after a few minutes, it felt wonderful.

Jensen gave me some of my bath toys, and despite my not wanting to be little on the weekdays, I couldn't help but play with my Barbies as he washed my hair and body.

"Alright, sweetheart. Time to get out." He helped me out of the bath and wrapped me up in a towel, then carried me into my little girl's room.

It was painted pink and had Barbie stickers all over the walls. I had a Barbie doll house with lots of Barbies, and I even had a Barbie comforter and sheet set! I loved Barbies.

He sat me down on the bed as he pulled out a pair of yellow flannel pajamas with little white stars and a pair of white panties. He helped me change into everything and then he brushed out my hair as I brushed out one of my Barbie's hair.

When he finished, it occurred to me that when I was little, I always spent my nights sleeping in my little girl bed, but I didn't want to not sleep with my husband for that long.

"Jensen?" I asked.

"Daddy," he corrected, turning from where he was placing my clean clothes in my dresser. That was one thing that he was firm about. When we were playing, I was supposed to always call him daddy. He said that it would keep me in my headspace.

Deciding not to fight him on this now, I said, "Daddy. Can I please spend my nights with you? I don't want to sleep alone."

"Of course you can, baby girl. Come on. It's nearly your bedtime. Let's go get your teeth brushed and let you go potty one last time tonight. Then I'll read you a bedtime story."

"Okay," I said, jumping into his open arms with a smile as he carried me out of my room and into the bathroom.

CHAPTER FIVE

I woke up the next morning feeling so refreshed. I hadn't slept for that long, or that well, in ages. I glanced at the clock to see that it was eight. To most people, that wouldn't have counted as sleeping in, but to me, it was. I was usually up no later than six every morning.

Last night, after I had finished getting ready for bed, Jensen had made me email my boss, and he'd emailed me back half an hour later saying that it was fine if I took off the next week and a half. I had been hoping that my boss would say said that it was impossible for me to miss that much work at one time.

"Good morning, sweetie."

"Oh my gosh!" I yelped, jumping out of bed. I hadn't realized that Jensen was there.

"I'm sorry, honey. I didn't mean to startle you. I thought you knew I was here," he said, putting his cup of coffee on the nightstand and placing a newspaper in his lap.

"It's okay. I was still waking up—that's why I didn't realize you were here," I said, climbing back in bed.

"Mm-hmmm… Did you sleep well, sweetie?"

"Yes."

"Good. Look what I made," he said, getting out of bed and walking over to his dresser. On top of it was a large covered tray.

"What is that?" I asked.

"Breakfast. I made it for you earlier, but you slept in later than you normally do, so I decided to wait for you," he said, as he moved the tray to his nightstand. He removed the lid to reveal two bowls.

"Thank you. That was really sweet, Jensen," I said, as he handed me a bowl full of oatmeal.

"Claire—"

"Hey! These have dinosaurs in them! I love dinosaur oatmeal," I said as I ate the small little dinosaur candy, then took a bite of oatmeal.

A smile crossed his face before he said, "I know you do. That's why I made it for you. Listen, Claire, I meant what I said last night. I want you to act little for the next week and a half. I think it will really help you. Unless you have any reason why this wouldn't work, for the next week and a half, I'm going to be daddy to you."

"But, Jensen," I began, then paused when he gave me a hard look. Putting down my bowl, I restarted, "But, daddy, I like being a big girl too. I can do plenty of stuff as a big girl and still relax. Like I could go and get my nails done and get a massage. That would be relaxing."

The look on his face told me that I was going to have to come up with a better reason than that if I didn't want to be treated like a little girl for the next ten days.

"Plus, being a little girl for a week and a half is going to be too long! I'll forget what it's like to be an adult."

"That's exactly what I intend to happen. You need to relax, and being little for that long and you forgetting your adult worries will help your health tremendously."

It felt like a hundred pound weight had just been dropped into my stomach. He wanted me to be little for so long and he wanted me to forget how it felt to be an adult. That sounded just like some of the boyfriends and husbands in a couple of the age play books I had read in the past. The men had ended up forcing their girlfriends or wives to be little all the time. I just couldn't let that happen!

I took a deep breath, trying to calm my fears. I knew that I was probably just being crazy. Jensen and I had been playing together for years and I trusted him to never force me to do anything that I really didn't want to do. *But, isn't that exactly what he's making you do now?* a voice whispered in my head.

"Claire—" he began, but I interrupted him. I suddenly didn't want to talk about this subject anymore because he would just think that I was crazy.

"I'm fine. Just super hungry," I said, diving into my dinosaur oatmeal with gusto.

Thankfully, it seemed he wasn't going to continue what he'd been going to say the first time.

"You do like your oatmeal. Try eating a little more carefully though," he said, taking a napkin and wiping my face.

"Thank you," I said, then finished the last bite of my oatmeal and put my empty bowl on the tray.

"You're welcome. Now drink your milk, little girl. It'll make you big and strong when you get older."

"Yes, daddy," I said, reaching for the cup with the crazy straw. I loved crazy straws with all of the loops and I loved watching my drink be sucked up through the straw. It was like watching a roller coaster! When I had drunk half of my milk, I started to blow bubbles. I giggled as they almost started to

come out of the cup.

"Claire, drink your milk. Don't play with it," daddy said as I saw him trying to cover up his smile.

"Yes, daddy." I continued to giggle and had to pause from slurping up my milk so I wouldn't choke on it. After catching my breath, I finished the last of my milk and then put my cup back on the tray.

"All done?"

"Yes, sir," I said, giggling and jumping out of bed. I had to admit, even if I didn't want to be little for such a long time, it was kind of fun at the beginning. I got to act goofy in a way that I wasn't able to when I was an adult.

I ran out of my adult bedroom and into my little one, then immediately sat down in front of my Barbie house and picked up two of the Barbies I had put down the last time I had been little.

I was just starting up a conversation between the two dolls when I heard daddy clear his throat from behind me. "Claire bear. You need to get dressed now. I'm going to take you to the park."

"The park?" I asked, turning around to look at him. I didn't want to go to the park now. I normally loved going to the park, but today was a Thursday morning. The only people who would be at the park now were littles who played this way twenty-four seven. I didn't want to be labeled as one of those types of littles. That was the label I was trying to avoid.

All of a sudden, that one hundred pound weight was back in my stomach. He had to know who would be at the park today and what other people who saw me there would say. That little voice in my head came back and was whispering that he wanted me to be little twenty-four seven from now on.

"Yes, sweetie. Now, let's see. It's supposed to be cold outside…"

I watched him pull out a pair of pants with little butterflies on them and a long sleeved pink shirt. Then he chose some pink and white knee high socks, and finally, a matching pair of frilly pink underwear and a bra.

"Come here, sweetie. Let daddy help change you, and then we can go to the park."

"Daddy, I'm five years old. I can change myself, and I don't want to go to the park today. I want to stay home and play with my Barbies!" I said, even though I was already walking over to him.

"Claire, you can play with your Barbies when we get home. And I know that you can change yourself, sweetie, but you're my little girl. It's my job to take care of you," he said. In short order, he removed all of my clothes until I was standing naked in front of him.

I didn't like this. Being completely naked while Jensen was still dressed made me feel extra vulnerable and like I truly was little.

"Okay, sweetheart, please step into these."

I put both of my hands on his shoulders as I stepped into the underwear.

He pulled them up and then continued getting me dressed. Once I was dressed, he picked me up and placed me on the bed.

"Time to get your shoes on. Since it isn't supposed to snow today, you can wear your pink light up shoes."

"Thank you, daddy! These are my favorite!" I exclaimed, as he put my right shoe on first, tied it, and then did the same for my left shoe. Then he bundled me up in my winter coat, and put on my hat, scarf, and gloves. I felt like I had gained an extra ten pounds by the time that I was dressed.

Thankfully, I didn't have to be this bundled up in the warm house for long. I was starting to sweat! He was soon changed and ready to go in a matter of minutes.

"Alright, sweetheart. Do you want to ride your bike or walk?" daddy asked, as we stepped into the garage.

"Ummm… ride my bike please," I said, running over to my bright pink bike. I loved my bike. It was perfect for me. It had a flowered basket in the front, a bell on the handle bar, and on each handle, glittery strings hung. Last year, daddy had finally taken my training wheels off so it was a big girl bike now.

I was just about to hop on when he said, "Claire bear. You need to wear your helmet, elbow, and knee pads if you want to ride your bike."

"Okay, daddy," I said, then reached for the knee pads in my basket and put them on, then put on my elbow pads, and lastly my helmet.

I was ready to roll. I hopped on my bike, kicked up my kickstand, and started to ride out of the open garage.

"Claire! Wait for me!" he called out and moments later, he was beside me on his bike. "You need to wait for daddy, honey. I don't want you to wander off on your own," he scolded.

"Yes, daddy. I'm sorry," I said, then continued to peddle. As I thought about it some more, I didn't think that anyone else would be at the park. It was a Thursday morning. Who would want to go to the park that early? All the littles who acted this way all the time were probably taking a nap, so I decided to not stress about my fears and just enjoy the time I got to spend with my daddy.

As we were riding to the park, I showed my daddy all the cool tricks I could do with my bike. I did a circle around him and then I did a figure eight. I even rode my bike with only one hand, but he really didn't like that.

We had just turned the corner to the park. I couldn't wait to ride the swings! I was so excited—until I saw there were about a dozen kids there with four adult supervisors.

I couldn't believe it! I thought the littles would be napping or would be inside. I didn't want to be at the park with them!

I was so focused on watching the children and so terrified that I would have to play with them… and that Jensen would talk with the supervisors…

and then sign me up for daycare… and I'd be a little forever… that I wasn't paying attention to where I was going until it was too late.

"Claire!" Jensen shouted as my bicycle crashed right into a pole. I fell to the ground, my chin hitting the unforgiving concrete.

"Claire! Baby, are you okay?" he asked, suddenly right beside me. He sat me up and I felt his hands move their way up and all around me, probably checking for wounds.

I was in shock and then embarrassed when I realized that the kids who were playing at the park were now all focused on me. Then I tasted something metallic in my mouth. I brought my gloved hand to my lip and then my chin and realized that I'd cut up my face badly.

Then the pain of my fall hit and I began to cry.

"Claire bear, it's okay. Come on, Dr. Roberts' office is just around the corner. We have to go see him."

"I don't want to go to the doctor!" I panicked, thinking of the last time I had been there. I had gotten a shot in my bottom and it had hurt so much. I didn't want that to happen again.

"Sweetie, this isn't up for discussion. Come on, we need to get you to the doctor. Up you go," he said, picking me up in his arms.

"Is she okay? We saw her take a tumble," one of the supervisors said as she came up to Jensen and me. Not wanting to look at this supervisor, I buried my head in his neck.

"It looks like she hit her chin very hard. I'm going to be taking her over to Dr. Roberts, just to have him double check everything."

"That's a smart idea. I'll grab your bikes and watch them for you. Whenever you'd like, you can pick them up from the daycare."

"Thank you so much. Come on, Claire, let's go visit Dr. Roberts," he said as he began to walk towards the office.

He walked past the park and as I realized that everyone was staring at me, I started to cry harder and snuggled closer into my daddy's neck.

"It's okay, baby girl. You're going to be okay. I know your chin hurts," he said, striding through the town while rubbing my back.

I didn't care about my chin hurting. I was humiliated because all those littles saw me crying like a little baby. I didn't pay attention to where we were until I heard the jingle of the bell that meant we were at the doctor's office. Suddenly, my nose was assaulted by the smell of antiseptic products.

"Oh! What do we have here?"

I glanced up at Nurse Kaitlyn and she let out a gasp.

"Oh, my dear Claire! What happened to you? Come on, you can take her right into exam room one. It's been quiet today, so Dr. Roberts will be able to see her right away," Kaitlyn said, leading my daddy down the hallway and to the exam room.

"Thank you, Kaitlyn," he said as he entered the room.

"No problem. Here, put these on Claire's chin," she said, holding out a wad of napkins. He gently did so as she left the room.

When he tried to put me down on the exam table, I clung to him because I didn't want to be let go. There were times when a little girl just needed to be held by her daddy, and this was one of them.

When he tried to put me down again, I cried out, "No, daddy! No!"

"Okay, honey. You just try and relax," he said, sitting down in one of the chairs that was in the room.

I snuggled closer to him. I didn't want to be here, and my face hurt. Daddy should have listened to me and let me stay home today and let me play with my Barbie dolls. Then none of this would have happened.

"Well, what do we have here?" Dr. Roberts asked, coming into the exam room with his wife, nurse Kaitlyn, behind him.

I hid my face in my daddy's neck as I heard the sound of the door clicking closed. Maybe if Dr. Roberts didn't see my face then I could get out of the shot that I knew would most likely happen.

"Hi there, Jensen. Hi there, Claire. What brings you two in today?" Dr. Roberts asked.

"Claire had an accident. She was riding her bike and got distracted and ran into a pole. Her face hit the ground and now she has a rather nasty cut on her chin. I was wondering if you could look at it and tell me if she would need stitches or not."

"Oh no. Accidents are no fun. Does your chin hurt a lot, Claire?" Dr. Roberts asked me.

I nodded but didn't move from where I was hiding against my daddy's chin.

"I'm sure that it does. But, you know, the only way I can make you feel better is if I see your cut. Do you think that I could look at your face, Claire?" he asked as I heard the sound of gloves being snapped on.

I shook my head. I did not want him touching my cut or giving me a shot and causing me even more pain. I'd had enough of that today.

"Claire, I promise that I won't hurt you. I just want to take a look."

"Let Dr. Roberts take a look, sweetie. He just wants to make you feel better," daddy said.

I knew that they were right, so I slowly turned my head toward Dr. Roberts while still holding tightly onto my daddy.

"That's a good girl," Dr. Roberts said, then took my chin in his hand and moved it from side to side. After a moment, he said, "Kaitlyn, dear, can you please hand me a wet paper towel?"

"Why?" I mumbled.

"I need to remove the dried blood on your face so I can see how bad your cut is," he said as he took the towel his wife gave him and started to wipe my face.

"Ouch! Stop… that hurts!" I protested, moving my face into my daddy's neck again.

"Claire, I need to do it. If I don't clean off your face, then I won't be able to see if your cut needs stitches or not."

"No! Let's go home! I'm fine," I said, beginning to panic. I realized that if I needed to get stitches that meant that I would need to get a shot, and Dr. Roberts would sew my skin up like someone would sew a hole in a shirt. I was not going to let that happen!

"Claire, you need to calm down and listen to Dr. Roberts. You want to be a good girl for him and me, right?" daddy said, beginning to rub my back.

"I… fine. Just hold me extra tight, daddy," I murmured so that only he could hear.

"Of course, sweetie. You're being such a good girl."

I turned back to face Dr. Roberts.

He started to clean my face again and it thankfully didn't hurt as much this time. When he finished, he said, "Hmm. It looks like that chin of yours needs a couple of stitches after all. I'll be right back and we can fix it up. Jensen, I'll need her to lie back on the exam table."

I let out a whimper at the thought of leaving the safety and comfort of my daddy's arms as Dr. Roberts left the room.

"Come on, Claire. I'll hold your hand the entire time," he said as he unwrapped my arms from around his neck and placed me on the exam table.

"Daddy…" I croaked, trying to keep my grip on him.

I normally wasn't this clingy. But when I got hurt, all I wanted was my daddy to snuggle me and make it all better.

"I'm right here, sweetie, see?" he said as his head appeared to the side of me. He grabbed both of my hands and gave them a little squeeze as Dr. Roberts came back into the room with some supplies.

Dr. Roberts whispered something in Kaitlyn's ear and she nodded before coming over to the bottom of the exam table and holding my legs. This did not make me feel better about what was to come.

"Okay, sweetie. I just need to give you a little shot. Then your chin will be all numbed for me to fix," Dr. Roberts said, coming towards me with a syringe in his hand.

I began to whimper and closed my eyes, turning my face away so I wouldn't have to see what he was doing. I really didn't like shots.

"It's okay, sweetie. This won't hurt. Right now, I'm just going to numb your mental nerve. Did you know that was what the nerve in your chin is called? Odd name for it, right? I always remember it because my anatomy teacher joked that if two people were wrestling, that would be the place to hit because it would knock the other person out and the two people would have to be mental to be fighting in the first place."

"Funny," I muttered, waiting for the shot to happen.

"You can open up your eyes, honey. I already gave you the shot. You were just focused on my great story."

I opened my eyes to see Dr. Roberts and my daddy smiling down at me.

"That wasn't so bad, was it, sweetheart?" daddy asked as he placed a kiss on my forehead.

A warm happy feeling spread through me. I loved it when my daddy was proud of me like that. It made me feel extra special.

"Okay, Claire, I'm going to stitch up your chin now. This should take just a couple of minutes. Just focus on your daddy."

I did just that. I kept looking at my daddy and ignored the tugging sensation in my chin.

"You're being such a good girl, Claire. I think that someone deserves a reward when we leave, Dr. Roberts," my daddy said proudly.

I nodded my head, excited at the idea of getting a reward. I would love another Barbie doll, or maybe I could get my daddy to buy me another Barbie book, or maybe even a Barbie house since I had been really well behaved!

"Stay still, honey," Dr. Roberts chuckled.

After a couple of minutes, the tugging sensation went away and Dr. Roberts said, "Okay, Claire, I'm all done. You can sit up now. You and your daddy just need to come back in a few days so I can make sure that the stitches have healed well."

"Won't you have to take them out?" daddy asked as he helped me sit up.

"No. Since Claire only needed four stitches, I used dissolvable ones. Within a couple of days, they should be gone."

"Okay. Thank you again, Dr. Roberts. We'll see you in a few days," daddy said, then picked me up and carried me out of the exam room.

"Wait, Mr. Boyer! I have a couple of stickers for Claire since she was such a good little girl today," Kaitlyn said, walking towards us.

"Thank you, Kaitlyn, and thank you for helping us out today," daddy said, taking the stickers and putting them in his pocket.

"I want them, daddy," I murmured, trying to reach toward his pocket.

"You can have them later, Claire bear. I want to get you home and into bed right away. It's a good thing that our house is so close to the doctor's office," he said, stepping outside and walking towards our home.

"Into bed? Daddy, I only had a couple of stitches in my chin. I'm not sick!"

"There will be no arguing, Claire. You're going straight to bed, and if you keep disagreeing with me, then it'll be with a sore bottom."

I pouted the entire way home. First daddy took away my stickers, and then he was going to force me to stay in bed like he always did whenever I was sick. How was that fair? I'd had a couple of stitches—it wasn't major surgery. I wanted to play with my Barbies, not be forced to sleep because it would make my body heal faster. Daddy was being so unfair!

"Sweetie, stop pouting. When we get home, I promise to give you your stickers right away and you can play with a couple of your Barbies in bed."

"Thanks, daddy," I said, smiling as we continued our walk home. My daddy always knew how to make things all better.

CHAPTER SIX

We made it home very fast, and true to his word, my daddy changed me into a pair of pink footie pajamas with little kitties all over them and put me straight to bed. Afterwards, he gave me my stickers.

"Thank you, daddy," I said, then put them into my sticker collection box.

"You're welcome, sweetie." He sat down on the side of my bed and brushed the hair out of my face. "We need to have a talk, sweetheart."

"About what?"

"I want you to please tell me what happened today when you were riding your bike. You're an excellent bike rider who always pays attention. You've seen other kids at the park before, but today it looked like you saw a ghost when you saw the other children."

Not wanting to admit why I had freaked out, I shrugged my shoulders. I was afraid that if I told him what I was thinking, he would either confirm my fears—that he planned to keep me little forever—or else he would be hurt because I didn't trust him enough to know that he wouldn't do that. Either option wasn't good, so I decided to just make up a fib that was part of the truth.

"I… I got distracted."

A small smile crossed his face as he said, "Yes, honey, I know that you got distracted, but do you want to tell me why you got distracted?"

"Because I saw the kids."

"Yes, Claire, I know that you saw the kids, but like I said before, I know that you've seen kids playing at the park before, but that never made you lose your focus. So, what changed this time?"

"I… ummm… I don't know. Maybe because it's Thursday?" I lied, shrugging my shoulders again. I really didn't want to have to tell him the truth. *Especially because maybe he hasn't thought about keeping me little all the time yet, but if I tell him about my fear, it could put the idea in his head and he'll do it,* a voice whispered in my ear.

"Okay. Anyway, Claire, you need to always pay attention when you're

riding your bike. I know that you saw the kids and you were probably excited to see them, but that doesn't mean that you can stop focusing on what's in front of you. You could have gotten seriously hurt, even worse than you did now," he scolded.

"Yes, daddy. I'm really sorry. I promise that it won't happen again." *Especially because I'm not going out again when I'm forced to be this small,* I thought.

"Okay, dear, but just to make it stick extra well, I think that an early bedtime for the next three nights is in order for you."

"But, daddy! It was an accident!" I protested. How could he seriously be punishing me when I didn't intentionally do something wrong!

"I know it was an accident, sweetie, and that's the only reason why you aren't over my knee getting a spanking right now. I just want you to remember very well, that you have to always focus on what's in front of you. That means when you're walking, riding your bike, driving your car, when you're an adult, or when you're my little girl."

"Yes, daddy," I said, defeated. I knew that I was getting off lucky, but since my bedtime was already nine when I was little, I wasn't a fan of going to bed at eight for the next three nights.

"That's my good girl. Now, why don't you play with some of your Barbie dolls while I go whip up some lunch?" he asked, as he got up, grabbed some of my Barbie dolls, and handed them to me.

"Okay, daddy," I said, taking my dolls.

He gave me a kiss on my forehead before walking out and leaving me to play with my dolls.

I picked up my story right where I'd left it off.

• • • • • • •

It didn't take that long for daddy to come back in with lunch on a tray. It was a simple meal of turkey sandwiches, with an apple and some chips. We ate together on my bed as I told him the latest gossip between my Barbies. It was fun!

Once I finished eating, daddy picked the tray up and put it on my dresser. He sat back down on the side of my bed and said, "Honey, I need to go and pick up our bikes."

"Why, daddy? That lady took them."

"I know, sweetie, but she can't hold them forever. She was just holding them for a little while, so I could take you to the doctor."

"Okay, daddy."

"I should be gone for half an hour, an hour at the most. You know that I normally never leave you alone when you're acting little, but I don't want to be rude and leave the supervisor with our bikes."

"I'll be fine, Jensen. Remember I'm really thirty-three years old? I know

not to burn the house down and stuff."

"Be that as it may, I would like for you to take a nap while I'm gone and if you need anything, you know what my cell phone number is."

"A nap? But, I normally don't take naps and I'm not tired!" I huffed.

"You just had quite an adventure today. I think that your body needs some time to rest and heal, so I want you to lie back and close your eyes," he said, gently pushing me down. Then he got up and pushed the covers up to my chin. "I won't leave for a little bit. If I'm not here when you wake up, then you can play with your Barbie dolls some more, okay?"

"Okay, daddy," I said, snuggling under my covers.

"Good girl," he said. He placed a kiss on my forehead, then left my bedroom and gently closed the door behind him.

I lay in bed for a little bit. I didn't want to take a nap, but truth be told, after the morning I had, I was tired. Still, I was hoping that I could stay awake long enough so that when my daddy left, I could get up and play.

Unfortunately, my body had other ideas. My eyes were soon closed and I was fast asleep.

CHAPTER SEVEN

I had a really odd dream. I had been riding my bicycle to the park and when I went to turn it, it wouldn't stop. Instead, my bicycle had a life of its own and drove me to the daycare. Then it stopped and since I was at the daycare, I figured that it wouldn't hurt to take a peek inside to see what it looked like. I was also hoping that someone could help me with my bike.

As I stepped inside the building, it was really weird to see what it looked like. It looked so normal, yet different. The walls were painted bright colors, and there were a couple of doorways that led into other rooms. I peaked in to one room and it looked like what you would expect a normal daycare to look like, except it had adult size toys, tables, and seats.

I left that room and walked down the hallway and peeked in to another room. This one looked the same as the last except this time, there were littles in there with three supervisors. I watched as the littles played together and it looked like everyone was having a good time.

A part of me, wanted to join in the fun with the other littles, but another part was screaming for me to run away and hide because this is what I was afraid was going to happen to me.

As I turned to leave the room, I bumped in to my daddy.

"Where are you going Claire bear? You need to stay here. This is where you're going to be spending your days now, while daddy is at work."

"What about my work?"

"Oh, sweetie, don't you remember? You quit your job. You're my little girl twenty-four seven now."

I woke up panting and sweaty. I tossed the covers off of myself, while trying to catch my breath. *It was just a nightmare, just a nightmare because I was too hot,* I had to keep telling myself to help calm my speedy heartbeat.

I hated nightmares, but I especially hated the first few moments after I woke up. I rarely had dreams and it felt like the only time that I did dream was when I had nightmares because I was too hot or cold.

Once I had calmed down, I hopped out of bed. My door was still closed,

so I went over and opened it.

"Daddy... daddy are you home?" I called out.

After a minute with no answer, I figured that he must still be picking up our bikes. I went back into my bedroom, grabbed a few of my Barbies, and headed downstairs. I knew that he probably wanted me to stay in my bed, but after my nightmare, I needed to move somewhere else and I figured that it would be okay if I turned a movie on while playing with my Barbies.

I left my Barbies on the couch and walked over to the TV stand. I looked over all of my options and decided on the classic *Cinderella*.

I put the movie into the DVD player, then sat back on the couch and began to play with my Barbies as the movie began playing.

Just as Cinderella was slipping on her glass slipper for the Prince, I heard the garage door open and daddy was walking into the living room.

"Hi, daddy," I called out, not taking my eyes off the screen. This was my favorite part. I thought that Prince Charming and Cinderella were just perfect together.

"Hi there, little girl. What are you doing out of bed?" he asked, then came over to the couch, picked my feet up, and sat down.

"I took a nap but woke up because I had a nightmare and decided to come down here." I said, just as the Prince kissed Cinderella.

"You had a nightmare?"

Crap! I wasn't supposed to tell him that.

"Yes," I said, hoping that he wouldn't want to know more about my nightmare, but of course, I didn't get what I wanted.

"What was it about?"

I debated telling him the truth, but I was so afraid that if I did, my nightmare would end up coming true, so I made up a quick fib.

"It was about Brussel sprouts. They were... they were the only food left to eat."

He let out a chuckle before he said, "I can see how that would be a nightmare for you. I know how much you hate Brussel sprouts."

"Yeah. Everyone hates them because they're yucky!"

"I have to agree with you there, baby girl. Brussel sprouts aren't that tasty."

"Mm-hmm..." I agreed as the last scene of *Cinderella* played. Daddy stayed quiet until the credits began.

"How's your chin feeling, sweetie?"

"It doesn't hurt that bad. It's a little sore, but I'm sure that it'll feel better in a couple of days."

"Good. Dr. Roberts only had to put in four stitches, so I'm sure that it will be healed in a couple of days."

A smile crossed my face at that thought.

"What's that smile for?"

"I can't wait for it to heal properly so I can kiss you properly." I giggled giving him an odd kiss.

"Hmmm... does someone need some special attention?"

"Yes, Jensen," I said, wiggling my bottom over his lap to feel his cock getting hard.

"I think I know just the way to make you feel better. Come on," he said, picking me up bridal style and carrying me into our bedroom. He placed me down in the center of the bed, then grabbed my footie pajama zipper in his teeth and pulled it down until it reached the bottom.

I couldn't contain the giggle that slipped through my lips at the funny sight.

"Are you laughing at me, young lady?"

"No," I said with a big smile on my face as another giggle escaped my lips.

"I think that you are. You know what the cure for that is, don't you?"

"No, what?"

A wide grin crossed his face as he shouted, "The tickle monster!"

"No, please! No!" I burst out laughing as his hands moved all around my body as he tickled me. I wiggled and pleaded for him to stop, but he didn't.

Finally, after what felt like an eternity of torture, he stopped.

I lay there, catching my breath as he removed my pajamas, panties, and bra, and then I was lying naked on the bed.

"Now for the best part," he said, licking his lips before he bent down and kissed my stomach, and then he kissed a line straight down to my soaked pussy. "Hmmm... someone sure is turned on right now," he breathed, running his tongue over my outer labia.

I let out a moan as each of his hands grabbed one of my knees and spread them farther apart as he settled himself between my thighs. He began licking my outer lips and then slowly worked his way in until he began to plunge his tongue in and out of my flooded channel.

"Does that feel good, Claire?"

"Yes!" I cried out, grabbing bunches of the bedspread in my fists. My entire body felt strung up with so much tension, I thought that I was going to burst.

"I want you to touch your breasts, Claire. I want you to play with yourself while I take care of your pussy."

I nodded my head, words failing me at the moment. I brought my hands up to my breasts, and I kneaded them, flicking my nipples and pulling at them. The slight twinge of pain when I twisted my right nipple too hard soon turned into pleasure and went straight to my core, and my pussy let out another burst of wetness.

"That is so hot, baby," Jensen said, making me pause to look up at him. I hadn't realized that he'd been watching me. I paused for a moment, slightly

embarrassed that he was watching me play with myself, but then he brought his mouth back down to my pussy and my thoughts turned to the incredible way he was making me feel with a few licks from his tongue and I began playing with my breasts again.

Jensen brought his tongue out of my channel and started to lick upwards sending stronger waves of pleasure to my core. I was so close to coming. When his tongue licked across my clit, I nearly bucked off of the bed. When he did it again, my pelvis rose from the ground as tingles started to travel all around my body. I was seconds away from coming.

I got so focused on what he was doing that I stopped playing with my breasts.

He stopped and growled, "Don't you dare stop touching yourself."

I nodded my head in obedience and began to play with my breasts again as he settled himself back down and this time began to suck on my sensitive bundle of nerves.

"Jen... Jensen..." I whimpered as he continued to suck my clit and I kept playing with my breasts. I was so close, I could feel tears leak out of my eyes.

I couldn't come until he said so.

"Come." I heard him mutter the magical word, and just as he brought his mouth back down to my clit, I lost control.

My muscles spasmed and I cried out. Jensen stayed in between my thighs the entire time and lapped my juices with his tongue.

Finally, my orgasm and the aftershocks passed and I just lay in bed and felt utterly spent.

Jensen appeared above me and I smiled at him and said the only two words that popped in my head after one of the most incredible orgasms of my life. "Thank you."

He grinned down at me before pulling me close to his hot body and giving me a kiss on top of my forehead. "You're welcome, sweetheart."

CHAPTER EIGHT

Daddy and I spent Friday and the rest of the weekend at home. He kept insisting that I needed to take it easy, even though I had only had a couple of stitches in my chin. Honestly though, I was happy that we didn't have to go out. I was sure that the incident with my bike had gotten around the community by now, and I was afraid that someone was going to make fun of me. I didn't want that.

However, by Monday morning I was going a little stir-crazy. There was only so long that I could stay inside relaxing before I went crazy—gossip about me or not.

Daddy and I were sitting at the breakfast table when I finally cracked. "Daddy! I need to get out of this house! Let's go out. Can we go to the store or something?"

He put his newspaper down. "You're right. We've been inside for a while. What do you think about going to the library?"

"The library?"

"Yes, you could check out some picture books and the latest James Patterson novel came in for me."

"Yes, please!" I said, clapping my hands together. I loved picture books! It was a nice change to look at the pretty pictures instead of the pages and pages of black words in a regular adult book. Plus, my daddy would read to me and it was very relaxing.

"That's settled then. Finish your breakfast first, sweetie, and then we can get ready and go."

"Okay!" I said and gobbled up the rest of my food.

Within minutes, I was finished and ran upstairs to my bedroom to change. I didn't want to go to the library in my pajamas. I'd look silly!

As I was sorting through my clothes, it occurred to me that I'd forgotten to ask daddy a very important question. Was I going to have to act little at the library... in front of all of those people?

I turned and thankfully daddy was just walking into our room.

"Daddy, do I have to act little when we're at the library?" If he said yes, I was liable to lose my breakfast.

"No, honey, not if you don't want to. I know that you still get a little shy around other people when you're acting little. You can act however you want, as long as you behave."

"Okay... good," I said as the icky feeling left my stomach. I wasn't going to have to act little... which meant that I was going to get to act like an adult. Suddenly a large grin spread across my face.

"Claire, before you get too excited, I want to remind you that once you get home, you'll still have to be little for the rest of the week, and just because you're going to act big at the library doesn't mean that I won't still punish you if you misbehave."

"Yes, sir. Oh, I'm so excited! I can't figure out what to wear," I said, flipping through more of my shirts.

"You have ten minutes to decide and if you haven't by then, I'll be the one picking out your wardrobe choice."

"Okay." That made my decision must quicker. I finally settled on a pair of well-loved jeans, with a pink long sleeve top and a sweater. I also grabbed a pair of fluffy polka dotted socks as I didn't want my feet to get cold. "I'm ready, daddy," I said, tugging my ponytail to make sure that it was extra tight.

He chuckled. "Almost, sweetie. Don't you want to brush your teeth first? We wouldn't want you to have stinky breath when you talk to anyone at the library."

"Oh yeah!" I giggled and blushed as I turned to go into the bathroom to brush my teeth. I couldn't believe that I'd forgotten to do that. I never forgot to brush my teeth because I had once read a sign that said not brushing your teeth was just as dirty as not wiping your bottom after you had gone to the bathroom... gross!

As I gently brushed my teeth, I thought about what books I wanted to pick out. Of course there would be some Barbie ones in there, but daddy had read those to me like a bazillion times, so I also wanted to get some new ones. They had some pretty-looking Disney Princess stories there. I thought that those sounded good. Oh! And a Junie B. Jones book too! She was so funny!

What really put me in the best mood was that I was going to be able to act like an adult, even if it was only for a while. You had to enjoy the small things in life.

I spit my toothpaste out and put my toothbrush back in its cup. I was ready to go to the library.

"How are we going to get to the library?" I asked, walking downstairs as daddy held my coat for me to step into.

"We're going to drive. I don't want any more accidents."

"Okay," I said as he zipped up my coat and we headed out the door.

• • • • • • •

The heat from the library felt wonderful as we stepped inside. It was just the beginning of winter and I was already sick of it.

"Good morning, Claire! Good morning, Jensen!" Mrs. Jones, the sweet older librarian said, greeting us from behind the circulation desk as she checked books in.

"Good morning," we both responded, then walked further into the library.

I started to head off towards the kids' section to look at some of the picture books when Jensen grabbed my hand.

"Honey, would you like me to come with you to look at some books?"

"No, thank you. I can pick my own."

"All right. Here's a bag you can place the books in. Remember, you have to be able to carry it all by yourself and if you can't, then you'll have to put some books back."

"Okay," I said, grabbing the pink canvas bag before turning back and heading towards the kids' section.

I knew right where the Barbie section of picture books were, so I went straight there. I sat down on the ground since they were on the lowest shelf and started to pick through them, deciding which ones I wanted to check out.

I was so absorbed in what I was doing that I didn't hear or see the older lady approach me.

"Hi there, young lady. You must be Claire."

I was so startled by the woman coming up to me that the two Barbie books I'd been holding in my hands fell to the floor next to me as I got a good look at the lady. I thought I recognized her, but I wasn't sure where I'd seen her before.

"I'm sorry. I didn't mean to startle you," she said, bending down and picking up the two books that I had dropped. "Barbie books, these are great choices. My students love Barbie stories."

She handed the books back to me and that's when I realized I knew where I'd seen her before. She was one of the women who ran the daycare center in the community.

"Oh! I forgot to tell you my name. I'm Mrs. Agnes," she said, sitting down next to me.

My brain finally starting functioning and I said, "Hi. It's nice to meet you."

"It's nice to meet you too."

A warm smile crossed her face. "Miss Claire, you and your daddy have been living here for a few years by now, yet I've only met you in passing and you always seem to be heading off to work. That's why when I saw you sitting here today, I wanted to stop by and properly introduce myself."

I suddenly started to feel myself get nervous. I didn't understand why she

felt the need to properly meet me. Wouldn't she only want to properly meet people who were going to be going to the daycare?

I swallowed hard and said, "Yes. My husband and I only play on the weekends and since I don't really like to go out then, it's just the two of us."

"That's a shame, honey. One of the best parts about being little is the friends that you make. I run the daycare around here and the littles who go there always have so much fun playing with one another. It's hard to get them to go home sometimes."

I shakily nodded my head. I did not need this woman giving my daddy any ideas about sending me to that daycare. That would be a disaster. He would make me act little twenty-four seven for sure, and I wouldn't ever be an adult. It would be just like those books. Suddenly, it felt like someone was squeezing my chest very hard.

Mrs. Agnes patted my knee and I jumped.

"Oh, honey, I'm sorry. I didn't mean to startle you again. That seems like all I've been doing to you today," she said, gently rubbing the spot on my knee that she had just touched. "It's just my job here in the community to make sure that littles are happy, and I think you would have a really fun time at the daycare—or even if you just wanted to hang out with a couple of littles outside of your house. I could give you some phone numbers. Around what age do you regress to?"

"Umm... around five years old," I said, thinking that it was a little strange to be having a conversation like this in the middle of the library. Then again, this was a community for people in age play relationships.

"Oh! You're one of the ones that likes to regress younger. I think that the younger a person likes to regress, sometimes it's even more fun. You get to color, play around, and wear the cutest clothes. I will definitely make sure to give you some other littles' phone numbers for you to call up."

"Okay," I said, not sure if I liked that idea or not. If she gave me other littles' phone numbers, then Jensen would get all excited and he'd want me to go play with them. I didn't want to do that because it would cut into his and my time together on the weekends, and even worse, one of the littles' mommies or daddies could put the idea in his head to send me to the daycare and make me act little twenty-four seven!

"Are you okay, sweetie?"

I nodded my head, not wanting to say anything.

"Okay, honey." Mrs. Agnes' phone beeped and pulled it out of her pocket and said, "Oh my, I have to go. There seems to be a problem at the daycare. It was very nice meeting you, Claire."

"It was nice meeting you too," I said, looking up at her as she stood.

"Stay warm, and please, feel free to call me anytime if you need anything."

"Thank you," I said, before she left to go deal with whatever problem she had.

I went back to perusing the Barbie books and finally settled on the two in my hand. Then I got up and chose a couple of *Magic School Bus* books, some Disney Princess books, and one Junie B. Jones book.

With my selections in my bag, I headed off towards the adult section in search of Jensen.

As I was walking through the library, I passed the DVD collection and I couldn't help myself as I went to take a peek.

I loved it when Jensen and I snuggled up on the couch together and shared a bag of popcorn as we watched a movie. I tended to fall asleep before the movie had even finished, but it was just enjoyable to be next to him, spending time together.

As I looked through the movies, I settled on three: *Parental Guidance, Zero Dark Thirty,* and *My Fair Lady*. I hadn't seen any of them, but some of my co-workers had recommended all three to me.

As I placed them in my bag, a girl I recognized came up to me. She was a little curvier than me and had tattoos running up and down her arms. I thought she looked beautiful.

"You're checking out *Parental Guidance?*"

"Yes."

"That movie is so funny! I watched it last week with my daddy and we were both in tears."

"That's so cool! I'm Claire."

"I'm Kara. It's nice to meet you."

"You too," I said, smiling at her. I was about to ask her what her favorite part in the movie was when Jensen came rushing over to us.

"Claire, there you are, young lady. I've been looking everywhere for you," he said, coming up to us.

"I'm sorry. I was on my way over to the adult section to try and find you, but I got sidetracked by the DVDs. Look at the ones I chose," I said, handing them to him.

"Hey, I have to go. It was nice meeting you," Kara said, then gave me a small wave before she turned and left.

"Bye!"

"Sweetie, you can't watch *Zero Dark Thirty,* and I'm not sure if I'd like you watching these other two movies either right now."

"Why not?"

"Claire, do you not remember what I told you? For the rest of this week you are to be acting like a little girl. Little girls do not get to watch movies like these. I think you should put them back and pick out some other ones that are more suitable for you right now," he said, handing the DVDs back to me.

Oh! That made me so angry! I wanted to watch those movies! I hadn't agreed to act little this entire week, and instead he had told me that I was

going to. I didn't understand why he couldn't let me act big for just a couple of hours to watch the movies.

"Are you going to put them back, young lady? You have five minutes to choose a few new DVDs and then it'll be time for us to go."

"No! I want these DVDs!" I said, placing them back in my bag.

"I said no, Claire. Now put them back and choose a couple of new ones, or else you won't be getting any at all," he said, crossing his arms over his chest. I should have stopped myself there and did what he was telling me to, but I was so frustrated.

"No! *I want these DVDs!*" I screamed, and to prove my point, I even stomped my foot on the ground and crossed my arms over my heaving chest.

It felt really good to stand up for my DVD choices—until I looked up and realized that all the eyes in the library were on me and what I had just done. I swallowed the lump that had formed in my throat as I realized that I had just behaved how an actual four year old would have behaved in a situation like this, and I suddenly felt like crying my eyes out.

The library was quiet as Jensen said, "Young lady. You will put those back this instant and because of your outburst, you will be going home with no movies."

"I—"

"No. Not one more word or else you'll be going home with no books. Do you understand me?"

I nodded, not wanting to risk saying anything for fear that I wouldn't get to check out my books if I did. I silently put the DVDs back, picked up my bag, and followed Jensen to the circulation desk to check out my books.

Mrs. Jones checked our books out without saying much until the books were back in our bags.

"Have a good day, you two."

"Thank you," I mumbled, then looked at the ground as we walked past and left the library. I felt tears pricking my eyes as we headed toward the car. I couldn't believe that I had acted so poorly today. I could already feel my bottom heating up at the thought of the spanking I knew I was getting when we got home.

· · · · · · ·

"Claire Patricia Boyer, you get down here this instant," my daddy called from behind me as I ran upstairs, tears streaking down my face.

I never should have agreed to go to the stupid library, I thought as I threw myself onto my bed. I pulled my stuffed elephant into a hug and began to cry harder.

Thinking back to how I'd acted, I knew that I'd acted very poorly. I was a guest in the library and I should have behaved better. I just got so frustrated that I couldn't check out a couple of movies that I wanted all because daddy

had decreed that I needed to act little for a week and a half. If he would have just let me act like an adult for a couple of hours, none of this would have happened.

"Claire."

I turned my head to see daddy at the doorway of my room.

"I'm… sorry, daddy. G-give me a f-few minutes and then y-you can punish me," I said, turning back and giving my elephant another squeeze. I knew that I deserved a spanking for what I'd done. He had always instilled manners in me, no matter if I was little or an adult. But sometimes it was hard to act polite when all you wanted to do was scream. Still, screaming in a public place was definitely not polite.

"Oh, Claire. What am I ever going to do with you?" I heard him ask before he picked me up and placed me in his lap.

I was not expecting that. I thought that he would punish me right away, but I wasn't going to miss a chance for a cuddle.

"I'm sorry, daddy!" I sobbed into his shirt as I wrapped my arms around his neck. He was warm and I felt safe. The sound of his heartbeat was soothing.

"Oh, baby girl. Can you stop crying, sweetie, so we can talk about this?" he asked, wiping the tears from my eyes.

"There's nothing… to talk about." I hiccupped, starting to calm down.

"Yes, there is. For starters, why don't you tell me what caused your tantrum? You rarely, if ever, throw them. So something must have been really bothering you."

I wasn't sure what I should tell him. If I told him the truth, he might think that I wasn't able to handle basic regular adult things and then he could start making me act littler more often. But if I lied to him, he'd undoubtedly know… he always knew when I was lying to him.

"Claire… I'm waiting," he said, tapping my thigh. It wasn't a hard swat, just enough to force me back to reality.

"I'm sorry. I got upset because people at my work have been talking about those movies and I wanted to see them too so that I could join in the conversation. I know that I'm supposed to be little right now, but I don't get why I couldn't have been allowed to watch them sometime this week. A week is a long time to act little. I'm also tired of always being the last one to join in the conversations at work about stuff like this. When you told me no, I just lost it."

As I was telling him my explanation, I could feel myself getting worked up again and then I felt horrible that happened because that's what got me in trouble in the first place. I needed to stay calm or else I would end up getting more spanks on my already sure-to-be-red bottom.

"That's what caused you to regress? Because you were thinking about work?"

121

"Yes… no… I don't know. It's hard to explain," I said, not sure if I wanted to tell him all of the truth.

"Well, why don't you try, honey? I can't help you if I don't understand."

I took a deep breath. "I was just looking at the DVDs and I saw the ones that I had chosen. Other people at work had talked about them and I wanted to watch them so the next time someone brought them up, I wouldn't feel like the dumb girl who had no idea what they were talking about. When you told me that I couldn't watch those DVDs, I guess I just got so frustrated that I just burst."

"Oh, baby girl. Don't you understand? This is why I wanted you to act little for a week. I wanted you to forget about work and just relax. You're always stressing out about work and that isn't good for your health. Also, I've taught you better than that. If you ever get that worked up, you're supposed to politely excuse yourself and go find a quiet place to calm down."

"I know," I said, looking down at my hands. Whenever I would get upset at home, I had become good at leaving the situation and going up to my room to relax and then coming back down when I was ready to work out the problem. That had saved me many a red bottom. "I'm sorry, daddy. I didn't think about that. I just got so mad and ended up going crazy."

He smiled a sad smile. "I know that, sweetie, but I still have to punish you. You caused quite a scene at the library, and I can't let that go without addressing it. First thing tomorrow, you're going to apologize to Mrs. Jones, especially because she's always been friendly to you."

"Okay, daddy." Despite my not wanting to get spanked, I knew that I had done a very wrong thing and needed to be punished for it. In fact, I knew that it would make me feel better as I felt so guilty for my rude behavior at the library. I wanted the guilty feeling to go away, and one way I knew that could happen was if my daddy spanked me.

"Over my lap then, sweetheart. Let's get this over with," he said, as he repositioned me so my bottom was on his lap and my torso and head were on the bed.

"Wait, daddy," I said before he began. I grabbed my elephant and gave it a hug before saying, "Continue, please." *At least I'll have something cuddly to hug while daddy gives me my punishment*, I thought to myself.

"Well, since you asked so nicely" he said, then began the spanking.

His hand rained down several smacks onto my jeans-covered bottom, and I jumped. It didn't hurt, but it definitely wasn't comfortable. Soon he removed my jeans and my panties, so I was butt-naked.

The spanking continued and daddy began to smack my bottom even harder. He hit all around and developed a fast pattern. With each smack, I was sure a red handprint appeared on my bare bottom, and each sharp pain made me think *this is how it would feel to have a firecracker set off on my bottom.*

I began to sob into my elephant as the pain radiated all over my bottom

and lower thighs. It helped to have the soft stuffed animal by my side, but it only helped a little.

When daddy hit a tender spot on my bottom, I cried out and tried to move away.

"Stay still, Claire," he commanded, slapping my bottom even harder, before he wrapped his leg around my legs to keep me from moving.

I continued to sob into my elephant as the spanking went on. It hurt so much! I hated getting spanked—hated it. But as I was sobbing into my elephant, I could feel myself letting go of the guilt I felt for the tantrum I'd had.

When the spanking was over several minutes later, I continued to lie over my daddy's lap and to hang onto my elephant for dear life.

"Claire, stay right there. I'll be right back," daddy said before shifting so I was lying fully on the bed. Then he got up and left the room.

I didn't pay much attention until he was back and was pouring cool lotion over my flaming cheeks. He rubbed it in and I couldn't help the moan I let out as the pain began to fade away.

"Does that feel better, sweetie?" he asked, gently massaging the lotion in.

I nodded my head slowly, now feeling very groggy. Between my tantrum and the spanking, I was tired.

"Okay, sweetie. I think that someone could use a bath, and maybe a nap and some lunch."

I just nodded again as he picked me up and carried me into the bathroom. I sat on the toilet as he filled the tub. Then he helped me undress before guiding me into the tub.

Once I was sitting in the warm water, I couldn't help but sink further down into it. It took the last of the sting out of my bottom as the warm water began lulling me to sleep. Before I knew it, my eyes had shut and I was sound asleep.

CHAPTER NINE

"Claire. Sweetie. Wake up, honey," I heard a voice call out as I felt someone shaking my shoulder.

"Mmm…" I moaned, not wanting to be woken up and moved out of my warm, cocooned area. I moved around slightly and could tell that I wasn't in the bathtub anymore and instead was in my bed. I didn't remember being moved, but daddy must have done it.

"Honey, Kara is downstairs waiting to see you."

Just like that, I was wide awake and jumping out of bed. I immediately went over to my bedroom mirror to look at myself. After the tantrum I'd thrown, I couldn't look like a slob.

I scoffed at my appearance. Daddy had dressed me in a pair of black yoga pants and a light pink long sleeve shirt and he'd braided my hair into one long braid. *At least you don't have tear streaks down your face,* I thought to myself.

"You look beautiful, honey," he said, coming up behind me and giving me a kiss on the cheek.

"I need to change. She can't see me like this… all messy," I said, trying to turn to reach my dresser, but he wouldn't let me.

"You look perfect, honey. You need to go talk to Kara. She won't judge you for how you look."

"Easy for you to say. You're a guy. You don't understand how women work."

"Oh, I think I do. Does your bottom need a refresher course?" he asked, looking me in the eye through the mirror.

"No, sir," I said, feeling my cheeks turn red.

"Good. Then why don't you go downstairs and talk to Kara? I'll be in my office if you need anything."

"Okay, daddy," I said and then took a deep breath before I walked out of our bedroom and headed downstairs. I wasn't sure why Kara would be here after how I'd acted, and I was hoping that I could get her to leave quickly so I could quietly lick my wounds in private.

I'd never thrown a tantrum before out in public. It was going to take some time for me to get over my embarrassment and be able to face everyone in town.

Kara was sitting on the couch in the living room. When she saw me at the entryway, she stood up and said, "Hi, Claire."

"Hi," I said, crossing my arms.

"Listen, I know that we just met, but I've heard some really positive things about you. I saw what happened at the library today. So, I just wanted you to have this."

She handed me a movie from the library—*Freaky Friday*.

"I know that it isn't one of the movies that you wanted, but it's just as funny."

"Thank you."

"You're welcome. It's due back in one week at the library, just so you know."

"Okay."

We stood in awkward silence for a couple of minutes. I didn't know what to say, and I was sure that she was just as confused about what to say too. How do you talk to someone who literally had a tantrum like a five-year-old girl?

"Claire, I wanted to say about today… it's okay what happened."

"What?" I asked, shocked that she would say something like that.

"I understand how you felt. Sometimes when I'm acting little and my daddy tells me that I can't do something that I can do just fine when I'm acting big, I get frustrated and have tantrums in public too," she said, taking a seat on the couch.

"You've had a tantrum in public too?" I asked, shocked as I sat down next to her.

"Yes, once or twice. I've gotten better, but it happens to everyone."

"I know that this might make me sound like a jerk, but I'm glad that I'm not the only one who sometimes has problems controlling their feelings."

She chuckled. "Oh trust me, you aren't the only one. I'm sure that everyone who lives in this community has had problems reigning in their emotions a time or two."

Deciding to take a chance and go with my gut that she was a great person, I said, "I really like your tattoos."

"Thank you!" she said, visibly brightening.

"Why do you have so many, if you don't mind my asking?" I had always been scared to talk to her before because of her appearance and because I knew she regressed to an older age than I did. Since she had been so nice to me, I wanted to know. I hoped that I wasn't rude for asking.

"Well, I got them because they make me feel pretty," she said, blushing and casting her eyes away as if she was embarrassed.

"But you're beautiful! I love your hair and your figure! I wish that I had boobs like you. Oh… I shouldn't have said that. I'm sorry," I said, feeling my face flush at my zero brain-to-mouth coordination.

She laughed. "Thank you. I'm just starting to accept myself as beautiful without the tattoos. It's nice to hear that someone else thinks I am too."

"It's the truth! I wouldn't lie," I said smiling back at her.

She and I talked for the good part of an hour before my daddy came to the living room and announced that Kara's daddy, Brody, had called and wanted her to come home.

"Thank you for thinking of me and checking this movie out for me. You and I are going to have to hang out again sometime soon," I said, as I walked her to the door.

"Totally. I'll give you a call soon."

"Okay, bye!" I said as she walked out the door.

I closed it behind me and turned to see my daddy standing there.

"Have fun, sweetie?"

"Yes, I did," I said as I walked up to him and gave him a hug. "Kara is super nice. I was always a little afraid to talk to her, but she was the best. She and I are going to hang out soon. Look, she also checked out this movie for me because she saw what happened at the library. Don't worry, it's rated PG, so nothing inappropriate is in it."

"I'm glad to hear that you made a new friend. What do you say to some lunch now?"

"Oh, yes please!"

Together we walked hand-in-hand to the kitchen.

• • • • • • •

It was eight at night and I was sitting in bed. Daddy had told me that I had half an hour before bedtime. I was tired, but my bottom was still bothering me from the spanking from that afternoon. Even though daddy had rubbed lotion into it, it was still bothering me.

"You okay, sweetie?" daddy asked as he walked into the bedroom.

I nodded my head, not wanting to complain.

"Claire, remember our rule about lying."

"Okay. My bottom is still hurting me from earlier."

"Hmmm… I have an idea I think will fix that. Come over here, sweetie. Let your legs fall off the side of the bed so I can examine your bottom."

I did as I was told, wondering why he wanted me in this position. When he pulled down my panties and pajama shorts and gave my bottom another smack, I was confused.

"Jensen! Stop!" I cried out, trying to cover my tender bottom with my hands. He grabbed both, holding them out of the way.

"Trust me. Just breath and this will feel so good in a matter of minutes, honey."

He continued the spanking, but this spanking was different from this afternoon's spanking. It was a lot more gentle, and instead of leaving a sting behind, these spanks left my bottom feeling warm in a good way and I soon began to feel my pussy getting wet.

I spread my legs slightly, hoping that he would stop spanking me and move his skilled fingers into my dripping folds.

The spanking continued and I felt like my body was on fire, except this was a very, very good fire. I began pushing my hips up so that my bottom met his hand smack for smack.

He finally stopped just as I thought I wouldn't be able to take any more of the pleasurable sensations without coming.

"Hmmm... someone seems to be very turned on," he said, plunging his fingers into my wet folds.

"Ohhh..." I moaned, balling my hands into fists.

"Do you want to come?"

"Yes... please."

He pulled his fingers out of me, then traced them all the way up to my engorged clit.

"Always the polite one, you are. Come whenever you wish," he said as I heard the clank of his belt and then felt his hard shaft enter me.

I could barely nod my head as Jensen began to thrust in and out of me and his fingers continued to play with my swollen clit. I tried to hold off my impending orgasm as long as possible because I wanted us to come together.

As he pulled me close and grunted, finding his release, I came screaming. I rode wave after wave of pleasure, finally relaxing as I felt him pull out of me.

A minute later, I felt a warm cloth against my skin, cleaning me.

"You okay, Claire?"

"Mm-hmm..." I mumbled, suddenly fighting to keep my eyes open.

"Go to sleep, honey. I'll take care of everything."

He didn't need to tell me twice as minutes later, I was sound asleep.

CHAPTER TEN

When I woke up Wednesday morning, I was not in a good mood. I opened my eyes and immediately saw that daddy wasn't in bed, then I turned my head to see that it was raining outside, which reflected my inner mood.

I was tired of waking up and doing nothing productive with my days. Sure, daddy thought that this was good for me. He said that my not going to work and being little for this long was reducing my stress. But I wholeheartedly disagreed. If anything, it was increasing my stress.

I liked acting little for two days a week. That was relaxing. But I was going on day seven of this treatment, and I was ready to climb up the walls. I needed to get out and do something productive with my day or else I was liable to start attacking someone.

With each thought, I felt my bad mood worsening, so I finally swung my feet out of bed and headed into the bathroom to brush my teeth and hair.

After that, I went to the kitchen and I saw daddy sitting at the kitchen table. He had his laptop open and was typing away. He was undoubtedly doing work. I wanted to scream at him, *why can you work during this time period, but I can't?* It just wasn't fair!

"Good morning, sweetheart."

"Mmmm…" I grunted at him, heading over to the cupboards to get a coffee mug. One of the absolute biggest things I hated about being little was daddy had this stupid rule that I couldn't drink coffee. *Who in their right mind would deny another human being the right to drink coffee in the morning? Jensen Boyer, that's who,* I thought to myself as I reached for the coffee pot.

"Young lady, you aren't allowed to have coffee right now," he admonished as I heard his the legs of his kitchen chair scraping back against the hardwood floor, signaling that he was getting up.

"Please. I need it," I gritted out, trying to keep my temper under control, but it was really hard to when I hadn't had coffee for almost a week. Missing coffee for two days wasn't that big of a deal, but seven days? He might as well have stabbed me in the hand—that's how it felt to go without coffee for

so long.

"Sweetie, five-year-old girls don't drink coffee. How about some milk, or maybe some juice?" he asked, going over to the refrigerator and opening it up.

I gripped the side of the counter and took a few deep breaths before I said, "No. I want coffee."

"Honey, I just told you that you can't have it."

"I know, damn it! But I want it! I usually have at least one cup every day, and I'm tired of not getting it!" I shouted, banging my hand against the counter, as if that would prove my point.

"Young lady. In the corner. Now," he said, taking my hand gently but firmly and guiding me to one of the corners in the kitchen. "You will stay in this corner for five minutes until you calm down."

"All I wanted was my coffee! You need to give me my coffee!" I pleaded, kicking the wall.

"Ten minutes, now. Keep up this attitude and I'll keep on adding time."

"Yes, daddy," I pouted, crossing my arms over myself and leaning my head against the wall. I couldn't believe that he was punishing me! All because I just wanted to have a cup of coffee.

Time seemed to slow down as I stood in the corner, just like it always did. I didn't understand why he was punishing me when all I wanted was just a cup of hot coffee. I would have loved to see how he'd have reacted if he wasn't allowed his morning cup of coffee for over a week. He would probably be just as upset as I was.

I took a deep breath, trying to reign in my temper. I knew that if I didn't, I was going to turn around and start arguing with him again, and that would just increase the amount of time I had in the corner, plus increase the number of swats I had coming.

This just wasn't fair. I had never really agreed to being little this long. Jensen just made me. If he could make me be little for this long, what was going to stop him from forcing me to be little more often?

"Okay, Claire, your time is up."

I turned around and grasped the hand that he held out for me. He led me into the family room and then he had me bend over the couch so my bottom was raised in the air. I rarely wore pants to bed, so I was already mostly naked from the waist down. He then made quick work of discarding my panties for my punishment.

He didn't say anything as my spanking began. I knew what I had done was wrong and there was no need for him to lecture me. Pain spread across my backside as he gave equal amounts of attention to both of my cheeks. He would sometimes hit my sit spots, and when he did, I really had to fight to stay still as the pain radiated through me.

I reached for one of the couch pillows and hugged it close to me as I

began to cry. I was the first one in line to get a spanking during sex, but not a punishment spanking. I hated pain and it seemed that's all that punishment spankings were—even though I knew he was holding back. He'd never give me a really hard spanking unless I did something life threatening, like drink and drive.

The worst part about punishment spankings was that he was much colder towards me during them, when all I wanted was for him to cuddle me and tell me that it was okay.

"Ouch!" I sobbed as he hit a very tender spot. I tried shuffling away from his hand, but he held me down and continued spanking me.

The sounds that filled the room were not pleasurable ones, nor was the pain that was coming from each one of his swats. I had to bite my lip to keep from begging him to stop.

Finally, I just sank into the couch and accepted the fact that this spanking was going to end whenever he thought I had learned my lesson. Thankfully, the spanking finally ended three swats later, and then he picked me up and cuddled me close in his lap as he sat on the couch.

"You're okay, sweetie. I've got you," he said softly as he rubbed my hair and back.

I cried into his shoulder for what felt like hours, but was probably about ten minutes. Finally, my tears stopped and I felt exhausted, despite the fact that I had woken up less than an hour ago.

"Feel better, sweetie?"

I nodded my head against his shoulder, not bothering to pick my head up.

"Are you ready for breakfast?"

I shook my head this time. I was content to stay right there.

"Okay, honey," he said, reaching for the blanket on the back of the couch and covering me with it. The extra warmth felt better and I soon began to feel myself drift off.

• • • • • • •

I woke with a start, momentarily confused as to where I was.

"Good morning again, sleepyhead. How are you feeling?" daddy asked from the end of the couch.

"Good," I said, sitting up and rubbing my eyes.

He smiled before saying, "You must be starving. It's nearly noon, I was starting to get a little worried that you were going to sleep the entire day away."

"Sorry about that," I murmured.

"There's nothing to be sorry for, honey. This is what I wanted you to do with your time off—relax. What would you like to eat? Breakfast or lunch?"

"Ummm… breakfast, please."

"Okay, honey," he said, getting up and going to the kitchen.

I leaned back against the couch, just thinking. It was nice being able to relax, but now that he had mentioned it, my thoughts turned towards Smith. I wondered if he had stolen any more of my clients since I had been away. It had been a week, so I was sure that he could have gotten one or two.

I glanced over to the kitchen to see that Jensen was busy cooking, so I quietly threw the blanket off and tiptoed out of the living room and upstairs to my bedroom.

My laptop and briefcase were in the corner of the room and I quickly reached for both, hoping that I could sneak a peek at my work before he noticed that I had left.

I had just opened up my laptop and booted it up when he appeared at the door.

"Exactly what do you think you're doing, young lady?" he asked in a very stern tone.

"Just checking the weather, daddy," I quickly fibbed, not wanting to add any more redness to my already red bottom.

"Sure... here, I'll help you out," he said, walking over to the windows and pulling open the blinds. "There you go. It's sunny out, but since there's still snow on the ground, you'll need to wear your winter coat."

"Yes, daddy," I said, closing my laptop. I knew when not to push him.

"Good girl. Now come along, breakfast is ready. I made you an egg, bacon, and cheese wrap, with apple juice."

"Oh! That sounds yummy!" I said, hopping off of the bed and taking his hand as he led me downstairs to the kitchen.

While I ate my breakfast, he ate a sandwich since he'd eaten breakfast earlier. "So, sweetie, what would you like to do this afternoon?"

I looked outside at the glistening snow and a thought hit me immediately. "Can we please go ice skating?"

"Hmmm... I'm not sure if we can go outside, but I know of a place where we can go inside."

"Okay!"

"Finish the rest of your lunch first please."

"Yes, daddy!" I said, excited for the first time in the past couple of days. Ever since the library incident, I had felt kind of down, but now we were going to do something that I used to do as a child that I really loved. "All done, daddy!"

"Good girl. Daddy is done with his lunch too, so let's go change and then we can be on our way."

"Okay!"

• • • • • • •

"We're here! We're here!" I shouted as the ice skating rink appeared in the windshield.

"Yes, we are," daddy said, smiling at me.

Despite my excitement, my bottom never left my seat and I kept my seat belt on. Last summer, I had made the serious mistake of unbuckling my seatbelt when Jensen was still driving the car and he had promptly pulled the car over to the side of the road and blistered my bottom until I promised that I would never unbuckle my seatbelt again until the car had come to a full and complete stop.

So, once the car was stopped, I threw off my seatbelt and hopped out of the car.

"Slow down there, skipper. Wait for me," he called as I bounded up towards the rink doors.

"Come on, Jensen."

"I'm coming, I'm coming," he chuckled, finally reaching the door and holding it open for me.

We went inside and I immediately noticed that there weren't that many people on the rink. There were maybe half a dozen kids, then two other couples were there. Jensen and I went over to the stand and we each got skates. Then we went over by the benches and I tried lacing my own skates up.

"Need some help, baby?"

"Yes, please."

He got off the bench and got down on one knee. Then he grabbed my foot put it on his knee and started lacing up my skate. When he finished with my first foot, he switched to my other one and made fast work of lacing up that skate. "All done. You ready?"

I nodded my head as I stood up and walked over to the rink. I stepped out onto the ice and started to glide. It was amazing—until I fell flat on my butt.

"Ouch!" I couldn't help but cry out as my already sore bottom smacked against the ice.

"Careful, sweetie. Here, why don't you take my hand?" he asked, easily skating over to me and offering me his hand.

Of course he can skate perfectly, I thought as I took his hand and he helped me up.

Together we skated around the rink in a big circle. It made me relax some more since there weren't too many people there—fewer people to embarrass myself in front of.

"Do you want to try skating alone? I'll still be right next to you and catch you if you fall."

I nodded and let go of his hand. At first my feet were wobbly without his strong arm holding me up and I thought I was going to fall. But then I

straightened myself up and started moving again.

After several minutes of skating without any worries of falling, I turned towards Jensen and said, "Look! I'm skating!" I knew that it was probably a childish thing to say and to feel proud of myself for, but I couldn't help how I felt. The look of pride on his face told me that he felt the same way.

"Great job, honey! Let me get a picture," he said, pulling his iPhone out of his phone.

"No!" I said, holding my hands up to my face.

"Come on, silly. You'll want to remember this."

"Fine," I groaned, and then pulled my hands down from my face and smiled at the camera for him. I secretly loved it when my husband went all proud-daddy.

For the rest of the afternoon, Jensen and I skated around until I was finally wiped out and I could tell he was too. Then we got off the rink and he helped me remove my skates. After we returned the skates and left the ice stadium, we saw a pizza place right next door. We decided to eat there, and I got the most delicious slice of sausage and mushroom pizza.

After we ate and finally began heading home, I couldn't help but think about how awesome today had been. I hadn't thought about Smith once and I couldn't remember the last time I had relaxed and had so much fun or laughed so hard.

I was still kind of upset that Jensen was forcing me to be little and relax when I didn't want to, but if this was what he planned for the rest of the week, I could get used to it.

· · · · · · ·

"Hey there, sleepyhead, you keep falling asleep on me today," daddy said, as I awoke when he picked me up from the car and began carrying me inside the house.

"Sorry," I said, then smiled as we entered our room and he sat down on the bed, still holding me in his lap.

"So, did you have fun today?"

"Mm-hmm."

"You must be really tired."

"I am, but there's one more thing I want to do before I go to sleep, unless you're too tired and want to go to bed now."

"Oh really? What's that?"

I wiggled my bottom into his lap and I could feel him get hard.

"Hmmm... I think that I still have some energy left to do that," he chuckled, then moved me onto the bed and hovered above me. "What do you want me to do, Claire?"

I thought the answer was obvious… *I want you to fuck me until I scream out*

133

your name. But something told me that wasn't the answer he was looking for.

"Kiss me."

He gave me a quick peck on the lips and pulled back with a smile.

"I said kiss me," I repeated.

"I did."

"Okay… kiss me like this is the first time you've seen me in a month."

He gripped my face in his strong hands and his lips devoured mine, sending what felt like little electric shocks to my core. My hands wrapped around his neck, pulling him even closer.

"Now what?" he asked, breathless.

"Kiss me again like my lips are the sweetest thing that you've ever tasted and let your right hand go underneath my panties and…" I could feel my cheeks getting so bright red. He had never made me do this before. He always took control in the bedroom and made his own decisions.

"And what, Claire?" he asked, a devilish smile on his face.

"And rub my… clit…" I whispered the last part and had to look away.

"You're too damn cute for your own good," he said, before reclaiming my lips and letting his hand slide down between us and slip underneath my panties. His hand brushed over my sensitive nub, and I let out a screech.

"Wow, you are soaked, baby. Does you telling me what to do… what to touch… turn you on?"

I shook my head.

"Hmm… I think that someone is lying. Admit it, Claire. This turns you on," he said, one of his fingers diving into my channel.

I gasped at the feeling as my vaginal walls closed around his finger and squeezed, eliciting a groan from him.

"I…" He was right. I might be embarrassed about this, but it was hot to tell him to touch me in a certain place and have him do it. He was still in control, but I got to make some decisions too.

"Admit it, honey, and I'll make you come like never before."

"Okay! Telling you what to do… turns-me-on-a-lot." I sped up the last part so it probably sounded all jumbled, but by the look on his face, he had heard me just fine.

"Good girl," he said and pulled his finger out.

"Hey! I thought you said you would make me come like never before."

"I did. All in good time, my sweetie. Tell me where you want me to touch again."

"Same areas as before," I said, pulling his neck down so he could kiss me again as he began to rub my clit.

Within minutes, I was a seething ball of need. I knew that Jensen knew I was ready to come, but the man wouldn't help me!

"Jensen!" I cried.

"You need to tell me what you want me to do."

"I want you to fuck me and to keep your promise."

"Alright, baby." Faster than lightening—or maybe it was just because I was so preoccupied with not taking matters into my own hands, literally—he got our clothes removed, put a condom on, and then he was back on top of me.

"One fucking, coming up," he joked before shoving his cock into me. I groaned and arched my back as he settled inside me. After a moment, he pulled out and then sank back deep inside me.

I couldn't speak as he continued thrusting in and out of me, each time hitting my G-spot.

My entire body was so freaking tense until finally, Jensen took pity on me and brushed his hand over my overly sensitive clit and I began coming for what felt like forever. I didn't even feel him come; I just heard him groan and I knew that he had met his release too.

I sank against the mattress with the biggest, goofiest smile on my face. Life was fantastic.

"You're too damn cute, Claire," I heard him chuckle as I refocused on him and realized that he was still inside me. "So, did I come through with the 'you'll come like never before'?"

"Oh, hell yes!" I couldn't help but say as I felt my vaginal walls still experiencing some aftershocks.

"Glad to hear it. But now, I think we both need a shower."

"*Ugh!*"

"Come on, lazy pants. I know you're tired, but I'm not going to let you go to sleep dirty."

"But I like being dirty. It feels so good." I smiled up at him, hoping that he'd just let me stay there.

"Yes, honey, dirty is good, but clean is good too. Now come on. You'll sleep even better after a nice shower. Besides, after the spanking your bottom got and the few times that you fell today, I'm not sure if you can take much more, and I'll be giving you a spanking if you don't get up."

"Okay, okay," I said, getting up and following him into the shower. I wasn't about to risk getting another spanking on my already sensitive bottom.

CHAPTER ELEVEN

It was Friday afternoon when daddy announced that he was going out in the evening. I was really happy as that meant that when he was gone, I could act like my adult self for a few hours. I was just itching to read a few chapters in the latest Mary Higgins Clark novel on my Kindle.

That was one of the things that I hated about regressing. It was nice, but I missed being able to read my adult books. After being treated little for so long, I was ready to burst at the seams and I couldn't wait until Sunday evening when my punishment was over and I could get back to acting like an adult.

I did love being little, but since I had been acting like a five year old for over a week, I was ready for Sunday. Every night since Tuesday I had been having the same nightmare that Jensen was going to keep me little permanently. I didn't like that thought and knew that tonight would help quiet my fears and get rid of the icky feeling in my stomach.

After he left, I would open up some wine, pour myself a glass, and then go and take a hot bubble bath and read my book. I was all set to do that, until daddy opened up his mouth again.

"Angela will be babysitting you. I shouldn't be gone too long though," he said casually as he checked something on his iPhone.

I dropped the chicken nugget I had been eating. *He just said... babysit. Someone is going to babysit... me?*

That icky feeling in my stomach suddenly grew tremendously and I thought I was going to be sick. I had never been babysat before. Daddy rarely went out on the weekends, but the times that he had, he had never gotten me a babysitter and had just let me act like an adult. He knew how I felt about someone else taking care of me when I was a little, so it scared the crap out of me that he was okaying it now.

"I don't need a babysitter," I said, my voice finally working.

He put down his phone and said, "Sweetie, we've talked about this. You're supposed to be little for this entire week, up to Sunday night. Today's only

Friday. You have two more days."

"Yeah, but what's a couple of hours of me not acting little going to do? I can take care of myself. I've already eaten, so all I was going to do was read my book." I pouted, crossing my arms over my chest. In hindsight, I knew that childish action probably wasn't the best thing to do when I was trying to prove to my daddy that I was old enough to take care of myself.

"Claire, my decision is final. Now eat the rest of your lunch. Afterwards, I think that it's time that you get put down for a nap. You've been in a cranky mood."

"I—"

He cut me off. "I'd be careful what you say next, little girl, unless you want a trip over my lap."

I ground my teeth together. I wanted to protest more, but I really didn't want to have a sore bottom when I got babysat.

"Good girl," he said at my quietness before he picked his iPhone back up and began paying attention to it again.

I sat there quietly, slowly finishing my chicken nuggets. I was angry. I didn't like being treated like this, but it seemed that I didn't have a choice.

Picking up my finished plate, I put it in the dishwasher and headed up to my adult bedroom. As angry as I was with him and even though I hated to admit it, he was right about one thing. I had been in a foul mood today because I kept having those stupid nightmares. Maybe a nap wouldn't be the worst thing in the world.

I pushed back the covers and climbed under them, then threw them back over myself. I gave my pillow a few good punches before I laid my head down and closed my eyes. Just because I was willing to take a nap didn't mean that I had to do it in my little room.

I sighed, trying to relax and clear my mind. I was really getting fed up with having to act little. Jensen was taking it to an extreme that I didn't feel comfortable with and I just couldn't get over the fear that he would want to keep me little from now on.

Even though I knew that he loved me and wanted the best for me, I also knew that he loved the control he got when I acted little. I just hoped that it didn't go to his head and he would try to keep me little for the rest of my life. I didn't know what I would do if that happened. I didn't think the community would allow that to happen, but what if they did? I would be forced to act like a five year old and there would be nothing I could do about it.

I squeezed my eyes tightly shut and told myself to relax. With that last thought, I drifted off to sleep, where my nightmares plagued me once more.

• • • • • • •

I woke up to the annoying ringing of my cell phone.

"Hello," I greeted the person, rolling onto my back to try and wake up faster.

"Hello, Claire. I'm sorry to be bothering you during your time off, but I wanted to let you know that we had to fire Smith. It seemed that he was breaking into your computer and going through your files to get information on your clients."

"Really? He's gone?" I asked, happily, shooting up in bed. It then occurred to me how I just sounded and so I quickly said, "Oh. I'm sorry to hear that."

"Yes, well, I just wanted to inform you of that so you knew he wouldn't be here when you got back on Monday."

"Yes, sir. Thank you so much for calling me."

"No problem, Claire. Enjoy the rest of your vacation. Goodbye."

"Bye."

I shut my phone, got up on the bed, and started to bounce up and down.

"Claire Boyer! Get down from there."

"I'm so happy, daddy!" I shouted, jumping into his open arms.

"Whoa there, kiddo. Why are you so happy?" he asked, sitting down on the side of the bed and placing me in his lap.

"I just got a call from my boss. They fired Smith! They caught him going through my files! I'm not going to have to deal with him anymore!"

"Oh, honey, that's fantastic! I'm so happy for you." he said, giving me a quick peck on the lips.

"Thank you. I can finally relax now. I don't have to worry about what Smith is up to anymore."

"That's excellent, honey. I'm really glad to hear that. I'm also glad that you got up. I have to leave in a couple of minutes and I thought I was going to have to wake you to say goodbye."

Suddenly, my happy feeling was replaced with nervousness about tonight as my worries from earlier came rushing back. I was nervous about meeting Angela. She and I had really never talked because I knew that she regressed to an older little and I didn't get out much to meet other littles.

I just hoped she was nice. It had been a long time since I'd had a babysitter. When I was a kid, I'd had a really mean babysitter who would make me go to bed at seven so she could sneak her boyfriend over and they could make out on the couch.

If Angela tried to pull a stunt like that, I'd be on the phone with my daddy so fast it would make her head spin.

I was pulled out of my thoughts when daddy asked, "You're going to be on your best behavior. Right, young lady?"

"Yes, daddy," I said, rolling my eyes at the same time.

"Young lady, I know that you didn't roll your eyes at me."

"I'm sorry, daddy," I quickly said, hoping that since it was nearly time for

him to be leaving that I wouldn't get a spanking.

Just as he was about to respond, the doorbell rang and I relaxed, knowing that he would never give me a spanking in front of people. That was something that we had talked about very early when we'd started dating. We'd agreed that we would never play with others or have anyone watch us when we were making love or when I was getting punished.

"We'll discuss your eye rolling when I get back home," he said.

I nodded my head and watched as he left our bedroom to go and greet our guests at the front door.

I jumped off the bed and glanced at myself one last time in the mirror. My hair was pulled back in a neat ponytail, which showed off my rosy cheeks. I had on a pair of black leggings, and I was wearing Christmas socks and a Barbie t-shirt.

This was not the outfit I would have picked out for myself when there were people coming over, but daddy had insisted that I wear my little clothing. He had said that it would help me stay in my little mindset for the night and make being babysat easier on me. Not wanting to start a fight, I had just agreed and hoped that Angela wouldn't say anything.

I heard daddy call me downstairs and I took one last quick glance at myself before I dashed down the stairs and into the living room where everyone was standing and talking.

"There you are," Jensen said, holding his arm out for me to come and stand next to him. I did as he wanted as he said, "Angela, Charlie, this is Claire. Claire, this is Angela and Charlie."

I gave a small wave while shuffling a little bit closer to my daddy. This wasn't an act. No matter if I was big or little, I always got super shy when I met new people. But once I warmed up to them, I was a chatterbox.

"It's nice to meet you, Claire. Your daddy has told me an awful lot about you. I hope that you and my Angela get along well tonight."

"We will, daddy," Angela said with a smile on her face as she got on her tippy toes and kissing him. She was dressed very fashionable tonight in a pair of skinny jeans, cute flats, and a form-fitting sweater. Even though it was a simple outfit, she looked like she'd just gotten off the runway.

"Alright then, Charlie, it seems like Claire is in good hands. We have to get going or else we'll be late."

"You're right, Jensen."

My daddy turned towards me and bent down. "Remember, Claire, I want you on your best behavior tonight. If I get a bad report, you know what the punishment will be."

"Yes, daddy," I repeated once again, this time without the eye roll.

"Good girl. Now if you need anything, Angela has my cell phone number. Charlie and I shouldn't be gone for long. Have fun tonight, baby girl," Jensen said before planting a kiss on my forehead. Then he and Charlie left.

I turned towards Angela, not sure what to expect. Was she going to make me stay little tonight? Or would she just let me act like an adult and do my own thing?

"What?" she asked, crossing her arms over her chest and giving me a look as though she were sizing me up.

"Ummm… I'm not sure what to do. I've never been baby sat before," I answered honestly.

"Ugh, you can do whatever you want. I'm going to go and watch some TV," she said, then turned and stalked over to the couch and sat down and clicked the TV on.

I watched as she turned the television to a program that I didn't like, so I just shrugged my shoulders and headed upstairs.

I was tempted to pull out my Mary Higgins Clark book and just read that. After all, Angela had said that I could do whatever I wanted, but I was afraid that daddy would see that I hadn't acted little like he wanted me to and that I would get in trouble. So instead, I walked into my little room, pulled out a few of my Barbies, and began to play.

I dressed the four Barbies I was playing with in hot dresses with matching high heels. Then I put them in their Barbie limo and drove them over to their hotel, where they were going to have their prom. Then I took them out of the car and put two of them over by the pool to swim and two of the others were dancing on the dance floor.

I wasn't sure how long I played with my dolls when Angela walked into my bedroom.

"What are you doing?"

"I'm playing with my Barbies. Do you want to join me?" I asked, hoping that she'd say yes because then I could add even more people to my prom!

"Um, no. Barbies are for babies. Don't they have a small sign on the box saying that they're for kids twelve and under?" she scoffed, crossing her arms over her chest.

"Barbies aren't just for babies. My daddy says that big girls play with them too. Come on, they're fun." I really hoped she'd say yes—now that she knew Barbies were not for babies.

"I told you no. Some of us aren't as obsessed with Barbie as you are. Look at you and this room. You have Barbie stuff all over, even on your walls. You're even wearing a Barbie t-shirt!"

"Yeah, so?" I asked, finally dropping my Barbies and standing up to face her.

"Maybe you're the baby here, and that's why you like them so much. Look at this room. It has stuffed animals everywhere. There's a rocking chair in the corner. This room screams little girl. I bet that you even wear diapers to bed. Do you wet the bed? Do you even act like an adult ever? I'm sure you act like a little girl all day, every day."

I couldn't help the tears that were beginning to start to fall down my cheeks. I liked acting little because it helped me relax, but when people thought that I was truly like a little kid even when I was an adult, it really hurt my feelings. I couldn't help that I liked to regress this young, but that didn't mean that I wasn't perfectly capable of being an adult too.

"I don't wet the bed or wear diapers, and I'm not a baby!" I said, wiping away the traitorous tears.

"Angela, what's going on here?"

Both of us turned to see Jensen and Charlie standing in the doorway.

"Nothing, daddy. Claire just dropped one of her baby Barbies, and I was helping her," Angela said too sweetly with a smile on her face as Charlie walked into the room to stand next to her.

I couldn't stay in this room anymore with everyone looking at me as Angela's words kept repeating in my head. She'd said the exact words I was terrified Jensen was going to say.

Wanting to just be left alone, I started to walk towards the door, but Jensen didn't move out of the way.

"Claire. Is what Angela said true?" he asked.

I tried to push past him, but he still wouldn't move.

"Claire, I asked you a question," he said, grabbing my shoulders gently.

"Just leave me alone, Jensen. She was fine. I just want to be left alone now," I said, pushing him so I could finally escape that room and the horrible stares of the other three people.

"Claire!" he called out.

"I want to be alone... as an adult!" I shouted, not bothering to turn to look back at him as I walked into our bedroom and then into the bathroom. I shut and locked the door, then turned the shower on.

I quickly stripped, then got in and sobbed my heart out. I couldn't do this anymore. I loved being little, but the fear that Jensen would turn me into a little twenty-four seven, like Angela had suggested, was too much for me. I couldn't handle that, so instead, I decided it would be better to not act little anymore.

Once I had made that decision, a part of me began to felt numb and the tears... just stopped. Wanting to wash away everything bad that had happened that night, I reached for the bodywash as the heated water cascaded around me.

I closed my eyes and just tried to forget what had happened, but it was difficult. Ever since I could remember, Jensen and I had a grownup relationship and an age play relationship. Now I was ending our age play relationship, and it felt like a part of our marriage was also ending.

But I had to do it. If Angela thought that I'd acted too childish and that I should just be little all the time, then undoubtedly so did he, and I wasn't about to chance him forcing me to stay little all the time. That would end up

killing me.

I wasn't sure how he was going to take this. He would definitely want to talk about it, but I was hoping that it could wait until morning. I wasn't sure if I was strong enough to talk about it tonight.

Shaking my head, I thought about the latest book I'd read. I just couldn't think about being little or anything anymore. It hurt too much.

Far too soon, the shower water ran cold and I had to get out. I grabbed a towel, quickly dried off my body, and then grabbed my light green bathrobe from the back of the bathroom door. I put it on, making sure to tie the sash tight before I opened the door.

Jensen was sitting on the bed, facing me.

"We need to talk, Claire," he said swinging his legs back to the floor and standing up, as I walked past him to grab the hairbrush that I'd left on my dresser.

"We really don't have to, Jensen. I don't want to act little anymore ever again, end of story," I said as I began brushing my hair.

"No. Not end of story," he said, walking towards me.

"What else is there to talk about?" I asked, taking a step back from him, which made him pause in his tracks.

"For one, why are you saying out of the blue that you don't want to have this type of relationship? We've had it since before we even got married."

"So? Marriages can change," I said, pulling a little too hard on my hair and letting out a whine.

"Honey," he said, taking the hairbrush from my hand. He began to brush my hair much more gently than I had been. "Are you upset because I had asked Angela to babysit?"

Why did he have to be so gentle? It made it that much harder to stand by my decision.

"No. I just felt like stopping, okay?" I said, wrapping my arms around myself and pouting... once I did that, I realized that it was very similar to what a young child would do. That just infuriated me even more.

"You know, sweetie," he said, putting the hairbrush down on my dresser once he was done getting all the tangles out, "you've always been bad at lying. Why don't you tell me the truth?"

"Fine, you want the truth?" I asked, spinning around so I could face him. "Yes, I was pissed that you hired Angela to babysit me! I was pissed that you made me take off work and act young this entire week! I'm a grownup and I'll be damned if I let you force me to be a little all the time. I won't give up my adulthood! I won't!" I screamed, ending with my foot hitting the floor.

"Oh, baby girl," he cooed, before he pulled me in to a bear hug.

I did not want to be hugged right now so I fought him, kicking and screaming, but he wouldn't let go. He just held onto me until I finished fighting and sagged against him and sobbed my heart out.

He picked me up and carried me into my little girl's room and sat down in the rocking chair with me in his lap. He slowly began to rock back and forth. I just lay there the entire time and cried.

Once I finished crying, I sat in his lap and quietly listened to the calming sounds of his heartbeat.

Our peacefulness was broken when he said, "So, this is what has been bugging you this past week. I knew that something was, but I didn't realize you were so worried that I was going to force you to be my little twenty-four seven. What gave you that thought?"

I didn't want to tell him, so I shrugged my shoulders.

"Claire, I'd really like to know so I can understand better."

"Fine. I got the idea from some of the books I've read. They were age play ones, and the littles were forced to act little without their consent, all day, every day."

His arms tightened around me as he asked, "What would give you the idea that I would want that for you? We've been together for so long. I've never forced you to do anything that you really didn't want to unless you were harming yourself. That's why I made you act young for this whole week. I saw how you were overworking yourself and that you needed a break. But if you ever really wanted to stop, all you'd have to do was say your safeword."

Gosh, when he put it like that, it made all of my fears for the past week and a half sound so silly.

"I know... I guess deep down I knew that. I just... I got the thought in my head, and then I got so scared. Then Angela teased me that my Barbies were for babies and asked if I wore diapers or wet the bed. It terrified me. I thought that if she thought I was a baby... then you must think it too."

"Claire, you must know that I will never force you to do something like that. When we got married, we agreed to certain limits and other things about our relationship. One was that you would be little for me on weekends, except if I thought that you really needed to act younger. In the years that we've been married, have I ever broken that limit?"

"No," I said, after a few seconds of realizing that he hadn't.

"Then why would you think I would break those promises now?"

"I don't know! I'm sorry!" I said, bursting into tears again. I was crazy. That was the only explanation as to why I would start freaking out like this.

"Hey, no more tears. You've been crying so much today. You're okay now. Now that daddy knows what has been bugging you, he can help make it all better."

"You can? How?"

"By promising once again that I will never force you to do anything, unless it's to protect you or keep you healthy. I also promise to treat you as my baby girl only on the weekends. Okay?"

"Yes, daddy," I said, snuggling extra close to him.

"I also think it would be a smart idea if I monitor what books you read on your kindle. I don't want you getting any more crazy ideas in that head of yours," he said, lightly tapping his finger against my head.

"No! I promise not to read any more of the scary age play books." I knew that was a promise I was going to keep. I didn't want any more crazy ideas going into my head either, but I didn't want Jensen to monitor what books I read either.

"Good. Now, I think it's time that we change you into some pajamas and get your tired body to bed."

At the mention of bed, I knew that I wanted to go there, but not to be put to sleep... yet.

"Jensen, ummm... I have another idea about bed."

"What is that, honey?"

I reached my hand up and slowly began to undo the buttons of his shirt until I had unbuttoned all of them, revealing his undershirt. I slipped my hand underneath it and rubbed over his strong six pack.

"Ah... you want some special attention?"

I nodded, giving him a quick smile before I ground my bottom into his lap. I began to feel him get hard and that just made me giggle.

"Are you giggling at me, young lady?"

"No."

"I think you are," he said, before picking me up, carrying me into our bedroom, and placing me on the bed. "You know what happens to young ladies who giggle at me?"

I shook my head.

"They get tickled!"

"No, please!" I yelled, as his fingers assaulted me. I was writhing on the bed as he tickled me all over. I tried stopping him, but he just grabbed my hands and kept tickling.

"I... I'm s... s... sorry!"

"Okay, since you said sorry," he said as he stopped tickling me. Then he bent down and kissed me, releasing my arms at the same time so I could wrap them around him.

"You're very wet for me," he smiled as he slid his hand underneath my panties to feel my pussy.

"Always."

His eyes darkened as I said that and he moved his hand up as he began to play with my clit.

I moaned and arched my back to push my clit farther into his touch. When he pulled his hand back out, I groaned.

"Easy there, girl. I just want to get you and me undressed," he said as he removed all of his clothes and helped me out of mine. Once we were each unclothed, he said, "Now, where were we?"

"Right here," I said, pulling him close to me so I could kiss him. As I kissed him, he grabbed my ass.

"Mmph!" I grunted as he squeezed my ass while picking me up and placing me on the bed.

Breaking the kiss, he moved so he was lying on the bed and I was on top of him. "I want you to ride my cock, baby."

I nodded, lifting myself up and then placing myself on his cock. I began to lift myself up and down, riding his cock, just like he wanted.

"That's it, baby," he said, grabbing onto my hips as he met me thrust for thrust. He put his thumb over my clit and rubbed it, sending waves of pleasure through me.

"You close, baby?"

"Yes!"

"Come for me," he said, pulling me close. I felt him grunt and lose control and the sight of that pushed me over the edge. I fell down to his side, his flaccid cock sliding off me.

"Let's go take a shower. Then it's bedtime for you."

"Cuddle me?" I asked, turning to my side so I could face him.

"Always," he said with a smile, before hopping off the bed, lifting me up, and carrying me to our shower.

CHAPTER TWELVE

I woke up the next morning with a huge smile on my face. I felt amazing. My body was sore in delicious places, and I had finally admitted my fear about Jensen turning me little and he had set me straight. After a week of worry, it was all gone. *I should have just told him right away, before this got out of hand,* I admonished myself.

"What's that look on your face for?" asked Jensen, already dressed in some jeans and a t-shirt, as he walked into our bedroom.

"I'm just happy that I have nothing to worry about anymore."

"I'm glad that you don't either, honey," he said, giving me an Eskimo kiss.

I giggled before asking, "Is breakfast ready?"

"Of course! It's Saturday, remember? Daddy always makes breakfast on Saturdays. That is, unless you want to be the adult you today, since you were little all this past week."

I thought about it for a second before saying, "I want to be little now. Let's keep with the schedule. Then starting Monday, I'll be an adult again."

"Okay, sweetie. Then I think it's time that I carry you downstairs," he said, holding out his arms for me to jump into.

I was about to when I remembered something. "Wait, daddy! I need to check my cellphone really fast. I know that I said I want to be little, but I haven't checked my phone all week. I need to make sure that I didn't miss any important calls, and then I'll be downstairs. Okay?"

"Okay, sweetie." He kissed my forehead and then left the bedroom.

I went over and grabbed my phone, but I didn't have any missed messages or phone calls. As I put it back down on my nightstand, I heard the doorbell ring, and then seconds later, I heard my daddy calling me downstairs.

Who could that be? I wondered as I walked down to the living room. Then I froze as I saw Angela. *What is she doing here?* I thought as I began to panic. I quickly walked over to my daddy, needing his strength.

Daddy wrapped his arm around me and that made me feel much better, and it gave me a chance to notice that Angela was dressed in a pink lacy dress

146

with lacy ankle socks, Mary Jane shoes, and pigtails. She looked nothing like the girl from last night who had been dressed so fashionable. Now she looked like the little girl that she'd teased me about being.

"Hello, Claire. Angela has something that she wants to say to you," Charlie said, giving Angela a stern look.

"I'm sorry that I made fun of you last night for acting so young. It wasn't polite and I didn't mean to hurt your feelings."

"It's okay," I said, and I knew that I truly meant it. I didn't like holding grudges against people. That just required too much energy.

"Thank you," Angela said with a soft smile that made me realize how beautiful a person she really was.

"Well, now that that's done, we'd better be going. Have a good day, you two," Charlie said, then he grabbed Angela's hand and the two of them left. As they were walking away, I couldn't help but notice the slight bulkiness around Angela's mid-section. It made me wonder if she was wearing a diaper.

Jensen closed the door and turned to face me.

"Well, that was a surprise," I said before turning around and heading to the kitchen. "Now, let's go eat! I'm starving, daddy!"

• • • • • • •

As I finished my last bite of scrambled eggs, daddy asked, "So, do you remember there is an indoor pool party at the community center today?"

"I forgot! Can we go? Please?" I asked excitedly. I loved going swimming and though I normally wasn't a fan of playing with other littles, I got to meet a couple of great friends these past couple of weeks and I was hoping they would be there. It would be so much fun to see Kara.

"Yes. I already packed a bag. You just need to get dressed and ready, and then we can go."

"Okay!" I said, before running upstairs. I couldn't wait to go! A few months ago when my daddy and I had taken a vacation, he had gotten me this really cute one piece Little Mermaid swimsuit. I couldn't wait to show it off!

• • • • • • •

"You can't be serious, daddy! I don't need water wings," I complained as he continued to blow up the hated things.

"Sweetie, I know that you don't know how to swim, so you can't expect me to allow you to go in the pool without them."

"But the shallow end of the pool is only three and a half feet deep, and I'm over five feet. I'm taller than the water," I countered.

"True, but what happens if you walk too far past the shallow end and go

in the deep end? That's over six feet tall."

"I promise I won't."

"I'm sorry, Claire, but I won't allow you to go swimming until you put on your water wings."

"Fine. Then I won't go swimming, I guess," I said, crossing my arms over my one piece Little Mermaid bathing suit.

"So be it. When you're ready to go swimming, I'll be sitting over there. I'll help you put your wings on and then you can go." Leaving the water wings next to me, he walked off and sat down at a table where a bunch of other grownups were sitting.

I huffed as I sat on the edge of the pool and flicked my legs in the water. I couldn't believe that he was trying to force me to wear those stupid wings. I knew that I couldn't swim, but I had promised that I would stay in the shallow end and he didn't believe me.

I was so focused on stewing that I didn't hear anyone approach.

"Hi," said a woman I recognized, but hadn't talked to much before, as she sat down next to me. "I'm Bailey."

A light bulb went off over my head as I remembered her. She was another one of the girls who liked to regress to a teenager mindset. I was pretty sure that she was good friends with Kara. I had seen them walking around together at the park, and Jensen had talked to her daddy for a while. I hadn't talked to Bailey much because she was an older little.

"I'm Claire. It's nice to meet you. I'm sorry that I didn't recognize you from before when our... when our husbands were talking," I said, stuttering a little over the daddy part.

"It's okay," Bailey said with a huge smile on her face, making me instantly like her. "Why aren't you in the water?"

"I... ummm... well, I need to wear these water wings because I don't know how to swim, but I don't want to. They're ugly... and babyish," I muttered the last part, looking down because I didn't want to be thought of as a baby again.

"I know what will make your water wings awesome to wear! I've got these really cool stickers. If we put them on your wings, would you like to get in the pool and show them off? I think it'd be cool to show the other girls. Does that sound good?"

I looked at Bailey and noticed how excited she was about the idea, so I nodded. "Okay. I like stickers!"

"I'll go get them! I'll be right back," she said, standing up and running over to where her daddy and her bag were. I heard her saying a few things to him before she fished the stickers out of her bag and came back to me.

"Here we go. Can I please have your water wings?"

I handed her my water wings and couldn't help but smile as she decorated my wings with flower and star stickers.

I was so focused on Bailey putting stickers on my dull water wings that I didn't notice my daddy approaching us.

"What's going on here?" he asked, wrapping his arm around my shoulder.

"Bailey sat down next to me and I told her that I didn't want to wear these stupid water wings because they'll make me look like a baby and she told me that she had stickers that I could put on them to make them cooler looking. Don't you think that they look cooler, daddy?" I asked, not taking my eyes off of Bailey as she started adding stickers to my second water wing.

"I do think that they look more unique. Even with these on though, I'd like you to stay in the shallow end, Claire. If I'm with you, then you can go in the deep end. Okay?"

"Yes, daddy," I pouted. If I was wearing the stupid water wings, I didn't know why I couldn't go in the deep end. If he was just going to make me stay in the shallow end, then I didn't really need the wings.

"Good girl," he said, placing a kiss on top of my forehead.

As he did that, Bailey had finished putting the last sticker on. "Here you go. I can help you get them on if you want."

"Yes, please," I said, sticking my arms out so she could put the wings on. Once they were on, she took my hand and started to lead me toward the stairs that were on the shallow side of the pool, but I had another idea.

I let go of her hand and ran over to the deep end. As I was going, I heard Bailey call out to me, but I didn't care. I wanted to do a cannon ball and show my daddy that with my water wings, I could swim just fine in the deep end.

I took a deep breath and shouted "Cannon ball!" before diving into the deep end. I was submerged in water, but my water wings did their jobs and pulled me to the surface.

When I opened my eyes, I saw that Bailey was in the water next to me and she looked a little shocked, which had me laughing so hard. That was so much fun.

"I want to do that again!" I shouted, as I grabbed her hand and Bailey pulled me towards the ladder.

Just as I was climbing out, I saw my daddy. He bent over, grabbed me, and pulled me out of the pool.

"Young lady. You were told not to go into the deep end. You're in big trouble, Claire."

Before I could say anything, I noticed Ian, Bailey's daddy, walking over, and he didn't look happy and was sending Bailey a scowling look. I didn't want my new-found friend to get in trouble for something that I did.

So I quickly said, "But I want to do that again. It was fun!" I couldn't help the grin that spread across my face as I led him towards where I'd done my first cannon ball. Bailey and her daddy followed and I hoped that I had gotten her out of trouble.

I heard Bailey talking to Ian, but I couldn't make out what she was saying

until Ian said, "Claire's having fun, Jensen, and no one got hurt. I think that we can agree that as long as we watch them and Bailey stays with Claire when they're in the deep end, everyone can go back to enjoying the rest of the day with no tears. How does that sound?"

I held my breath, hoping that he would agree to that. *Please, please, I just want to have fun,* I thought to myself as I waited for his answer.

"Alright, as long as Bailey promises to watch Claire and stay with her whenever they're in the deep end, then it's okay with me."

"Okay! But, Claire, let's stay more towards the shallow end, so we can play together," Bailey said.

I pouted, but I caved in the end as I decided that Bailey had a point. If she had to always pull me through the deep end because I couldn't swim, that wouldn't be too much fun for her.

Together we went to the shallow end of the pool and had a blast playing together. We had a splash fight, and then we just floated around and talked about stuff. After a while our daddies came in and we played with them. It was so much fun, and I was really glad that I had gotten over my fear of letting others see me as my little self. It was the best day that I'd had in a while.

· · · · · · ·

"Did you have a good day, honey?" my daddy asked as we lazily held hands and walked home together in the crisp air.

"I did. I didn't realize how much fun it would be to play with other littles." I had done it before a time or two, but I had never played with any little like I'd played today with Bailey.

"I'm glad that you had a lot of fun. So did I. We'll have to do this more often."

"Okay, daddy," I murmured. I was really tired. All of the swimming, talking, and giggling I'd done with Bailey had taken the energy right out of me. We'd also eaten right before we left, so I had a full belly too. I knew that the minute we got home I was going to go straight to sleep.

"Are you getting tired, Claire bear?"

I nodded my head and let out a loud yawn to further confirm my response.

"I figured you would be. You were swimming all day today. Here, I'll carry you."

"No!" I said, but he ignored my protest and picked me up anyway.

"Wrap your arms around me. I don't want you to get loose."

I did as I was told and snuggled closer to my daddy as he held me like a little kid. I even laid my head down on his shoulder and let out a contented sigh.

"Go to sleep, Claire. I'll take care of everything."

"You always do, daddy. I'll stay awake until we get home." I didn't want my daddy to have to undress me, dress me in some pajamas, and then put me to sleep. That would be a lot of work for him. The least I could do was stay up to help.

"Okay, honey," he said, before he began to slowly rub my back.

Within minutes, I was really battling to keep my eyes open. My daddy was so big, and I felt warm and safe in his arms and couldn't help my eyes constantly closing.

"I love you, daddy."

"I love you too, my Claire bear."

Happy and safe in my daddy's arms, I lost the fight with my eyelids as I drifted off to sleep.

THE END

Brody's Little Brat

ADALINE RAINE

CHAPTER ONE

Kara Mitchell waved to the security guard as she drove her car past his booth. She lived in a gated community named Little Haven, whose residents all participated in or encouraged a certain type of lifestyle—age play.

Some of the residents believed all age-players engaged in role play. Many did see age-playing as a form of role play, but some age-players let themselves regress to a younger, happier mindset, one without bills, job stress, or other adult-oriented issues. The length of time in a younger mindset varied. Kara knew of some members of the community who chose to be "little" twenty-four seven, while others made a schedule that limited the time spent age playing. The members were encouraged to choose whatever rules made them the happiest as a couple.

Kara's boyfriend, Brody Thomas, decided to move them here one night about a year ago, when after a mental overload, Kara had lashed out badly and refused to calm down. Their argument had escalated past her boiling point, and she'd almost hurt herself—although not purposefully. Still, it had forced Brody to add additional rules to their already active domestic discipline dynamic and to decide that moving to Little Haven would be a good idea.

Kara already followed certain rules about respecting herself and Brody, as well as balancing meals and taking time for herself, but the new rules were different. On nights she chose, or when Brody decided her stress had built up too much, he would be in a new role: daddy.

If she acted out while in her teenage mindset—sometimes she felt about fifteen and some days she felt older—she got punished. Usually the consequences involved a spanking, but not always.

If she broke the rules while in a more adult state, there were also repercussions. Those usually involved a spanking as well, but sometimes Brody was more creative than that.

They both functioned well in the arrangement, though at first, Kara had to get used to Brody being her daddy. She kept it a secret from her family and friends since she still needed to sort out in her head how a twenty-six

year old woman could let her boyfriend take such a role, but to be honest, she didn't have many people to keep it from anyway. Her siblings were all much younger than her, and she could count the friends she had back home on one hand.

Kara blew out a breath. She needed to get to the house and apologize, instead of thinking about the past. She'd slid and broken the rules more than once over the past two weeks. Brody would no doubt punish her when she arrived home. Kara had legitimately forgotten to contact him and let him know she was hanging out with two classmates to finish up a project, and hours had passed by without her checking in with him.

Shit. What would I do if he didn't tell me something like that?

She knew she would be out of her mind with worry. She'd really messed up tonight.

As she pulled her car into the garage and turned off the engine, she wondered if she should just run inside and beg for forgiveness right off the bat.

Sighing, she opened and closed the car door, then headed inside. The entry door led straight into the kitchen, and Brody sat as still as stone at the table, worry splashed across his features.

"I'm so sorry…"

"Are you okay?" he stood and met the distance between them. "Did your cell phone battery die?"

Brody Thomas didn't look like the sort of man who would hold his girlfriend accountable, a man who had a hand as hard as a paddle and a belt that left red stripes after it kissed her bottom, but he definitely was that kind of man. In many ways Kara was the luckiest woman in the world, but she didn't feel lucky at the moment.

His stern demeanor didn't change, so she focused on his brown eyes. They normally sparkled when locked on hers, but now they were dark chocolate and angry.

Kara looked down as the blood rushed to her cheeks and she studied the tiles on the kitchen floor. She thought about the first time she had approached Brody and—after only two short weeks in a relationship with him—had asked him if he wanted to be in charge. He had laughed at first, and she remembered she'd initially giggled and played the silly girl card, but then he'd grabbed her close to him and sat her in his lap. Then he'd captured her chin and whispered against her ear, "There was never a question of that."

Kara had nearly creamed her panties when he'd held her in such a fashion, but then just as quickly he had moved back and kissed her nose and told her how cute she was. Any woman with functioning eyes would have rated him as extremely hot, but Kara noticed that he never acted cocky.

"Kara."

Brody's voice pulled her back to the present and she snapped her head

up.

"I'm sorry, no, my battery is just fine."

She bit the inside of her cheek as he reached for her hand. She knew better than to hesitate and she fought a huff.

"Then let's go into the bedroom and address your lack of courtesy." Brody's voice was stern and incredibly sexy at the same time.

Kara shuffled her feet as she held onto his hand, and he reached back and wrapped his arm around her. His touch made her wet even though the threat of the paddle loomed just over her head like a dark cloud. He had let the first two times slide, and she wished in that moment she had submitted to his rules earlier. "I really don't want a spanking right now."

Brody sighed as his hand touched the bedroom door and twisted it open. "I should have addressed your lack of consideration when you forgot to tell me earlier in the week."

Kara pulled back from him and angry words suddenly flew from her mouth. "The first time was because I got stuck in traffic and it would have been highly irresponsible of me to flip open my phone in the middle of the freeway just to text you that—" Her mouth shut immediately as he shook his head.

"Kara, we came up with these rules together."

He stepped inside and sat down on the black and gold comforter spread across their bed, then motioned for her to sit next to him. "When we first got together, you were about to get evicted, you had unpaid bills, and you were living off the dollar menu. You could never find any time for friends or family, and your grades were slipping. You begged me to hold you accountable this way."

Kara sat down next to him and pulled her legs underneath her. She stared into those gorgeous eyes of his and tried to come up with an appropriate response.

She had been craving this type of attention since her childhood but had never found a way to ask for it. Brody refused to let her slip up with any of her commitments—including bills or studies—and he never faltered to discipline her when her choices had to do with personal responsibility. And his discipline was even more serious when it came to her self-esteem and negative emotions.

"I won't let this slide again. You mean too much to me." Brody took her hand and gently but firmly slid her over his lap. He reached under her hips and unbuttoned the blue-black jeans. She turned over quickly and clutched the waistband.

"Can't you just spank me over them?"

She had splurged last week on a tattoo that danced across her lower back just above her tailbone. It had seemed like a good idea at the time, especially since Brody hadn't spanked her in several weeks. She'd arrogantly thought a

few more weeks would go by until she needed to tell him. She loved her ink, but he would probably be angry that she hadn't asked to budget for it.

"What is going on with you tonight?" Brody pulled her up to look into her eyes. "Tell me what the problem is."

"I didn't tell you about something that I went out and bought, and it wasn't that expensive, but I should have told you." Kara bit her lip. How much more trouble could she get into?

"Honey, just tell me now."

"I'm not in the mood to be spanked, and these jeans are tight. Just let me go to bed." She watched as the deeper meaning of her statement hit him and his grip tightened around her waist. The pants fit her fine, but she'd hinted at her weight.

"I've been patient with you tonight, but that's it. Stand up and take them off. Now."

Something strange came over her and she jumped up and off his lap. She pulled off her jeans in several breathy movements and threw them at his face. "Here! Take them!"

"Kara—"

Kara stomped her way out of the bedroom, ignoring his attempt to talk any more. She stormed down the hallway and threw herself onto the couch. She had no idea what the real root of her problem was, but she knew it was the first time in over a year that she had thrown such a tantrum. It was just a stupid tattoo, not even a very expensive one, but she knew he would see it as a lack of respect to his rules about the budget. And all this on top of her ignoring the rules about checking in with him for the past few weeks.

Kara knew Brody's recent lack of attention was probably the underlying cause of her brattitude. He worked as a freelance contractor and recent projects had been keeping him busier than usual. But knowing the cause didn't help her emotions, or help her relax. She really wanted his attention, and the lack of it always sparked a chain of events. She ended up lashing out, forgetting to inform Brody of where she was, coming home late, etc.

"Ugh…" Kara settled deeper into the cushions. She needed to apologize now, but she wished she'd simply talked to him, instead of throwing a fit.

● ● ● ● ● ● ●

Brody watched Kara stomp off, a vile tone to her words, but he remained on the bed. It would be pointless to spank her now with the type of mood she was in.

What emotions was she holding inside? Since they had moved to the community, much of her stress had been eliminated. This place allowed her to act in a teen type of mindset on days she felt like it or whenever he sensed her becoming overwhelmed. They moved to this place to help, not to give

her more stress.

He stood up as he formed a plan. Her tantrum could not be ignored, so he would have to come up with something to show her she was still responsible for her behavior.

His eyes drifted to the large sequined box that held Kara's favorite naughty playthings. She always liked the treasures—vibrators, butt plugs, ball gag, and lots of lube—but tonight those things would be included in her punishment. Hopefully when everything got settled, Kara would tell him what the real problem was.

Brody reflected on the past few weeks, then realized that his skills had been contracted out to three different clients, and lately his time had been dedicated solely to those projects.

"Shit… Kara…" Brody ran his hands through his hair. She'd slipped on their rules a few times, and he'd completely overlooked her gentle push for attention. When the two of them first got together and he'd set rules, she'd pushed a lot. Her poking had been short-lived though, since his consistent responses had showed no budging on the rules.

But his working hours had trumped everything lately—especially his time with Kara. He still needed to respond to her tantrum, but the situation pulled at his heart. He made a mental note to set aside more time for them this week, then he left the bedroom to get Kara.

• • • • • • •

Kara flipped the television on, but her attention kept going back to the situation with Brody. Why hadn't he followed her out here? Why hadn't he grabbed her and spanked her as promised? A large knot formed in her stomach and she grew uneasy.

Why was I so disrespectful? I could have just told him about the tattoo. I know it would have been all right.

She glanced at the hallway again. *What if I pushed him too far this time?*

Her face grew hot and wet as unexpected tears poured down and over her cheeks. How could she have been so disrespectful? Brody had literally taken care of everything the past year, even adding in a travel budget so they could return to their home state to visit family a few times a year. He was the one who put everything together, without ever getting angry or lashing out, and she really owed it all to him.

She'd switched to a local college, which was roughly a half an hour or so away from their house, and she'd filled in the gaps with online choices, which gave her more time to focus on herself and slip into her younger persona.

But Brody had decided she needed to cut back her credits at school, so she only had four classes this semester. Twelve little credits instead of her usual load of fifteen. She was so much smarter than that!

Tonight was one of the nights she was supposed to come straight home and get into her younger clothes so she could tackle the rest of the week. Her classes were stacked over three days, and she seemed to have the tendency to brat off by the third day of classes. But if—after all the homework or projects were completed—she regressed to her younger space at night on the same days she had classes, she got through the week without any issues.

Brody knew that, of course. Not only was he super smart, but he paid attention—close attention—to what she responded to and how she reacted to certain situations.

In the beginning, back at their old apartment on the East coast, he would sometimes end up punishing her every night straight for a week. That hadn't happened all that often, but she'd had the tendency to push him and rebel. Since moving to the new community, and since Brody had added more rules, she hadn't bucked too much. Well, at least she hadn't until now.

Kara wiped pitifully at her cheeks and peeked over at the hallway. A strong sounding set of footsteps echoed on the hardwood floor, and she returned her attention to the screen. She did not want to see the disappointment undoubtedly etched on his handsome face.

Brody said nothing as he walked over to the television and turned it off. He produced a tissue with a flourish and carefully dried her eyes, then extended his hand and waited.

Kara drew a sharp breath at the sight of his outstretched palm. She raised an eyebrow up at him and set her hand in his.

"But—" she started to say but he held a finger to her lips.

"We'll talk about it later." In moments they were headed back to the bedroom. "Right now, we need to reset the course you're on."

"I... I... I... kn... know," she stammered as her heart raced. He probably had darker things in mind than just using a paddle.

Brody let her go and reached behind her. He easily unclasped the hooks of her bra and let it spill out into his hands. Kara immediately drew her hands up to cover her breasts, but he swatted her hands until she let go.

It was not modesty that had brought Kara's hands up, but instead it was her notion that she had an imperfect body, and he knew it. He slid a finger into either side of the waistband of her panties and removed them effortlessly.

Kara squeaked as he stripped her. He was not in a sexy mood and she wasn't sure what he was planning. "But—" she started again.

Brody took great care to wrap one long piece of her dark chestnut-brown hair around his hand before he pulled her close to him. She admired how pretty her dip-dyed teal, purple, and magenta pieces looked tucked between his fingers. She wished she had a camera! Then she glanced up at his face, and it reminded her he was not playing around.

"No more talking."

Kara gasped as he tugged her hair, but she shut her mouth. He led her over to the bed by her hair, then slowly bent her forward at the waist until her arms were on the bed and her butt was in the air.

A cool gel tickled her ass moments before a plug slid deep inside. It met with little resistance, but she clenched and groaned as the sensation forced her to focus on what he was doing.

"Stand up."

Kara straightened and turned around. She opened her mouth to protest when he popped a small red ball gag between her lips. As mortified as she had been to be plugged in her ass, the new sensation of the rubber in between her cheeks and tongue distracted her from the slight humiliation.

"Kara, I want you to stand here and think about what it does to me when you put yourself down. You made a snide comment about your pants being too tight, which sounds like you're picking on your weight again. And that is on top of your earlier actions, and why you're being punished right now."

He led her to the corner and stood her against the wall. "You are beautiful and sexy, and I want to be with you. Whenever you put yourself down, you put me down too." He laid two good smacks on her ass. "Now, put your hands behind your back and lace your fingers together."

Kara stood there with tears streaming down her face—not from the burn from his hand but from the guilt she felt about the tantrum. She quickly put her hands behind her as instructed.

"Good girl," he whispered against her ear.

Kara stood straighter after his word of praise and he ran his hand over the top of her intertwined fingers and assured her he would be back.

"If you freak out because of the gag, just remove it. I won't be angry since we haven't used it much, but I'd like you to keep it in."

She nodded, determined to do as he'd asked. He patted her behind once before stepping away. She heard him leave the room but she kept in place. She really needed this tonight.

• • • • • • •

Brody wanted to stay in the room so she would not feel abandoned, but he had to make it clear her behavior was not acceptable. He admired her beautiful curves for a moment longer before he stepped to the door. Kara's body was such a sensitive topic, and trying to find where her self-esteem issues stemmed from boggled his mind. His gaze lingered on her shapely butt with the plug inserted deep inside, but then finally he stepped into the hall.

He left the door open and glanced down at his watch. He couldn't go far since she had a gag on. He'd told her she could remove it, if needed, but he knew she would do her best to obey him. If she panicked, she could forget how to release it. It was risky enough to have her turned away in the corner

without eye contact. He had intended to let her stay still for five minutes, but since she had the gag, he decided to shorten the time.

He leaned against the wall and jabbed his fingers through his hair.

Why else is Kara pushing me?

He had already seen the tattoo when he'd observed her movements and her occasional wince while it healed. The plug, gag, and corner time had nothing to do with the expense of her body art. If anything, he loved when she came back with more ink. It added such beauty to her already sexy features.

Normally, he let her do what she pleased when it came to her ink, but if she were going to act up, he had to consider rules about that as well. What it came down to was that she had kept something from him in addition to not following the guidelines already in place.

Brody straightened and walked back into the bedroom. He removed the gag from Kara's mouth and led her to the bed. Then he carefully sat her down and wiped her face and nose. She dropped her eyes, but he caught her chin and slowly tilted her face up towards his.

"I won't let you slide on the rules again. Is that clear?"

Kara's face flushed red as he gripped her chin, and she let out a choked sob. "Yes, sir. It's clear."

He smiled at the title, something she added to show respect when he punished her in a more adult way. He didn't recall asking her to use it, but it made him feel even more connected to her.

He moved to the dresser and pulled out a soft pair of black yoga pants and a grey V-neck sleep top, then handed them to her. "Put these on. We're going to go eat dinner, and then you're going to come back here and go to bed early."

Kara inhaled sharply but said nothing. She stood up, then reached a hand back towards the flare of the plug.

"Leave it," Brody admonished and took Kara's hands in his. "You are going to sleep with that in, all night, and then in the morning when you wake up, you will be spanked as originally intended." He let go and stepped back. "I'm going to go heat up dinner. I expect you to follow me."

Kara bit her lip as he strode to the door, but she didn't protest. Good. Maybe she would go back to listening to him.

When Brody reached the kitchen, he heated up the rice. He'd left chicken in a pot on the stove, simmering in sauce, and he checked on it as well. His overall day had been busy and boring, but he'd made sure everything would be ready for Kara when she arrived home. His plan had included cuddling on the couch and watching old movies, but now she was all out of sorts. Hopefully they could eat dinner and she would get into a better mood.

• • • • • • •

Kara slid her clothes on, sans panties with the plug in place, then dragged her feet to the kitchen. She was not in the mood to eat, and she flopped down on the chair. The plug moved a little and she felt a rush of wetness in between her thighs. Kara wiggled her butt awkwardly on the chair as Brody set a plate down in front of her. "I'm sorry I didn't ask about the tattoo."

Brody dished out their meals and sat down. "The tattoo isn't my concern. I already figured it out days ago." He scooped a mouthful of teriyaki chicken into his mouth and chewed. "But you're sliding on the rules, and I'm not happy about that."

Kara followed suit. The chicken and rice were each in a different sauce, and the spices and flavors mingled perfectly in her mouth.

"I've been busy," she huffed. She wished she could really eat. On her way home she'd stopped for a fast food run and had filled up on fries. And a shake. It had seemed a good idea at the time, and it had satisfied her hunger. Still, she knew she'd made poor choices, and the fast food hadn't made her body feel as good as a balanced meal did. But she didn't want to give Brody yet another reason to lecture her.

"Being busy doesn't give you an excuse to break our rules."

"Busy like you've been? You've been way too busy to even notice—" Kara clamped her mouth shut as she bit back more nasty remarks. She didn't want the night to play out any worse.

"I know." Brody reached across the table and took her hand. "I have been really busy with some projects. I've got multiple clients all blowing up my phone, and we haven't spent much time together."

Kara tugged her hand back. "Just because I can't spank you doesn't mean you should get off scot free—but nope, no consequences for Brody."

"Finish your dinner and go to bed. I've lost my appetite." Brody stood up. He busied himself with putting the food away. Leftovers never tasted as good as the original, and that thought added guilt to her already spinning emotions.

"I didn't have one to start with," Kara spoke through gritted teeth. "But you made it, so I'm eating it." She picked her up her fork and scooped another bite into her mouth. "I don't want you angry at me because I'm wasting food," Kara spoke around the food, not caring about her table manners.

"Get up and go to bed. I'll get to the bottom of the problem after I spank you in the morning. But for now, your day is over."

She didn't move and continued to put large forkfuls in her mouth.

"Kara, go to bed, or I will put you there."

Kara had half a mind to throw the food, the plate, and the silverware onto the floor, but it would only serve to land her in hotter water. "Fine. Daddy." She threw her chair back and stood up, then stormed up the hall.

She felt guilty about putting more responsibilities on him than on herself, but she didn't want to explain all of her feelings to him. He encouraged her to give up some of her responsibilities, but she sometimes wondered if he ever felt resentful about their choices. His work was way more stressful than her current classes, and he didn't take enough breaks for himself.

She really had it coming tomorrow.

Kara finally got into bed and pulled the covers up to her chin. She would eventually explain it all to Brody, but not tonight.

• • • • • • •

Brody cleaned up from dinner—or what was supposed to have been dinner, and then he made his way to the bedroom. He should have taken care of her a few weeks ago when this behavior started, but he'd mistakenly believed it would sort itself out. He pulled his jeans and t-shirt off, then got into bed without bothering to put on his normal lounge pants. He was still very worked up about the events as they transpired, and he just wanted to sleep.

After several minutes, he felt Kara's hand take his, hesitantly at first, and then she linked her fingers in his. He didn't respond verbally but tugged her until she turned over to lie on him.

Hating that they were going to bed under such crappy circumstances, Brody kissed the top of her head, but he had nothing else to say. She had a hell of a spanking coming in the morning, and hopefully she would explain what was on her mind after he disciplined her perky little ass.

CHAPTER TWO

Brody got up and went downstairs. He didn't have to be physically at work at his consulting job today, but he did have another project he could work on from home. It would give him enough time to discipline Kara, have breakfast, and shower before signing onto his work station.

Kara greeted him with a cup of coffee. She had added whipped cream and pink sprinkles—not a real tough looking mug, but it made his mouth melt into a smile.

"Good morning. Did you make this for me or you?"

Kara nuzzled his cheek, then went back to the table. She was eating oatmeal with blueberries and honey. When he'd met her she used to have three or four frozen waffles slathered in butter and maple syrup for breakfast. She'd said the sugar was the only thing that got her hyped up enough to make it through to lunch. Of course, he pointed out that some sort of protein or another balanced choice would have a better effect on her body. Her breakfast this morning showed that at the very least she was listening to that.

"Hi! I made it for you." She giggled then scooped a mouthful of oatmeal into her mouth. "I'm really sorry about last night. I won't forget to text you if I run into something that will keep me out later than usual."

"That sounds very responsible." Brody nodded as he took a sip from the cup, and he saw her watching him for a reaction. It actually tasted delicious. "Thank you for the coffee."

"You're welcome." She finished with her meal, then stood to clean up. "My afternoon classes got canceled. They were with the same teacher and she had some sort of family emergency. So do you think I can just be, you know, less adult today?"

"Of course, babe." Brody took another sip, then set the drink down. "But you and I need to make time for a talk. I think it would be best to get it over with now."

Kara sucked in a breath. "Yeah, sure. I mean, I kinda hoped you had forgotten about that."

"Go up into our room and wait for me."

He watched her eyes widen, but she nodded her compliance and hurriedly made her way out of the kitchen.

Brody took several long and thoughtful sips from his coffee. He wanted her to squirm a little bit, but not too long. It was better to punish her early so she could have the rest of the day to let her adult obligations go. Finally, after five minutes, he made his way upstairs and down the hall into their room.

When he punished Kara when she was in a younger mindset, he made sure it was done in her teen room, surrounded by her things. It was never overly harsh—not that he handled his normal discipline that way—but it was done lighter. Today, he would punish her in an adult way.

He walked in to their room and smiled. Kara had already bared herself and had bent over the bed. Brody could see the flared end of the plug still resting firmly inside of her. She had listened to him, despite her outburst last night.

Brody wasted little time in removing the plug and setting it on the nightstand. His focus immediately returned to her glorious, full bottom. He quickly ran his hand over it as he tried not to linger. Kara's butt was perfectly bubble shaped, with two round pillow-like cheeks jutting out just enough for him to easily smack them. He slapped his hand expertly on one side and then the other and admired the blush of pink underneath.

Brody targeted the sweet juncture of her thigh and ass. Then he adjusted the intensity while slowing down the blows to allow her breathing to even out. After five particularly hard slaps, he paused. "Why am I spanking you, Kara?"

She had curled her fists into the comforter after the first crack, and it remained clutched in her hands as she answered. "Be... be... be..." she choked back a sob. "Because I forgot to tell you I would be late more than once. And then I got all nasty with you."

"Hmm. So, are you going to let me worry like that again?"

"No." Kara shook her head back and forth. "I'll be sure to tell you even if it's already past the time. I don't want you to think something bad happened to me."

"Do you think it was fair to ruin a good dinner with your bad attitude?" Brody smacked his open hand against the center of each of her globes rapidly until they blushed.

"No! No! You made such a nice dinner! I'm so sorry!" Kara kicked her feet and yelled as he continued on. "Please! Please! Brody!" she wailed.

"Our time together is special. Last night we were supposed to spend it watching a movie, all cuddled up on the couch. You made the decision to let it play out the way it did."

Brody kneaded his fingers into each cheek as he spoke, rubbing and

pinching before setting his sight onto the lower curve of her bottom. His hand throbbed, already reminding him that he would feel the same burning sensation for a while, and he flexed it. "Six more and we're done."

Kara braced herself, knowing from prior punishments that they would be the worst of the bunch. "Yes, sir."

He delivered the blows swiftly, three hard smacks to each cheek, before settling his arms on each side of her body. Brody leaned down until his torso rested very lightly against her back so he could kiss her head. "It's over, baby. Let's not do this again, okay?"

Brody truly hated to cause her any discomfort, but he wanted her to understand that every action had a consequence. Kara had been the one to approach him about being held accountable via physical discipline. She'd reacted the strongest and the most positively to spanking, and so it was used the most often.

Truth be told, he really didn't have to spank her for punishment very often. In the beginning, about three years ago, she had pushed all the time. But when they'd moved to the new community just over a year ago, she had initially acted up, but that had died down.

So, what was it? Why had she started slipping back into her old ways?

He slowly raised himself up and scanned the room for her black yoga pants. He could trace every curve with just his eyes when she wore them. Brody wished she could love her body as much as he did.

"Here. Let me help you get these back on."

Kara turned over and allowed him to pull them up her legs and over her hips. She held her arms out wordlessly, sobbing now, and he wrapped himself around her so they could lie on the bed.

Brody rubbed her back and held her tight until finally the crying stopped. "I love you."

Kara nuzzled against his chest. "I love you too. Can I nap for a bit? Then when I get up, I'll shower and stuff?"

"Yeah, babe. Sure." Brody kissed the top of her head. "Make sure you put away the toys from last night and clean them," he said, referring to the plug and gag.

She nodded. "Of course." She kissed his cheek, then scooted out of his arms to get under the covers. "And I love you more!"

Brody got out of bed. "Nuh-uh." He leaned back down and tickled under her chin. "I love you more."

She giggled but didn't retaliate. Their tickle fights were epic and she usually lost. "See you in a bit."

"M'kay," she replied and pulled the blankets over her head.

Brody grinned at the cocoon bundle, then left the room. She had taken the correction well, and he hoped they could continue on a good path.

• • • • • •

Brody looked over as Kara entered the room. She had showered and was still wrapped up the towel, and nothing else. He raised an eyebrow as she sauntered over.

"Hey…"

"Are you really busy?" Kara looped an arm around his shoulder and kissed his cheek.

"Uh, well…" Brody checked the time on his laptop. "I have a conference call in about twenty minutes. Why? What's up?"

Kara tugged his chair back, and the wheels moved him away from the desk. "I know what I said before, but um… I've been so busy with class that we haven't… you know…"

Brody swallowed hard. She wanted to do this now? He glanced at the time again. "In less than twenty minutes?"

Kara smiled coyly and dropped the towel.

Well, that's all the encouragement he needed. "Aw, fuck, that's plenty of time."

He got up, took her hands, and led her over to the bed. He pushed her backwards only far enough so her legs dangled off the end. Brody rested his hand above the tiny triangle of hair in between Kara's legs and used his fingers to part her lips. He gave her a wicked grin and dipped his head down to kiss her clit. She moaned and arched her hips up.

"Please… don't torture me…" Kara groaned as he sucked and licked, tasting her sweet juices, then she gasped when he slid two fingers inside her pussy. "Oh! Oh… babe…"

"Mmmm?" Brody loved the way she responded to his touch. He released her little nub and slowly licked along her thigh. "Is there something you want?"

"Yes! Yes, please…"

"Tell me."

Her pussy clenched around his fingers and he moved them faster.

"What do you want?"

Kara didn't answer, too lost in bliss to reply properly. Brody trailed the fingers of his free hand along her skin until he reached her breasts. He pinched one nipple, hard, and she moaned loudly.

"What was that? Come on, we're wasting time…"

"Please, Brody!" Kara rose up on her elbows to meet his chest. "I want you to fuck me." She kissed him deeply, and he knew she could taste herself on his tongue.

Brody raised an eyebrow as she pulled away and he captured the back of her head with his hand. He drew her to him and kissed her again, hungrily, until he released her. "It isn't nice to distract me while I'm working. Maybe I

should keep you like this, naked and horny, and make you wait until my call is over."

"Please, babe, don't do that. I'll be really good," Kara pouted. "Please?"

Brody wasn't mean-spirited and he didn't want to punish her, but on the other hand, it would teach her a thing or two about barging in while he was sending out a reply to an important discussion via email. Of course, she had a thing about rejection too, so if he hadn't been sweet on her advances, it would have messed up the rest of her day. He decided to go with a more playful route.

"Maybe we should fuck while I'm working? Then you'd have to be as quiet as a mouse."

Kara's eyes went wide. They both knew how loud she was. "Brody! Please! I'll knock next time!"

Brody gave into her pleas and withdrew his hand. Then he quickly unzipped his pants and slid into her heat. She was so wet and so ready for him. They didn't use condoms since Kara charted her cycle and took daily birth control pills. The sensation was increased with no barrier between their skin, and she felt so good around his cock. Brody pumped his hips as she put one of her legs over his shoulder. Kara was seriously the most flexible woman he had ever seen, and this position allowed him much better access. She moaned loudly, letting him know he'd hit her sweet spot.

"Does that feel good, baby?"

"Yes! Yes! More, please!" Kara scratched her nails down over his back and arms. "Harder... baby... fuck me harder!"

He obliged, loving when she begged for what she wanted. If only she could do it more often. "Come on, baby, I want to make you come."

"Yeah, right there..." Kara arched upwards. "I'm so close..."

Brody moved her other leg over his other shoulder and pumped faster. He teased her clit with his fingers, able to do both in this position, and then she lost her mind. She bucked underneath him while she made high pitched moans of pleasure.

"Come on... I've got three minutes, babe. Come on." He shifted his hips slightly to get an even better angle and she hit her climax first. Then Brody brought her body to another orgasm as he came, his cock releasing his seed into her core.

He collapsed next to her on the bed, and she swung her legs around so that they lay entwined, grinning at one another.

"I could never be quiet." Kara winked as they got untangled.

"It's a good thing I forgot about your gag..." Brody winked back as a look of shock crossed her face.

"You wouldn't!" Her eyes were wide, but it wasn't with fright. She licked her lips, waiting for some type of response to her exclamation.

"I've got all kinds of tricks up my sleeve, baby." Brody kissed her, her

juices still lingering on her lips, and he cocked a grin. "My call is in thirty seconds. Be good today and we can do this again."

Kara giggled. "Is that all I have to do?" She smiled as he moved away. "I can totally behave."

Brody sat down at the computer and brought up the conferencing application his boss used. "Good. Let's plan on it."

She ran her hands along his shoulders, then he watched her leave, a swagger in her step. She didn't usually act up when he was working, and since he'd set a good tone for the day, he hoped she did as she said she would.

CHAPTER THREE

It had been about a week since Brody punished her. She'd been making sure he knew what she was doing and where she was going. She'd also explained why she felt guilty, but he'd assured her he wanted her to focus on what she needed. She'd agreed, but lately her head felt clogged. Today she actually felt dizzy on top of everything but hadn't brought it up to Brody. Instead, she'd retreated to her teen room to relax. It was the spare bedroom, but Brody had helped her turn it into a special haven which allowed her to express herself. It had a girly-gothic look with a bit of punk mixed in, and it made her happy.

Her stomach gurgled, and a sharp pain hit it. Kara had been eating a lot of junk food lately, and it was wreaking havoc on her stomach—something else she didn't want to tell Brody about. The past few days had been painful. She was constipated, embarrassed, and now had cramps.

She hoped she could keep it from him a little longer. She knew he wouldn't allow her to keep going in the state she was in, and he would probably try to tell her about what his great-great grandmother used to do to fix tummies. None of the stories he mentioned were ever pleasant, and they usually involved something being stuck up one's bottom.

Kara slid a bead onto the nearly transparent thread in her other hand and tried not to think about her stomach.

Brody had bought her a simple jewelry making kit a few weeks ago to keep her happy and content when she was in her teenage mindset. It was surprisingly easy to allow herself to slip into a time in her life that she'd never had the opportunity to enjoy.

Yesterday, they'd spent their time together at the mall. He'd let her pick out a few new pieces for her wardrobe. She never used to be into fashion at all, but ever since she'd allowed her younger self more freedom, a lot of her wardrobe choices reflected it.

Some things she could wear to school, but a few things—like her tutus—were for around the house and neighborhood only. Those rules were self-

imposed of course. She could technically wear whatever she wanted anywhere.

Under Brody's watch she had been eating better and working out and had dropped about thirty pounds in just the past year. That was the second reason for her interest in clothes. Things just fit better. She was happier with her body, which was still curvy in all the right places, and it made her feel good. Of course, she was thrilled at the idea of shopping with him, especially for the punky style she had grown fond of, and he supported what made her happy.

Her outfit today consisted of a black fluffy skirt over rainbow leggings topped off with heavy motorcycle leather boots and chains. The top of her looked vastly different with a pink and gray sparkly sweatshirt with skulls all over it. Her hair was braided into pigtails with pink ribbons woven in and through them.

Overall she looked like she could work in one of those gothic retail clothing stores and fit right in. Most of her tattoos were covered in this outfit, but in the spring and summer she planned to pick out styles that flaunted her ink.

Pop!

The tiny seed bead flew off the tip of her finger, escaped off the folding table, and hit the floor.

Damn it.

She couldn't pay attention long enough to finish one measly bracelet. Trying to block out how bad her head felt, she had been lost in her thoughts and had gotten distracted.

Kara selected another bead and planned to thread it on top of the other brightly colored ones in the row. She managed to place it without issue and then wove the fishing line back through the top bead to form a flower.

But Kara lost her concentration as a sharp stomach pain hit her and she tore the line, sending all of the tiny beads scattering across the table.

Instead of filling herself with good food and keeping her stress level down, part of the whole point of being in this mindset, she had been doing the opposite. It had only been the other day that she'd tried to get her meals back on track. Why couldn't she just listen to what Brody had been telling her?

She glared evilly at her tummy, as if it could help the way she had been treating it lately, then tried to focus again.

"Fuck it all!" She pounded the table and sent everything to the floor in her rage. She kicked the wall then moved to the other side of the room and ripped down the posters she had lovingly hung the day before, purchased on the way home from the mall. She banged her fists again but then another pain hit and caused her to immediately stop her ranting.

Suddenly, she heard someone moving towards the room.

"Kara!" Brody's concerned voice came through the door. "What's wrong?" He opened the door, stepped inside, and surveyed the mess. "What happened in here?"

She shook her head back and forth, tears streaming down her face, and hung her head down. She wanted to curl up on him and beg him not to be mad, but for now she could only cry. It was so stupid to throw a fit over a bracelet, but she had been keeping things in again, and now it was affecting her physically too.

"I can see you're upset," he reached down and cupped her chin, "but your attitude isn't appreciated. Use your words. Tell me what happened."

"Why don't you use your super intelligent brain to figure it out?" She could barely stop the attitude flowing out of her mouth, though she didn't care that she was making the situation worse. "Wait—"

Before she could apologize, he had taken her by the ear and forced her to her feet. She stood but kept her hands over her belly.

"Young lady, I don't know what's gotten into you today, but you're going to regret speaking to me like that."

"Nothing has gotten into me. I'm a terrible little bitch every day."

Brody shook his head and she immediately wished she could take back her words. He looked down at her hands, then nodded to the door. "Go into the bathroom and wait for me."

She nodded, then shuffled her feet out of the room and up the hallway.

Sure that she had some sort of punishment coming, Kara went into the bathroom and sat down on the edge of the tub. He'd never disciplined her for bad language before, but she had been really disrespectful.

He appeared in the doorway a few minutes later, then stepped inside to join her.

"First of all, when I ask you a question, I expect an answer. Secondly, do not curse at me—especially in a way where you also put yourself down." Brody motioned for her to come towards him. "I'm going to wash your mouth out with soap, and since you've been holding things in again, I've got something else that will loosen you up. I've seen you holding your stomach the past few days, and this will help."

Kara didn't like the sound of that at all! She padded over to him and watched in a mixture of fascination and horror as he lathered up a washcloth with soap and water. Suds appeared in the soft rag, and in seconds it was brought up to her lips. She opened her mouth obediently but gagged as the bitter taste hit her tongue.

"No matter how old you are, you do not speak to your daddy in such a manner."

Why couldn't he just shut up? His words made her feel terrible and caused her stomach to churn in knots on top of the other issues. Sometimes his punishments tugged her into a more adult mindset, but this one kept her

firmly rooted in her teenaged one.

"Go ahead and spit it out." Brody pointed to the sink and she hurried to comply.

"I'm sorry. I will try my best not to give you such an attitude or to curse." She forced a small smile, her mouth still gross from the soap, and blinked up at him.

"Bend over the tub and take down your pants."

Confused since they were still in the bathroom, Kara trembled a little at the order but moved as he instructed. "Yes, daddy." She bent so that her butt was up in the air, then reached back to tug her leggings past her knees. One of Brody's hands rested on the small of her back while the other took her panties down as well.

"When you keep your emotions in, it causes stress which can mess your stomach up. When you hold back your feelings, you throw yourself off balance. What I'm going to do will literally irritate the heck out of you at first, but it will help you go to the bathroom. It will be uncomfortable, but I promise it will make you feel better…"

Oh no! He had a very valid point, and truth be told she was doing exactly as he said. It had probably been the real reason why she couldn't concentrate on her beads. She whimpered at the thought of anything going up her bottom, but she knew he would never do anything to harm her.

"Try to relax."

Brody moved his hand to her back hole and then rubbed some type of ointment around and inside it. She clenched, not wanting to allow whatever it was in, but that earned her two sharp smacks on either cheek.

Kara sucked in a breath and let it out, desperate to be done with it. Then something slid up inside of her along with his finger. He kept it there, no doubt to hold it in, but the pressure felt strange and his fingers weren't small.

"I don't like it."

"You're about to like it even less." Brody withdrew his finger and suddenly she realized what he'd done.

An unpleasant burning sensation ignited deep inside her bottom. He had given her a soap-stick suppository! He had mentioned them in the past and she had immediately done an internet search. The last time she'd balked at the idea and instead had suffered for days before going to the store and picking up some pills. The ones that you swallowed. This was different.

"Brody!" she whined and wiggled her bottom. "It burns! Please let me get it out!" Two sharp slaps hit against each of her upper thighs. Kara screeched. "I mean, daddy! Please!"

"Then you shouldn't be keeping things in and away from me. Everything I do is to help you." Brody laid one more round of smacks on her sit spots, then stopped. "You're going to stay like this for a few minutes to let the soap do its job. I'd rather not spank you through it, so just relax and stay still."

Kara nodded and stayed bent over. If she continued to push, especially after her tantrum earlier, she would wind up with a spanking on top of all this. "Can I talk to you after this?"

"Of course, but first you're going to go get on your pajamas and take a nap. When you wake up, clean up the room you wrecked, and then we'll talk." Brody rubbed her back. "Okay?"

Still embarrassed to be half naked with a suppository melting inside of her, she didn't respond right away, but finally bobbed her head up and down. "Okay. I will."

Finally Brody tugged her upwards. "The soap should work soon. Go ahead and go to the bathroom, and then go to bed. I'll come check on you in a little bit." He kissed her forehead, then left, closing the door behind him.

Kara relieved herself, though she could still feel some of the suds inside. It really made her feel better, though her earlier actions still left her mortified. She'd snapped at him for no reason, and what's worse, she now had a mess to clean up.

Kara took time to remove her make-up, then went up the hall to their bedroom. She climbed in bed, pulled the covers up, and snuggled down. At least she would feel better in a little while.

• • • • • • •

"Kara? Hey…" Somebody shook her shoulder. "Hey, honey, wake up."

Kara blinked her eyes open, and looked up at Brody. Her head throbbed, and her whole body ached.

"I can't," she mumbled but sat up anyway to do as he said. Tears of pain and exhaustion trailed down her cheeks, and she flopped back down. "Ugh."

Brody's palm touched her forehead, and then he kissed the spot he'd touched. "You're burning up. I'm going to go call and see if I can get you an appointment with the doctor."

"No!" Kara pulled herself up again. The only place worse than the doctor's office was a torture chamber. She was not going there no matter what he said! "No, please! You can't make me go!"

Brody raised his eyebrows as he stood there watching her, and she wondered why her voice had come out so bratty sounding.

"This isn't open for discussion. Get your socks and shoes on." He walked out of the bedroom and she heard him go downstairs.

She couldn't get in any more trouble, so she might as well stay in bed. Why had she sounded like she was in her younger mindset though? Was she slipping into it because she didn't feel good?

"Whatever." She tucked herself back under the covers and tried not to think anymore. She had gone to bed in that mindset, so it was probably best not to question it.

"Kara?" Brody's strong baritone filled the hallway seconds before he reached the room. "Come on. You got the last appointment. We have to go."

"I'm fine. Just let me sleep." Determined to just ignore him, she turned away from the doorway and pretended to be half asleep.

"We can do this two ways. Either you get up and put your shoes on and I help you to the car, or I get you up, spank you, and carry you to the car. What's it going to be?" His voice had grown more stern over the past few years, and though she wanted to obey it, she also found herself not wanting to cooperate. "Kara? You have thirty seconds before I decide for you."

"I'm not getting up! I feel like crap, but it's just nothing." Kara pulled the blankets tighter. If he really did decide to go with the second option she wanted to a have something to hold onto.

"Fifteen seconds."

"Cut it out! I told you that I'm fine!" she snapped, but she couldn't really be angry with his reasoning. Truth be told, she didn't get sick very often, and for her to feel sick enough to stay in bed meant something was wrong.

"Eight seconds."

"For fuck's sake!" Kara flipped around, still holding the covers to her, and glared up at him. The simple movement made her dizzy and she had no choice but to close her eyes tight. "Ohh…" She began to cry again. "Please don't be mad at me!"

Brody sighed somewhere over her head. "My patience with you is running very thin, young lady."

She felt him untangle the blankets from around her body. A few minutes later he had gotten her socks and sneakers on, like he had asked her to do before, then scooped her up in his arms. She didn't struggle, though she really wanted to.

Kara didn't like anyone picking her up, but Brody had proven more than once that he could handle her—all of her. She opened her eyes again as he moved down the stairs, but she saw only concern in his features.

"I don't like going to the doctor's office."

"I know, but we need to make sure you're okay." Brody continued to the garage and set her down into the backseat of the car. She buckled her seatbelt and dozed.

CHAPTER FOUR

"Come on, Kara. Wake up a little." Brody's voice tugged her from her dreams as he shook her shoulder. She finally opened her eyes, took his hand, and got up. He led her into the waiting room and up to the reception desk.

The woman behind the counter had on scrubs and wore a stethoscope around her neck. Usually a nurse didn't run the desk, so who was she?

"Hi!" The woman smiled cheerfully but shot a look of concern to Kara. "Is this Kara?"

Brody nodded as Kara linked her arms in his. "Yes, I just called. She's not feeling very well and since she doesn't get sick very often, I thought it was worth coming in."

"I'm so sorry to hear that. I'm Nurse Kaitlyn. Usually we have a receptionist but she moved away a few weeks ago and we're a bit behind. Here is some paperwork to fill out. Please follow me into exam room three. We're running low on staff and time, so I do apologize." The nurse handed him a clipboard with a pen attached, and he walked around the side of the desk to follow her.

Kara shuffled along behind him, occasionally stopping to lean against the wall, but said nothing. He squeezed her hand reassuringly, then urged her inside the exam room.

"Please get on the scale for me." Kaitlyn motioned for Kara to comply, but she shook her head, vehemently opposing the idea.

"No way. My weight hasn't changed." She sounded a little more adult than she had in the bedroom, but there wasn't time to argue and she knew that.

"It's standard. Please cooperate so we can help you feel better." Kaitlyn changed her tone to sound more authoritative, but Kara wasn't having it.

"You can clearly see from my chart—" Kara trailed off as Brody crossed his arms over his chest. She was sure he trusted her to read his face and know that if she didn't do what she was told, he would spank her right there. "—that it's been a year. Yup." She climbed up onto the scale without another

word.

Nurse Kaitlyn nodded her thanks, then made a note. "Okay, please get undressed and get into a gown. You can leave your bra and panties on, but everything else needs to come off." She pointed behind a small privacy screen. "Usually I would leave, but we're out of time so I'll just wait here until you're ready."

Kara looked at the flimsy robe and opened her mouth, as if to argue, and Brody shot her another look. She glared right back but resigned herself to go behind the curtain. She yanked off her top and pants then got the flimsy gown on and stepped around the curtain. The gown fit her surprisingly well, and didn't make her feel like all her bits were hanging out. She reached down to take off her shoes and fell to the floor.

"Oh, honey. Are you dizzy?" The nurse reached for her feet but Kara scooted herself backwards.

"I can do it myself." Kara swallowed hard. She wanted the nurse to treat her like an adult, but she knew her actions kept screaming 'little'. The nurse approached again and offered her hand but Kara had already made up her mind to do it herself. "Damn it! I'm fine!"

A huge bear of a man walked into the exam room and Kara shut her mouth. She didn't know who he was but she had a bad feeling he was the doctor. He'd probably overheard her tantrum because he didn't appear happy.

"Go finish with the files for today. I'll get Kara's vitals. If I need you, I'll call you." He touched her cheek, and the petite nurse smiled warmly up at him. She went up on her tiptoes, kissed his cheek, then turned to Kara.

"I hope you feel better. You're in good hands." Kaitlyn nodded to Brody then moved out of the room.

Kara had a terrible feeling about what was now about to happen. She had bratted off to the nice nurse, and now she was in trouble. She began to cry, something she normally didn't do in public, and quickly covered her face with her hands.

"Kara? I'm Dr. Roberts. I'm sorry you're not feeling well today, but we have to do a few things to see what's wrong." A large hand pulled her to get feet. To add to her embarrassment, he lifted her onto the exam table, as if she weighed nothing, and stepped back. He swiftly removed each of her sneakers and socks, then set them on the floor. "Can you please lie down and roll over on your tummy?"

"I'd rather not." Kara watched him shake down a thermometer, a glass one like she remembered from her childhood, and his request pointed to an uncomfortable-sounding conclusion. "In fact, now I'm sure of it."

"If you can't turn on your side, then it's going to be over my lap. After I take your temperature, I'll let your daddy grab the paddle over there on the wall and teach your bottom a lesson—one which will remind you how

important it is to listen, especially when we both want you to feel better."

Kara choked back a sob. She couldn't understand the words 'over my lap' along with the process of taking her temperature. Only little kids had it done that way!

"I don't want to—" She wiped furiously at her cheeks.

The doctor took her chin in his hand and very slowly tilted it up until she could see his eyes. They were a warm mix of hazel and brown, and they appeared very concerned as they studied hers. "This is your last chance."

"Can… can you please help me?" Kara bit down into her trembling lip, but to her surprise, he immediately nodded. It hadn't been completely about her behavior, she realized. He wanted her to voice what she needed.

Dr. Roberts released his hold and helped her roll over, and she felt grateful for his help—even though she didn't want any part of this exam.

Brody watched as he stood near the window, and she reached her hand out to him. "Will you come over here, please?"

"It's okay," Brody quickly responded and made his way to her side. He laced his fingers in hers and planted a kiss on her forehead. "Just relax."

"It's going to be cold and a little uncomfortable, but I promise it won't hurt." Dr. Roberts' voice came from somewhere behind her, and she tried not to think about what he was about to do. "Lower your panties, please."

Kara tugged them down over her hips with one hand, then rested her head on Brody's arm. "I'm sorry." She felt an icy gel tickle across her bottom hole. Then a slim rod, almost as cold, slipped inside. She groaned a little, but it didn't hurt. She was more embarrassed than anything else.

"This is the most accurate way to obtain a temperature. Don't you do it this way at home?" Dr. Roberts questioned Brody.

"Uh, well, to be honest, I never thought about it. Kara is old enough to keep a thermometer in her mouth," Brody stated simply.

"I see. Well, make sure Kaitlyn gives you a gift basket on the way out. It's for new patients, but since we haven't seen Kara before, it counts. There's quite a few things in there I'm sure you'll find useful." The doctor was carrying on a conversation with Brody as if he wasn't holding a thermometer in her butt!

"We saw our doctors back in New York before we moved out here. Neither of us gets sick very often, but we should get better about physicals." Brody nuzzled against her head. "Just another minute."

"I don't like it. It's cold and feels weird." Kara wiggled her hips impatiently.

Brody reached over and pressed his free hand down on her lower back. "You need to stay still. It's almost over."

Finally, Dr. Roberts removed the thermometer and read it. "You have a low grade fever. It's just over one hundred and one. You can fix your panties and sit up slowly."

Brody helped her get her panties back over her hips. She started to cry again as she struggled to sit up. "I'm sorry. I'm dizzy too and it's bothering me."

The doctor checked her blood pressure and pulse then looked into each ear.

"I was okay before. I mean, a little off, but not like this."

"Your right ear is infected, so that must be what's throwing your balance off. We'll get you some antibiotics to clear it up. Your daddy also noted on your chart that your tummy is backed up?"

Ugh! Why did Brody do that?

Kara sniffled and brushed away a tear. "Yeah, I mean, not as much anymore. He, uh, gave me something to help."

"Lie down again." The doctor washed his hands and then returned to the table. "I'm going to press my hands all around your stomach. If something hurts, even a little, I want you to tell me."

"Okay." Kara let Brody move her up the table a little so she could give Dr. Roberts the access he needed.

She took a deep breath and let it out slowly. His hands were surprisingly warm as they roamed in an odd pattern all over her belly. She realized he was poking at certain places, and though it wasn't overly painful, it definitely was no picnic. "Ow! Oh, right there hurts."

Dr. Roberts dropped his hands and straightened. "I'll have Kaitlyn administer an enema to relieve some pressure, but I also want to check one other thing." He focused above her head for a moment. "Has she ever had a rectal exam?"

"No, no, no!" Kara popped up into a sitting position, though her head protested the movement. "No fucking way!" Brody set his hands on her shoulders but she bucked against him. "You're not doing that! I'm still an adult and I can refuse any treatment or test I deem unnecessary."

"If you are severely constipated, your bowels aren't moving properly. If it's been going on a while, there could be something more serious causing it." Dr. Roberts sat down next to her. "I would never suggest an invasive procedure or exam unless I thought it was warranted."

"You have really big fingers!" Kara blinked back tears. "I mean seriously!" The doctor smiled at her observation, and she realized it was something he probably heard all the time.

"Let's get you cleaned out a bit first, then we can talk again."

"I don't want an enema either," Kara pointed out, but she knew deep down it would help her. Part of her also knew, the part that kept pushing her back into a younger mindset by the minute, that he was right. Of course he wouldn't suggest something without a good reason.

"I normally have a wheelchair, but one of my patients broke their foot last week and is borrowing it. Since you've become unsteady on your feet,

I'm going to carry you to the other room, okay?" Dr. Roberts ignored her comment about the enema and stood up. *Just how tall is he?*

Kara glanced over at Brody, who nodded encouragingly. "Go ahead and let the doctor help you."

"I, uh, really don't like being picked up. I'm too heavy," Kara said offhandedly, hoping the doctor would let it go.

Dr. Roberts chuckled. "Honey, I'm strong enough to lift you over my head and bench press you. I'm not going to, but I could do it without even thinking."

Kara huffed. "Fine, break your—"

Brody interrupted her put down with just one word. "Kara."

Why do I keep going all teen?

"Sorry, whatever. It's your chiropractor bill." Kara blinked innocent eyes at Brody, who crossed his arms over his chest. He seemed to be doing that a lot today.

"We all come in different shapes and sizes. I don't like the negative comments I'm hearing about your body." Dr. Roberts lifted her easily into his arms, and she looped one arm around his neck. "I'm just bringing Kara down the hall, then I'll be back in to talk to you." He nodded over her head to Brody and walked out of the exam room.

"Yeah, well, you and my daddy..." Kara frowned. What the hell was going on in her head? "I mean, my boyfriend say the same thing."

"It's okay to call him daddy here. Almost all of the patients I see slip into a younger mindset when they come in—whatever makes them feel comfortable."

"I'm not comfortable at all. I feel like I keep switching back and forth, and it's so confusing."

"So, stop fighting it and just relax." Dr. Roberts turned into a large room with another exam table. He set her down gently, then rested his hand on her shoulder. "Kaitlyn will be with you in a few minutes. I expect you to do what she tells you."

"Yes, I will." Kara didn't like being on that table and knowing what was about to happen, but her stomach hurt so bad that at this point, she would let the nurse do whatever she needed. "Can I ask you a question?"

"Of course."

"Are you a daddy too?" Kara glanced away awkwardly, wondering why the hell she had asked him that. It wasn't any of her business. Finally, she returned her eyes to him, not sure what else to say.

Dr. Roberts smiled warmly, as if knowing the sort of things running through her head. "Yes, I am actually. I moved the two of us here so we could run a family practice that catered to a community like Little Haven," he released her shoulder. "I'm sure Kaitlyn would love to talk to you about it someday."

"After she sticks a tube up my butt?" Kara flushed, now mortified at the words she had spoken out loud.

"I've made friends in odder ways," Kaitlyn retorted as she poked her head into the room. "Honestly. I really have."

For some reason her reply made Kara grin. "Seriously?"

"You tell Kara about the interesting situations you find yourself in. I'm going to go talk to her daddy." The doctor smiled again at both of them and then left the room.

"Is he like your daddy even at the office?" Kara rolled onto her side, still trying not to think about the humiliating prospect of this woman becoming very familiar with her bottom, and sighed.

"Um, not really at the office so much." Kaitlyn touched the waistband of her panties. "Can you take these off? Some of the water may drip and I don't want to get them wet."

Kara managed to hook a finger at the top and shimmied them down over her hips and off. She felt a bit odd in her current position but that was just the sort of day she was having.

"Try to relax. You'll feel my finger first and then the tube. I promise it won't hurt, but it does feel a little uncomfortable."

"Do you, uh, do this a lot?" Kara gasped as the tube slid inside her. To the nurse's credit, she'd made it ease in without any pain. Of course, it wasn't an overall unpleasant feeling. It was just that Kara wasn't used to having much back there.

"I love your tattoo!" Kaitlyn rested one hand just above it and Kara imagined her looking at the doves and flowers that stretched across her back. "Enemas? Yeah, sometimes. Some people get really embarrassed about stomach problems, but I wish they didn't."

"Um… oh." Kara tried to think of something else to talk about. "What's weirder way than this procedure to meet a friend?"

Kaitlyn laughed so hard she snorted, as if remembering one of those times. "Well, one time I was on a date with this guy and we were hiking in the forest. He wasn't watching where he was sitting, and um… oh lord, it wasn't funny at the time, but… he sat on a porcupine! So, the next several hours were spent with me bent over his behind and pulling out quills."

"Do you mean Dr. Roberts?" Kara tried to imagine the look on his face and how embarrassed he must have been at the time.

Kaitlyn giggled and snorted again. "Wait, wait… yeah, but wait. I'm going to start the water now. It should feel nice and warm. Let me know if you get any cramps. Once all of the water is in, I have a tiny plug—" she moved one hand in front of Kara's face to show her the tiny black object "—to hold the water in."

It looked similar to her plugs at home. It couldn't be that bad. "Okay." Kara glanced over her shoulder. "Did Dr. Roberts really sit on a porcupine?"

"Oh my goodness! Yes, yes he did! From that day on he has checked and re-checked every time he sits down. Even in the office! I don't blame him though. Those quills hurt like something wicked."

"Do you um, do this age play thing? Or is it like role-play to you?" Kara fretted after she asked the questions. Maybe the nurse didn't want to talk about it.

"So, we've role-played in the past, but when I'm little, it's real. He's treats me just like a daddy would take care of his girl. I'm getting the feeling that you go into a sort of teenage mindset, but I go younger." Kaitlyn rubbed her back. "You're doing great, honey."

"Yes, I guess. It's weird because I don't usually go out in public and act this way. I'll be at home in my room by myself. Even after we moved here, I don't venture out, you know?" Kara shifted a little. The water felt okay but made her feel full.

"So, we've been here just over a year, right? If Joe didn't encourage me to get out, I would stay locked inside too. I go to this spot, and I can't really describe it, but in my head I feel like I'm around nine or ten. I don't have to worry about anything but playing. It's the most amazing way to relax."

"But you're also old enough to get your own food and not wear diapers." Kara pulled her knees up towards her chest. "Not that there's anything wrong with that," she quickly added.

"Yup, you're right about all of that. Now, we're almost done. I'm going to take the tube out and put the plug in. Just breathe."

She felt the nurse slowly remove the tube, then slide the black plug in. It didn't feel any worse than anything else that had been up her bottom today.

"Thank you for helping me. I'm really sorry I gave you a hard time."

"You're welcome. But next time I expect you to be a little more respectful." Kaitlyn walked around to the other side of the table. "This is going to feel really weird, but I promise it will help get everything out. I'm going to massage your tummy."

"Oh gross!" Kara shook her head. "No, please don't do that."

Kaitlyn's eyebrows shot to the top of her head. "With what I just did, you balk at me putting my hands on your belly?"

Kara couldn't stop the tears that suddenly flooded down over her cheeks. She didn't want Kaitlyn touching her fat.

"Please let me help you."

Kara shook her head again, unable to explain what the problem was.

Kaitlyn frowned, then did something Kara would never forget. She took her scrub top off and turned around. To Kara's shock she saw terrible looking scars along the top of her shoulders. They looked like blisters that never popped and were raised and shiny. She had a few deeper lines zigzagging down to cross the middle of her back and some even further down. Kara reached up to run her hand along the edge of one. She yanked

her fingers back, as if aware that she had just done the thing that she didn't want Kaitlyn doing to her.

"It's okay. I'm not ashamed of them anymore." Kaitlyn turned around to show her more around her collarbone and down. "The experiences I lived through to have these on my body were terrible. For many, many years I hated my body. I covered it up with high shirts and never wore a tank top or a bathing suit. I was embarrassed instead of being angry at the monster who did this to me."

"I'm so sorry you went through that." Kara watched the pretty nurse put her top back on and nodded when she hovered her hands just above her stomach. "I have stretch marks, but I helped put them there."

Kaitlyn began to work her hands in a circular motion, gently pressing. It did feel very strange with the water inside of her, but it didn't hurt. "Some people use food to hide their feelings. Did you do that?"

Kara had literally gained fifty plus pounds in less than three months just before she went to high school. She was in so much pain emotionally from the constant stress of watching her younger brothers and sisters. She had been a kid herself and never got to relax.

She had taken over the role of caregiver since her mother had worked so much. Her duties had included cooking, cleaning, bathing, and all the other tasks involved in raising children. She didn't blame her siblings. Her blame fell on the non-existent man who should have been there—her low-life father who had bounced to start a new family. He had been abusive to her mom too, but she'd never let her mother know she knew about it. Thinking about it now, it had been better without him around.

Kara had yo-yo dieted during high school and the following years but had finally learned that the game was mental. It didn't matter what food plan she tried, she needed to get her head on board with whatever she chose and stick with it. She had been overweight on and off since then, and now she couldn't imagine what she would be like without her protective barrier. That's all it was, after all. A barrier to hide behind—like her tattoos. No one could see the real you behind it.

Hot, wet tears poured down her cheeks, though she tried to mask the sniffles. "Mm-hmm."

"Oh, honey. I didn't mean to upset you. I just meant that I understand what it's like to be unhappy with part of your body." Kaitlyn rubbed for another minute or so, then stepped back. "I know you've been off balance. Let me help you to the chair in the bathroom. When you feel the urge to go, you'll already be in there. It's private, so just take your time."

Kara brushed at her cheeks and let the sweet nurse help her up. She looked down at her panties, scared to try and lean down with the way her head was.

"Here, it's okay." Kaitlyn knelt down and removed them from around her

ankles. She handed them to Kara. "Go ahead and take my arm. We'll go slow."

Kara let her lead her into the bathroom. "I think I have to… you know…"

"Yeah, sure. There are rails on either side of the toilet. When you're finished—go ahead and sit on the chair near the sink. Push the call button and someone will come walk you back to the room."

"Thank you."

Kaitlyn left her to do her business, and she was grateful for the privacy.

· · · · · · ·

Kara cleaned herself up and realized she felt a lot better without so much pain in her tummy. Of course, there was still the matter of Dr. Roberts wanting to do an internal exam of her bottom. She did not want anything to do with that!

Of course, her rational brain pointed out that in all the years she had been going to the doctor, it had only been suggested and performed one other time. He was surely looking out for what had caused the issue to start with, but she was very unhappy at the idea of his finger going there.

She thought about the butt plug that Brody had popped inside the night he'd punished her. That had to be bigger than the doctor's fingers. Right? She decided to leave her panties off, unsure what her decision would be.

Ugh, why can't we just go home now?

Kara pressed the call button and waited for someone to come and help her back. To her surprise, it was Brody. He kissed the top of her forehead and wrapped his arm around her waist.

"Are you feeling any better?"

"Yeah, a little. I just want to go home."

"I know, honey. Just a little bit longer."

Kara leaned against him as they made their way back into the room. She took in a breath but only Kaitlyn was in there. She couldn't see what was next to her, but the nurse had a look on her face that made her uncomfortable again. She was in there for some reason, and whatever it was, it wasn't pleasant.

"Kara? I need you to bend over the table slowly. We've got some antibiotics that will make you feel a lot better."

"If you think that you're giving me a shot, you can go to hell."

"Okay. Then I'll let Dr. Roberts come in and administer it." Kaitlyn sucked her cheek in between her teeth, then focused on Brody. "There's a paddle on the wall, and I highly suggest you use it. I know Kara isn't feeling well, but we don't tolerate bad behavior."

"Wait! Please!" Kara cried again. She hated to be so emotional in front of strangers, but she was mortified at the way she was treating Kaitlyn. "I'll

listen! I'm really sorry!"

"I appreciate your apology. Dr. Roberts will be right in."

Crap! This was not how she wanted things to play out. The lovely nurse was probably really mad at her. Why the heck had she told her off?

Kara felt her lower lip trembling but resigned to move away from Brody and bend over the table as instructed originally.

"I'm going to take advantage of this position. And I hope it's the last time you ever get a shot on a spanked butt." Brody rested one hand on her back and let the other meet her cheeks. He punished her swiftly with his bare hand. It was short but intense, and she was grateful he hadn't followed the suggestion about the paddle.

Kara said nothing as the discipline continued, though she did squeak a few times when his hand met her sit spots.

"I have the right to refuse it! I'm an adult!" She danced up on her heels when she got one hard smack on each upper thigh. "Ouch! Ouch!"

Dr. Roberts walked in, and Kara buried her head in her hands. "Kara, do you think it's nice to be disrespectful to someone who is helping you?"

She shook her head and refused to turn around or reply.

Brody didn't bother to fix her gown as he stepped away, but she figured the doctor would just pull it open again anyway. They seemed to be very bottom-oriented today.

"I told Dr. Roberts I agreed," Brody told her. "You'll feel better a lot quicker, and you won't be sick for your test at the end of the week."

"I really hate the way you made a decision without talking to me about it." A much more adult sounding Kara retorted as she shook off his correction. She reached back and held the hem of her gown closed, then straightened. "Maybe if you'd talked to me, I wouldn't have pissed off the sweet nurse."

"I don't like being ignored." Dr. Roberts focused on Brody. "I think she's being even more difficult since you spanked her."

"I don't have much experience with paddles. I usually use a hairbrush." Brody inclined his head to the wall. "If I knew how to swing it, I'm sure Ms. Kara would get a better picture of how I expect her to act when we're out."

Kara felt a pit of ice form in her belly. His tone had gone to a funny place where he sounded amused, as though he was miles away from what was happening. She bit down into her lip as Dr. Roberts approached the wall and maneuvered the large wooden paddle out of its holders. He cracked it once against his hand, causing her to jump.

"I'm rather handy with a paddle."

Brody can't let him spank me! Kara shot a horrified look to Brody, who nodded his agreement.

"You are! I'm so impressed! Do you think you could demonstrate your skills?" Brody cocked his head to the side. "I'm sure it would leave a lasting

impression."

She had really messed up this time. Brody had her best interests in mind, as did Dr. Roberts, and she just kept giving them both lip. Not to mention how rude she had been to Kaitlyn when they had shared a really special moment earlier. She had no right to be acting like this.

"I believe you're right." Dr. Roberts took two large steps until he was back at the exam table. "Your daddy thinks your behavior is out of line, young lady."

Kara blinked back another round of tears. She'd had it with the damn tears today!

The doctor drummed his fingers on the top of the exam table. "Bend over. After I get your bottom a little rosier, we'll get the shot over with, okay?"

Kara sucked in a breath but did as he commanded. Brody wanted her to listen after all, and she had been so awful to the doctor's wife. She still didn't want either one, but a shot would speed up her recovery. She bent and opened the gown.

"Good girl." Dr. Roberts placed one hand at the base of her spine and then smacked the paddle hard against her right cheek. She yelped from the sting and then again as he repeated the gesture on the other side of her bottom. He did this two more times, then laid the implement down. "Let's not have to repeat this next time."

"I'm sorry I was so mean to Kaitlyn!" Kara babbled as the next round of tears began to fall. "I really like her!"

"I understand, and you can tell her you're sorry when you come back next week and straighten out the file cabinet. You cannot treat the staff in this office the way you did." He rubbed an alcohol pad in circles close to the top of her bottom and she clenched. "Try to relax. It's a big pinch, and a big burn. The medicine goes in slow so the burn lasts a bit."

Kara blew her breath out and was happy to feel Brody's hand against her face. "I won't do it again!" She tried not to tense up as the needle hit home, but she failed. "Ow…"

"Just breathe. It's almost done." The doctor certainly had experience. At least he didn't give a bad shot. "Keep your head down for a minute, then get up slowly."

She felt him remove the needle, then heard him move away.

Brody kissed the top of her head. "You did well." He helped her slowly straighten up.

"Are you serious about me coming back here?" Kara watched Dr. Roberts wash and dry his hands.

"Yes. You can move the files from the front desk back to the archive in the record room down the hall. That is, when you're feeling better. I'll arrange it with your daddy."

"Can we skip the last part that you mentioned before?" Kara didn't want anything else near the general area of her behind.

"I really want to make sure there isn't anything else going on. You do have the right to say no, but I'm concerned about it happening again." Dr. Roberts folded his arms across his chest. "I promise it will be over with fast."

"Do I have to bend over again?"

"It will be easier if you get back on the table. The edge of it drops to allow a better angle." Dr. Roberts had a blank expression on his face, and she understood it came from his concern over something else going on. Kara was too nervous to agree verbally, but she maneuvered herself back up on the table.

"I'm going to call Kaitlyn back in here to assist. Do you want your daddy to stay in here too?"

Kara felt the tears start again and she nodded—so overwhelmed in her head again.

Brody leaned over and whispered in her ear. "It will be over really soon, and we can go home and snuggle, okay?"

She nodded again.

"I love you, honey."

"I love you too." Kara looked down at the end of the table. Kaitlyn had come back in, and she patted her foot with a comforting touch. "I'm sorry I'm being awful."

"I forgive you. I'm right here too." Kaitlyn gave her a small smile, then focused on handing the doctor something.

"Kara, I need you to scoot down to the end of the table, okay?" Dr. Roberts could seriously be a hostage negotiator with his voice of perfect calm and perfect reason. It was firm, gentle, and just a tiny bit demanding. How did he and Brody both know how to get her to cooperate?

She managed to move her body down. "Will it hurt?"

"You'll feel a bit of pressure, but it shouldn't hurt. If you do feel pain, I want you to tell me immediately." Dr. Roberts laid a sheet over her lower half. "Let your knees fall open to the sides."

"Uh-huh." Kara sucked in a breath as she opened her legs. Brody took her hand in his and kissed the side of her head. "I don't want to do this."

"I know. It's okay." Brody gave her hand a squeeze. "Just try to relax."

"Breathe, honey. We'll be done really soon." Dr. Roberts assured Kara.

Kara felt the now familiar gel press up against her bottom hole, then the tip of Dr. Roberts' finger as he worked it around the edge. He inserted his finger deeper, and she could feel him poking around. It didn't hurt, like she had imagined before, but it did feel odd. Plus, she was embarrassed to have so much attention there. Another finger entered slowly but did not go in all the way. She tried to focus on her breathing, but the tears started again and she sniffled.

"Does that hurt?" Dr. Roberts glanced up and over the sheet to meet her eyes.

"N… no." Kara inhaled deeply and let it out. "No. I don't know why I'm crying again."

"You're doing great. It's almost over." Brody gave her hand another squeeze. "I'm very proud of you. I know it's uncomfortable."

"All right. We're all done." Dr. Roberts withdrew his fingers slowly, so he wouldn't cause any pain on the way out. "You did great. I didn't feel anything which would indicate a problem. You can get up and dressed. Make sure you pick up your basket on the way out."

"Thank you." Kara watched him dispose of the gloves and wash his hands. "Thank you both so much."

Kaitlyn patted her head as she left. "You're welcome. We'll see you when you come back. Feel free to call me if you ever want to talk. My number is in the basket."

Kara got dressed slowly, and then she took Brody's hand. He grabbed the pretty gift basket as they passed the front desk, then helped her out to the car. She got into the backseat and stretched out. "I'm sorry I acted up. I just really don't like going to the doctor."

"It's okay. I think you learned your lesson. We'll go home and relax and then you can go to sleep."

"Thank you for taking care of me."

"That's what daddies do."

Kara snuggled down into the seat. She was damn lucky. Brody really knew exactly how to take care of her.

CHAPTER FIVE

It was a few days after her visit to the doctor and Kara was camped out on the couch. She was bundled up in blankets, and though she felt a little better, she still didn't feel well enough to do anything. Brody walked into the living room and stopped to touch her head.

"How are you feeling, honey?"

"Mmugh," she replied with a pout. "Can you please stay home today?" He had told her about an hour or so ago that he had been called in for an important meeting.

"I can't, but I have someone coming over to sit with you."

Kara rolled her eyes. "I want to be alone then. Just call them back and tell them it's fine," she snapped before she could stop herself.

Brody narrowed his eyes and leaned down so they were at the same level. "Hey, none of that. You were still dizzy last night, and I don't want you moving around if you don't have to. I have Joe coming over with Katie."

Kara's mouth dropped. "You don't mean like, Dr. Joe, do you? And what do you mean Katie? She's not a kid."

"Yes, I do mean Dr. Joe, and today Katie is in her younger mindset. She wants to come over and help, but she's not in her nurse mode. He's doing me a favor by coming over, so I expect you to be very good."

"I'm not a little kid." Kara spoke through gritted teeth. She was not happy with this arrangement! She didn't need a babysitter! "I'll just go in my room. I swear I'll be okay!"

"Do you need a punishment before I go? I'd rather not spank you when you're still sick, but I think it will change your tune really fast." Brody straightened. "What's it going to be?"

"I'll listen to Dr. Joe." Kara smoothed out one of the blankets. "He's not going to be all like, doctorish when he's here, right?"

"I'm not sure what you mean. Yes, he's a doctor, but he's also Katie's daddy. He's not going to come over here and spank you and give you a shot, if that's what you're referring to."

"He spanked me in his office like a damn little kid!" Kara snapped, reliving the memory of the way he'd paddled her bare bottom before the shot of antibiotics.

"He most certainly did. If I recall correctly, you told his lovely wife to go to hell." Brody sighed then looked down at his watch. "You need to be on your best behavior. Being sick doesn't excuse bad choices. Besides, I already told him that he has my permission to act on my behalf."

"I'll try," Kara sighed. His words sent a terrible shiver up her spine. She didn't like the idea of Dr. Joe having permission to do anything since she was so embarrassed from being exposed in his office. But, he was so gentle too, especially with Katie. She hoped she could be good like she'd promised.

"What was your temperature?" Brody rested his hand against her forehead. "You still feel warmer than usual."

"Like ninety something," Kara mumbled as she shifted uncomfortably under his hand.

"You didn't check it, did you?" Brody glanced at his watch again as he dropped his hand. "I asked you an hour ago so I could give you med—"

"I couldn't find the digital one and I'm not using... that... other... one." Kara knew exactly what he expected, but interrupted him anyway.

The oral blue digital one had died a terrible death. It had slipped off the counter the other day when she'd cleaned the kitchen and it had fallen into the drain. Kara, terrified of the garbage compressor from all those movies that showed people losing their hands, had clicked the switch to off, but in her panic she'd accidentally turned it on. Good-bye, adult thermometer. She hadn't told Brody yet since he'd told her to stay on the couch and rest.

"Where is the red one?" The doorbell rang, interrupting their conversation. "Quickly. I have to answer the door."

"It's upstairs somewhere!" Kara snapped. "The other one got crushed in the sink. I'm not using a damn baby thermometer!"

Brody rubbed his chin, as if contemplating how much time it would take, then nodded. "Okay, you can tell me all about it when I get home. In the meantime, I'm sure Joe can help you find it."

"Ugh!" Kara flipped herself around to face away from the door. She didn't have to see either of them. What if Dr. Joe got strict with her? Would he check her temperature again? Brody would probably ask him to.

"Hey, Joe. Thanks for coming over," Brody said warmly and closed the door.

"It's no problem. I've got a call or two later on in the day, but nothing else. I don't have to be in the office today." The low baritone of the doctor's voice carried across the room.

"Hi, Katie," Brody addressed the doctor's wife. "Kara isn't feeling well enough to play, but we've got a lot of movies. Kara also told me she wanted to get into more crafty things, so I picked up a few kits. They're on the kitchen

table if you want to look at them in a bit."

"Thank you!" a younger-sounding Kaitlyn piped up as she entered the room. She gasped when she arrived at the couch. "Is she sick-sick?"

"Kara isn't contagious or anything, but her head is dizzy. Maybe you can watch a movie later?" Brody's voice sounded closer and she felt him press a kiss to her head. "Dr. Joe and Katie are here, honey. Please listen. I'll be home in a few hours."

"Mmumph," Kara mumbled, not wanting to let them know she wasn't sleeping.

"Can I sit on the couch next to Kara, daddy? I brought my favorite blanket, and I'll be really quiet," Katie begged.

"Yes, but don't wake up Kara." Dr. Joe's voice sounded closer. She imagined him sitting in the armchair nearest the couch.

Kara felt Katie tentatively climb onto the couch. She situated herself at the far side of it but her feet reached hers. She poked at Kara's feet a little, soothingly not annoyingly, and that made Kara smile. Even in her littler mindset she wanted to comfort.

Kara heard the TV turn on and then several minutes later the low hum of cartoons filtered across the room.

"I love ponies," Katie whispered. "I hope when you feel better you can come over and play with me."

Kara thought about her statement for a long time. She was in her teen type of mindset—she'd been stuck in it since the other day at the doctor's office—but the idea of going over to Katie's house to play sounded incredibly appealing. Could she do something like that?

"I can see you smiling. I know you're awake…" Katie whispered again. "We can brush their hair and make them go on an adventure…"

"Katie…" Dr. Joe warned from his spot. She was certain he was near the couch now since Katie's voice had been very low. "Let Kara be."

"I just want her to know she can like, come over and stuff."

Kara imagined the sweet woman pouting, and finally she turned outwards. "It's okay, and um, I'll think about it." She tugged her feet closer to her body so she didn't take up the whole couch. "Thank you for staying. I'm still not quite all better."

"Did your daddy give you Tylenol this morning?" Dr. Joe set his laptop down on the coffee table. He was dressed casually in jeans and a t-shirt, but even without the lab coat and stethoscope he looked authoritative.

Kara bit her lip. After the whole fiasco, she never got around to asking for the Tylenol.

"Um, well… he was supposed to." Kara cuddled deeper under the blankets. Dr. Joe raised an eyebrow, and she had a funny feeling she would have to explain. "But, um, he had to go to work and all."

"That doesn't sound very responsible. Did something happen?"

Katie piped up loudly, "I bet Kara didn't do what she was told!"

Kara shot a glare at the smaller woman, who glared right back.

"When I don't feel good my daddy takes my temperature and gets me medicine. So, I don't think you listened!"

"Katie, you have to remember not everything that happens in our house happens everywhere. Apologize to your friend for yelling." Dr. Joe motioned for Katie to hurry.

"I'm sorry, Kara, but I bet you really didn't!" Katie got up from the couch and went over to him. "Her eyes are all tired. She looks sick, daddy!"

"Katie, why don't you go into the kitchen and see what craft sets Brody bought for today? I'll come check on you in a few minutes." Dr. Joe's tone went deeper than normal, and Kara worried about what him sending Katie out of the room meant.

"I'm sorry." Katie threw her arms around him in a bear hug. "Yes, I'll go." She passed by the couch and patted Kara's hand. "I just want you to get better so we can have fun."

"I know. It's okay," Kara assured her, then watched as she dashed off to find the kitchen. For the first time, she noticed how adorable Katie's outfit was.

The other woman had on tights with bubbles of all colors randomly splashed over them, a long purple tee-shirt, and a pink and black sweater on top. Her short black hair was pulled up in a high ponytail that bounced as she went out of the room.

Kara wasn't surprised at her choice of clothing but instead at the notion of her coming out in public. She liked her bravery and hoped spending more time with her was on the horizon.

Then Dr. Joe cleared his throat, and she realized he had asked her something.

"I'm sorry, I was... well, it doesn't matter. What did you ask me?"

"Did you have a fever today?"

Kara swallowed hard as she tried to think of a way to reply without prompting him to verify the information. "I didn't really get around to checking it," she admitted, though somewhat reluctantly.

He had been insistent in his office about the more accurate method, and she didn't want to argue with him. It hadn't been an entirely unpleasant experience, especially with everything else she had gone through later on, but now they were at her house. It felt different.

"Did your daddy ask you to?"

Kara nodded slowly but didn't answer.

"But you refused?"

She nodded again.

"Where is the thermometer now?" Dr. Joe folded his arms across his chest.

"It's upstairs in the bathroom." Kara swallowed again. "In the cabinet over the sink," she squeaked, "next to the toothpaste."

"For someone who didn't want to listen, you sure remember where you left it." Dr. Joe reached down to feel her head, then straightened. "Why don't you go get it so we check and see if the fever is back? Then you can take some medicine."

"Yeah, I guess." Kara shoved the blankets off and stood up. "I have to get up anyway." She teetered slightly and Dr. Joe helped her steady herself. "Thanks. I was on the couch like all day."

He let go of her slowly, and she carefully moved to the stairs. She wasn't thrilled about the idea of him sticking the thermometer in her bottom again, but she knew if she'd only done it this morning when Brody told her to, it would have been a non-issue.

Kara went into the bathroom and found the instrument. She studied the tiny glass rod in its red case for a minute before using the bathroom. She washed her hands, remembered the tiny jar of petroleum jelly that had been included in the gift basket, and took the items back downstairs.

Kara could have refused to let Dr. Joe do it, but Katie had said he took her temperature when she was sick. Maybe she should just let him take care of her instead of worrying about every little thing. He already saw lots of parts of her the other day.

She saw Dr. Joe walking back into the living room from the kitchen. Kara didn't say a word, but made her way carefully to the couch. She set the objects on the coffee table, then looked up at him.

"I went to check on Katie. She's working on this really complicated paint-by-numbers on velvet." Dr. Joe picked up the thermometer and shook it down. "It's neat because you can use paint, or markers, or really any materials to color it in." As he spoke, he opened the jar and twirled the instrument twice.

Kara raised an eyebrow. "You did that without even looking." How many times a day did this man do this procedure?

She carefully lay back down on the couch. Did everyone who visited the office get it done this way?

"I guess I've had a lot of practice." Dr. Joe smiled warmly. "Go ahead and roll onto your tummy for me."

Kara took a deep breath and quickly situated herself. She tugged her fluffy kitty-cat pajama bottoms down past her hips and did the same with her panties. Dr. Joe sat at the edge of the couch and covered her with one of the lighter blankets. He folded the top down just far enough to get to the spot he needed, and then he spread her cheeks. She squirmed as the tip of the rod touched her most private place, but she relaxed as soon as it was in.

His cell phone chirped just as he fixed the blanket over her. "I'm sorry, but I have to take this. Stay still." Dr. Joe answered on the second ring.

"Hello? This is Joe. Uh-huh… uh-huh. What is it?" The person on the other end babbled into his ear. "Who?"

Kara felt her face grow hot. He was talking to someone while he took her temperature! She knew the other person would have no way of knowing what he was doing, but she wiggled impatiently. Dr. Joe sensed the movement and rested his hand on top of the blanket on her lower back.

"It's almost done. Stay. Still," Dr. Joe whispered. Then he raised his voice again, "Yes, she is allergic to that medication. It should be in her file. Oh, the server is down?" He shifted his hand away once Kara stopped moving. "Uh-huh. Okay, so if it's not fixed when I'm back tomorrow, I'll call for a technician to come out."

Kara huffed, really wanting this ordeal to be over with. She felt acutely aware of the slim object inside of her, and she wanted it out.

"Hasn't it been in long enough?" Kara pouted, but kept her voice really low.

"No problem. Right. Call me again if you need me. Thanks." Dr. Joe ended the call. He clucked his tongue at her as he removed the thermometer. "A doctor I work with called to ask about one of my patients." He smacked one hand against each of her sit-spots—not really hard, but it stung enough to send a message. "Next time, do what your daddy tells you when he tells you to. Then you won't have to worry about interrupting a business call."

"Ow! I'm sorry, Dr. Joe. I won't act up again!" His hands were massive and they stung as bad as a paddle. "Do I still have a fever?" Kara shimmied her panties and pants back up.

He gently tucked the blankets around her and she realized she was grateful for his presence, despite her protests.

"You do have a fever, young lady, all the way up to one-hundred and two. No wonder you feel so miserable." He set the thermometer on a napkin next to the case, then got to his feet. "I'll get you something to lower it. Rest, honey. I'll let Katie come back in too."

"Thank you. I'm sorry I didn't listen. I'll tell my daddy about it when he comes home." Kara gave him a small smile, then curled herself up on her side. Brody had been right to worry about her. One-hundred and two was a pretty high fever, and she felt crappy.

Katie came back into the room and cuddled up on the couch again. This time she snuggled against Kara's legs. "I'm sorry I said mean things to you. Your eyes just looked sad and all, and I thought my daddy could help."

"It's okay. Your daddy did help. I'm glad you're both here with me."

Kara took the medicine that Dr. Joe brought to her. Then he patted Katie's head and they both fell asleep, happily watching a movie about cartoon ponies and their friendships. Sometime later she felt something lift off of her, and opened her eyes.

Dr. Joe had picked Katie up into his arms and she had somehow stayed

asleep. He reached down and patted her cheek. "We'll see you when you're feeling better."

"M'kay. Thanks." Kara's eyes fluttered shut again, too tired to force herself awake.

• • • • • • •

"Kara?" Brody shook her shoulder gently again, and this time she opened her eyes. "How are you feeling?"

"Oh? Um… better I think." Kara sat up and rubbed her eyes. "Is it still today?"

Brody smiled. "I let you sleep on the couch because you looked so peaceful. I think your fever broke last night. You don't feel warm anymore."

Kara quickly eyed the coffee table, and he followed her gaze.

"I didn't check it, but I heard you let Dr. Joe do it. I'm happy you listened while I was at work."

Truth be told, when Joe gave an overview of their afternoon, Brody had beamed with pride over Kara's acceptance of the doctor. Of course, Brody had asked her to listen, but sometimes she had other ideas.

"I should have taken care of it when you asked me yesterday morning." Kara wrapped her arms around his neck. "Katie had a lot of fun with the craft stuff, but she, uh, asked me to come play with her someday. I told her I'd like to, but I'm not a kid, you know?"

Brody was having trouble reading her at the moment. She sounded a bit like she was in her teen mindset, but it was a bit unclear. "You know you can be whatever age you want to be when you have your time, right?"

Kara frowned, as if not quite understanding. "But, I'm not little."

He smirked and ran his hand down her cheek. "You don't have to act five, babe. It's your thing, and I hope you know I'll support your choices."

Kara flushed almost as red as her hair. "No, Brody. I'm not physically little. How could I possibly go over to Katie's and pretend I'm like seven or something when I'm… this?"

"If you refer to your body as a 'this' again, you won't have to worry about going over to Katie's or anywhere for the next week. Don't feed your brain negative thoughts. The size of your body has nothing to do with your mindset."

She sucked in a breath, then nodded. "Fine, I'll think about it. Oh, before I forget. Thank you for having Dr. Joe and Katie come over. They helped me feel a lot better."

"I'm glad. Joe and I also spoke about you going to the office next week to do some filing. They are desperate from some extra hands. What if you picked up about fifteen hours a week? It would get you out into the community. Maybe you'd even make more friends."

Kara shrugged. "I don't know. I'll think about it. You know how I feel about doctor's offices."

"My other thought was that it would help you get over your fear. Anyway, it's something to think about after you go there. We can talk more about it later." Brody squeezed her hand, then got to his feet. "I've got a project to wrap up later on, but I'm home today. Is there anything you need?"

"I feel sort of gross. I really want to take a shower, but I don't think I can stand up that long. Plus it takes forever to wash my hair."

"What if I fill the tub for you? Then you can sit down so you're not unsteady on your feet. Wash up, and I'll come in to help with your hair."

"You'd do that?" Kara whispered in awe. "I mean, you're so busy—"

"It's no big deal." Brody kissed her forehead, then slid her arms away from his neck. "Come on, you'll feel like a different person." He helped her to her feet and supported her as they went upstairs.

"Thanks…" Kara trailed off as they went into the bathroom. She sat down on the closed toilet lid and watched him as he tested the water and added her favorite lilac smelling bubble bath.

"Go ahead. When you get to your hair, call me." Brody patted her shoulder, then left the bathroom.

• • • • • • •

Kara got undressed and sank down into the bathtub. The water felt amazing on her skin, and she smiled. Brody always knew exactly what to do to make her calm down and relax.

She took her time washing her body, but not too long since she didn't want the heat to disappear. After the last part of her body had been scrubbed clean, she called, "Brody!"

He came in about thirty-seconds later. True to his word, he leaned down against the side of the tub and used a cup to wet her hair. "I guess I never realized how long your hair is."

"Yeah, it's all the way past my butt." Kara leaned into his hands as he lathered the shampoo into her scalp. It smelled wonderful, like coconut, but felt even better. She loved the way his hands worked the soap into her hair, and it felt even better when he used fresh water to rinse it out. He repeated the process with her conditioner and she nearly moaned from the sweet sensations. He had such amazing hands, and having them focused on her head made her tingly. "You have great hands."

"Oh yeah?" Brody nuzzled against her neck. "I'm glad you enjoy them."

"Can you show me what else you do with your hands in a much more adult way?" Kara dipped her head back to lick along his bottom lip. She rotated outwards so she could face him, and captured his mouth in hers. "Please, baby?"

Brody broke the kiss and ran his hands down her face. "Are you sure? If you weren't feeling well yesterday…"

"I read online, you know on one of those smart sounding medical websites, that fucking is the best medication."

"I think you confused articles. Laughter is the best medicine."

"Only if you're fucking a clown," Kara deadpanned but couldn't keep the wicked grin off her face.

"You little brat." Brody nearly smacked the faucet release to get the water to drain. "Come on, stand up. I'll show you my greatest talent involving my hands."

"It better not involve my ass." Kara gasped as he picked her up and out of the tub and wrapped her in a towel. He had a strange smile on his face and she couldn't tell exactly what he had in mind. "Unless, of course, we're trying new things?"

"I guarantee you won't be laughing when I get through with you," Brody warned, but his serious face dissolved into a huge grin. "Come on, baby. I've got evil plans." He wrapped his arm around her waist to keep her steady, and they moved up the hallway towards their room.

Kara let the towel drop somewhere along the way and lay down on the bed. Brody crawled on top, licking her as he moved from her knees to her thighs, then up and over her hips, and stopping at her waist. He nuzzled her there before placing his mouth against each of her breasts and sucking on each nipple as he made his way higher, nibbling on her collarbone and finally kissing her neck softly. She melted into a puddle when his lips brushed across hers, and she moaned loudly. "I want you."

"You've already got me, baby." Brody positioned his hips over hers and slowly slid inside her. "Always."

Kara arched upwards to match his rhythm. "Now, about those hands?"

Brody gave her a sly smile, then trailed his hands down and over her body. His hand stopped when it got to her clit, and he tugged the tiny nub in between two of his fingers as he pumped deep inside her. The action elicited a cry of pleasure from her lips, and she moaned loudly.

"You like that?"

"Oh, yes! Please… please keep going…" She lost herself in the endorphin rush fluttering through her body, then came hard when his cock hit her g-spot. He knew just how to move to push her buttons. "Brody!"

He reached his own peak and came in spurts. Then he wrapped his arms around her body and collapsed on the bed from the exertion. "I warned you about my hands…"

"And evil, evil plans!" Kara giggled as she shifted around so they lay face to face. She leaned forward and kissed him deeply. "Thank you for taking care of me. I know some of it stems from the crap I've been doing to myself lately. I know you always have my best interests at heart, and I'll do better

with listening."

"I'm glad you know." Brody planted a kiss on the top of her forehead. "I'll go make brunch. When you're ready, come downstairs." He got out of bed, dressed, then left her to her thoughts.

He took care of her in ways she never could have imagined, not even in her wildest dreams. And he never lost his cool, not even when she bratted him! She needed to do her best to follow the rules to show her appreciation. Their relationship fit her every want—and even fulfilled desires she didn't know she had.

She got out of bed with a huge smile on her face. *Wicked plans and wicked hands.* It sounded like her next tattoo.

CHAPTER SIX

Kara arrived at the doctor's office at eight in the morning. She entered hesitantly, her deep fears hitting her as she stepped inside, and she took a deep breath.

Kaitlyn met her immediately with a grin. "Kara! I'm so happy to see you this morning! We've got a ton of patients today since we're doing our first round of flu shots today."

Kara tried to force a smile, but the thought of all those needles made her very uncomfortable. No doubt she wouldn't be able to escape her own dose. "Yippee..."

"So, follow me to the back room. We're about two weeks behind on filing. After that, if you can just check in each person as he or she comes in, that would be great. It's super easy—" Kaitlyn led her up the small hallway "—mostly just grab the name and give them a time slot. Joe and I will both be administering vaccines to move faster." She pointed to a row of filing cabinets.

"Uh-huh." Kara rubbed the back of her neck. She felt flushed all of a sudden.

"What is it?" Kaitlyn arched an eyebrow. "Are you okay?"

"I really hate shots... The thought of so many people coming through here for that one purpose makes me shiver." Kara shook off a round of goosebumps.

"Don't think about it right now. Focus on the folders. I'll come back and check on you in a few. We're not starting until eleven o'clock, so you've got plenty of time. I have to draw them all up, so we should finish at about the same time." Kaitlyn patted her arm encouragingly, then left the room. It was small but held several dozen cabinets. Kara would be lucky to finish by eleven.

• • • • • • •

"Kara? Hey, it's quarter to eleven…" Kaitlyn entered the back room just as Kara finished with the last file. "Oh! Yay! I'm so happy! I can actually find things again."

"Huh? Oh, yeah." Kara grinned. "There were tons of files out. It was no big deal. I like organizing… all those little letters… so much fun."

"It's really going to help us out a lot! Joe wanted to see you in his office. It's the third door on the right." The petite brunette smiled warmly at her. "I'd love if you came in once a week."

"I'm pretty freaked out right now. I don't like being in any sort of medical office, but I like you and Dr. Joe a lot. I'll think about it."

Kara moved past her into the hall and found the door Kaitlyn mentioned. She knocked on it once and waited for the doctor to tell her to come in.

"Hey. Come in and shut the door. I have a favor to ask you."

Dr. Joe smiled as she followed his instructions. She took a seat across from his desk. "Sure, what is it?"

He threw a glance to the door to confirm it was shut, then focused on her. "Kaitlyn's birthday party is tomorrow. Total fairy princess theme."

Kara nodded, unsure what that had to do with her. "That sounds lovely."

"I hired a woman to come paint faces, and her son got sick. She can't make it. I know you're super creative. Brody told me about some of the artistic projects you work on. Can you face paint?"

Kara giggled a nervous laugh. His face looked so sincere, so different than the stern doctor who'd told her to bend over a few days ago. "I can. I mean, I used to as a side job after I graduated high school, but that was a while ago. But do you really think I'm fairy princess material?"

"I think anyone can be a fairy princess. I'm sure you could put together a cute outfit. I'd even go as far to guess that you have wings somewhere." Dr. Joe waggled his eyebrows. "Please? I'll give you money for the paint, of course. I just don't want to let Kaitlyn down."

At the mention of her name, Kara tried to picture how she would react when she heard about the lack of an epic fairy princess face painter. Her lower lip trembled at the thought. "That's not playing fair. You know how much I like Kaitlyn."

"I never said I played fair." Dr. Joe gave her pleading eyes. "It's only for two hours. You can stay for dinner once everyone else leaves. I'm sure someone there will want a Hello-Kitty on her cheek."

"You also know how much I like that pretty cat." She rolled her eyes playfully. "Okay, okay. I owe you both anyway for taking such good care of me."

"No, you don't. We're both just really good at that. To be serious, I really don't think I can find anyone else on such short notice, and I knew mentioning Hello-Kitty would get you thinking!" Dr. Joe tugged out his wallet, opened it, and fished out two twenties. "If the supplies are more, just

let me know and I'll make up the difference."

Kara reached forward, accepted the cash, and pocketed it. "I have one more question. You're not letting me leave today without a flu shot, are you?"

"Probably not, but I was going to mention that way later." Dr. Joe shrugged. "It's still optional, even though it's highly suggested this time of year. If you decide to come in a few times a week, it will be mandatory."

"Ugh!" Kara rose from the chair and rolled her eyes again. "I didn't say I'd come back. This could be a one-time only thing. I really, really hate medical places."

"I think being here, in a really positive environment, might help you get over that fear. But it's up to you."

"Thanks, Dr. Joe. I'll let you know later." Kara nodded before she stepped to the door, opened it, and went out into the hallway. Only five minutes until the office opened for flu shots. She imagined it would be a mad house.

· · · · · · ·

Kara came home after being at the doctor's office all day, and she crashed on the couch. So many of the patients had visited in younger mindsets, and they'd acted exactly how you would expect a child to act. It had felt strangely satisfying to hand them lollypops and stickers at the end of the visit. She liked how each one of them had smiled at her and made her feel important—as if her gesture made up for the shot!

Brody came in from the kitchen and joined her on the couch. He set three large bags on the coffee table and nudged her leg. "Hey, babe. I picked up something for you."

Kara groaned as she pulled herself into a sitting position. She kissed his cheek, though, and smiled. "Thanks. What is it?" She tugged the largest bag to her and peeked inside. Face paints, brushes, sponges, glitter, and containers! "Oh! Brody!"

"Joe called me this afternoon and let me know about the party tomorrow. I think it's a great idea. Kaitlyn will be so surprised. Oh, and he told me he wants you to keep the money he gave you. You worked so hard today."

"I got a shot too," Kara pouted, but peeked in the other two bags. More supplies. She spied stickers, fake rhinestones, and eyelash glue to attach them! "These are fantastic!"

"You willingly agreed to get a flu shot? I'm really proud of you. Does that mean you're going to go to the office more often?" Brody smiled as she let out a sigh of contentment.

"Well, I'm not sure about it yet, but it's a good idea to do something preventative to ward off sickness." Kara let go of the bags and curled herself up on Brody. "Thank you for encouraging me to go there. I really felt like they needed my help. Plus, I got to talk to Kaitlyn a lot today!"

"You're welcome, babe. I'm happy you went there today. I made dinner, so let's go eat. You can tell me more about the party."

Kara nodded. "I'm going to go get in my pj's, but then I'll be right down." She kissed him sweetly once more, then stood up. "Tomorrow will be great too."

"All right. I'll be here." Brody winked. "I also picked up those brownie bars you like so much and fresh strawberries."

"Perfect! Be right back." Kara danced up the stairs. Even after her long day, she was in one of the best moods she'd been in in a long time.

CHAPTER SEVEN

Kara returned home from the birthday party covered in paint and in a slightly foul mood. She loved how happy Kaitlyn had been to see her, but a group of women all in seven to twelve-year-old mindsets had certainly tested her patience. It was like baby-sitting for her siblings all over again.

Kara changed her clothes into two differently colored knee highs, along with her short black boots to balance out the black and pink plaid mini-skirt and black graphic tee-shirt. Her hair was then done in a high ponytail with a bright ribbon wrapped around the elastic. While collecting her make-up, she got into an argument with Brody, and he took away the privilege of wearing any. He knew how much she loved her make-up! So she settled on a sparkly chapstick with a bit of sheen, then clomped downstairs.

After fifteen minutes of whining about not having anything to do, she was sent out to take a walk. After another ten minutes of protesting, and a light spanking, Brody practically kicked her out the door.

Snow showers threatened later on in the day, but for now it was dry and only a little chilly. Kara wandered along the street and made her way to the playground. She scanned the area, hoping to find someone hanging out from the teenage crowd, but she didn't see anyone.

Happy her clothes were warm enough so she didn't need a heavy coat, Kara pulled her fur-lined Hello-kitty hoodie up over her head, then moved towards the edge of the fence. She hadn't gone far when something smacked her hard in the shin. Tears blurred her vision from the quick blow, and she blinked them away.

What the hell had hit her?

A woman about her age stood with her hands over her mouth and a look of horror on her face. "I'm so sorry!"

Kara looked down to see a purple skip-it toy looped around the woman's ankle, then she looked back up to her face. It was mostly her own fault, Kara decided, for not paying attention to what she was doing. She could have knocked the poor thing right over!

"No! It's okay. I wasn't watching where I was going." She knew this was a great opportunity to introduce herself, but what if she wanted to be left alone? The toy looked so much fun though, and finally, after thirty awkward seconds, she pointed to it. "Do you think I could try?"

"Yeah, sure. Just don't break it." The other woman took the object off her foot then reached down and clasped it around Kara's foot. "It's super easy. Just swing it around and hop over this part."

"I'm Kara." Kara extended her hand. "It's nice to meet you."

"I'm Bailey." The woman straightened to shake her hand, then stepped back. "Go ahead and try it. It will count how many jumps you do."

"I'll try not to hit you!" Kara grinned and began hopping. After a few minutes of Bailey cheering her on and giggling at the game, she stopped. Something had changed in the air and the wind had picked up. Some flurries fell around them, and she knew it would be a long, cold walk home. Kara quickly undid the toy and handed it back to Bailey. "It got cold really fast!"

"Come on! My house is just over there. You can come over." Bailey pointed across the way and the two of them took off. "My daddy won't mind."

Kara nodded as she hurriedly followed her new friend. She hadn't made many in their community, so being invited over, even for the purpose of getting out of the snow, made her giddy with excitement. "I'll call and get picked up. Thank you!"

• • • • • • •

Brody picked her up from Bailey's house after he finished work as she'd wound up staying for most of the afternoon. Kara got into the car, then leaned over to plant a kiss on his cheek.

"I made a friend." She smiled sheepishly. "Her name is Bailey, and she's really sweet. I met her daddy Ian, too. They, uh, do some of the things we do."

"I'm really happy you met someone to hang out with. I missed a call while I was in a virtual meeting, and the voicemail was from him. He asked me to give him a call back and let him know if you are allowed to have a sleepover tomorrow." Brody reached over and patted her thigh. "Do you want Bailey to come over?"

Kara nodded excitedly. "Yes! I've never experienced a real sleepover. Bailey is going to bring movies, and we're going to stay up late! Then we can have breakfast and hang out," she concluded with a grin.

"It sounds like you've got it all planned out. I'll call Ian back when we get home and finalize things. Aren't you happy I made you go outside today?"

She giggled as he moved his hand to her nose and tapped it twice. "Yes, daddy."

"Good. I'm also proud of you for being so responsible this afternoon. You let me know what happened immediately and made a good decision to stay out of the weather." He smiled warmly at her.

"I hope you remember this tomorrow night! Bailey and I were giggling like crazy today. You know how loud I laugh."

"Sweetheart, you're still going to be respectful of the rules. Giggling is fine, but no funny business." He waggled his eyebrows at her. "I mean it."

"Okay, okay." She held her hands up, palms out in surrender. "We'll behave!"

They pulled in to the driveway and ended the conversation. She knew Brody meant what he said, but tomorrow it would be about her and Bailey and their amazing sleepover adventure.

• • • • • • •

Kara was on pins and needles as she waited for Bailey to come over. She had never had a real sleepover before, and though it sounded silly, she wanted everything to go right. Brody had promised to take care of dinner and said that he would be on his best behavior.

His best behavior! As if he ever acted up.

Kara walked through the kitchen about a dozen times until Brody chased her out with a wooden spoon. He was making spaghetti sauce and told her it would be super easy to find another spoon. She retreated, clutching her behind and squealing. She did not want any of that! Especially before her friend came over.

Finally, she saw Bailey nervously walking up the stairs towards the house. She kept stopping and glancing over her shoulder. *Did she change her mind and not want to stay?*

Kara bit her lip and tried to shake off her own nerves. Then with a huge smile, she opened the door and called out to greet her new friend, "Hi, Bailey! I'm super happy your daddy said you could come over."

Bailey arrived on the porch, bags in hand, and smiled a little. "Thanks. I'm excited."

The other woman didn't seem too excited, but she imagined it was a slightly awkward situation for both of them. They were grown women as it were, and both had confessed the want to relive a younger, happier time.

Kara didn't have too many happy moments from her childhood, and she had told Bailey about some of the harder things she'd experienced. Then they'd both decided at that moment to have an even better than high school sleepover! Of course, now that they were both standing in the doorway, looking at each other, it seemed uncomfortable.

Brody, always knowing just what to say, made his way to the front door and urged Bailey to come inside. "It's cold out, ladies. You're letting all the

heat out."

Kara shut and locked the door.

"Thanks. The bill is high enough without leaving doors open." He went back into the kitchen and they followed. He paused to wipe his hands on the towel hanging from the stove before he checked the sauce.

"I'm Bailey."

Brody frowned. "What terrible manners I have." He turned around and shook Bailey's hand. "I'm Brody. It's nice to meet you." He released her hand and smiled warmly at the two of them.

"We're going to watch lots of movies and stay up late and eat junk food." Kara shot a look to Bailey, who nodded.

"Yeah? What movies?" Brody raised an eyebrow. "Are they rated R?"

Ugh! He was acting like a total… well… like a total party pooper. Except, Kara wanted him to be interested in her plans. She wanted him to question her decisions when she was in a younger mindset, but she hadn't planned on him doing that in front of her friend.

"What movies did you bring, Bailey?" Kara popped the question over to her since her own movie collection was filled with romantic comedies and they had vetoed those down earlier.

"Just some Simon Pegg movies. Yeah, they're rated R. All the best movies are." Bailey shrugged at Kara. "We totally agreed about that before."

"What's wrong with that rating?" Kara shot back to Brody.

"Woah-ho. You better change your tone or I'll send your friend home right now." Brody checked on the sauce then turned up the pasta water. "I just asked if they were rated R. Help Bailey bring her things upstairs. Dinner will be ready in about twenty minutes."

"I'm sorry, daddy," Kara huffed. She had thought he was going to shoot down their movie ideas. She skipped over to the stove and planted a kiss on his cheek. "If it's too inappropriate, we'll turn them off and watch cartoons."

Brody grinned. "Uh-huh." He tapped his finger on her nose. "Hurry up, because I've got to watch these pots."

"Okay!" Kara motioned for Bailey to follow her. "We're staying in my, um, teen kind of room." Would she think she was stupid for having a whole room just to be a teen in?

"You have a room too!" Bailey's voice was thick with excitement. "That's so cool!"

Kara led her inside and helped her spread out her stuff so it didn't get mixed up in hers. She sheepishly watched Bailey eye her little fairy statues, alternative rock posters, celebrity crush photos, and purple Christmas lights that were tacked up to give the room a gothic feel.

Kara's room was painted a light teal with darker teal sponge painting along the top border. There were also butterfly stickers and some pretty purple flowers dancing up and down the walls. She imagined it was an odd mixture

to someone who didn't know her very well.

"Are you like a girly gothic girl?"

"I'm just me. I love butterflies 'cause they make me happy. Just like I like the biker boots and black makeup." Kara shrugged. "I don't know. I just have my own sort of style, I guess."

"I like it." Bailey pointed to one of Kara's arms, the one with a half sleeve tattoo. "I like your tattoos too. I mean, they're so different. And it's like, you really express yourself with them."

"They make me happy. My mom used to tell me that only whores and sailors got tattoos, but she's like, not the one who has to look at them." Kara covered her mouth. "Oh, that's awful, isn't it?"

Bailey shook her head. "You should do what makes you happy. It doesn't matter what anyone else thinks of them."

"Ladies! Dinner is ready!" Brody's voice carried up the stairs and down the hall. He could be crazy loud when he wanted to be.

"Come on! My daddy's sauce is like, to die for. I hope he made garlic bread too!" Kara giggled as they made their way out of the room.

• • • • • • •

Kara took a huge forkful of pasta into her mouth so she didn't say anything else stupid. She had a hard time concentrating with Bailey at the table since she didn't normally eat meals in her younger mindset. It seemed silly, and maybe something she should explore more, but her terrible relationship with food made it hard. She made a mental note to mention the problem to Brody. If she purposefully went younger before a meal, maybe she could retrain her brain to approach food with a whole different outlook.

Suddenly, she realized two sets of eyes were on her and she dropped her fork. "What?" She snapped before she could stop herself.

"Your friend asked what sort of snacks there were for tonight. Twice. You were miles away…" Brody stated plainly. There was no anger in his voice, but his face made it clear that he didn't appreciate her not paying attention to her company.

"Oh." Kara felt a wave of heat flood her cheeks. "Geesh, I'm sorry. I was just thinking about something, and I didn't hear you. We've got movie theater style popcorn with extra butter."

Bailey had finished her spaghetti and took a piece of garlic bread. She buttered it generously and took a bite. "That's cool. I like butter." She smiled as Kara raised her eyebrows. "I mean popcorn!"

Kara giggled, easily tugged back to her younger self, and grinned. "Seriously, it's all about the butter." She stood then to clean her plate even though she hadn't eaten much. She'd just had a lot going on in her head. If Brody noticed, which he probably did since that man noticed everything, he

didn't call her on it.

"You can leave it, Kara. I'll clean up from dinner." Brody stood and took the dish. He planted a quick kiss to the side of her head. "Go have fun."

"You ready?" Kara asked after politely waiting for Bailey to finish her bread. Her friend nodded and stood as well. "Okay, let's go." She led them back up the stairs and into her room. "Do you want to get your pj's on now?"

"Yeah, but can I ask you something really quick?" Bailey sank down to the floor and rolled out her sleeping bag. "I mean, if you'll answer."

"Sure, you can ask me anything." Kara agreed, then helped her fix the bag. "What's up?"

"What was with you at dinner? Are you upset I'm here?"

"Oh! No, not at all." Kara bit her lip, now feeling awful about drifting off during dinner. "It's just, I'm not used to being around anyone when I'm... you know... it's hard sometimes."

"It's only hard if you fight it. So Ian and I talked about it in the beginning, about the rules, I guess. Who initiates, what happens, or if one of us just isn't in the mood, and when we really need to be adults."

Her reply snapped her right out of her teen mood and she was suddenly grown-up Kara. "Do you think we could talk about that a minute? I've never had anyone else I could talk to about it."

Bailey nodded, encouraging her to continue.

"I usually have a set day, or time, or you know, Brody might suggest it if I'm having a really hard day. So, who starts it at your house?"

"I usually initiate the little stuff. It's visual. I'll change my clothes or wear my hair differently. Those are simple things Ian can see, and he knows how to act. But more than that, it tells me who I am. It tells me how to act. The physical reminder is for both of us." Bailey reached for her bags, rummaged through them, and brought out her pajamas. "See? These are really soft, but they have little hearts and flowers all over them. It's an instant thing for me."

"Oh!" Kara had an 'aha' moment. "Like when I get all my punky stuff on? You know when we met at the park, and I had my tutu and leggings and all?"

"Yes! Exactly. When you get dressed, you're thinking about how you're going to feel when you're wearing each piece. So, if you went to school tomorrow, would you put on your Hello-kitty sweatshirt?"

Kara contemplated it for a moment. Hello-kitty was back in a big way, but not really appropriate in an adult setting. "Not so much. You're right, I would choose a fleece or a hoodie that was a bright color or something, but not that one."

"See? So, you get it." Bailey stood up as if to get ready for bed, and Kara jumped to her feet.

"Wait, before we watch movies and all, can I ask you something personal?"

Bailey bit her lip, as if unsure where this conversation was about to go, but she nodded.

"Does Ian spank you?"

"Yeah, when I get punished, but sometimes when we role-play too. It all depends on where I'm at in my head." Bailey looked like she either wanted to share more, or she wanted to get on with their night. But Kara really wanted to know more. She rarely opened up to anybody about the sort of relationship she and Brody had. Especially the spanking!

"Do you like it?" Her voice came out in a hush and she was sure her face was red.

"I like it… most of the time." Bailey shrugged. "I like the spanking, the heat, and pain. The pain is exciting when we use it as foreplay."

She squeezed her eyes shut and Kara fretted. Was she getting too personal?

"But I don't like them when I've done something wrong."

"Have you ever done something wrong on purpose, just so you get the spankings?" Kara plowed on instead of letting her friend answer. "Because I've done that. And it's not right, but in the beginning when we had just started this, and I didn't know if, you know, Brody was going to follow through—"

"Hey!" Bailey interrupted her. "Just take a breath and start over. You don't have to be embarrassed around me. We're friends."

Kara beamed, her whole face lighting up at Bailey's words. "Yeah, it's just I'm not used to that either. I have friends at school, but they don't get me. So, my question was about acting up on purpose. I did that a lot before I realized that Brody would follow through."

"I never thought of that, so I don't really know. I hate it when he has to punish me, but the spankings are amazing."

"Does Ian like spanking you?" Kara fiddled with her hands. He seemed like such a nice guy that it was hard to imagine him spanking Bailey at all. She supposed the same could be thought of Brody, though. The idea of Brody giving her a good girl spanking instantly made her aroused, and she almost didn't catch Bailey's answer.

"Oh, yeah. It's the control he likes… well, that's part of it." Bailey cocked her head to the side and grinned wickedly. "He really gets off on that. We both do. But by that time, we're out of role-playing, and it's all as adults."

"Do you think Ian could talk to Brody? I mean, about all this stuff?"

"I can ask him…" Bailey shrugged. "I don't know how he'll feel about the topic, but I'll talk to him. But not until his work has settled down. He's under a lot of pressure right now."

"Yeah, sure thing. Thanks." Kara grinned as she rummaged through a small dresser. "So, let's get on our pj's and watch movies!"

Bailey grinned back. "Then we can stay up like, all night!"

• • • • • • •

Kara curled up on her side and aimlessly threw popcorn into her mouth. She must have already eaten a whole bag at least! Plus, the huge bowl they were sharing was still half full. They had spent the rest of the night watching a bunch of movies and drinking soda. Brody had come in about an hour or so ago and told her good-night. She had kissed him on his cheek and happily hugged him. She was so excited to have Bailey over and couldn't wait to tell him all about it!

It was well past midnight now and Kara was going back and forth between her teen self and her normal everyday self. She was craving a cigarette like something wicked, so she got up and fished her pack out its hiding spot. As she found her lighter and ashtray and brought them to the floor, Bailey's eyes went wide.

"What is that? Do you smoke?"

"Uh, sometimes… I mean, not a lot. Come on, have one with me." Kara held out the pack.

Bailey raised an eyebrow and looked over the warning on the side of the package.

"My daddy is asleep, he won't even know."

"Fine!" Bailey took one and Kara quickly lit it for her. They popped in the next movie and had several cigarettes each while it played. "You don't have beer too, do you?"

Kara laughed so hard she snorted. "No! Beer is gross!" Her ridiculous statement on top of already feeling giddy made the two of them laugh very loud—so loud that the door swung open to reveal a tired looking Brody.

"You two need to keep it down. Some of us need to go to work…" He trailed off and looked at something on the ground.

Oh shit! The ashtray! It was almost full of cigarette butts, and if the two of them were supposed to be teenagers, it was against the rules.

"What the hell have you been doing?" He glared down at Kara.

Kara swallowed hard and glanced over at Bailey. She didn't know what to say. "I'm sorry, daddy. I wasn't going to have one, but Bailey wanted to try."

He picked up the ashtray, shook his head, and let out a long breath. "If it wasn't the middle of the night, I'd take you home, Bailey. You're both in trouble. Go to sleep. Now. Movie and lights off."

The two of them nodded without another word. He seemed really upset, but what was worse, she had placed the blame on her friend. She hoped Bailey wouldn't be too mad.

Kara turned off the DVD as Bailey got up to shut out the lights. They crawled into their sleeping bags at the same time, but neither of them laughed.

"Why did you do that? He's really pissed," Bailey huffed under her breath.

"I mean, really mad. Like a real daddy."

"He hates that I smoke. I thought if you were here, maybe he wouldn't be so mad at me." Kara fiddled with the edge of the pillow. She'd really messed up.

"Well, that didn't work out so great."

"I'm sorry. I'll explain it to him in the morning."

"Yeah, well, that won't get me out of trouble," Bailey retorted.

Kara wanted to apologize more and assure her friend she would sort it out. But her eyes felt heavy and in moments she drifted off into a dreamless sleep.

CHAPTER EIGHT

Kara cleaned up the room from last night by herself. She felt crappy for lying to Brody about the cigarettes and promised herself she would find a way to make it up to Bailey. She begged Brody to make pancakes, her favorite, and she hoped it would sweeten the apology she'd give Bailey.

She got down on the floor and shook Bailey's shoulder lightly. "Bailey, wake up." Kara shook her shoulder again. "Hey, come on, wake up!"

"What time is it?" Bailey sat up, resting on her elbows. "I want to go home."

"It's just after eight. Brody has breakfast. Please don't be mad. It was a joke, and I'll explain it all later. I just didn't want to get in trouble last night. I really am sorry." Kara got to her feet. "I put your movies and stuff back in your bags and set them near the door. Just come downstairs when you're ready."

Bailey snorted a laugh but it held no amusement. "Funny joke." She struggled to get out of her sleeping bag, as if she wasn't used to it, and stood up. "It wasn't funny."

"Okay, you've made your point." Kara didn't know what else to say. She knew they were still in a younger type of head space, but seriously, it wasn't like Bailey would actually get into trouble. "I'll see you in a few."

She left her friend, or someone she hoped would still be her friend after all this, and went down into the kitchen. She loved watching Brody cook, and one of his specialties was pancakes. He could flip one like nobody's business. Kara forced a smile but didn't say a word as she sat down at the table.

"Are you okay, honey?" Brody set two short stacks of pancakes in front of her.

She moved one towards where Bailey would sit, then nodded. She adored the table! It was wonderfully prepared with options of butter, real maple syrup, honey, blueberries, and raspberries. When had he found the time to do all this?

Bailey entered a few minutes later and sat next to Kara.

"Morning, Bailey. Want some orange juice?" Brody asked her as she tugged the stack of food towards her.

"Yes, sure," Bailey mumbled but didn't meet his eyes. Geesh, she was really upset with her!

Brody moved to get them each a glass of orange juice but as he reached for the freezer door, Bailey shook her head back and forth, vehemently. Kara, unsure of what had come over her friend but wanting to please her, followed suit.

Brody looked back and forth between them and raised his eyebrows. "What?"

"Ice is bad for you," Bailey stated simply, then nudged Kara with her elbow.

"It's the worst form of water," Kara agreed quickly.

"What?" Brody sighed. "What's gotten into you two?"

"When liquid freezes it loses all of its nutritional value." Bailey had a firm confidence in her voice that made her sound knowledgeable.

"And frozen things are bad for your teeth!" Kara decided to keep the game going, though she had no idea what it was about.

"Ladies, I don't know why I'm getting a science lesson this early, but I'd like some ice." Brody opened the freezer, grabbed one of the trays, and took out two cubes. He dropped them into his glass then opened the door again.

Kara watched as Bailey's hands clenched and opened several times as she bit her lip. What on earth had come over her friend?

"Bailey?" She turned towards her to ask what was going on when Brody cursed under his breath.

"Bailey?" He set an object down on the table in front of them. "Do you care to explain this? I highly doubt Kara froze her own bra."

Kara felt her jaw drop. The brilliant teal-colored satin and lace bra with matching panties—her favorite set—that Brody had gotten her for their anniversary came into view. When had Bailey managed to take them, sneak downstairs, and pop them in the freezer? To make it worse, she saw terrible brown colored stains on the lingerie from where it had been wrapped around her crushed cigarette pack.

"It's just a joke." Bailey shifted uncomfortably as Brody kept his eyes on her. "It was much funnier last night."

"I'll go thaw it out." Kara stood and retrieved the item in question. "Be right back." She did it in a nonchalant way, even though she wanted to slap Bailey for ruining her special lingerie.

She took her time pining up the frozen straps and panties via clothespin on the small drying line in the laundry room just off to the side of the kitchen. Kara would have to wait until the ice melted to attempt to do serious stain removal. She wasn't really angry at Bailey for getting her back, but she also didn't want either of them in trouble.

She flounced back into the kitchen. Bailey was clearing the breakfast dishes, rinsing them, and loading them into the dishwasher. Kara shot a questioning look at Brody.

"After she finishes the dishes, you're going to walk your friend home, and you've got a task. I want you to make sure Bailey tells her daddy that instead of sleeping, she decided to go on a little midnight adventure. I'm sure she already has a lot to tell him with the tobacco incident as well." He finished his glass of juice, then set it in the sink.

Bailey quickly picked up the dirty glass, washed it, then set it on the top rack. "So, you're not going to tell my daddy?" She returned her attention to Brody as Kara looked on.

"No, you're going to tell him yourself using your own words." Brody reached forward to rest his hand on Bailey's shoulder. "There's something I want to share with you. You're the first person in a long time to make my Kara giggle like that. So I hope you two can work through this. I know you were just being funny, but sometimes you can hurt someone's feelings that way."

"I know. I won't do it again." Bailey nodded several times. "I'm very sorry."

"I believe you." Brody smiled, then moved away to Kara. "Go walk your friend home."

"I think Bailey was just being silly and I really want her to come back." Kara threw her arms around Brody, hugging him tight. "So can't you let this one go?"

"Sweetheart, there is a lesson in all of this. I will call her daddy, whose number is right in my phone, later on today. If I find out you two tried to keep a secret, then you will be punished. Is that clear?" Brody tapped the top of her nose. "Kara?"

"Yes, daddy, it's clear," she mumbled, feeling like it wasn't entirely fair. It was just a stupid prank and now Bailey would probably get spanked!

Kara found their jackets and handed Bailey hers.

"I've got a project to work on so if you want to stay a little while at Bailey's, you can." Brody waved to the two. "I hope to see you again soon, Bailey."

"Thank you for letting me stay." Bailey accepted the jacket and put it on.

"Bye!" Kara shrugged her hoodie on, then led them out the side door.

As they made their way to the road, she noticed Bailey was dawdling. She linked her arm through Bailey's and poked at her. "Is your daddy going to be mad?"

"I guess we're about to find out." Bailey yanked her arm away. Of course she was mad, especially since it had all been Kara's idea.

"Look, that was a really shitty thing to do…"

"And what you did wasn't?" Bailey spat the words out, surprising Kara

with the tone. "Listen, all role playing aside, it was a really childish thing to do."

"But you put my underwear in the freezer! Isn't that childish too?"

They stopped and stared at each other for almost a full minute before dissolving into laughter. Bailey nodded in agreement. "Yeah, it was. And as far as the tobacco stains, I hope they come out."

"So do I. Or you can buy me a new set." Kara stopped laughing as she looked up to see the kitchen light on. She glanced over at Bailey, who sucked in a breath as Ian moved past the window.

"Maybe," Bailey sighed. "But then you owe me a cheesecake. A real one. That is my most favorite dessert. You so owe me for last night."

"Deal," Kara replied as they walked across the small street and onto the front lawn. She followed Bailey up to the house, though she really wasn't sure what to do. Was she really going to listen to her friend tell on herself?

Bailey unlocked the door and stepped inside. She suddenly sucked in a breath and turned back to Kara. "You know what? You should just go home."

"Yeah, well, I can't. Brody said I have to make sure you tell your daddy or we're both in even more trouble." Kara shuffled her feet, now more uncomfortable than before.

"Trouble that you started! If you didn't give me those stupid cigarettes to smoke—"

"What's going on?" Ian, fresh out of the shower and in nothing but gray sweats, appeared at the top of the stairs. "Why are you back so soon? Did something happen?" He proceeded to come down the stairs, then pulled Bailey in for a hug.

"Yeah, something did." Kara leaned against the door. She didn't want to tattle, but the tension grew as he studied her.

"All right. Come tell me about it." Ian motioned for them to follow him into the kitchen.

This couldn't be good. She just wanted Bailey to tell him what happened so she could be on her way. Of course, Bailey had taken all the blame for something that she had thought up. Why had it been such a big deal anyway? They were both adults!

"We smoked cigarettes," Bailey blurted.

Ian's eyebrows shot up, and he blinked at her. The corner of his lip twitched, as if something amused him, but he kept quiet.

"And then I put Kara's bra and panties in the freezer."

He cleared his throat, turning away from Kara to set his coffee cup in the sink.

"So, Bailey, do you think that was a nice thing to do to Kara? She invited you over to her house. Fed you dinner, then breakfast." He gave her a sidelong glance from the sink.

Oh! Kara knew that look. He was not happy with her antics. Should she mention that most of it was her fault? *Ugh! Should I say something?*

"Well, no... but she lied. She said it was my idea, but it was hers. They were her cigarettes."

Kara opened her mouth to reply, but Ian hit her with a look as well. She immediately shut it and shrugged at Bailey.

"Right. But are you supposed to smoke cigarettes? Is that something you think is a good idea?" He turned around, folded his arms, and leaned against the sink.

"Well... no. But that's not the point." Bailey bit her lip as she stared at her daddy. The man had a point. Kara hadn't twisted her arm to smoke!

"I think it is the point. It's my point. You did something you know you're not supposed to do. You did something wrong. And you know what that means." Ian titled his head to the side. "Don't you?"

"But that's not fair. She..." Bailey sputtered and pointed in her direction. "She went and got them."

"I did! Bailey is telling the truth!" Kara took a step towards Ian, as if to explain, but he narrowed his eyes and they darkened when they met hers.

"Do I have to put you in the corner so I can properly adjust Bailey's attitude without your mouth running?" Ian spoke with authority and it made a ripple run up her spine.

Kara shook her head several times.

"Go back to where you were standing. Now. And no more talking."

"I'm... I'm sorry." Kara retreated to the edge of the kitchen and shut her mouth. Damn, his tone had taken on a serious threat. Just like a real daddy would be acting after such a stunt, she imagined.

"Bailey, you inhaled that cigarette. No one made you do that. You did it all on your own." Ian returned his attention to the trembling woman standing a few feet from him.

"Fine. When Kara's gone..."

A small, slightly evil-looking smile appeared on Ian's mouth. "Come here." He pulled out a kitchen chair, brought it to the center of the room, and sat down.

What he did next made Kara shudder. It was a very simple gesture, but it held a ton of meaning. He patted his knee.

Bailey threw a worried glance in her direction, then quickly focused back on Ian. "But... now?"

"Now."

"Wait!" Kara yelled from her tiny space across the floor. "I really should go home! I shouldn't—"

"If you distract me again from the matter at hand, you'll be next."

Kara's stomach dropped to her feet at his warning. *Holy hell.* Her palms were sweaty now as she took in the overall picture. Was he serious? She didn't

want to push him to find out. No, she was in enough trouble already. Kara mocked a zipper across her lips, locked it, and pretended to throw a key over her shoulder.

"Good. I'm glad you believe me." Ian held out his hand to Bailey, who had knelt down at his feet, and he settled her across his lap.

Kara prayed he left her pants on! She knew her friend didn't need all of her bits on display!

The first smack landed hard across Bailey's behind and surprised both women. Kara jumped, very much in awe that he'd decided to do this in front of her, while Bailey twitched from the impact. Ian laid several more slaps across each of her cheeks while her legs kicked. She clearly was not enjoying this. As several agonizing minutes went by, his hand smacked across every inch of her bottom.

Kara stood in rapt attention as Ian rubbed each cheek in turn, then tugged Bailey to her feet. He stood up and returned the chair to the table.

She couldn't believe she had just watched him so thoroughly spank Bailey. She tried to imagine what it would feel like for someone to watch her get punished. What if Brody had spanked her like that in front of Bailey? She opened and closed her mouth a few times, as if wanting to offer another apology or something, but nothing came out.

Bailey crossed her arms over her chest and refused to meet Kara's eyes. "I really want you to go home now."

Kara nodded but her feet stayed planted to the floor. Finally, as if seeing her problem, Ian approached and took her arm. He firmly but gently guided her to the front door. "Bailey is grounded for the next two weeks and I'll be sure to tell your daddy that." He twisted open the knob and she stepped out onto the small landing.

"I didn't mean for Bailey to get into trouble. I really didn't." Kara bit her lip hard. She had so many emotions rushing through her, but none of them were from a childlike mindset.

"Then make sure you don't do it again. Get home safe, Kara. Thank you for inviting Bailey over." With that, Ian closed the door and she heard it lock behind her.

Damn! She needed to get home to Brody right away. Kara skipped down the steps as fast as her feet would go and rushed home. She wished she had taken the car instead of lollygagging along with Bailey, but it didn't matter since she had only a few blocks to go.

Kara walked back in a tizzy. She had been upset to know that Bailey was about to be punished, but then to witness it! She didn't like to see her friend in trouble, but she had become so aroused at how Ian had handled the situation. He took control, much like Brody did, but there was an added element that had her head spinning. She had wanted to slide her hand down the front of her pants and pleasure herself as the punishment had continued.

I'm awful to feel this way!

She finally reached her own front door and went inside. Brody had told her on more than one occasion that if she wanted or needed sexy adult time, all she had to do was ask. But she was not in an asking sort of mood. She needed him right now!

Kara pulled her sweatshirt off, followed by her leggings and boots and the rest of her outfit until she was left with just her sparkly black and pink bra and panties. She moved through the house, room to room, searching for Brody.

She finally heard him coming out of the bedroom and she practically threw herself at him. She sank to her knees and all but assaulted his zipper.

"Kara—"

"Sexy time," she managed to mumble before taking his cock in her hand and licking around the head. "Bailey did what you said. No more teen." Kara took him into her mouth and he grew hard as she sucked.

Brody tangled his hand in her hair. "Okay..." he trailed off as she increased her speed and bobbed up and down. "Oh, baby..."

She continued to work her mouth on him, then sneakily began to pump along his shaft with her hand. He groaned as she hummed, and she felt the corners of her mouth turn up. She loved giving him head more than anything else, and his pleasure made her so happy.

"Oh, God... you feel so good. Let me make you feel good too." Brody tugged on her hair until she looked up. "Come on."

Kara let his cock escape her lips but pouted her displeasure at the sudden ending. It was short-lived though as he pulled her to her feet and nearly carried her to the bedroom, the promise of amazing sex on the horizon. But a thought hit her as they got closer to the room, and she felt the need to tell him what happened.

"I watched Bailey get punished. It shouldn't have... I mean... I have to confess..."

Brody waggled his eyebrows at her. "Watching your friend get disciplined got you all horny?" They went inside and he sat them on the edge of the bed. "Really?"

She felt a wave of heat come over her and shut her eyes. She was mortified at her reaction—but even more at his surprise. Kara felt him tug her panties down. She arched her hips up as he slid two fingers inside her.

"Oh my..." Brody moved them out and in again. "You're dripping, baby."

"I mean, I didn't like... like it..." Kara moaned as he found her g-spot and tickled it. "I'm an awful friend!"

"No, you're not." Brody kissed her hard and she opened her eyes to see his expression. "I think you wanted to be in that position. I think you wondered what it would be like for someone to watch you get spanked. To

know that your intimate parts were all on display like that."

She nodded, truly embarrassed now. "Well, he left her pants on."

"Hmm? Well, I can't say for sure that I would do the same."

"Ah, oh…" Kara arched up as his fingers strummed against her. "Right. So, yes… I pretended in my head that I was getting punished too."

Brody withdrew his fingers and flipped her onto her back. She jumped as his hand took both of her ankles and raised her legs up. He landed two sharp smacks to each side of her ass. Then another set, then another, and she bucked as the intensity ramped up.

"Ouch! Ouch!" This position hurt the worst since her sit-spots and thighs were so accessible.

"You pretended Ian was punishing you while she watched?" Brody rubbed along each thigh then smacked his hand on each cheek.

"Ouch! Let me think!" Kara didn't know how to answer that. She had pretended she was in Bailey's position, but it had nothing to do with Ian. She'd just admired the way he'd handled everything.

He was so calm about it! When he admonished Bailey and disciplined her she could see how much love bloomed between them. He was certainly easy on the eyes too, but it wasn't like she was crushing on him. She just couldn't help what she felt.

"Hmmm?" Two more sets, more intense and faster than the previous ones, met each side of her bottom. "You were trying to let your friend get off the hook before and it made you feel a little guilty, didn't it?"

"Yes," she managed to reply through the steady stream of blows on each cheek. The spanking had started out in a playful way, but now it held the hint of a punishment. "Ow! Sort of."

Punishment for the pang of guilt that had shot through her when Brody had made his decree about making sure Bailey told her daddy exactly what happened. Yes, it had been a silly prank, but they both had rules last night, and neither woman had listened. "I should be punished too."

His hand stopped immediately and moved up to her shoulders. "Why? What do you think you did wrong?"

"She froze my bra! It's not like she punched me in the face or something. Why would you make her tell her daddy about something so stupid? I didn't do anything wrong other than do what you told me to!" Kara bit her lip hard after the words flew from her mouth.

There were so many emotions jumbled up inside that she couldn't properly express them. But when she heard the sharp intake of breath over her shoulder, she immediately knew there would be consequences for her outburst. It wasn't that she had to agree with Brody, but she had just challenged him in regards to how he had handled things this morning.

Shit.

Her line of vision changed quickly as Brody spun her around and sat her

on his knee. He took her chin in his hand and tilted it upwards.

"Before we go any further here, we need to clear the blurred lines. You begged for sexy adult time, but your attitude screams for an adjustment. I'm happy to push the reset button, but I need to know where you're at in your head."

"I'm not feeling very adult anymore," Kara confessed. She didn't want to interrupt their sexy romp for his correction, but she knew they needed to move past the recent events. "And I have something to tell you."

"Okay. Go find your clothes, put them back on, and go wait for me in your room." He didn't look happy to stop their fun, and she didn't blame him, but Kara knew honesty trumped all.

"I'm going." Kara leaned over to kiss his cheek, then slid off his lap. She padded out of the room, stopping only to pick up a tank top before going out into the hall.

· · · · · · ·

Brody shook his head. The events from last night and this morning pressed heavily on his mind and he wondered if letting the other woman come over had been a good thing. He shook his head again and tried to sort it out.

Of course, he didn't really know what sleepovers were like. His younger sister had always been too busy watching over the three youngest siblings and she'd never had friends over.

It had been one part of Kara's story that always tore at his heart strings. She, like his sister, had constantly had to supervise the younger ones and never really got to experience the joy of growing up. All of her time was spent being a mom to her siblings. It wasn't fair to have that sort of experience held back.

After a few minutes, he went into the room Kara retreated to whenever life got too overwhelming. It was a beautiful space for her to be herself.

Right now, he needed to find out what was going on. He walked in to find her perched on the bed with her arms crossed over her chest. She didn't look like she was in the mood for a punishment at all.

Brody ran his hand down over his face. "Kara—"

"I lied to you last night. So, what are you going to do about it?"

Brody swallowed hard. He honestly couldn't believe the words she'd just spoken. *What the hell had she lied about?*

He brushed off her tone, stepped to the bed, sat, and yanked her over his knees. He smacked her bottom several times on top of her flimsy yoga pants, then tugged them off. He repeated the movement, this time targeting her sit-spots, then pushed her panties down towards her knees. The spanks were harder than usual, and she screeched like a banshee, but to her credit she

didn't kick.

Brody moved his hand back to her cheeks, bringing each stinging blow down with gusto.

"I'm sorry! I'm sorry, daddy!" Kara began wailing now as the intensity grew, and she finally beat her fists into the pillow in front of her. She grabbed it tightly, and her knuckles were white as she clenched them around it. "Please!"

Brody shifted his focus to her upper thighs, but slowed down the pace. "What did you lie about?"

He paused to knead the tender skin at the juncture of her thighs and bottom. One more round in that area would leave more than a lasting impression. It would remind her of her misbehavior whenever she sat for the next few hours.

"I wanted a cigarette and I talked Bailey into smoking. She didn't really want one! I'm so sorry! Her daddy was really disappointed in her."

Brody let out a long breath. "Is that why you didn't want to tell her daddy about the frozen clothing?"

Kara sniffled a few times, then nodded. "Yes. I should have fessed up, but I didn't want you to be mad at me."

"So, do you think Bailey got punished for no reason?"

"Well, no…" Kara managed to reply before he brought his palm down on the already sensitive skin just under the curve of her bottom. "Ow! Oh! It hurts there!"

"We're not done yet."

Brody decided to move the spanks back up to her blushing cheeks. They were only rosy, rather than the deep pink a paddle would have made them. His hand fell into a steady rhythm as it danced across her skin and left a handprint in several spots. Kara sobbed openly as all the fight drained and she lay limply across his knees. She let go of the pillow and laced her fingers in his free hand.

"I'm really sorry."

Brody pulled her pants and panties up, then situated her on his lap so he could pull her against his chest. "Despite you placing the blame on her, Bailey made the choices she did. She didn't have to have a cigarette and she didn't have to ruin your pretty lingerie."

"I know. I hope I can find a way to get out those stains." Kara curled herself closer to him. "I won't lie to you again. I should have accepted responsibility for what I did. I won't blame someone else either."

"Good." Brody slid her off his lap. "Stay here until dinner. I'll call you, and then it's an early bedtime for you. For the next two weeks you're grounded. I hope your sudden free time gives you plenty to think about, young lady."

"Yes, daddy," Kara pouted. "I'll listen this time."

Brody patted her head and kissed her cheek. "You better."

Then he left her alone in her room to sort out her thoughts. He'd never grounded her before this, though he supposed there hadn't been a reason up until now. Lying and having her friend take the blame was serious. He only hoped she would understand as much.

· · · · · · ·

Kara bit her lip as Brody strode into the kitchen. She'd woken up early since he set an early bedtime for her last night, and she'd been cleaning like a crazy person this morning. The hall, living room, dining room, small bathroom, and stairs almost shined from her hard work. She normally handled the cleaning since Brody's hours varied so much, but she really outdid herself today.

He raised an eyebrow as he met her at the counter. She had just set the coffee machine to brew, but his presence in the room distracted her from the coffee.

"You've really outdone yourself. The house looks amazing!" Brody kissed the side of her head, then planted another kiss on her lips. "Maybe I should send you to bed earlier a few times a week."

"I'd rather you not. I just wanted to say sorry again. I shouldn't have lied to you. I also got my friend in trouble, and I really didn't mean to."

"I accept your apology, Kara. Find a way to make it up to Bailey. I'm sure she will understand when you explain yourself."

"Yeah, I hope so." Kara's mind drifted back to their sleepover. What could she do to make it up to her?

CHAPTER NINE

It was four days after Bailey and she had their sleepover, and Kara still couldn't believe Brody had grounded her! Now she had to wait until he left for work to survey the fridge.

Thank goodness she had the right ingredients to make Bailey one of her amazing cheesecakes! She had bought raspberries earlier in the week and had the perfect sauce recipe to use them in for the topping.

Kara ransacked the cabinets and freezer and found some expensive white chocolate. *Oooh!* She could sliver that into shavings to sprinkle on top of the fruit.

She tied a pretty apron around her waist and turned up her iPad so she could listen to music as she baked. The cake itself didn't need to bake but the crust did, so she popped it in to firm it up. Kara bobbed around the kitchen, happily thinking loving thoughts so when Bailey ate the dessert she would feel them. It was true about adding love to your recipes. It made everything taste better.

Kara brushed a piece of hair out of her face and texted her friend.

Hey! You home?

Thirty seconds or so passed and a message came back.

Is this a trick question?

She giggled.

I have to bring you something!

Two minutes passed while Kara glared at the screen, waiting.

Like a get-out of jail free card?

Was Bailey mad at her? *She should be,* her brain reminded her. She had blamed their sleepover antics solely on her friend when they were both responsible, which was why Kara was now grounded too.

Brody is at work. Be over soon.

Bailey wrote back immediately.

Don't get in trouble!

Kara rolled her eyes. No one was home, so it didn't matter.

The oven beeped and she quickly opened it. She carefully pulled out the pie plate and set it on the counter on top of a pot holder. It cooled down as she cleaned up the kitchen and then scooped the cream cheese mixture into the bottom of the plate and spread it all out evenly. Next she carefully spooned the sauce with the berries on top. It looked so yummy!

She set the masterpiece in the fridge and went to change into her punky clothes. Brody had taken her car keys so she would be walking over to Bailey's house.

• • • • • • •

Kara studied her outfit in the mirror one last time, then headed back downstairs. She glanced at her cell phone and confirmed that Brody was still several hours from coming home. It would be plenty of time for her to run the dessert over and get back. She put the finishing touches on the cake, carefully wrapped it in Saran wrap, and headed out with a huge smile on her face.

Her smile faded as she got halfway between the houses. She had completely forgotten to lock the door! She contemplated going back to lock up but decided against it. It was a gated community after all, so hopefully no one would notice.

Kara nearly skipped up to the door and knocked. Bailey would have to forgive her now!

After a minute without an answer, she pulled out her cell phone. It would be impossible to text one handed, though, so she turned around and cradled it against her cheek to try to text talk. That would work.

Suddenly, the door opened behind her and she spun around.

"Oh! I was just about to text you!" Kara thrust the pie towards Bailey, but it wasn't her friend. She swallowed hard as Ian raised an eyebrow.

"You were about to text me?" Ian stood there with his arms crossed over his chest.

"No… I… what I mean…" Kara fumbled for words. "I felt really bad about Bailey getting punished because it was all my idea. I made her favorite dessert. It took me all day!"

"Did you get permission to come here?" Ian's mouth turned up at the edge in a surprised smile. "I thought you were grounded."

Kara pouted. She didn't know what else to do. Of course Brody had talked to him. They'd gone out the other night and had done whatever manly adult men did. She felt her lower lip tremble and she suddenly made the decision to lie. Maybe he'd just assumed she was grounded and hadn't actually talked to Brody.

"Of course I got permission." Kara gave him her best smile. "I baked Bailey a cheesecake. It's got raspberries and white chocolate on top!" Her cell phone rang, still clutched awkwardly in the crook of her neck. From the ring tone playing she immediately knew it was Brody.

Shit. I'm about to be in a lot of trouble…

Ian's smile widened. "I'll get that for you."

His eyes didn't look amused as he tugged it away from her, and before she could protest had clicked 'answer'.

"Kara's phone? Yes… uh-huh… really? Well, why don't I put you on speaker?"

Kara felt sweat pool around her armpits and trickle down. She was really, really in for it now. She didn't say anything as Ian clicked the speaker button.

"Go ahead and say that last part again." Ian cocked his head to the side as he studied Kara.

"I came home early to surprise Kara but I didn't find her at home. In fact, not only is she not here, but the door was unlocked. Anyone could have just waltzed in and taken whatever he wanted." Brody's irritated tone filtered through her phone. "I texted her without an answer, so I called thinking she was busy, but the last thing I expected was someone else to answer."

"I'm sorry, daddy!" Kara finally began to cry. "I felt terrible about what happened with Bailey and—"

"Kara, I don't really want to hear it right now," Brody firmly stated, then cleared his throat. "Hey, Ian, keep her there, will you? I'll come get her in about five."

"Sure thing. Not a problem." Ian took the pie plate from Kara, then stepped back to allow her to go inside. "See you in a few." He clicked 'end' and handed the phone back.

Kara took the phone but didn't go through the front door. She really just wanted to go back home so she resigned herself to taking very tiny baby steps. Maybe if she barely moved by the time she actually got all the way into the house, her daddy would be there and she wouldn't have to face Bailey's daddy alone.

"Go sit in the kitchen. Hurry up. I don't like being lied to, and when your

daddy hears about that on top of what you did, I'm sure it will be very hard for you to sit down for quite a while."

Kara nodded as she hurried to the kitchen. Bailey sat at the table and was reading while drinking something out of a mug, and she raised her eyebrows when Kara strolled in.

"I told you not to get in trouble!" Bailey shot a look at Ian. "I didn't tell her to come over!"

"No, wait, I didn't say you did. I felt really terrible about blaming you at our sleepover. So, I, uh, made you a cheesecake." Kara sank down into the chair next to her. "I lied to your daddy and mine, so I'm in a lot of trouble."

Ian set the dessert down in front of Bailey. "Next time make sure you ask for permission. It's easier than asking for forgiveness, not the other way around."

A loud knock sounded on the front door and he went to answer it.

"This looks delicious. And I do forgive you," Bailey whispered into her ear. "But please, don't get in more trouble. Just be good so you can come over for real."

Kara sighed. "I'm really sorry."

Ian returned to the kitchen with Brody tailing him.

Brody took her chin in his hand and tilted it upwards to catch her eyes in his stern gaze. "I thought something terrible happened to you. I was ready to call security because surely you couldn't have done something so irresponsible..."

"Well, I did. So can we just go now? I'm sure as hell not welcome back here anytime soon." Kara not only interrupted him, but she shook off his hand and stood up. She was embarrassed to be scolded in front of her friend and just wanted to get out her house.

"If Bailey spoke to me like that after already being in hot water, she'd be sent to the corner for five minutes," Ian spoke up, though Bailey shook her head. "Do you have something to add?" he asked Bailey sternly, and she dropped her head down and looked at her book.

"Hmm? Do you have any corners around here?" Brody tapped his chin, then shifted slightly to look at Ian. "I mean, I hear they are the latest fad."

"You are in luck, my friend!" Ian grinned. "I happen to have four of them in this room alone."

Brody took Kara's hand firmly in his and led her over to the corner nearest the kitchen sink. "I think this one is quite lovely. Kara, turn around, please."

She did so, hesitantly, and glared over her shoulder. It earned her four well placed smacks against her bottom and drained all her fight. Now she was beyond mortified.

"I've got a paddle upstairs if you need one." Ian had a hint of amusement in his tone, but there was a serious note there as well. She didn't want to push

either one of them.

In fact, Kara didn't appreciate their tones at all. They actually sounded like real daddies, and it confused her for a minute. She thought it would make her mad to have them playfully talking about her being punished in front of everyone, but it didn't.

It was that they both cared enough to correct her behavior. That was something she wasn't used to, and that thought alone made the floodgates open up. She hung her head and cried, no longer ashamed to let it out.

After a few minutes, Brody came over and placed his hands on her shoulders. "Come on, honey. Let's go home and we can talk about it."

Kara wiped at her eyes and shuffled out of the corner. "I'm sorry I lied to you." She raised her head to catch Ian's gaze, then glanced to Bailey. "And I'm really sorry I came over without asking. I hope you like the cake."

Bailey stood up and made her way over. She reached for Kara and hugged her quickly. "I really do forgive you, and I'm sure it will be awesome."

Brody guided her to the door. "Thanks for letting Kara borrow the corner. I should get some of those installed."

"No problem. Once these two get their privileges back, Kara is welcome to come over." Ian shot a look to Kara, who still had tears falling down her cheeks. "But not before then."

Kara nodded. "I promise." She looped her arms around Brody and the two of them went outside. She would be in for a heck of a punishment once they got home, but for now she was just happy to see him. He really loved her. Even with her crazy antics.

• • • • • • •

Brody pulled the car into the garage and shut it off. He hadn't said a word to Kara, and though he hated to let the tension build this way, she needed to understand how scared he'd been.

Earlier, when he'd walked inside and seen the front door unlocked, her car in the driveway, and no sign of Kara, he had immediately freaked out. He had called Joe Roberts, wondering if she had gotten sick or hurt or something worse, but the doctor had assured him she hadn't stopped by.

Then he'd called Ian's cell phone, but it had gone straight to voicemail. He'd been ready to call the main security office but had taken a chance and dialed Kara's cell phone. Of course he'd never expected, not in a million years, to have Ian answer her phone. And even worse, the other man's voice had sounded slightly amused, as if anticipating the sort of events that were about to play out.

They had talked at length yesterday about Kara and Bailey, respectively, and how each of them had set rules and expectations. Ian had told him a lot about their dynamic, but it was obvious they were both still learning. Every

day was a new challenge, either in regards to how to be a daddy, or just how to be a good partner in general. Brody hadn't thought that Kara would sneak out, not even once. But now they needed to go through another punishment, and he needed to do something different to get through to her.

When he'd grounded her and had taken away her car keys, except for during an emergency or for school, she had turned into a little hellcat. She'd argued and set out counter points like a politician caught in a scandal, but he'd meant business. And now she'd lied again after getting her new friend in trouble over something silly. All of this could have been avoided if Kara had simply listened and obeyed the rules set for her.

He motioned for Kara to get out of the car and the two of them went inside.

"I know I did wrong by going out when you grounded me," Kara started as they entered the kitchen. "I didn't think you would be back, but that just adds to the awful choices I made."

"Give me your phone." Brody extended his hand and waited for her to hand over her bedazzled, pimped-out pink cell phone case with the expensive smart phone inside. She used it constantly to text, play games, and connect with her friends online.

"Okay." Kara easily handed it over, obviously not realizing why he'd asked for it. "Are you going to spank me for sneaking out?"

"Go get your laptop and bring it down here."

"My… laptop? What do you mean, bring you my laptop? I bought it with my own money!" Kara glared daggers at him.

Brody reached into the top cabinet and pulled out a thick wooden spoon. He laid it on top of the counter. "Your laptop. Now. Otherwise, I'll bend you over the table and spank you until you go and get it."

"You wouldn't dare!" Kara shot another look at him. "You can play dance of the wooden spoon fairy all over my bongo drums and I still won't give it to you." She sounded bratty with a capital 'B' as she threw her arms across her chest defensively.

"Okay, but I'm thinking *Flight of the Bumblebee* will get my message across." Brody took the spoon in his hand and quickly rounded the counter. Kara took two steps backwards, as if seeing too late that he meant business.

"No… no… no…" Kara protested but he had already reached her and had taken her upper arm in his hand. He led her firmly to the kitchen table and as promised bent her over until her hands were spread out across the top. "You can't just take my stuff away!"

Brody reached under her, unbuttoned her jeans, and worked them down over her hips. He followed suit with her panties, but to his surprise, Kara reached her hands back and covered her cheeks. He lightly rapped the spoon across her knuckles.

Kara let out a string of curses, but yanked her hands away. "What the—"

Her words died on her lips as he spanked her upper thighs with the spoon. He knew that would sting and get her attention. "Ow! Ow!"

Brody moved his focus up to her cheeks and smacked the implement hard. It cracked loudly across her bottom, delivering a solid reminder. He changed the speed and rapidly fired the spoon across her behind until it kissed every inch—from the perfect curve of her cheeks to the top of her pinkening rounds. She stopped cursing and now sobbed into her arms.

"Do you want to reword your question?"

"I'm sorry, daddy," Kara babbled through tears. "Can I ask for a compromise?"

"I'm listening." Brody brought her panties and pants back up, then helped her to stand. He sat down on one of the kitchen chairs and tugged her onto his knee. "What is it?"

"Can you move the laptop down here? I'll only use it for school and research. You can limit the time and password it." Kara curled her fingers in his.

"I suppose…" Brody planted a kiss on her forehead. "But you're limited like you suggested for the next two weeks."

"That's past the time I'm grounded." Kara looked up at him and pouted. "I thought…"

"Do you want to go to the library to do your research?" Brody shot back, and she immediately shook her head back and forth.

"No, no, I accept your punishment. It won't happen again."

"Good." Brody patted her thigh and she got off his lap. "Now, let's eat something and move on with our day."

"There's still some beef and broccoli in the fridge. Do you want me to heat it up?" Kara brushed the last of her tears away.

Brody nodded and watched as she fixed the leftovers. She had grown a lot over the past few weeks, and his heart filled with even more love for her. She trusted him to do good by her and it made him feel more complete than he could put into words.

Kara stopped and stood still when she caught him watching her.

"I'm just really happy you're home safe," he said.

"Me too," she agreed and went back to her task.

He really was the luckiest man in the world. She was such a good girl—in both her adult and her more innocent mind spaces, and even when she bratted. Kara genuinely wanted to please him and do what he asked. Brody planned to take her out once the semester finished, and she would flip over the moon when she realized why. Now, if only he could keep it secret until then.

CHAPTER TEN

Three months flew by and her college semester was finally over. She had done very well in all of her classes and had volunteered at the doctor's office during the week. Dr. Joe had offered her a part time position answering phones, making appointments, and filing like he and Brody had talked about, and Kara had finally agreed once her classes wrapped up.

Working at the office got her out of the house more, and she also got to spend time with Kaitlyn. The two of them were becoming fast friends, and Kara had agreed to come over soon for a play date. She wanted to try to go back to an even younger mindset than she normally did, and both Brody and Dr. Joe had readily encouraged her.

Bailey had become her closest friend and had forgiven her for the stupid antics on their sleepover night. The other woman had a lot going on, but they still found time to meet up a few times a week to share stories and just let go. More often than not they were in their younger mindsets, but next week they were planning a trip to the mall as adults. Shopping therapy broke through both of their bad moods and also steered Kara clear of her previous attempts with food therapy.

Kara had also been spending more time outside of the house than before. She'd interacted with many different littles and their mommies and daddies, while always remembering to be polite and accepting. She thanked her lucky stars each day for the wonderful man who'd brought them to this point. Her Brody. Her daddy.

"Kara?" Brody's playful tone snapped her happily out of her thoughts.

"Babe?"

"Dr. Joe told me about this amazing hike through the woods with a waterfall at the end. It's not steep or anything, and it's about a twenty-minute drive from here."

"Uh-huh?" Kara met the distance between them and wrapped her arms around his waist. "But what about the bugs and the poison ivy and the weird animals...?"

"I'm not a weird animal!" Brody pulled her up off the ground and twirled her before setting her back on her feet. It was a gesture she used to balk at, but now she felt very loved when he did it. "Seriously, though. I have it all planned out! The forecast is warm and sunny."

"Okay, Brody the explorer…" Kara winked. "I'll go pack some trail fuel." She turned to go towards the kitchen, wiggling her behind as she went. Brody followed and landed two swats across her bottom.

"Hey!" she screeched, not angry but definitely surprised as she spun around. "What was that for?"

Brody grinned and kissed her hard. "If you bounce it like that, it makes me want to smack it… then of course, it makes me want to do other things."

Kara waggled her eyebrows playfully. "Okay, okay! Let me go now or we'll never get out of the house!"

• • • • • • •

Brody drove to the park but didn't say much. He was too nervous about the plan he had for them.

Finally, Kara blurted out, "Are you gonna tie to me a tree and leave me in the woods?"

"What?" He shook his head, then moved his hand to take hers. "No, I would never tie you to a tree!" Kara let out a sigh of relief as he cocked a smile. "A log maybe…"

"Brody!" Kara giggled. "You seem far away." Her tone dropped its playfulness. "If you want to turn around, we can hike some other day."

"Nah, we're here. It'll be fun." Brody pulled into the wooded park, paid the entrance fee, and parked. He hadn't thought his attitude had caused a red flag, but apparently Kara knew him better than he knew himself.

"I've got a cooler with an extra water bottle for each of us. I can't wait to get to the top! I have to tell you about next semester too. I got the pamphlet in the mail last week…" Kara continued to babble on and on about how many credits she needed to take versus how many were online or in a real classroom. She explained various projects, some which were community-based, which needed to be completed before she could do her thesis for her final project and be able to finish her degree. He listened, mostly, trying hard to seem interested even though something really important had taken over all of his attention.

"Babe? You've gone all quiet again. Are you going to push me over the water…?"

Brody stopped walking and bent Kara over a log near the edge of the trail. He landed four hard slaps on the seat of her cute jeans. "The only thing I'm going to do at the top is spank your butt until its burning if you don't stop making up terrible ways for you to die on our hike." He punctuated his

statement with two more smacks.

"Ouch! Ouch!" Kara bucked. "I'm sorry! For crying out loud, Brody, let me up!"

He straightened and set her back on her feet. "For crying out loud?" Brody couldn't keep the grin off his face. "Really?"

"It's just you've barely made any comments at all about school. I'm so close to my degree, and it's been a really hard semester. You dragged us out here to have fun, but you don't seem to be having any." Kara bit her lip as he leaned over to kiss her. Finally she gave in and gave him several kisses back. "Are you really okay?"

"Yes. We're almost at the top and I hear the view is amazing. I've heard if you reach it at a certain point when the sun is in the sky, you can see a rainbow, and I know how much you love them." He took her hand and tugged her towards the path.

"I do love rainbows," Kara agreed as she wiped the dirt from the lap of her jeans with her free hand. She picked up the cooler which had slipped from her hand during her quick dip over the log, and then she continued walking.

Five minutes later they were standing at the end of the trail and facing a huge waterfall, and sure enough, they could clearly see the sparkling hues of a rainbow coming off the sun's rays in the mist. Kara clapped her hands together excitedly and dug her phone out of her pocket. She held it up to take a picture but instead nearly dropped her phone when Brody got down on one knee.

"Kara—"

"Oh my God!" Kara threw her hands over her mouth. Tears streamed down her cheeks as she took in his pose and what he meant to say.

Brody carefully cracked open a small velvet box. He had wanted this moment to be perfect and hoped she understood why he'd acted so oddly. "I brought you up here because I wanted to tell you how much you mean to me. I love the times we spend together, no matter what age you act like, but it's more than just that. You've blossomed into this amazing, confident woman, and I want to spend the rest of our lives together."

Kara moved her hands to brush away the flow of her tears. She nodded several times, listening to his words, clearly moved. "I love you!"

"I love you too." Brody picked up the white-gold band with its dazzling heart cut diamond and held it up to her left hand. "I promise to always be good to you as a husband and as a daddy. Kara Mitchell, will you marry me?"

"Oh! Brody!" She nodded several more times, as if unable to get the words out. "Yes! Yes, I will marry you!" Kara made a sound that was a cross between a laugh and a sob as he slid the ring onto her finger. "Of course!" She opened her arms wide and he got to his feet to embrace her. "I'm so excited!"

"I'm so happy you said yes." Brody kissed her deeply. "Come on. Let's go back down the trail. They've got this nice secluded spot where we can eat."

Kara giggled. "I know what I'd like to do more in such a nice secluded spot..."

"Kara!" Brody tickled her sides. "Come on. We have plenty of time to engage in extracurricular activities later."

"Ooooh!" Kara raised an eyebrow. "I bet I can guess what those include!"

They headed back down the path, arms linked, happiness shining in their eyes as they began their next adventure together.

THE END

Bailey's Little Adventure

SUMMER GRAYSTONE

CHAPTER ONE

I drove home pushing the speed limit, shooting through yellow lights I should have stopped for, totally blowing through the stop sign at the end of my street. All I wanted was to be home, get out of this hateful dress and heels, and forget my day at work. It was stressful, full of arguments and missed deadlines, and the sooner I could get away from it, the better.

I hit the garage door opener, waiting impatiently as the door trundled up. Ian was a fanatic about me putting the car in the garage, and even though I was tempted to leave it in the driveway—leave it on his side of the driveway, no less—I knew that would be pushing the boundaries of our agreement. Outside the house, unless we'd made it clear ahead of time, I was an adult, a twenty-six-year-old grown woman with a job, and all the responsibilities that went with being that grown woman. Even though the garage was, technically, inside the house, I was driving the car, meaning I was the adult. Meaning the car got parked where it belonged. But inside, I was someone totally different.

Inside this house, I was daddy's little girl. And more than anything, I wanted to be that little girl.

The kitchen was clean, more or less. The breakfast dishes were in the sink, the coffeepot half full of elderly coffee. Dinner was a distant dream, and there was a basket of laundry by the laundry room door. All of that was my responsibility, my afternoon chores.

"Fuck it. I'm not doing any of that crap." I kicked off my heels, tension starting to leave my body. As I made my way to my room, I shed the rest of my adult outfit, walking into my room in just my bra and panties. They were lime green, trimmed with black lace. Ian had bought them for me last week, a reward for being a good little girl and giving him a blowjob. I loved both giving him head and the underwear. Hopefully I'd have the chance to do something else for him. There was another set of undies at Hot Topic in electric pink that I thought were wicked.

But today, I wanted nothing to do with being good. I wanted to relax, kick back, and chill. I yanked my hair into a ponytail and pulled on my

sweatpants, and a worn, too-small football jersey that daddy told me needed to be thrown out. Or given back to the child I'd borrowed it from. Sometimes I thought about getting rid of it, because it bothered daddy. But I thought he secretly liked it, liked the way it stretched tightly across my chest.

I logged on to Facebook and started reading what my friends were up to. There was the usual drama and the drama queens behind it, breakups, cat fights, bitch fights, all of the usual suspects with nothing to do and all the time to do it. I flopped down on my stomach on the bed with the laptop, getting totally caught up with what was going on.

I was in the middle of texting with a friend when the bedroom door flew open. I jumped, rolling over, slamming the laptop shut. Daddy stood in the doorway, and by the look on his face, he was not happy.

"Bailey, there's no dinner. The laundry is still where you left it this morning. And you're on Facebook." He pointed to the laptop. Guiltily I slid the computer under the blanket.

"No. I was... doing homework."

He shook his head. "Don't lie to me, Bailey." He crossed the room. "You know what happens when you don't do your chores? And you know what happens when you lie about it, don't you?"

A thrill went through me. I knew exactly what was going to happen. I was going to be punished. I hoped I was going to get a spanking, but there was no guarantee. Not doing chores was pretty serious, but he could just make me do them. It might mean doing them in my underwear, or washing the floor naked while he watched. But that wasn't the punishment I wanted, or needed.

I nodded. "Yes, daddy."

"Then stand up."

I slid off the bed, standing with my head down, hands folded in front of me, like he'd taught me. I could see his shoes as he walked toward me He stopped right in front of me. My breathing was already faster, anticipation building.

"I thought I told you not to wear this anymore." He plucked at the sleeve of my jersey.

"Yes, daddy. But I like it." I looked up at him and I caught the look of shock on his face. "It's comfortable." I arched my back just a little, the fabric pulling tight. Daddy made a noise I knew meant he liked what he saw. But I was pushing him and I wondered how far I could go before he'd get really angry.

"You're my little girl, and I expect you to listen to me, Bailey. Is that so hard?"

I rolled my eyes, and that was the final straw.

"That's it, Bailey. Now you're going to get a spanking."

I tried hard not to squee, but I knew he knew how I felt about spankings,

and why I wanted them.

He sat on the bed, legs spread a little. It was pretty obvious he was sporting an erection, which meant this was going to be intense for both of us.

"Come here."

I held back, hesitant, until he held out his hand. I took it, letting him pull me to him. The numbers of my shirt were practically in his face and for a moment that's all he looked at.

"Turn."

I knew the drill and turned to the side. He ran his hands up my thighs, thumbs hooking into the waistband of my sweats. Slowly he pulled them down until they landed on the floor, his hands resting on my thighs. There was a heartbeat of silence and then he drew in a ragged breath.

"You're my little girl, Bailey, and when you don't behave, you need to be punished. Do you understand?"

"Yes, daddy."

"Tell me why you're being punished." He slipped his fingers beneath the edge of my panties. They fit me like a second skin and it took a little more work for him to get them down over my curves.

"I didn't do my chores. I'm wearing the shirt you told me not to wear." I hesitated. If I didn't recite every last infraction, there'd be more punishment.

"You were..." He waited, his fingers tensing against my legs, moving higher. "There's more, Bailey."

"I rolled my eyes."

"Yes. And?"

I tuned to look at him. "I don't know." Was there something else?

He smacked his hand against my ass and I jumped, letting out a yelp. The sting was intense, mostly because I wasn't expecting it, but he'd hit me harder than he ever had. He'd never spanked me like this, before I was in position, lying across his lap. Something was really bothering him.

"Bailey, you lied to me. And now you're lying again." He smacked me again, the pain radiating across my ass.

"Lied about what?" I turned to look down at him, hands on my hips. "I didn't lie."

"You said you were doing homework, and you weren't, and now you're lying about lying." There was another smack, and I rocked forward from the blow. The pain sank into my skin.

"Oh... I'm sorry, daddy. I... it... I didn't remember." This had never happened before and I wasn't sure what he would do.

He was breathing hard, his erection straining against his pants. I knew I was ready for punishment, and what might happen afterward, and it was pretty obvious he was too. But I couldn't push him, or it wouldn't be the same.

He caressed my ass, soothing the area he'd smacked. I wanted him to spank me, let me cry, let out all the stress and tension from the day. But this was unexpected, and it was pretty intense. There were too many emotions running through me, and I was confused.

"Fine. It's time for your punishment then. You know what to do."

With something like relief, I went through the ritual of moving to the side, kneeling down, and laying myself across his knees. It was always the same, and it set off the same anticipation inside me. And the same sense of safety. This was what I wanted, and this was how it was supposed to be.

When I had settled across his knees, he set one hand on my back, the other on my ass. I wiggled against him, feeling his cock pressing against my side. It seemed impossibly hard and hot, and it excited me to know I could make him feel this way.

The first hit was hard, and I winced at the sting. My skin was already tingling and this smack lit me up in a way I'd never experienced before. It was still confusing, but being spanked like this was familiar and comforting.

The next smack made me cry out, the pain sharp and intense. Then he rubbed his hand over me, caressing me for a moment.

"You know you're my little girl, Bailey. And you need to be punished when you misbehave, don't you?" His voice was low, just as soothing as the hand rubbing my ass.

Before I could answer, he spanked me again, and my answer turned into a gasp. As he gently rubbed my skin, I squirmed as the pain subsided from sharp and stinging into something warm and delicious—like caramel topping on ice cream, thick and sweet, running down over the cool treat.

The heat sank through me, like it always did, pooling between my legs. Instantly I was wet and as much as I wanted the spanking to continue, I was ready for what would come next.

But Ian's hand came down on me again, quickly followed by another slap, and another. My cries went from gasps and moans of pleasure, to tears and cries. This hurt, it stung, and my tender skin felt like it was on fire. I gritted my teeth, hands clenched in fists, enduring each slap.

"Daddy, please." I turned, looking up into his eyes. Ian blinked down at me, his hand resting on the burning skin of my ass.

"You lied, Bailey. You know the punishment for lying is this, right?"

I nodded. "Yes, daddy."

His hand moved in a circle over my ass now, and I thought he was done with the punishment. But then I froze. I wasn't allowed to ask him to stop. Tears sprung up again, and I looked back to his face.

"I'm sorry... I forgot..." I sniffled. "It won't happen again."

"You're right. It won't." His hand came down once more and I burst into tears. "I'm your daddy, Bailey, and I know what's best for you. I take care of you, don't I?"

I nodded, sniffling again. "Yes, daddy."

Beyond the pain, as always, was relief. The tears washed away the adult stress of my day, leaving me clean and free, allowing me space to be the Bailey I wanted to be.

"I'm sorry, daddy. I promise to be a good girl." I wiggled in his lap, just a little, testing him. Beneath me his thighs tensed, his hips rolling up slightly. It was okay; things would be okay now.

His hand moved lower down, fingers slipping into the cleft of my ass. I wiggled harder, but his fingers stopped. This was what Ian needed: control. Too much independence from me, and he felt lost. I struggled to lie still.

"Good girl." His voice was a low murmur, and his fingers moved again, sliding further, teasing the edge of my slit. I drew a breath, biting my lip, as one finger slid into me, slowly moving back and forth. God, I wanted to arch my back, rock my hips, push back against him.

But I stayed still, eyes squeezed tightly shut, muscles tensed. Ian was always telling me to be patient, that I couldn't always have everything the moment I wanted it. And now I wanted Ian, badly. But I'd have to be patient. He was in control and I needed to follow his lead.

"That's my good girl, just like that." His fingers moved faster, his hips rising beneath me, breathing short and fast. Just a little longer, and I'd have what I wanted, and what I knew he wanted as well.

But if my mind knew I had to wait, my body had a different idea. I was trying to hold still, but my muscles were trembling, and the harder I tried not to move, the harder it got. And the harder it got, the more excited I became. I was quivering inside, my pussy clenching around Ian's fingers. I knew he felt this, and hoped he didn't count this as me moving, because there was no way I could control that.

I was so close to coming, and I tried to hold back. But Ian knew how to finger me, how to drive me crazy. That's what he was doing to me now, and even without looking at him, I knew he had that half-smile on his face—almost a sneer, but not quite. He enjoyed this, loved the control.

I was just there, right at the edge, my body shaking uncontrollably, and then Ian pulled his hand away from me. I couldn't help myself; I cried out, pounding my hand on the floor, my body thrumming with arousal, but unable to come.

"You thought you were off the hook, didn't you, Bailey?" His voice told me he wasn't quite smiling. "You've been a very bad girl tonight. I think I might just send you to bed."

I didn't think he'd do that, but I wasn't sure. Ian was full of surprises, most of them wonderful. But sometimes he exerted control in perverse ways. Sending me to bed alone was one of them. I wanted to protest, but I held my tongue.

"But I think that would be cruel. Besides…" He stood up and I slid to

the floor, landing on my hands and knees. I looked up at Ian, towering over me. From here his erection pushed out the front of his pants, and I practically came looking at him. He moved behind me and I waited, panting, knowing what was coming next. I heard his zipper, and the harsh sound of his breathing behind me.

Time stood still as I waited. I pictured him standing behind me, looking down at my ass, his cock rising up from the apex of his thighs, waiting for whatever he needed to make it perfect for both of us.

There was a thud as he dropped to his knees behind me, his hands grabbing my hips, and then he was there, his cock sliding into me. I came almost instantly, crying out, back arched, mouth open. It went on and on, my body contorting, shaking, the world going black for a minute.

Everything after that was quick, brutal, and everything I wanted—everything I needed. Ian thrust hard and fast, pushing me forward and I struggled not to pitch face first onto the carpet. I pushed back up, bucking against Ian, my body on overdrive, the orgasm I'd had never really ending, peaking over and over.

Ian's fingers dug into me and I heard him make the noises I knew meant he was close, really close. I wanted to feel him come, to hear that growling noise he made. And I wanted what came after sex.

He was bottoming out now, his balls slapping my ass. I braced myself, focused now on him, holding steady as he pummeled into me. Then I heard it, that low sound that started deep in his chest, kept building, his thrusts faster.

The growl reached a peak as he buried himself in me, and I felt every pulse as he came, every spurt of hot come filling me. Amazingly I came again, weakly, my body shaking against Ian's hips as he continued pumping into me.

We both collapsed at the same time, Ian falling beside me, pulling me against him, arms around me. It was dusk outside and we lay in the dark, breathing hard, hot and slick with our lovemaking.

• • • • • • •

Much later, we decided to go to bed. My ass stung from the spanking, but I bore the pain like a badge of pride. I'd connected with Ian just the way I'd wanted to, needed to. I'd purged the crappy ass day I'd had, and I was pretty sure Ian had done the same thing. It's what worked for us, pretty much every time.

We decided to sleep in the master bedroom that night, not my room down the hall. It was my cue that I could be the adult Bailey, and we could talk about our day, about our lives, about us, as adults.

"Do you want some wine or something? I'm going to get a drink." Ian stood in the bedroom doorway, gray cotton sweats hanging off his narrow

hips. I loved him best at the end of the day, like this, relaxed and happy.

"Um… just a bear, please."

He smiled and disappeared. It was a kind of a joke between us. After we were first married, I'd bought a set of '50s children's drinking glasses with animals on them. I fell in love with the bear glass, and because the glass was small—a child's glass—I'd started asking for it when I wanted just a little something to drink.

I lay back against the pillows, absently clicking through the TV. There really was nothing to watch, but I didn't want to be alone, and until Ian came back, I could pretend there people here with me.

Ian came back, handing me my glass. I clicked off the TV, tossing the remote onto the bedside table. I saw he had Scotch, and I was pretty sure that wasn't his first glass. Sadness washed through me. When Ian had a bad day, I felt it keenly, in my bones.

"You want to talk about it?" I took a sip of wine, the crispness bright on my tongue. "Or should I go first?"

"You first." He took a long swallow of his drink, then turned on his side, resting his head on one hand, the drink cradled in the other against his stomach. I always worried he'd spill it, but that hadn't happened yet.

"Marcus had one of his 'talks' with me today." Marcus is my manager, but he's also a control freak, an egomaniac, and a really nasty man.

"Did his talk involve you sitting and him standing?" Ian took a sip of his drink, the ice clinking in the glass.

"Yeah, it did. If I'd have known I'd have worn a turtleneck." Marcus had a habit of hovering over me during his little pep talks, or while I was working, and looking down my blouse. I wasn't given to wearing really revealing stuff, but he always made me feel exposed and extremely uncomfortable.

"What was the talk about?"

"Same old crap. I need to raise my productivity, but not sacrifice quality. I need to be responsive to my clients, but not spend too much time chit-chatting with them. And I need to be on time more."

"Is that all?" Ian laughed, finishing his drink. He rolled over, set his glass on the bedside table, and rolled back to me. He set his hand on my thigh, just above my knee, fingers gently caressing my skin. I loved his touch, no matter how he touched me. I felt connected and grounded, and loved.

"He's probably got a really tiny penis."

I snorted wine as I laughed. Ian could always make me laugh.

"So, what happened in your day?"

Ian was a lawyer in a pretty prestigious firm downtown and was on the fast track to make partner. The pressure was immense, and it made Marcus and being late seem trivial by comparison.

"Same as most days, Delaney is riding my ass. Not billing enough hours, not being… what did Marcus tell you? Not being responsive to my clients.

Delaney wants me to give him a minute-by-minute breakdown of what I'm doing, without cutting into billable hours." Delaney was Ian's boss, a managing partner, and supposed mentor. He sounded more like a tyrant to me.

My job as a graphic designer was fast-paced, but I didn't have to assign every minute of every working hour to a client. For that I was profoundly grateful.

"You could ask to move into Delaney's office. He's got enough room in that suite of his."

Ian nodded, a faint smile on his face. "His secretary's office is bigger than mine."

"You can't move into her office." I finished my wine, putting the glass aside. I slid down next to Ian, tracing a finger across his chest. "I don't want to think of you sitting in the same space with Cassie. She's too cute."

"You sound jealous." He looked down at me, his eyes heavy-lidded, one eyebrow cocked in that sexy way I loved. "You're my girl, Bailey. You know that."

"And you're my guy. I love you, Ian."

He leaned down, kissing me softly. In this space, this room, I was Bailey, Ian's wife, and we were equal partners.

"I love you too, Bailey. Very much."

His next kiss was less gentle, more assertive, his lips moving over mine, parting them with his tongue. I responded, wrapping my arms around his neck, pulling him closer. His chest rested against my breasts, the heat and hardness of him weighty, solid, comforting. He was my rock, my anchor.

He moved a hand down to my waist, fingers working beneath the edge of my t-shirt, slowly exploring my waist, up my body, flirting with the underside of one breast. I arched my back slightly, pushing against his hand. I felt his smile against my mouth and he moved his hand just enough to cup my breast. He squeezed gently, his thumb flicking across my nipple. I gasped against his mouth.

I loved having him touch my breasts, play with my nipples. Ian was happy to oblige and he broke the kiss, giving me a hazy, sexy smile.

He slipped down in the bed, tugging the edge of my t-shirt up my stomach. I wrapped my fingers through his thick hair, waiting for his touch.

He kissed my stomach, his tongue flicking around the edge of my belly button. I giggled, squirming beneath his touch. He raised his head, looking up at me.

"North or south?"

Another inside joke. I laughed. "You're the navigator, you pick the direction. I'm happy wherever you go."

Ian winked, then lowered his head, his lips brushing against my stomach, moving lower. A frisson of excitement shot through me, and I shifted

restlessly, moving my legs apart in anticipation.

He slid his fingers beneath the edge of my panties, and I lifted my hips just enough for him to slide them down over my hips. Then he pulled them over my legs, down my calves, and off over my feet.

Slowly he moved down to the foot of the bed, lifting one leg, cradling my calf in one hand. He gracefully ducked beneath my leg, coming up between my feet, smiling up at me. This was his method, slow and languid, taking his time. He'd told me so many times he loved every inch of me, loved how I tasted, how I felt, both beneath his hands and beneath his lips.

He kissed the arch of my foot, his lips and tongue caressing my skin. Sometimes his touches tickled, and I spent minutes giggling beneath his hands. But tonight, after what we'd experienced earlier, I wasn't giggly. I was calm, open, and getting very aroused.

Every kiss, every touch left a trail of fire on my skin. Ian moved from my foot to my ankle, his hand rising to beneath my knee. His fingers caressed me, his lips moving over my skin.

In the same slow motion Ian had used, I pulled up my t-shirt, running my hands over my stomach, then higher, cupping my breasts.

Ian watched me, moving further up my leg, past my knee, to the inside of my thigh. I arched my back, squeezing my breasts, caressing myself, pinching my hardening nipples.

Arousal exploded low in my stomach and I exhaled sharply, my legs twitching apart. Ian lifted his head from his path, gaze focused on my hands, on what I was doing to myself. I arched further, rolling my nipples between my fingers, meeting Ian's eyes. He liked to watch me touch myself, play with myself, and it was one of our favorite adult pleasures.

Ian stretched out between my legs, pushing them further part. I let him, willingly, aching for his touch. He teased a finger over my swollen folds, moving it over me, touching me everywhere except where I wanted. But he knew my limits, knew how much teasing I could take before I started begging. Tonight I didn't want to beg, and Ian sensed that.

He slipped a finger into me, and I rolled my hips to meet his first thrusts. Before long he had two fingers pushed into me, sliding them slowly in and out. His thumb brushed against my clit, and I gave a soft cry, hips rising to meet him.

Then his hand went away and I was left waiting, eyes closed, still fondling my breasts. I felt his breath before I felt his kiss, his tongue following the same path his fingers had taken. He licked and sucked, kissed and tasted me, fanning the fire he'd lit. Before long I was moaning, arching and shifting beneath his hands, his mouth.

Ian had always had a miraculous ability to read my movements, to understand my inarticulate noises, and to follow my desires without me having to explain. I wanted him inside me, I wanted his hard cock, filling me

the way nothing else could.

He lifted his head, meeting my eyes, and wordlessly climbed up over me. Somewhere along the way he'd lost his sweatpants and now he lay between my legs, his hard cock pushing against my inner thigh. He shifted again, and then he was where I wanted him.

I reached for him and he lowered himself onto me. Arms around his neck, I pulled him down to me, kissing him greedily. I felt his smile; I'd told him I liked how I tasted, and he'd said he did too. We shared the kiss, shared that intimate and erotic taste, somehow more heady than any wine.

But my body demanded more, and Ian's did as well. He pushed my legs with his hard thighs and I rolled my hips up, drawing my legs up his hips, locking my ankles at the small of his back.

He pushed forward, his cock sliding into me, slowly, achingly slowly, fitting perfectly. I exhaled, hips rising to meet his first delicious thrust.

But we'd gone past slow and Ian began the familiar dance between us, pulling back, thrusting hard, repeat, thrusts getting harder, deeper. My gasps and soft exhalations grew louder, harder, moans and cries intertwining.

Ian moaned deeply, adding music to this dance between us. Hearing him excited me more, sending me higher, and Ian responded to that, his breathing becoming faster, a light sheen of sweat on his chest and back.

I was ready, my body on the edge, Ian right there with me. He lifted his head, eyes locked with mine as his thrusts reached a fever pitch. I held his face between my hands, watching him as he watched me.

His final thrusts were short and sharp, each driving home that he was reaching his climax. And when he came, I did too, joining him with cries and caresses, hips meeting his, him grinding down on me, me forcing myself up against him.

Ian's orgasm filled me with a heat like no other, and then I was filled with my own special release, my body taking on a life of its own, the heat inside me transmuted into something else, something dark and primal, animalistic and overwhelming.

I threw my arms wide, fingers grabbing the sheets, arching up hard in one last crescendo of orgasmic release. Then I went limp, my body falling away from Ian, falling away from consciousness.

Ian was lying on his side beside me, his hand on my stomach when I came back to the world. "Hey there. Welcome back." He leaned over and kissed me. "You were gone again."

"Yeah. Sorry."

"Don't be sorry. I wish I could go with you." He pulled the blankets over us, trying in vain to untangle them. We wrestled with them for a minute, then finally got them straight. Ian turned out the light and I snuggled into his warmth. We were quiet and I was on the edge of sleep when Ian's deep voice brought me back to the surface.

"Thank you, Bailey."

"For what?"

"For being who you are, now… and before. For marrying me." He hugged me, patting my ass. "For everything."

I reached up and kissed him. "I love you, Ian. And thank you for being you."

Ian was asleep in a few minutes, but I lay in the dark, wondering about this man I married, a man who loved me for being me, for being someone who was a part-time little, an adult woman who played at being a teenager. A man who could deal with all of my eccentricities, and still love me.

CHAPTER TWO

Ian was working on a Saturday, and I wasn't happy about that. Weekends were, for me, the absolute best. I could be any age I wanted to be, any time. I would spend the entire weekend in little mode, and it was wonderful. If we were going out, we'd have an adult date night, where daddy's little girl got to play dress-up, wearing makeup, a grownup dress, and heels. More often than not it ended up with me in hysterical laughter watching confused waiters and bartenders trying to decide just who I was. I loved it, but most of all I loved being out with Ian.

But today I'd been alone. I'd wandered around the house, halfheartedly doing my chores. I was so bored, I'd actually done the laundry and put it away, and cleaned the kitchen. I missed Ian, missed our routine. But his push for partner had gone into overdrive, and that meant working on Saturdays.

Facebook was lame today—a bunch of scrubs and whiners taking over the conversations. I'd checked a couple of times, finally gave up, opened Pandora, and listened to my favorite station. For once it gave me something new and I lay on my back on the bed, headphones on, blissed out listening to basement trance music.

But even that only lasted for a couple hours. I yanked off my headphones, closed the laptop, and wandered back through the house. I could make dinner... but we always ate out on Saturdays. Ian wasn't sure he'd even be home for dinner. If he wasn't, I'd just order pizza.

I ended up in the living room, looking out the window. It was sunny. Ian was always telling me to get out more, get some exercise. I pinched the tiny roll around my tummy, wondering if Ian thought I was getting fat. That couldn't have been what he meant, could it?

A walk would be something to at least pass the time until Ian came home. It was kind of windy looking, so I grabbed my new Chibimaru hoodie, wishing that I'd gotten the Vans skate shoes. But the day we'd been at the mall, Ian had been in a hurry, and we'd only had time to make a quick pass through Hot Topic before he had to go back to work.

It was colder than it looked outside, but it felt good to walk. I headed down the path to the playground... yeah, a playground. I lived in this gated community called Little Haven. They had a lot of neat things inside, but the coolest part about it was the fact that there were a lot of woman like me who pretended to be a different age. They wouldn't be judged and neither would I. As I walked to the park I shivered slightly; it was too cold for anyone to be out, and I was happy to have the whole place to myself. I dragged along my purple skip-it toy until I made it to the playground and began to play. A couple of minutes had passed when suddenly my skip-it crashed into something... or someone. I gasped and put my hand over my mouth. I hadn't made a single friend and now I never would. I'm a mess. "I'm so sorry!"

"No! It's okay. I wasn't watching where I was going. Do you think I could try?"

I breathed a sigh of relief that she wasn't injured. "Yeah, sure. Just don't break it." I took the toy off my foot, then reached down and clasped it around her foot. "It's super easy. Just swing it around and hop over this part."

"I'm Kara." Kara extended her hand. "It's nice to meet you."

"I'm Bailey." I straightened to shake her hand, and then stepped back. "Go ahead and try it. I'll count how many jumps you do."

"I'll try not to hit you!" Kara grinned and began hopping. After a few minutes of me cheering her on and giggling at the game, she stopped. Something had changed in the air and it had grown colder. Kara quickly undid the toy and handed it back to me. "I think it's going to snow!"

Sure enough, the wind had picked up without either of us noticing, and the sky opened up. Seconds later before we knew it there were flurries everywhere. It wasn't just a light snow and it was freezing! "Come on! My house is just over there!" I pointed across the way and the two of us took off. "My daddy won't mind!!"

"Thank you!"

We ran through the back door into the laundry room, squealing with laughter. Cold snowflakes that had melted seeped through my hoodie, and I unzipped it and got out of it as quickly as I could.

"Hey, let me have it." I extended my hand for her wet Hello Kitty hoodie. "I'll throw it in the dryer with mine and then you can go home when the snow lets up. Or you can call your daddy now." I watched as her face turned scarlet and added, "I mean if you have one..."

Kara nodded and handed it to me. "I don't usually tell people I have a daddy. I mean we've been together a while and I've been doing this... um, thing."

I could tell she was uncomfortable. "We don't have to talk about it if you don't want to." I set the dryer and then motioned back toward the kitchen. "Do you need to call home, let someone know where you are?"

"In a minute. You have a really nice house." Kara walked into the kitchen

while I started the dryer.

"Thanks." I followed her, watching as she poked around looking at Ian's lawyerly magazines on the island, frowning at them. "How long have you lived here?"

"Brody... that's my..." She looked up at me. "You're into age-playing, like me, right?"

"Yeah. Right." I let out a breath. "You want some hot chocolate?"

"Sure. My daddy and I moved in over a year ago. I go to school a couple of times a week." She took the cup I handed her. "Thanks. Brody... my daddy... he's working."

"Mine works too." I took my cup and motioned her to follow. "Come on up to my room. We can listen to music, if you want. Trent Reznor's got a new album out."

"Yeah, cool." I kicked off my shoes at the bottom of the stairs, and Kara did the same.

"Is this your room?" Kara stood in the doorway, staring at my total disaster of a bedroom.

"It is. It's a mess."

"Yeah, but so's mine."

We hung out the rest of the afternoon, listening to music and talking about our lives. Kara was explaining her history with Brody, and I looked at her from where I lay on my stomach on the bed, head resting on my hands. Kara was lying on the floor, her feet in black and white socks and propped up on my bed.

"How long have you been a little?" she asked.

"About two years. Ian and I had been married about six months, and we started playing around with some stuff... some bondage, nothing extreme... Ian likes the control. I like this..." I looked around my room, at the posters on the wall, the colors, the mess. "And we just play at what we like, until we get it right." I rolled over, hugging my pillow, looking up at the ceiling. "It's the most amazing thing, when we're both in the same space at the same time. Sometimes he's more into it, and I just play along. It's fun, but it's for him then. But when we're both into it... yeah, it's pretty intense. I can't explain it. I feel safe and protected, so cared for."

The rumble of the garage door brought me upright on the bed and I looked at my alarm clock. "That's my daddy." I jumped off the bed, running down the hall. The excitement of him coming home had me almost forgetting Kara was there.

"You're home!" I met him just as he was coming up the stairs. He pulled me against him, and I reached up, kissing him hard. He held me for a moment, and then stiffened, looking past me up the stairs.

"Hello. And who are you?"

I turned around, arms still around Ian. "Oh, sorry. Ian, that's Kara. Kara,

this is Ian. This is my daddy." I turned back to Ian. "We met in the park, and it started to snow a lot, so we ended up here. Is that okay?"

"It's fine with me, if it's okay with…" He glanced up at Kara, one eyebrow raised. "Did you call home?"

Ian had gotten it right away, knew what Kara was. I smiled. He was amazing. And I loved him so much for it.

Kara nodded. "I did. It's okay that I stay, until you got home, and then I'm supposed to go home."

"I'm sure your daddy is missing you." He disentangled me from his neck, and I followed him down the stairs, Kara coming down behind me.

"This was fun. Too bad I have to go home." I could almost hear the pout in Kara's voice.

"Too bad you have to go home," I agreed.

"Well, you could spend the night at my house…?"

Kara looked so hopeful. And it would be fun to have a sleepover, to stay up all night, and just be a girl. "Can I spend the night at Kara's?"

Ian was at the refrigerator, pulling out ice from the freezer. He looked tired—exhausted, in fact. I wanted to take back my words, to see if he needed me. "If it's okay with… what's your daddy's name?" Ian was great at staying in his role. Sometimes he was better at it than I was.

"Brody. We live across the park."

"If you call and he says it's okay, then it's fine with me."

Kara broke into a big grin, reaching into her pocket for her cell. "Okay. Thanks." She turned away, flipping open the phone.

I went and stood beside Ian, leaning against his shoulder. He slipped an arm around me, kissing the top of my head.

"Are you sure it's okay that I go to Kara's? I can stay home, if you want?"

"Don't worry about it, baby girl. Have fun."

CHAPTER THREE

I was so excited to go over to Kara's tonight. It had been a long time since I had gone on a sleepover. But, I was also kind of nervous. Kara seemed like a really cool girl, but I hadn't spent the night away from Ian since we first met. I hoped that I would be okay without his strong presence by my side at night.

I packed my backpack with my PJs, my toothbrush, hairbrush, and other little things to bring with me to the sleepover. Once I finished, I picked it up and walked in to the family room where Ian was working.

"I'm going to go, daddy."

"Okay. You have fun," he said, getting up and giving me a kiss.

"We will," I said, waving goodbye to him and leaving the house.

The walk to Kara's wasn't that far, which was good. I kept checking over my shoulder to see my house where Ian was. *It's only for one night. You can do this,* I kept telling myself.

Just as I reached Kara's house, she opened up her door and called out, "Hi, Bailey! I'm super happy your daddy said you could come over."

I couldn't help the smile that crossed my face, despite the fact that I was still a little nervous. "Thanks. I'm excited."

Just then, Brody, Kara's husband, appeared in the open front door and said, "It's cold out, ladies. You're letting all the heat outside."

I followed Kara inside and watched as she shut and locked the door before Brody said, "Thanks. The bill is high enough without leaving any doors open."

I nodded before remembering my manners and said, "I'm Bailey."

A frown crossed Brody's face, making me think that I had done something wrong, but then he said, "What terrible manners I have." He reached his hand out to shake mine. I took it hesitantly, as he continued, "I'm Brody, it's nice to meet you."

"We're going to watch lots of movies and stay up late and eat junk food." Kara shot a look to me and I nodded in agreement.

"Yeah? What movies?" Brody raised an eyebrow. "Are they rated R?"

I noticed that Kara looked annoyed at Brody when he asked that, but she didn't say anything; instead she turned toward me and asked, "What movies did you bring, Bailey?"

"Just some Simon Pegg movies. Yeah, they're rated R. All the best movies are." I shrugged, not seeing the big deal since Kara and I had already discussed this. "We agreed on that."

"What's wrong with that rating?" Kara shot back to Brody.

"Whoa-hoh. You better change your tone or I'll send your friend home right now." Brody checked on the sauce, then turned up the pasta water. "I just asked if they were rated R. Help Bailey bring her things upstairs. Dinner will be ready in about twenty minutes."

I watched the interaction between Kara and Brody and had to bite my lip. They reminded me of Ian and me.

"I'm sorry, Daddy," Kara huffed and she skipped over and planted a kiss on Brody's cheek. "If it's too inappropriate, we'll turn them off and watch cartoons."

I wanted to protest that idea because the movies that I brought over were great. I didn't want to watch cartoons instead. That would be lame.

Brody grinned down at Kara. "Uh-huh. Hurry up, because I've got to watch these pots," he said, tapping Kara's nose.

"Okay!" Kara said excitedly before motioning for me to follow her upstairs. "We're staying in my, um, teen kind of room tonight."

I got really excited at that. Kara had a teen kind of room just like me! I thought that I was the only one who had a room like that. "You have a room like that too! That's so cool!"

Kara led me inside to a room that was painted teal and had butterfly stickers on the wall. There were little fairy statues, rock posters, and purple Christmas lights all around the room. I thought that it was awesome! It also reminded me of a kind of gothic room, but with girly touches.

"Are you like a girly gothic girl?"

"I'm just me. I love butterflies 'cause they make me happy. Just like I like the biker boots and black makeup." Kara shrugged. "I don't know. I just have my own sort of style, I guess."

"I like it," I said, before really noticing one of the half-sleeve tattoos that Kara had on her arm. "I like your tattoos too. I mean they're so different and it's like you really express yourself with them."

I had always wanted to get tattoos, but I was too afraid of the pain. I also was afraid that I would make the wrong choice and one day regret getting the tattoo.

"Thanks. They make me happy. My mom used to tell me that only whores and sailors got tattoos, but she's like not the one who has to look at them." Kara paused, realizing what she said could be interpreted as not the nicest

thing to say about one's mother. "Oh, that's awful, isn't it?"

I shook my head. "You should do what makes you happy. It doesn't matter what anyone else thinks of them."

"Ladies! Dinner is ready!" Brody's voice carried up the stairs and down the hall.

"Come on! My daddy's sauce is like to die for. I hope he made garlic bread too!" Kara giggled as we made our way out of the room.

· · · · · · ·

Brody, Kara, and I sat down to dinner.

"So, Kara, what sort of snacks are there going to be tonight?"

Kara just ignored me and took a bite of food. Finally, after a few minutes of Brody and me staring down at her, she dropped her fork and snapped, "What?"

"Your friend asked what sort of snacks there were for tonight. Twice. You were miles away…" Brody stated plainly. There was no anger there, but his face made it clear that he didn't appreciate her not paying attention to me.

"Oh." Kara said, her cheeks heating up. "Geesh, I'm sorry. I was just thinking about something and I didn't hear you. We've got movie theater-style popcorn with extra butter."

"That's cool! I like butter," I said, as I was buttering my garlic bread. Kara raised her eyebrows, making me realize my mistake. "I mean popcorn!"

Kara giggled and grinned. "Seriously, it's all about the butter." Kara stood up and moved to clean her plate off.

"You can leave it, Kara. I'll clean up." Brody stood and took the dish. He planted a quick kiss to the side of her head. "Go have fun."

"You ready?" Kara asked me politely just as I was finishing eating my garlic bread. I stood up as she said, "Let's go." She led me back upstairs in to her teen room and asked, "Do you want to get your PJs on now?"

"Yeah, but can I ask you something really quick?" I asked, as I knelt down on the floor and rolled out my sleeping bag. "I mean, if you'll answer."

"Sure, you can ask me anything," Kara agreed, fixing her sleeping bag right next to mine. "What's up?"

"What was with you at dinner? Are you upset I'm here?"

"Oh! No, not at all." A guilty look crossed Kara's face and I felt bad for asking the question. "It's just I'm not used to being around anyone when I'm… you know… it's hard sometimes."

"It's only hard if you fight it. So, Ian and I talked about it in the beginning, about the rules, I guess. Who initiates, what happens or if one of us just isn't in the mood, when we really need to be adults."

An expression crossed Kara's face before she said, "Do you think we could talk about that a minute?"

I nodded, encouraging her to continue.

"I usually have a set day, or time, or you know, Brody might suggest it if I'm having a really hard day. So, who starts it at your house?"

"I usually initiate the little stuff. It's visual. I'll change my clothes or wear my hair differently. Those are simple things Ian can see, and he knows how to act. But more than that, it tells me who I am. It tells me how to act. The physical reminder is for both of us." I reached for my bags, rummaged through them and brought out my pajamas. "See? These are really soft, but they have little hearts and flowers all over them. It's an instant thing for me."

"Like when I get all my punky stuff on? You know when we met at the park and I had my tutu and leggings and all."

"Yes! Exactly. When you get dressed, you're thinking about how you're going to feel when you're wearing each piece. So, if you went to college tomorrow, would you put on your Hello Kitty sweatshirt?"

"Not so much. You're right; I would choose a fleece or a hoodie that was a bright color or something, but not that one."

"See? So, you get it." I stood up as if to get ready for bed and Kara jumped to her feet.

"Wait, before we watch movies and all, can I ask you something personal?"

I bit down into my lip, as if unsure of where this conversation was about to go, but nodded.

"Does Ian spank you?"

"Yeah, when I get punished, but sometimes when we role-play too. It all depends on where I'm at in my head." I bit my lip, wondering if I should say more. I really liked Kara, but I wasn't sure how much information I should tell her. People got weird when it came to spankings.

"Do you like it?" Her voice came out in a hush as her face grew even redder.

"I like it... most of the time." I shrugged. "I like the spanking, the heat and pain. The pain is exciting when we use it as foreplay." I squeezed my eyes shut, not sure if I should continue, but decided since Kara was asking the questions that she wanted to know. "But I don't like them when I've done something wrong."

"Have you ever done something wrong on purpose, just so you get the spankings?" Kara asked, but before I could say anything, she kept talking. "Because I've done that. And it's not right, but in the beginning when we had just started this and I didn't know if Brody was going to follow through—"

"Hey!" I interrupted her. "Just take a breath and start over. You don't have to be embarrassed around me. We're friends."

Kara beamed. "Yeah, it's just I'm not used to that either. I have friends at college, but they don't get me. So, my question was about acting up on purpose. I did it a lot before I realized that Brody would follow through."

"I never thought of that so I don't really know. I hate it when he has to punish me, but the spankings are amazing."

"Does Ian like spanking you?" Kara fiddled with her hands as she asked that question.

"Oh, yeah. It's the control he likes... well, it's part of it." I cocked my head to the side and grinned wickedly. "He really gets off on it. We both do. But by that time we're out of role-playing, and it's all as adults."

"Do you think Ian could talk to Brody? I mean, about all this stuff?"

"I can ask him..." I shrugged. "I don't know how he'll feel about the topic, but I'll talk to him. But not until his work has settled down. He's under a lot of pressure right now."

"Yeah, sure thing. Thanks." Kara grinned as she rummaged through a small dresser. "So, let's get on our PJs and watch movies!"

I grinned back. "Then we can stay up like all night!"

· · · · · · ·

It was well past midnight when Kara pulled out a cigarette and an ashtray. I was shocked! I never expected her to be a smoker.

"What is that? Do you smoke?"

"Uh, sometimes... I mean not a lot. Come on, have one with me." Kara held out the pack.

I raised an eyebrow and looked over my shoulder, almost expecting my daddy to step out and punish me for even thinking about smoking.

"My daddy is asleep, he won't even know."

"Fine." I took one and Kara quickly lit it for me. We popped in the next movie, each of us enjoying several cigarettes while it played. "You don't have beer too, do you?"

Kara laughed so hard she ended up snorting, causing me to burst out laughing too.

Kara finally settled down enough to say, "No! Beer is gross!"

The two of us must have been pretty loud because the door swung open to reveal a tired-looking Brody.

"You two need to keep it down. Some of us need to go to work..." He trailed off and looked at something on the floor.

I realized that he was looking at the ashtray, which was almost full of cigarette butts. Shit!

"What the hell have you been doing?" He glared down at Kara.

Kara visually paled, glancing over at me before saying, "I'm sorry, daddy. I wasn't going to have one, but Bailey wanted to try."

Brody picked up the ashtray, shaking his head and letting out a long breath. "If it weren't the middle of the night, I'd take you home, Bailey. You're both in trouble. Go to sleep. Now. Movie and lights off."

The two of us nodded and didn't say another word. We both knew that we were in big trouble.

Once Kara had turned off the DVD and I turned off the lights, we crawled into our sleeping bags.

"Why did you do that? He's really pissed." I huffed under my breath. "I mean, really mad. Like a real daddy." I closed my eyes, just imagining what my daddy was going to say when he found out what we'd done. I was so going to get a spanking, probably an even worse one since Kara made it sound like it was my idea to smoke.

"He hates that I smoke. I thought if you were here, maybe he wouldn't be so mad at me," Kara said, fidgeting with the edge of her pillow.

"Well, that didn't work out so great."

"I'm sorry, I'll explain it in the morning."

"Yeah, well, that won't get me out of trouble," I retorted before closing my eyes and trying to fall asleep while imagining myself over Ian's lap, bottom in the air.

Kara was asleep. I could tell by her breathing. I had this insane desire to get back at her for getting me in trouble. As quietly as I could, I got out of my sleeping bag. On the floor in the tangle of her clothes I found Kara's cigarettes, the pack we'd started, and a fresh, unopened pack. I took them and then spied her bra and panties.

At some point during evening, we'd changed into pajamas, hiding under the sleeping bags while we shimmied out of jeans and t-shirts, and pulled on bigger t-shirts and pajama bottoms. Kara had dropped a brilliant teal-colored satin and lace bra and matching panties on the floor, beaming as she did.

"Brody bought these for me, a present for our anniversary."

I scooped them up and ran out of the room. I stood for a minute in the kitchen, and then an idea hit me. I can't say it was inspired, but it was almost dawn, and I was sneaking around with someone's underwear in my hands.

I ran her bra and panties under the tap, then wrapped the wet clothes around the cigarette packs. I squeezed them hard, taking a perverse satisfaction as the cellophane crackled, and I felt the cigarettes squish between my fingers.

Looking wildly around the kitchen, I finally spied the refrigerator. I wrapped the panties around the whole dripping mess and yanked open the freezer door, shoving the clump of bright material into the back of the freezer.

I ran back to Kara's room and crawled into my sleeping bag. I lay for a few minutes, watching the sky lightening outside, the light in the room turning a soft gray. I turned over, punching my pillow, angry at Kara for her hare-brained scheme and for including me in it.

• • • • • • •

I woke up to Kara shaking me awake.

"What time is it?" I asked, sitting up on my elbows. "I want to go home." After what Kara did to me yesterday, blaming me for cigarettes, I wanted to get home as soon as possible.

"It's just after eight. Brody has breakfast. Please don't be mad. It was a joke and I'll explain it all later. I just didn't want to get in trouble last night. I really am sorry." Kara got to her feet. "I put your movies and stuff back in your bags and set them near the door. Just come downstairs when you're ready."

I couldn't help the snort that left me. Kara thought that blaming me for her cigarettes was funny. "Funny joke," I said, getting up and rolling up my sleeping bag. Once it was rolled up, I turned toward her and said, "It wasn't funny."

"Okay, you've made your point. I'll see you in a few." Kara left the room and I sat down on her bed. I was still furious with her for what she'd done, and I didn't like being blamed for something I hadn't done.

Then a smile crossed my face when I thought about what I'd done for revenge. *When Kara sees, it'll be the last time that she blames me for something that isn't my fault,* I thought before heading downstairs to the kitchen.

I was greeted to the sight of Kara sitting at the kitchen table and Brody was at the stove. There was a big stack of pancakes on the table. I couldn't help licking my lips as I sat down and pulled the food toward me.

"Morning, Bailey. Want some orange juice?" Brody asked, as I served myself some pancakes.

"Yeah, sure."

When I noticed that Brody was reaching for the freezer door, a sense of dread went through me. He couldn't open that door! I shook my head vehemently at Kara, trying to get her to stop Brody from opening the freezer door.

"Stop!" Kara called out and I thanked my lucky stars that she did.

Brody looked back and forth between us and raised his eyebrows. "What?"

"Ice is bad for you," I stated simply, then nudged Kara with my elbow.

"It's the worst form of water," Kara agreed quickly.

"What?" Brody sighed. "What's gotten into you two?"

"When liquid freezes, it loses all of its nutritional values," I lied, hoping that Brody would buy it and not open up the freezer.

"And frozen things are bad for your teeth!" Kara said, and I was so happy that she was agreeing with me without knowing why.

"Ladies, I don't know why I'm getting a science lesson this early, but I'd like some ice." Brody said, opening the freezer door and reaching for the ice. I knew the exact moment when he found my little present for Kara. He let

out a curse under his breath.

"Bailey?" Kara asked. I wasn't sure what to say to her. I had planned to be gone when she found my present.

"Bailey?" Brody asked, setting down the frozen object on the table. "Do you care to explain this? I highly doubt Kara froze her own bra."

Kara's jaw dropped as I muttered, "It was just a joke… it was much funnier last night."

"I'll go thaw it out. Be right back," Kara said, grabbing the frozen items and leaving the room.

"Bailey. I'm very disappointed in you. What you did was wrong."

"Yes, sir," I said, casting my eyes downwards.

"I want you to finish your breakfast and then you will do the dishes until Kara gets back. Understand?"

"Yes, sir," I said, suddenly not feeling that hungry.

For the next five minutes, under the watchful gaze of Brody, I began washing all of the dishes. I knew that I had made a mistake by freezing Kara's underwear. I was just so upset that she had gotten me in trouble. I just wanted to get her back. I did, but it appeared that I was also going to get punished for that too.

Kara came back in to the kitchen and Brody started to talk to her immediately.

"You're going to walk your friend home and you've got a task. I want you to make sure Bailey tells her daddy that instead of sleeping, she decided to go on a little midnight adventure. I'm sure she already has a lot to tell him with the tobacco incident as well." He finished his glass of juice, then set it in the sink.

I quickly picked up the dirty glass, washed it, then set it on the top rack. "So, you're not going to tell my daddy?" I asked, hoping that washing the dishes was going to be my only punishment for what I had done.

"No, you're going to tell him yourself, using your own words." Brody reached forward to rest his hand on my shoulder. "There's something I want to share with you. You're the first person, in a long time, to make my Kara giggle like that. So I hope you two can work through this. I know you were just being funny, but sometimes you can hurt someone's feelings that way."

"I know. I won't do it again." I nodded several times. "I'm very sorry."

"I believe you." Brody smiled, then moved away to Kara. "Go walk your friend home."

"I think Bailey was just being silly and I really want her to come back." Kara threw her arms around Brody, hugging him tight. "So, can't you let this one go?"

My heart swelled at what Kara had said. She was trying to get me out of a punishment when I knew that I had hurt her by what I had done. She truly

was a great friend for trying to do that. It made me respect her so much.

"Sweetheart, there is a lesson in all of this. I will call her daddy later on today. If I find out you two tried to keep a secret, then you will be punished. Am I clear?" Brody tapped the top of her nose. "Kara?"

"Yes, daddy, it's clear," Kara said, handing me my jacket.

"I've got a project to work on so if you want to stay a little while, you can." Brody waved to the two of us. "I hope to see you again soon, Bailey."

"Thank you for letting me stay." I accepted the jacket and put it on.

"Bye!" Kara shrugged her hoodie on, then led the way out the side door.

We made our way to the road and I couldn't help but take slow steps. I wasn't that excited to go home to get a spanking. Ian probably wasn't going to let me go to another sleepover because of my behavior last night.

"Is your daddy going to be mad at you?" Kara asked, pulling me from my thoughts.

"I guess we're about to find out."

"Look, that was a really shitty thing to do…"

"And what you did wasn't?" I spat the words out, and if Kara's face was any indication, I had surprised her. "Listen, all role-playing aside, that was a really childish thing to do."

"But you put my underwear in the freezer! Isn't that childish too?"

I stopped in my tracks and just stared at Kara. I knew that she was right, but I didn't exactly want to admit it. She had hurt me and I had gotten even. We stood still, staring at each other for a long time before a small smile fluttered across her face and within seconds she and I were laughing, deep belly-aching laughs.

"Putting your underwear in the freezer was childish." I said, once I finally caught my breath.

"Yes, and so was blaming you for the cigarettes. How about this, you can buy me a new set?"

"Maybe," I sighed. "But then you owe me a cheesecake. A real one. That is my most favorite dessert. You so owe me for last night."

"Deal," Kara replied as we walked across the small street and onto the front lawn.

I walked up to my house, unlocking the front door and stepping inside. I turned around and said, "You know what? You should just go home." I hoped that she would. I didn't need anyone around for when I told Ian what I had done.

"Yeah, well, I can't. Brody said I have to make sure you tell your daddy or we're both in even more trouble."

"Trouble that you started! If you didn't give me those stupid cigarettes to smoke—"

"What is going on?" Ian, fresh out of the shower in nothing but gray sweats, appeared at the top of the stairs. "Why are you back so soon? Did

something happen?" He proceeded to come down the stairs, then pulled me in for a hug.

"Yeah, something did." Kara leaned against the door.

I sent Kara a glare. She could have given me at least a minute to tell my own daddy what I had done.

"All right, come tell me about it." Ian motioned for us to follow him into the kitchen.

When we were in the kitchen, I blurted out, "We smoked cigarettes." Ian's eyebrows shot up, and he blinked at me. The corner of his lip twitched, as if something amused him, but he kept quiet. "And then I put Kara's bra and panties in the freezer."

I waited for Ian to say something, but instead he took a leisurely sip of his coffee. Finally, he put it down and faced me.

"So, Bailey, do you think that was a nice thing to do to Kara? She invited you over to her house. Fed you dinner, then breakfast?" He gave her a sidelong glance from the sink.

Oh! I knew that look.

"Well, no… but she lied. She said it was my idea, but it was hers. They were her cigarettes."

I saw Kara open up her mouth as if she was going to say something, but Ian gave her a look that had her closing her mouth before he turned back to me.

"Right. But are you supposed to smoke cigarettes? Is that something you think is a good idea?"

"Well… no. But that's not the point." I bit my lip as I stared at my daddy.

He was right. I knew that I wasn't supposed to smoke, but it wasn't my idea! I had just gone along with it because Kara had asked me.

"I think it is the point. It's my point. You did something you know you're not supposed to do. You did something wrong. And you know what that means." Ian tilted his head to the side. "Don't you?"

"But that's not fair. She…" I sputtered and pointed in Kara's direction. "She went and got them."

Why were people forgetting that? It was like everything was my fault, but nothing was Kara's!

"I did! Bailey is telling the truth!" Kara took a step toward Ian, as if to explain, but Ian gave her another look that stopped Kara in her tracks. *Crap!* I was really in for it.

"Do I have to put you in the corner so I can properly adjust Bailey's attitude without your mouth running? Go back to where you were standing. Now. And no more talking," Ian said in a very stern tone toward Kara that had chills running down my spine.

"I'm… I'm sorry." Kara retreated to the edge of the kitchen and shut her mouth.

"Bailey, you inhaled the cigarette. No one made you do that. You did it all on your own." Ian returned his attention to me.

"Fine. When Kara's gone…" I began, but Ian stopped me with a look that sent chills through my whole body. I knew that look. I wasn't about to like what was coming next.

"Come here," he said, pulling out a kitchen chair, moving it to the center of the room, sitting down, and patting his knee.

I glanced over at Kara. Ian had never punished me in public before.

"But… now?"

"Now."

"Wait!" Kara yelled out. "I really should go home! I shouldn't—"

"If you distract me again from the matter at hand, you'll be next," Ian said, and I knew that no matter what either Kara or I said, I was going to be getting a spanking in front of her.

Kara stepped back and made it look like she was zipping her lips.

I sighed. *Better get this over with,* I thought as I walked over to Ian. He grabbed my arm and tugged me over his lap.

The first smack that landed across my behind was hard and I couldn't help but twitch from the impact. Ian laid several more taps across each of my cheeks, and I couldn't help but kick my legs. It hurt so much.

Ian continued his spanking, not giving me a moment to catch my breath. I was quickly brought down to a babbling mass of pain and I was humiliated that my new friend was watching me get punished.

My ass sizzled with pain and all I wanted was the spanking to get over with so the world could open up and suck me away, because there was no way that I was going to be able to hang out with Kara after this.

Finally, Ian ended my spanking, stood me up, and pushed the chair back.

I turned to Kara and noticed that she had a look of awe on her face. It was as if she wanted to apologize more. That made me feel worse! It was so embarrassing!

"I really want you to go home now," I said to Kara, looking at the floor. I didn't want her to stare at my tear-soaked face.

Kara nodded, but made no movement, making this even worse for me. Finally, Ian approached her, tugged on her arm, and guided her out of the house to leave me standing alone in the kitchen.

Once he came back I turned to Ian, both my pride and my ass stinging. "Why did you do that? You've never punished me in front of anyone before!"

He stood up, looking far too pleased with himself. "Want some coffee, Bailey? You look like you didn't get much sleep."

• • • • • • •

I sat at the kitchen table with my coffee, gingerly shifting in my chair.

He'd given me a really hard spanking. Most of my spankings happened at night, and I ended up in bed, where by morning the physical remnants of my punishment had faded.

"Your ass hurts, right?" He sat down opposite me, watching me.

"Yeah. Why did you do that?" The coffee was hot and strong, and my head was finally clearing. And I was getting mad.

"You did something you weren't supposed to, Bailey. And I don't want you doing it again. I thought if you got your spanking in front of Kara, it might make more of an impact." He smiled, and I winced. "Pun intended."

"Yeah, well, it was a rotten thing to do." I finished my coffee. "It was still her idea."

"She's not my girl, Bailey. You are. And I'm responsible for you, not her. What she does, that's up to Brody to decide how to handle." He stood up. "You, though, still have more punishment coming."

I stared at him as he went to the refrigerator. "More? Why? I got my spanking." This was unfair, really, monumentally unfair.

"That was for the cigarettes. You did something else, right?"

"Oh, well... yeah. But that was just..."

He'd taken out an ice cube tray, setting it on the counter. He turned to me, and he had that look I'd seen before, something dark and dangerous lurking in his eyes. But there was something very erotic there, too. I was equal parts afraid and curious.

"Take off your shirt, Bailey. And your jeans." He still had his back to me, talking over his shoulder. "Leave your panties and bra on."

I stood up, stripping out of my clothes, heart thumping against my ribs. Ian could be devious in his punishments and I had no idea where he was going with this.

When he turned back, he had an ice cube held between his fingers. My eyes went to that, and then down to the outline of his cock against the thin material of his sweats. Something loosened up inside me, and I thought maybe this punishment wouldn't be so bad.

I took a step toward him, reaching out to cup his erection. But instead of welcoming my caresses, he grabbed my wrist, pulling my arm up.

"Not so fast. This is my punishment. You need to do as I say. Alright?"

He held my wrist, eyes locked with mine. I nodded, swallowing hard. This wasn't going the way I'd thought, not at all.

"You like to play with ice?" He pushed me back against the kitchen chair, twisting my wrist just enough to force me to sit down. I looked up at him, mouth open. He stood over me, the ice cube dripping chilled water onto my chest.

"No... I mean... it was just a joke."

He let go of my wrist, looking down at the water running between my breasts. He reached out, tracing with one finger where one drop ran over my

skin, his finger hot against me.

"It wasn't very nice though, was it, Bailey?" His eyes rose to mine. I shook my head.

"I said I was sorry…"

"Are you sorry? You still need punishment, Bailey. You still need to know you did something wrong."

I followed the ice cube as he brought it down to my chest, touching it to the top of one breast. It was colder than I thought it would be, and I shivered. Ian made a sound, something like a laugh, but not quite.

"Take off your bra, Bailey." His voice had gone soft and hypnotic. My hands trembled as I reached behind me and undid the clasp on my bra. The straps slipped off my shoulders, and I let it fall to the floor.

"You're so beautiful…" Ian knelt in front of me, his eyes roaming over my exposed breasts. I was pretty sure we were out of my role-playing and into his thing now, and I sat still, waiting for whatever he wanted… or needed… to do.

He held the ice cube out, water dripping on his knee. With infinite slowness he touched the ice cube to my nipple. I jerked away, and Ian looked up at me.

"Sit still, Bailey. I don't want to have to tie you up." His voice dropped even lower. "Unless you want me to?"

I shook my head. I knew I was in trouble and deserved to be punished. I know when we do the bondage sessions, it is always amazing; I just wasn't sure I wanted to be restrained when he was using all the ice on me.

"Then sit still. And don't talk, unless I ask you a question. You're under obedience."

He brought the ice cube back against my breast, circling my nipple, but not quite touching it. For a second I couldn't tell what it felt like. It was painful, and I thought I wanted him to stop, but I knew I couldn't ask for that.

I gritted my teeth as he ran the ice cube in smaller and smaller circles, teasing, flirting, grazing my hardened nipple. I knew it would be intense and I was right.

When he touched the ice to my puckered nipple, I cried out, grabbing his wrist. He looked up at me, one eyebrow raised.

"Let go, Bailey." He held my eyes, waiting patiently until I reluctantly let go of his wrist. "Hang on to the edge of the chair. Don't let go. If you do, I'll find something else to do with you."

I was breathing hard, but I did as he asked, grabbing the edge of the kitchen chair. Ian smiled, then went back to his patient task, making slow circles again, starting the whole thing over. My only hope was the ice cube would melt.

He ran the ice cube across my nipple again, and I bit my lip. It was intense,

but almost instantly he pulled the ice away. Before I could even process what I felt, he leaned forward, licking my nipple. My body reacted to the familiar, arching against him, but before I could even enjoy the feeling, he pulled away. The ice cube came back, rubbing against my now-softened nipple.

He kept switching, rubbing the ice cube over my nipple, pulling it away, then sucking my nipple into his mouth. He moved between my breasts, kissing and sucking me, then rubbing my nipples with the ice.

I'd spread my legs, an open invitation, aching for his touch somewhere besides my breasts. I knew he was aroused. There was no way I could miss his erection tenting the front of his sweats.

I was gripping the chair so hard my knuckles were white. As much as I wanted to be touched, I wanted to touch Ian.

But I knew he had the patience and self-control to keep this up far longer than I could stand. He knew this, and it was something he exploited.

By the time the cube melted, I was gasping, shaking, and so totally aroused I could barely hold still.

Finally he sat back on his heels, hands resting on my knees, looking up at me. "Did you like that, Bailey?"

"Yes." My voice was a breathless whisper.

"Do you want me to do that again?"

I shook my head. "No. I want..." I bit back what I was going to say. Part of obeying him during times like these meant that I could only say yes or no. It was hard for me, and no matter how hard I tried, I usually broke obedience.

He raised an eyebrow. "What do you want?"

I shook my head, not falling for his tricks. He smiled. "You're learning. You can talk now."

"Fuck me, Ian. Please... I can't stand not to be touched."

His look was opaque, and for a horrible moment I thought he was done with me, with my punishment, with anything else. Then he stood quickly, grabbing me by my upper arms, pulling me to my feet. He kissed me hard, a messy kiss, sexy and passionate, and I didn't care about anything other than him holding me.

He pushed me back, out of the kitchen, and into the living room. Before I could catch my breath or my balance, he lowered me down to the carpet. He grabbed my panties, and I lifted my hips so he could pull them off.

I was on my back, my legs falling open, my body already thrumming with arousal, primed for him to take me.

He knelt between my legs, undoing the string on his sweats. When he pulled them down his hips, the same rush I got every time I saw his cock flooded through me. I reached for him with both arms, and he lowered himself onto me.

There was no hesitation, no gentle foreplay. He thrust into me, knocking the breath out of me with the force of it. I tried to brace my feet on the floor,

but Ian slid his arms beneath my legs, lifting my feet off the floor. He rose up, kneeling between my legs, my thighs resting on his shoulders. I was under his control again, no leverage, no way to thrust back. I was at his mercy.

I could tell by the sound of his breathing, the look on his face, the tilt of his hips, that he was on the edge, just like me.

He ran his hands beneath my ass, and I winced as he touched my stinging skin, but I didn't care. He grabbed me hard, pulling me up his thighs. I watched his cock sliding into me as he fucked me, giving me what I wanted. What he wanted as well.

It took only moments for him to be close to his release. He looked down at me, eyes locked with mine, his breath rasping from his open mouth. His fingers were sunk into my hips, holding me as he drove his cock into me, his chest covered with sweat.

"Bailey… oh, God…" He growled out my name again, and then he thrust hard, my name lost in a moan. Inside me I felt the first pulses of his cock, the hot spurt of his seed as he pushed himself into me.

I arched against him, my body contracting around his cock, and I shuddered in his hands. I screamed, pushing up against the floor with my hands. For a heartbeat or two the world went dark around me as I strained against him, my mind spiraling into some kind of other dimension.

Then I was lying on the carpet, Ian falling across me, his cock still buried inside me, still moving, the final thrusts slowing as he buried his face against me, nuzzling my neck. "I missed you last night. I woke up, wanting you. I could smell you on the pillow."

"I missed you too."

"Neither of us had a good night then, did we?"

He rolled onto his side, pulling me into his arms. I wondered what would happen if someone came to the front door, but then I really didn't care. I wanted to be close to Ian, to be an adult for a little while.

"It was okay. At first. It was fun. But Kara wanted to… you know. And then it just went downhill. I thought about coming home…"

"But you were a good girl, and stayed." He gave my shoulder a squeeze.

"Well, you always tell me not to go out at night, so, yeah, I wasn't going to walk home at three in the morning. Besides, I didn't want you to think I was a burglar and hit me with the baseball bat."

"Yeah. Probably not a good idea."

Ian shifted onto his back, and I rested my head on his shoulder.

He pulled me to him. "You know, our relationship, it's a big commitment, and it takes a lot of trust between both of us."

I thought about trust. Maybe I didn't trust Ian enough for him to let us really experience what he wanted, bondage-wise.

He gently pushed me off him, sitting us both up. He kissed my forehead. "You want lunch?"

I did, and he made it for me. We sat in the kitchen, wearing pajamas and sweats, for the rest of the afternoon. Ian had work to do, but we ended up in the living room, curled on the couch, at first watching television, but eventually falling asleep, wrapped in an afghan and each other.

CHAPTER FOUR

I left work early that Friday. Ian had found out he'd made partner, and he told me we were going out to celebrate. There'd be a big firm dinner sometime later, but this was just for the two of us. I was excited, but also a little scared.

A long time ago, back when we'd first started role-playing and stuff, we'd talked about some of the rules. Well, not really rules, not even expectations, but guidelines. Something to give us a path to follow. And one of the things we'd decided early on was that for special occasions, like our birthdays, or like Ian making partner, that person got to decide not only where we'd go or what we'd do, but how we'd act. For me, it usually meant a trip to the mall as a little, getting new clothes, and then a movie and pizza. Simple stuff.

We'd lain awake the night he'd been told he'd been made partner, and Ian had told me what he wanted for his night out with me. I'd laughed at first, but then I'd realized he was serious.

"I want you to be Bailey, role-playing like you do on weekends, but then role-playing as an adult."

"Not me just dressing up?"

"Not just that, because when you dress up on weekends, you're still role-playing as a teenager. You're sixteen-year-old Bailey, wearing heels and a dress. I want sixteen-year-old Bailey to role-play as an adult."

He rolled onto his side, propping his head on his hand. "Think you can do that?"

I lay on my back, looking up at the ceiling. It was kind of a mindbender, but I thought about it.

"Yeah. I think it'll be fun."

Ian kissed me quickly, and then grinned. "There's more."

"More?"

"I want you to be in submissive role too. Under obedience from when I come home, until I tell you you're not."

"Oh." Some of the fun seemed to go out of the evening. "Okay."

"It's something you'll enjoy. I know you have a hard time being a sub, but I'd like you to try. Okay?"

He sounded so hopeful, and because it was such a special occasion, I knew I'd try.

"Yeah. Okay. I'll do my best."

He kissed me again, longer this time. When he pulled back, I was amazed by the love I saw in his eyes.

"All I ask is you try. That's all. Thank you."

And so here I was, leaving work early, much to the dismay of my boss. But he could go to hell. This was Ian's night, and mine, and I was excited for it to start.

Ian had picked out everything for me to wear, right down to my underwear. The dress was a simple black dress, but the neckline was plunging, and so was the back. I couldn't remember when I'd gotten it, and I hadn't worn it before. The shoes were my regular black heels.

But the lingerie was brand new. Ian had come home on Thursday with a small—very small—package. I opened it and pulled out a gorgeous bra and panties. They were black, lacy, and very sexy. I wanted to try them on, but Ian had made me promise that I'd wait until Friday.

I pulled the car into the garage and practically ran into the house. Ian had wanted me to be dressed and ready when he came home. I had maybe an hour before he'd be there, and I wanted everything to be perfect.

I took probably the fastest shower of my life, washing my hair, touching up my legs and armpits with the razor. I dried off, then took time to dry my hair, getting the curls tamed into waves that hung down over my shoulders. Ian had given me a wonderful body lotion, scented like lavender, and I slathered myself with it until my skin was as soft as satin and I smelled like France.

I pulled out the bra and panties, and put them on. They fit perfectly, like everything Ian got me. I stood in front of the mirror, turning in a circle, looking at my reflection. The bra pushed my breasts up and out, and the lace showed just enough, the satin covering the rest of me. The panties were hardly there, just a brief bit of lace and satin. I felt amazingly sexy, and for a minute thought I would meet Ian at the door in just these.

But his instructions had been clear; I needed to be ready. So I pulled on the black dress. The bra made the dress fit like a second skin, and I did a twirl in front of the mirror, wearing my heels. I rarely thought I was beautiful, but tonight, I was stunning.

The garage door rumbled open and I ran downstairs. Ian was just coming through the kitchen, but he came to a halt when he saw me.

"Holy... Bailey. You look amazing."

I remembered I was supposed to be under obedience, but screw it. "You really think so?"

"I do." He set his briefcase on the island. "Are you ready?"

"I am. All dressed, down to these." I turned, flipping up the edge of my dress, flashing him a good view of my ass.

He laughed. "Okay. I get it." The smile lingered on his face as he walked toward me. "Remember what we talked about? How you're supposed to act?"

"Yes. I'm under obedience... unless you ask me a question." I frowned. "I guess I screwed that up already."

"You're forgiven. But from now on, you're my sub. You do as I say, when I say. I'm daddy here, and Ian outside. Right?"

"Right... oh, sorry. Yes, daddy."

"Right. If you have a question about how you're supposed to act, or what you're supposed to do, you can ask permission. Understood?"

I nodded, not risking saying anything.

"Good. I'm going up to change clothes." He walked past me, then turned. "I want you to watch."

I stared at him. "Okay. Um... yes, daddy."

Ian went upstairs, and I followed, hand trailing over the banister. He walked into our bedroom, dropping his suit coat on the bed.

"Sit." He pointed to the chair beside the bed. I dropped down onto it.

He kicked off his shoes, then undid his belt, pulling it out of the loops. It made a slithering sound, and for a moment I wondered what it would be like to be spanked with that instead of his hand. Something dark unfurled inside me, but I pushed it down, focusing on Ian.

He'd started unbuttoning his shirt, slowly, his eyes never leaving mine, then he pulled the shirt open, exposing his chest. Ian isn't muscular; he's built like a swimmer, broad shoulders and flat stomach, narrow waist. His chest was perfect for resting my head, for falling asleep against.

Now it was doing something else to me as I watched him slowly take off his shirt. I wanted to touch him, reach up and run my hand over all that warm skin. But I sat still, looking up at him.

His eyes never left mine as he reached down and slowly pulled down his zipper. I bit my lip, waiting as he pulled his slacks down over his hips. They fell slowly to the floor, and he stood in his boxers, the front tented with his erection.

He was standing so close I could smell his aftershave, feel the heat of his body. The temptation to touch him was so strong I sat on my hands. I didn't want to make a mistake, to ruin being in obedience.

"Bailey..."

I looked up at him, lips parted. "Yes, daddy."

He hooked his fingers in the waistband of his boxers, pulling them down. They caught briefly on his cock, and I wanted to reach out, to pluck them away from him, to let that gorgeous cock free of his boxers.

But I sat on my hands, my toes curling in my shoes, as I watched him

drop the boxers to the floor. He took a step toward me, his cock just inches from my face.

"Suck it, Bailey. Suck me how I like you to. Suck my cock."

I blinked up at him, then looked down at his cock. I reached with one hand, circling his thick shaft with my fingers, stroking him slowly for a moment before leaning forward. Slowly I licked the head of his cock, circling it with my tongue. His hips flexed just slightly, just enough to let me know he liked what I was doing.

"More, Bailey... more."

I opened my mouth, pulling him inside, swirling my tongue around his shaft, letting my mouth soften around him. He thrust slowly forward, pushing himself further into my mouth, the head of his cock hitting the back of my throat. I gagged for a minute, and he pulled back a little.

For the next few minutes I sucked him like there was no tomorrow, pulling him out to run my tongue over the head of his cock, taking him back into my mouth, as deeply as I could.

He reached out, grabbing my head, winding his fingers through my hair, holding me hard, his hips jerking forward. He thrust deeply into my mouth, and I gagged again, but he held my head and I couldn't move.

His grunts and moans grew louder, and he moved closer, legs apart, my face pressed against his stomach. I raised a hand, pushing against him, holding myself up.

I thought he was close, and I waited for him to come in my mouth. It was something I loved, and I knew he did too. But suddenly he let go of my hair and pulled away, and I almost fell off the chair. He staggered back a step or two, breathing hard.

"...good girl."

I sat in surprise, not sure what to do next. Ian stood in the middle of the room, his cock rising up hard and long and glistening with my spit. I was just as wet as his cock, and I wanted so badly to touch myself, to run my hand over my panties.

"I'm going to take a shower."

"Yes, daddy." For a minute I was disappointed, but then I thought I could have a minute alone, and take care of the ache between my legs.

"And you're going to watch."

"I'm... watching?"

"You are." He turned and walked into the bathroom. I heard the shower start and got up off the chair, following him.

He was standing by the shower door, waiting for me. I walked in, body still thrumming with arousal. Seeing him standing there, knowing I'd just had him in my mouth, had brought him so close to coming... it was almost enough to send me over the edge.

"Watch me, Bailey. Sit there and watch. No touching... just watch."

I stared at him as he stepped into the shower, closing the glass door behind him. I perched on the edge of the window, breath catching in my throat as the water coursed over his shoulders, ran down his back and over his legs. His cock was still hard, still thrust out in front of him.

He grabbed the soap, working up a lather and then slowly began washing his chest and arms, the bubbles running down over his stomach. It was driving me crazy, watching as he took his time, his hands moving over his body. He turned toward me, eyes meeting mine through the watery glass. I held up my hands, showing him I was being a good girl. He nodded, a crooked smile on his face.

But he seemed determined to torment me, and his hands slid lower, sliding his hands over his cock, washing himself, the bubbles running down his legs. The washing turned to stroking, and I watched as he closed his eyes, his hand moving slowly at first, then faster, the head of his cock disappearing in his hand.

I watched, and I got wet, my breath coming in short gasps. I wanted to touch myself, to rub my hand between my legs, to bring myself off as I watched Ian.

But he'd said I couldn't, and I bit my lip in frustration as I watched him come, his hand almost a blur over his cock, as the first thick streams of come spurted from his cock. I heard his moans over the sound of the water, and I cried out, almost coming with him. I watched as long as I could, finally turning away, taking a deep shuddering breath as he finished.

The water went off and he stepped out of the shower. I glanced at him, caught the half-smile on his face as he reached for a towel.

"Enjoy the show? You were a good girl, Bailey."

I wanted to tell him this wasn't fair, and the normal Bailey would have risked punishment. But I was supposed to be Bailey role-playing as a little, who was role-playing as an adult. I was dizzy from watching Ian, and from trying to remember how to act.

"Okay." It was all I could manage. "Um… yes, daddy."

"Good girl." He dried himself off, giving me another show of his body. I wanted nothing more than to pull him down and take him, right there on the bath mat.

"I'm going to get dressed." He stopped at the bathroom door. "But… you know, you should use the bathroom before we leave."

I stared at him. "You're serious?"

"I am. I know you, Bailey. You're a sneaky little girl. I know you would love to just touch that pretty pink pussy in the bathroom but we can't have that, so pee now… so you won't have to later."

"Fine." I tried to close the bathroom door, but he put his hand against it.

"Just go. Leave the door open."

I went, trying to work up a little friction with the toilet paper, but it wasn't

enough, not nearly enough. I flushed, pulled up my panties, and followed Ian into the bedroom. I sat on the bed, watching as he dressed. When he was finished he turned to me.

"How do I look?"

"Pretty good. Like a partner." I closed my eyes, wincing, knowing I'd spoken out of turn.

"It's okay, Bailey. I asked you a question." He sat on the bed. "Listen, this sub thing and obedience… just relax. You'll make mistakes. And you'll be punished. But I'll give you a warning, and I'm not going to embarrass you in public. And if it makes you feel better, we can decide what your punishment is now, so if you break obedience, you'll know what to expect. You can answer, no punishment."

"Okay. It's hard though. I want to be perfect for you. But it's hard."

"You're not going to be perfect, Bailey. No one is. It's not about that… being perfect." He put an arm around my shoulder. "The whole thing is about giving me control, letting me take control, make decisions. To take care of you. It's kind of like why you want to role-play. You want to be taken care of, to give up all your responsibilities for a little while. We play at what makes us happy. I want to take care of you, and I want you to let me do that. Does that make sense?"

I nodded. "I think so. It's just sometimes I think I'm always messing up, making mistakes. Like I don't love you enough and so I make mistakes. Or I want to be punished, so I make mistakes."

He pulled me close. "Whatever happens, just have fun. For punishment, just the usual, okay? Nothing too harsh."

"Okay. I'll agree with that." I reached over, kissing his cheek. "Now what?"

"Back under obedience, okay? I want you to try, okay?"

I nodded again. "Yes, daddy." It felt good this time to agree, to say yes, and know why I was saying it, that it was okay to not be perfect.

"Then let's go to dinner."

He stood up, pulling me up from the bed. "I'm happy to be going out, and I'm very happy to be going to dinner with such a beautiful woman." He kissed me hard then, and the desire that had faded just a little rose up, hot and wild. But the kiss was over too soon. He started toward the door, me following. But then he stopped in the doorway, turning back to me.

"Oh, one more thing."

"Yes, daddy?"

He held out his hand. "Your panties. Hand them over."

"My… you want my panties?"

"I do." He wiggled his fingers. "Off with them."

I reached beneath my skirt, wiggling out of my panties, slipping them down my legs. For a moment I stood and held my new panties out to Ian.

He took them, fingering the satin between his fingers.

"They're warm… and very wet." He brought them to his nose, inhaling, closing his eyes briefly. "You smell like lavender, and sex. Quite a heady combination."

He tucked the panties into his jacket pocket and left the room, as if he carried women's panties in his pocket every day.

• • • • • • •

The restaurant was full, but Ian had a reservation in the back, in one of the booths with a table that faced the rest of the restaurant. It wasn't our usual spot at all, and I stared at Ian as the maître d' led us to our table. Ian slid in first, leaving me on the end. I loved being so close to him and sitting side by side.

A waiter appeared, reciting the specials, filling our water glasses, leaving behind menus. I took a drink of water, then reached for the menu. But Ian reached across, taking it out of my hand.

"I'll order." He set the menu where I couldn't reach. I opened my mouth, but then I remembered I was under obedience.

"Yes, Ian."

He smiled, then put his hand on my knee. "Good girl."

The waiter appeared and I listened as Ian ordered salmon for me, on a bed of something I wasn't quite sure about, but thought were vegetables. I was a little put out by him ordering, and I struggled for a minute, wanting to interrupt and ask for what I wanted. But I bit my tongue, literally, until the waiter left.

"You're doing really great, Bailey." His voice was low, soothing, and his fingers tightened briefly on my leg. "Relax. It's okay. You're fine."

I took a deep breath. It was okay. It was just dinner, and I liked fish. Being here with Ian was more important.

His fingers relaxed against my leg, but he started moving them up my leg. He slipped them beneath the edge of my skirt, resting on bare skin.

"You're so soft…" He drew a soft circle on a spot he knew was a ticklish one for me, and I instinctively clenched my legs.

"Bailey… relax." He pinched me, not hard, but enough to let me know he was serious.

I made the effort to unclench my legs. Ian moved his fingers against my skin and I relaxed as his fingers moved higher. I wondered how far he would go in a public place. He wasn't given to public displays of affection anyway, so this was new for both of us.

His fingers were way under the edge of my skirt now, touching places he'd only touched when we were alone, when we were…

The waiter appeared with our salads, and Ian calmly took his hand away.

I looked at the salad in front of me, not the least bit hungry.

"Eat, Bailey. It's good."

I picked up my fork, spearing a piece of lettuce, putting it into my mouth. The dressing was tangy and sweet, and very, very good. I took another bite, and then dove in.

"See? I know what you like."

Ian was smiling at me, and I grinned back. "Yes, daddy. You do."

The salad was quickly gone, and I found I was looking forward to the main course. As if reading my mind the waiter appeared, clearing our salad plates. I watched him walk away, now impatient for my dinner.

But Ian had something else in mind. His hand was under the table, his fingers right back where they had been before the salad. Only this time his movements were more deliberate, more insistent. He moved his hand further, fingers in the crease of my thigh.

My heart rate went up and my breathing got shallow. He was inches away from all the places I craved to have touched… that craved his touch. Without even thinking I let my legs move apart just a little, sliding closer to him on the seat.

"Easy, Bailey. We're in public."

I drew a sharp breath, glancing up at the packed restaurant. He was right; we were in full view of a dozen tables. I glanced around, but everyone seemed to be more interested in their own little world than mine. Besides, the tablecloth hung down far enough that whatever was happening beneath it couldn't be seen. Or at least I hoped it did.

He slid his fingers along my thigh, over the top, back between my legs, skirting the issue, never quite going where I wanted him to go. I slid a little further down on the leather seat, resting my head against the wall. Maybe if I concentrated on the sensations inside me, I could have one of those hands-free orgasms I'd read about online.

There was a bang and clatter, and I shot upright. The waiter was at our table, sliding a huge tray of plates onto one of those folding tables. Ian's hand vanished from beneath the table, and he leaned forward expectantly, as if there was nothing more important right now than the food being set before us.

But there was something more important to me. The ache between my legs, the desire… need… to have that satisfied was almost unbearable. I wanted something, anything, to relieve this.

"I need to use the ladies." I pushed against Ian. "Please, Ian."

"No, Bailey."

I blinked at him. "You're kidding, right?"

"Bailey, this is a warning, okay? And no, no bathroom."

This was all whispered as the waiter placed our food in front of us. I sat back, trying not to pout. He really was serious. And he really did know me.

But the food distracted me, and Ian hadn't put his hand back on my leg. I squirmed away from him a little and picked up my fork. I inhaled the rich aroma of lemon and butter, salmon and something else I didn't recognize. As I took a bite, I closed my eyes. This was heaven.

Ian had a beautiful steak, and he cut off a piece, looking over at me. "Like the salmon?"

I nodded, mouth too full to even say yes. He smiled, and we went back to our meals. I discovered I was starving, and the salmon was perfectly cooked. The fire Ian had lit inside me faded a little.

Just as I was finishing my salmon, trying hard not to pick up the plate and lick the delicious creamy sauce off of it, Ian put his hand back on my leg. The instant he touched me, all the heat and passion he'd built up earlier flared up again, hot and insistent.

But this time it wasn't just teasing. His fingers slipped between my legs, skimming over my freshly shaved skin.

"Hmmm, you are smooth." He leaned toward me, his lips against my ear. "You feel amazing... and I can't wait to get you home..." He ran his finger against me, and with each word I melted a little. "I want to start with your toes, work my way up all that smooth skin... to here."

He thrust one finger into me, and I jerked forward, knees hitting the underside of the table. An empty water glass fell over. Ian's laugh ruffled my hair.

"Good girl."

The waiter was headed our way again, and I expected Ian to pull his hand away, but he didn't. I looked up at the waiter, pretty certain the look on my face gave away what was going on under the table. But he blandly put down a single plate with a piece of cheesecake on it, and then set one fork on the table.

"Is there anything else I can get you?"

Ian looked up, smiling. "No. I think we have everything we need right here."

The waiter left and Ian started a slow repetitive movement, his finger sliding in and out of me, his thumb brushing against my clit. I was so fucking close to coming I was trembling. I looked at him, begging him with my eyes to let me come, or to stop what he was doing. But he gave me that half-smile of his, with a lift of one eyebrow, that told me he was thoroughly enjoying himself.

"Do you want some cheesecake? It's your favorite... white chocolate raspberry." He picked up the fork, spearing a piece of the dessert.

"Open up."

I opened my mouth and he slid the fork between my lips. Down below his finger slid further in to me. Between the luscious silken dessert in my mouth, and the sensation of his finger probing inside me, I was lost. I closed

my eyes, moaning around the mouthful of cheesecake.

"Bailey…"

I swallowed the cheesecake and turned to Ian, meeting his gaze. My breathing was so shallow I thought I would pass out. There were no words I could say, nothing beyond what I could tell him with my eyes.

His fingers shifted inside me, moving against some magic spot that brought a muffled cry to my lips, and a sheen of perspiration across my upper lip. I didn't care that I was in the middle of a packed restaurant. I didn't care about anything other than being here with Ian, knowing he was in this with me, that it all made sense to him.

I leaned my head against his shoulder, my hand gripping his arm, closing my eyes. His fingers thrusting faster, his thumb pressed against my clit.

My body was shaking uncontrollably, my legs jerking as Ian's hand moved faster. I held back another cry, fingers digging into his arm. I could feel the muscles of his arm moving as he pushed deeper. I pressed my feet against the floor, every muscle in my body tensed, taut, on the edge.

Ian said something and I belatedly realized the waiter must have dropped off the check. But I was focused on what Ian was doing to me, to the sensations crashing through me, to the spiraling heat low between my thighs.

"Bailey… come for me. Now… let go, baby girl, and come."

My hips flexed upward, my thighs falling open in complete abandon as the floodgates opened, and I came hard. I bit my lip, turning my face against Ian's neck, tears running down my cheeks. My legs jerked again, and I felt totally out of control, but didn't care.

Everything inside me felt fluid and soft, and even though I tried to hold back, a gush of warmth ran from me, seeping down the cleft of my ass, soaking my dress. I arched my back, pressing my ass down against the leather seat, the last intense waves of my orgasm racing through me.

Ian exhaled loudly, and I wondered how the hell he'd managed not to come with me.

"Good girl." His voice brought me back to the restaurant, the noise of the other diners reaching my ears. I straightened up, looking around in amazement. I expected everyone to be staring at us, and I turned to Ian.

"That really happened?"

"It really did, baby girl. You were amazing." He wrapped an arm around my shoulder, pulling me against him.

"And no one even noticed?"

"No one. The waiter dropped off the check, and never blinked an eye."

I sat back, wiping my cheeks with a napkin. "Am I out of obedience?"

"Yes, for now." He smiled, wiping his thumb across my cheek. "How was it?"

"Incredible. Beyond incredible." I held his hand. "How are you? That must have been… hard." I giggled, then pulled a face. "Sorry. No pun

intended."

He shrugged, taking a drink of water. "No big deal." But his hand shook as he set the glass back down, and I noticed he'd drained the glass.

"Should we go home?"

He reached for the check, catching the waiter's eye. "Let me take care of this and then we can leave." The waiter took Ian's credit card, disappearing again into the back of the restaurant.

"I can hardly wait to get you home." He nuzzled my neck and I put my hand on his thigh. But he reached down, gently taking my hand away. "Not yet. Not until later."

I sat back, making a face at him. "You're no fun." But this was fun. More fun than I'd had in a long time.

· · · · · · ·

Ian drove home, pushing the speed limit, driving through lights he'd normally stop at. I sat primly on my side of the car, back under obedience per Ian's instructions. I was content to sit and be quiet, after the amazing experience in the restaurant. I was looking forward to going home, tearing Ian's clothes off and repaying him for the amazing time I'd had at dinner.

But when we got home, he'd led me into the kitchen, and said I was still under obedience. I frowned, but followed him upstairs. My dress stuck to my ass, and I plucked at it. I'd walked quickly out of the restaurant, slightly self-conscious, almost running to the car.

"Sit there." Ian pointed to the bedroom chair. I did as I was told, hands folded in my lap. He went to his dresser, rummaging in one of the drawers. I couldn't see what he had in his hands. But my heart started beating faster, my hands going cold. I was pretty sure I knew where this was heading.

Ian knelt down in front of me, hands on my knees. "Bailey, I want to use these with you." He held out a length of red silk.

My eyes went wide and I opened my mouth, shaking my head, ready to say no. But the look on Ian's face told me he really wanted this, that it was important to him.

"Can I talk?"

"Yes. You can."

"I want to, but I'm scared. You know that. Being tied up… it's your thing, not mine."

"I know. Here's what I want to try." He reached out, gently taking my hand, wrapping the silk around my wrist. It was soft and slithery, cool to the touch. But it was a binding, a way for him to tie me down.

"This is what I want to use. And I want to tie you like this…" To my amazement he quickly tied a knot in the silk around my wrist.

"Where did you learn how to do that?" I held up my arm. "It's beautiful."

He didn't answer right away. He was looking at the silk on my arm, at the knot he'd tied. "You can untie this knot, just by pulling on this part." He grabbed one end of the tie, gave it a tug, and the red silk fell to the floor.

"See? It's really all in your control. If you want to stop, then we'll stop. But I'd really like you to try this."

I picked up the silk, running it through my fingers. It didn't seem so bad. It was just a length of silk, soft. And it was Ian, not some stranger, who was going to do this. I looked from the silk to his eyes, then held it out to him.

"Yes. Okay. I'll try."

The smile he gave me said everything. He leaned forward, kissing me on the lips. I wound my arms around his neck, and let the kiss consume us. After a small eternity Ian pulled me up from the chair, lifting me in his arms and carrying me to the bed. He laid me down and I tried to pull him with me, but he reached behind his neck, pulling my hands away.

"Not yet."

He slid his hands up my legs, beneath my dress, pulling it up over my hips, higher, over my waist. When he'd gotten it as far as it would go, he reached up, undoing the closure at the neck, and the short zipper at the side. He sat me up and effortlessly pulled the dress over my head. I was left in the beautiful bra he'd bought me. Out of habit, I reached behind me to undo the clasp of the bra.

"No, Bailey. Leave it."

I looked up at him. He'd reached down, scooping up the silk tie from the floor. My heart sped up, and I was pretty sure Ian could see it beating. I put my hands on the bed, waiting for what would come next.

"Lie back, Bailey. Up near the head of the bed."

I scooted back until my head was on the pillow. Ian sat on the edge of the bed.

"Give me your arm."

I held out my arm and he took my hand, wrapping the silk around my wrist. I turned my head and watched as he wound the silk around the bedframe. He deftly tied another knot, and snugged it against my skin.

"You're under obedience, but anytime you're scared, or want me to stop, or if something hurts, you need to tell me. Okay? You can just say what you want, no safeword, nothing special. Just tell me."

I nodded. "Okay... oh... yes, daddy." I laughed a little, more from nerves than anything else.

Ian smiled, then leaned across me. "Other arm." He repeated the same procedure with the other arm.

"Does that hurt? Is it too tight?"

I tugged on my restraints. I could feel the give in the silk, but I could also feel the tightness of the material against my wrist.

"It's okay, I think. At least it is now."

"Okay. Good."

He sat back, eyes roaming over me. "You're so beautiful, Bailey. I'm so lucky." He leaned down, lips catching mine. I tried to lift my arms, but they pulled up against the silk. It startled me and I pulled back from Ian. He smiled, running a finger down my cheek.

"It'll take time to get used this. Just relax, let me do the work. Breathe, okay?"

I nodded, taking a deep breath. He stood up, pulling off his tie, undoing the buttons on his shirt. This wasn't the slow strip tease he'd done for me before. There was a restrained urgency to his movements, as if his clothes were suddenly constricting him.

He undid the button and zipper on his pants, letting them and his boxers fall to the floor. He stood by the edge of the bed, and in the soft light he was beautiful. He was my husband, the love of my life, and for him, I wanted to try this bondage thing.

He moved to the end of the bed, climbing up between my feet. He knelt, gently taking one foot, kissing the arch, slowly moving up to my ankle, his lips lingering over my skin. He cradled my calf in his hand, caressing me as he kissed the inside of my knee.

I wanted to hold still, but it was impossible. My legs moved, my hips rolling and rising, my ass pressing down against the mattress. I was still on a high from dinner, still thrumming with excitement.

Again I reached for Ian, and again I was held back by the ties. A shiver of panic raced through me, and Ian must have felt the tension in my muscles. He looked up, eyes heavy-lidded, a bit unfocused. But he smiled, and the panic receded.

"Just relax, Bailey. You're fine. Remember, if you want, I can let you go. Do you want me to untie you?"

"No... no, I'm okay." I relaxed my arms, unclenching my fists. Ian sat back, rubbing my foot, watching me as I got myself centered.

"You sure?"

I nodded and he gave me a smile in return. I wanted this to be right, to be as good at this as Ian wanted me to be. Maybe if I focused on Ian's touch, what he was doing, and less on what I couldn't do, it would be better.

It wasn't all that difficult to pay attention to Ian. He'd pushed my legs apart and was lying between them, paying a whole lot of attention to a spot on the inside of my thigh, just above my knee. It was the same spot that he occasionally tickled, but when he kissed me there, it was heaven. I closed my eyes, letting my head fall back onto the pillow.

He changed to the other leg, slowly kissing and nibbling his way north, over the tender skin of my inner thigh, his breath hot against my skin. I was getting as aroused as I was at the restaurant, only now I was free to moan and move and enjoy this experience.

Ian moved higher, his hands sliding under my ass, lifting my hips. He looked up at me briefly, eyes dark with passion. He bent his head, all teasing and gentleness gone. I felt like dessert, being devoured by someone who was ravenous.

I arched against him, my legs spread wide, pulling against the silk ties. But this time, instead of panic, there was something else. I was controlled and restricted, but I was the center of Ian's attention. I had no choice, unless I asked to be untied, than to submit to whatever he wanted to do to me.

And what he was doing to me was nothing short of amazing. Ian could do things to me with his tongue, his lips that drove me wild. It wasn't long before I was twisting in his hands, pulling against the ties.

The silk rubbed against me, and there was a not unpleasant burning sensation on my skin. As Ian thrust his tongue into me, as he sucked and nibbled on my swollen clit, I found myself twisting my wrists, the heat that built up a strange counterpoint to the fire that Ian was making happen.

I strained against the silk, twisting in Ian's hands, on the verge of something I had no control over. Ian knew me, knew my sounds and movements, and brought me to that edge, then slowed, pulled me back, teasing me, then building to another crescendo, over and over.

But Ian knew when to stop, or when to change, when to let me go over that edge. I was crying now, tears of happiness and ecstasy—and a tiny bit of frustration—running from the corners of my eyes.

When I thought I would burst, when I didn't think I could stand another minute of this delicious torment, Ian pulled away from me, rising quickly over me. I let my legs fall open, welcoming him as he fell against me.

He was inside me, thrusting hard and fast, and I came almost right away. I arched hard up against him, feet pushing against the bed, head twisting side to side. I pulled hard on the silk, my arms straining, aching to hold Ian.

Ian's body tensed suddenly, and he set his hands beside my shoulders, pushing up from me.

"Bailey... I love you, Bailey."

He buried himself in me, pushing hard, his heat melding with mine, feeding me, fueling my orgasm. We came together as only we could, and together we were more than we could ever be apart.

I closed my eyes, and something happened. I lost the world, spun away into some place I'd never been before. I heard music, saw colors, smelled things that didn't even exist. I was gone, no longer part of this world.

"Bailey? Hey... Bailey. Talk to me."

I opened my eyes. Ian was holding me cradled against his chest, brushing the hair away from my forehead.

"I'm awake. I'm up." I thought I was awake.

"Yeah." His smile was more relief than happiness. "Yeah. You are."

I sat up, the world spinning a little. "Can I have some water?"

"Yeah. Sure." Ian climbed off the bed, heading to the bathroom. He came back with a glass of cold water. I drained it in messy gulps, the icy chill cutting through the fog in my head. I handed him back the glass.

"I'm untied." I looked down at my wrists. There were faint pink marks on my skin. I touched them. There was no pain, but I could remember the heat of the silk as it rubbed against me.

"I did that. You... I think you went into subspace, Bailey."

I looked up at him. He took my hand, touching the marks like I had, softly, almost reverently.

"What's subspace?"

He looked up, his eyes shining. "Submissives can get there, if what they're doing is really intense. You have these amazing orgasms anyway..."

"And this happens to submissives?" I thought being a submissive might not be so bad after all, if this was the reward.

"Not all, and not every time. I can't make it happen... it can't be forced. It's a good thing, but totally unpredictable."

I yawned, a wave of exhaustion washing over me. "Sorry. I'm just really tired." I reached behind me to undo the clasp on my bra, but my shoulders screamed in protest. I winced, hugging my arms around my chest.

"Here, I'll do that." With infinite care he undid my bra, pulling it off my body. "You're going to be sore for a day or so. Just take it easy."

I yawned again, seemingly unable not to. "Sorry."

"You've had a big day, Bailey. Come on." He took my hand, standing me by the side of the bed. "Let me fix this..."

He did the best he could to straighten out the sheets and blankets. In the tangle of sheets were the red silk ties. I reached down, picking them up. I held them as Ian finished straightening the bed.

I held them out to him. "Can you tie me up again?"

He looked down, then back to me. "Bailey, you've had enough. You're exhausted..."

I shook my head. "No, not for sex... just tie me up."

"Are you sure?" He took the ties, holding them as if weighing them. "You really want this?"

"I want to feel them on me, to wake up with them on."

He gently turned me toward the bed, and I sat on the edge. He sat down beside me. "I'll tie them loosely, so if you want, you can just slip your wrists out of them, okay? I don't want you to panic in the night."

I nodded, yawning again. "Okay. You can do that." I lay down in the bed and Ian pulled the sheet over my shoulders. I held out my arms, and he looped the silk over my wrists, tying the ends to the bedpost. He looked down at what he'd done, and then to me. There was a look in his eyes I could only label as pride. I didn't think it was pride in his knot-tying ability. I was pretty sure it was pride in me.

But sleep was coming fast, and I closed my eyes. Ian climbed in beside me, wrapping his arms around my waist, molding himself against my back. He said something, but I was too far gone to make any sense of the words. I thought I'd ask him what he'd said in the morning.

• • • • • • •

I was awake, but I couldn't tell how long I'd been asleep. It could have been minutes, or hours. I blinked once, and decided it had been hours.

The room was bright, and I could tell that it was probably close to afternoon by the way the light slanted through the blinds. They were closed, but sometimes, if I took a nap on the weekend, I woke up to this same light, the same pattern across the blankets.

I rolled over, but something stopped me. For a split second confusion washed through me, but then memories of last night came flooding back. I looked up, saw my hands still tied to the bed, the red silk wrapped loosely around my wrists. But the knot was undone, and I was holding the ends of the silk in my hands. I let go, and the silk fell to the bed.

"Hey, sleepyhead."

I rolled onto my back, pushing up against the head of the bed. Ian was in the doorway, wearing jeans and a t-shirt, barefoot, looking rested and amazingly sexy. And he had my big mug, which I sincerely hoped held hot coffee.

He walked across the room and the aroma of my favorite blend reached me. I sat up a little more, pulling the blanket around me.

"Here. You earned this." He handed me the mug and I took it gratefully, taking a big swallow of hot strong coffee.

"This is just what I need. Thank you." I took another swallow. "I feel bad though. About last night... about this."

"Why? What's wrong?" He set his hand on the sheet covering my leg. "Didn't you have a good time? Does something hurt?"

I shook my head, laughing. "Slow down, Ian. It's not that. All that was amazing... beyond amazing." I set the coffee on the bedside table. "It's just that this was supposed to be your night, to celebrate making partner. And it turned into being all about me. I feel guilty."

Ian smiled, giving my leg a gentle squeeze. "It's what I wanted, Bailey. Every minute of it. To be there with you, to experience what happened last night... it was perfect."

"But..." I still had a hard time wrapping my head around Ian sometimes. "So that was a perfect night for you?"

"More than perfect. It was the best night I've ever had. You were perfect."

"Oh." I felt my face grow warm. "Even when I messed up?"

He leaned forward, kissing the end of my nose. "Even when you mess up.

I love you, Bailey. Like I said, I don't expect you to be perfect. I just want you to be open to things, to try. And if you make a mistake…" He shrugged. "Then you make a mistake."

His hand had slid up my leg, and now he was slowly pulling the sheet away from me. "And when you make those mistakes, you get punished, right?" His voice had gone all rough and sexy, low and almost scary sounding. A scary sound that I loved. A little thrill ran through me.

"Yes, I do."

"And I think I missed a few punishments last night. Don't you?"

My breath came up short. I'd messed up, broken obedience, talked out of turn, more times than I could count. I swallowed hard, nodding.

"Then maybe you're due for a punishment now?"

I blinked, staring at him. "Yes."

He'd pulled the sheet down my legs, and I was completely exposed. "The usual? A spanking?"

I was getting wet just from the sound of his voice. I nodded again, and found my voice. "Yes. But…" I panicked, amazed at myself for even wanting what I was going to ask for.

I held out my wrists. "Tie me up."

It was Ian's turn to look surprised, but only for a second. Then he smiled, reached behind me for the silk ties. He slowly wrapped them around my wrists, tying the ends in a bow.

"Nice knot work." I grinned at him.

"You're my present."

He took my wrists, pulling me forward. I rose up on my knees. It was awkward not being able to use my hands, but Ian was there for support. I thought he'd put me across his lap, but he pushed me down onto my stomach in the tangled sheets. I struggled for a moment, trying to raise my head. He grabbed my hips, pulling my ass into the air, until I rested on my knees and my elbows.

And then he started my punishment. I lost count of how many times he spanked me. The familiar sound of his hand on my skin, the sharpness of the first smacks, the heat that sank into me… it was all there. But then it went past that, into something else. I could hear Ian's breathing, hear my own cries in cadence with his hand hitting my ass, but it all bled together into one rush of sensation.

I came, suddenly, hard, my body almost convulsing on the bed. I knew Ian had stopped spanking me, but somehow I still felt him. With each wave of ecstasy that washed through me I felt the touch of his hand on my skin, the sharp sting, the incredible heat, the deep throbbing.

Finally, I collapsed on the bed, breathing hard, my body still moving to some inner rhythm. I felt Ian moving beside me and I opened my eyes. He was looking at me, something like awe on his face.

"Bailey, my God. You've never done that before."

That didn't make any sense. "I've had orgasms before." Awkwardly I rolled onto my side, my bound hands in front of me. "You've been paying attention, right? You've seen me come."

He shook his head. "I mean just from the spanking. I usually... do something else, touch you, or something. But this was just from the spanking."

It finally dawned on me what he meant. I held out my hands. "Maybe this had something to do with it?"

He pulled the end of the silk and the bow came undone, the silk sliding off my hands. He held it for a minute, then folded it carefully and set it beside my now cold coffee.

"Maybe it did."

CHAPTER FIVE

"It's about time you showed up," Ian exclaimed before I could get my jacket off. "I was beginning to think I was gonna have to get Dan drunk so I could take advantage of him later." He winked at the bartender.

My breath caught in my throat. He had done it. We were really going to do this. We had always talked about how I needed a big girl night away from everything and it had really happened.

It felt like hours ago I'd gotten off the plane and checked into the hotel with him. We'd left Little Haven and taken a vacation to California. We were in the beautiful hotel when we talked about our fantasy night and he'd made it real in just a matter of hours. He'd purchased the cop Halloween costume and had rented out the nearby bar just for us—for me and my big girl fantasy night.

"Oh, shut up and get me a drink," I said. I don't know why I told him to shut up. I wouldn't do that normally. This entire big girl night was putting me on edge, but apparently he could tell. He was already coming up to me with four shot glasses.

"You have the right to be sexually harassed," he joked, holding his gaze on my ass until I noticed what he was looking at.

"Yeah? If I say your tongue, will you hold it against me in some dark alley?"

"Of course," he said, taking the seat next to mine.

"Your tongue, your tongue, your tongue," I said, grinning.

"Keep it up," he said, pushing three of the four shots across the table to me. "One of these days I may just take you up on that."

"If you do, you're the one who better *keep it up*," I said, slamming the first shot of tequila and reaching for another. I don't know what was going on with me. I had been a little for so long that I didn't know what the right thing to say anymore. I was being flirty and fun with my husband and I loved it... but somewhere deep down I missed being his little girl too.

"Don't you worry about that, little lady."

"We'll see," I said, pointing at the jukebox in the corner of the bar.

"What, you want that I should serenade you?"

"I'm sure you're a fine singer, but I think I'd prefer Nine Inch Nails."

"Coming right up," he said, pushing the fourth tequila across the table. "Now drink up, so I can take advantage of you later."

"You gonna frisk me, officer?" Ian winked at me as he got up.

"Nah, I'm gonna handcuff you and then I'm gonna protect and serve the hell out of you."

"Promises, promises." I said weakly. I couldn't deny the thought of him using handcuffs on me sent a thrill of pleasure through me.

Trent Reznor, exclaiming he wanted to fuck some woman 'like an animal' belted out just the first of a long list of songs Ian had picked out, and I couldn't help but notice Ian was acting a bit bolder than normal, pushing the very limits of what could still be considered joking. We hadn't ever done this before and I was terrified of doing something wrong, but as the next hour passed, I became aware that this could very well be the night I had longed for since the day I first met Ian. A big girl night. A normal couples night out away from Little Haven. Just a crazy night of passion without me being little and having little girl responsibilities. Ian knocked me out of my own thoughts when he asked if I was ready to leave.

"I don't know," I said. "What's to stop you from taking me out someplace dark and having your way with me?"

He leaned in close to me, so close I thought for a moment he was going to kiss me right then and there. I was already beginning to close my eyes, expecting, hoping that was what he had in mind.

"Can I be honest with you?"

"Of course."

"Right now, and any other night since I'm being honest, the only thing that could stop me from fucking you, would be if you told me I couldn't."

"Is that right?"

"That's right," he said.

"Well, then, let me be honest with you too," I said, my hand sliding under the table and come to rest on his leg, just inches from his hard cock. I felt him tense just slightly and the denim under my hand moved slightly, a reaction that surprised, as well as excited me.

"By all means."

"There is absolutely no chance in hell I would ever tell you no."

It was different for me to be so... in control. With my daddy he was always in charge; he always led things and did them exactly how he wanted them and I was totally fine with that. I loved that. It made me happy to not have to make those decisions... but this was different. I allowed my hand to slide up his leg to his crotch. When I found his swollen cock, I squeezed.

His head went back slowly as he closed his eyes, and a light guttural moan

escaped his lips. I shivered and, finding his neck with my teeth, gently bit him just below his jawline. He winced slightly, but his hand found the back of my neck and pulled me into him. I pulled back, holding his skin between my teeth a few moments longer before releasing it and running my tongue up his neck to the bottom of his earlobe. After gently nibbling on it as well, I whispered into his ear.

"I live pretty close," I said seductively. "Let's go see just how many laws we can break."

Ian opened his eyes and looked into mine, his hand finding the nape of my neck and placing a light kiss on my cheek.

"I've got a better idea," he said, taking my hand and pulling me from my chair. I let him lead me out the door, and as we reached his car, I was about to ask him just what his brilliant idea was exactly. But I didn't have to. In that moment, he turned me and with an effortless move with his left hand to the middle of my back, just between my shoulder blades, bent me over the hood of the car. I stifled a moan. I loved when he took what he wanted and didn't ask. The big girl in me was so excited.

"I'm afraid you've been a bad girl," he said, pulling one of my hands behind my back. Before I could say anything, I felt the cool steel of his handcuffs as he clamped them over my wrist. I happily put my other hand behind my back and soon it was connected to the first. I felt a quick slap to my jean-covered ass and gasped softly. A second and a third smack came fast before I could ask him to stop. I felt myself getting wet and blushed. "You are in big trouble, missy. You didn't pay for your drinks before you left." A sliver of fear went through me as I realized that he was right. We didn't pay for the drinks. I was really in big trouble.

"Hey, easy, Bailey. Look at me."

My eyes snapped to his and I saw my daddy looking back at me.

He spoke in that voice he knew I responded to. "It's alright. Relax, baby girl, I'm just trying to play the part of the cop. I paid for the drinks. Calm down, sweetie…" He held my gaze until I had relaxed. "Do you still want to be a big girl?"

"Yes, daddy…" I giggled. "I mean yes, officer." He opened the back door of the car, I slid into the back seat.

"I know a quiet place we can go," he said, sliding behind the wheel and pulling out of the parking lot.

"Is it where you take all the girls?" He laughed at this.

"No, I've never taken anyone there," he said, smiling at me in the rearview mirror, "though I have gone out there by myself before when I got to thinking about you."

"Is that right?"

"That's right… on more than one occasion, I don't mind telling you."

I could feel that warm tingle between my legs as I imagined him out in

the middle of nowhere, masturbating to images of me inside his head. I sat quietly as he drove, listening as he told me of a long-held attraction that mirrored the one I held for him. He was playing his part perfectly. The cop friend who had never been bold enough to ask me out. I shivered slightly when I thought about how the night would end.

When he turned off of the main highway onto a gravel road, I knew where we were headed. It led to the lake, to a deserted picnic area that I imagined kids liked to use for partying. The spot was perfectly engineered for such activities since the road topped a hill several miles from the spot and you could see the headlights of any approaching car long before they got to you.

When we came over the last big hill, the spot was empty. There were no headlights and there wasn't a sound. As Ian pulled up to the edge of the picnic area and turned off the headlights, I glanced back out the back window to make sure we were alone. As he opened my door and helped me out of the car, I realized he had turned the radio up so we could hear it even outside of the car.

"Are you going to leave the handcuffs on, officer?"

"Why yes, I am, young lady, now come with me," he said, leading me by the arm to the front of the car after closing the door behind me.

I walked beside him, my anticipation growing with each step as Tom Petty's voice drifted harmoniously through the night air around me. When they reached the front of the car, Ian turned me around to face him, looking down at me with quiet admiration. I could see the reflection of the moon as it shimmered across his eyes. He took my face in his hands and gently held me there for a moment.

We were a good ten feet from the edge of the water, but my emotions were swimming as I stared into those dark eyes, longing to taste his kiss. When he leaned in, his thumbs each caressing one of my cheeks, I lifted myself up on my toes to meet him. His mouth was hot and my breath wilted as his tongue found mine and began to dance. I pressed myself against him, feeling his hard chest against my breasts, and for a moment wished my hands were free so I could wrap them around him and never let him go.

As he darted around my tongue, playfully teasing me as I tried to catch up with him, he unbuttoned my shirt and it fell along my arms, coming to rest on my wrists behind my back. My hair fell loosely back onto my shoulders, but he brushed it back behind me with his hands and kissed me on my neck, just below my chin. As I leaned backward against the car, I felt his cock pressing against me through his clothes, indicative that his desire clearly matched my own.

My bra was black lace and it opened in the front. He had no trouble removing it and leaving it resting against my arms. I marveled at the hunger in his eyes when he first saw my naked breasts. His approval was evident, as a telling smile crossed his lips.

He lowered his head, and taking one of my breasts in his hand, circled the nipple of the other inside his mouth, his tongue flicking against it in an elongated circular motion. His hand cupped my other breast with a firm gentleness, his thumb sliding easily across its peak with the steadiness of a surgeon. In one swift motion he had pinched my nipple and squeezed hard, causing me to whimper as I arched my back.

"I've dreamed of this moment," he whispered with a labored breath in the brief time it took to rise again to my neck, kissing me forcefully. "Do you want me?"

"Yes," I managed, my words coming out almost in a breathless plea.

He pulled back from me slightly, and as he stared into my eyes, seemingly into my very essence, I felt his hands find the button on my jeans. I stared back, content to swim helplessly into those dark shimmering pools of passion, knowing nothing else existed but this moment we had come to together.

I finally was free as my pants unclasped under his fingertips. I was dying, my panties were soaking wet, and finally he was going to help me. A gentle tug to each side sent my zipper as low as it was ever intended to go, that metallic sound announcing a finality to my waiting as the cool night air found its way onto my bare skin just above the low-cut panties I had chosen on the off chance they might be seen by the man in front of me now. I let out my breath, only then knowing I had been holding it in the first place.

His hands slid around my hips, his fingertips slipping below the seam of my jeans and leading his hands to my ass. With a handful of ass cheek in each hand he pulled me against him again, his fingertips pressing into my flesh, his ready cock again throbbing against my bare stomach. I felt the horizontal metal bar that ran in front of the car's grill and I gripped it tightly with both of my bound hands to steady myself as he leaned against me, his tongue again finding its way into my mouth, replacing my breath with a seemingly unquenchable fire.

As he pulled away from me, I caught his bottom lip in my teeth and held him, but the need to taste his tongue again was too much and as I felt it come out of his mouth, I greedily sucked it into my own. Ian pushed the back of his hands against my jeans, forcing them away from my body and then slowly guided them down over my hips. Once past my waist, they slid easily to my ankles, leaving me standing there in nothing but the scanty black silk panties, wetter now than I could remember them ever being.

I followed his eyes as they found their way down my body to the prize I had been longing to award him for too long now, and again I saw them burn with a hunger as he stood breathlessly in front of me. I caught just a glimpse of his tongue licking his lips before he was kissing me again. The skin just below my stomach flinched when I felt his fingers touch me, but before I could appreciate the gentleness of his touch, he gripped the fabric with both

hands and pulled to the sides, separating my panties from my body in two pieces. I gasped in unexpected delight at the barbaric energy pulsating from him. His lips were turned up in a lustful snarl as he held the remains of my panties in each of his hands.

As his hands went around my waist, I felt the steel on my left wrist loosen, and before I realized what he had done, he had taken the cuff from one hand, wrapped the chain around that metal bar I had been holding and secured my hand again. My hands were again bound together, only now I was also chained to the car itself. A quick wink reflected in the dark eyes as he lifted me up and onto the hood of the car.

Leaning over me, Ian kissed me briefly before finding his way between my legs. With one of his shoulders under each of my thighs and his hands clasped together on my stomach, he lowered his head. I felt his wavy hair, soft and long as it brushed against my inner thighs, tickling me slightly. But any humor or urge to laugh was gone before it had time to take root as I felt the tip of his tongue touch me just below my pussy.

My eyes clenched together tightly, blocking out the stars above me as his tongue slid slowly upward, separating my lips and finding its way inside me. When he reached my clit, he reversed his direction and I felt the back of his tongue make its way back down toward the slippery opening between my legs. This time, he buried his tongue as deep as it would go inside me, causing me to cry out in pleasure.

I no longer had any need for gentleness, he sensed it, and he began lapping at my pussy roughly with his tongue, making long, full strokes from deep inside me upward to flick against my swollen clit before darting back inside me. He drove it deep into me, his upper lip slamming against my clit while his chin slammed against my ass. When his tongue dropped lower and flicked against my asshole, I thought I might scream. It was unthinkable, but at the same time, I found myself wondering if he would dare do what his tongue was suggesting he might. *No, don't do it,* I wanted to beg him, but somewhere inside me was a curiosity that kept me from saying it, a willingness—almost a need—to let him do anything he wanted.

As his tongue pressed against my clit again, this time even harder than before, I felt a surge shoot through me, causing my legs to tremble against the sides of his head. It was at that moment that he did the unthinkable, the unspeakable. His tongue shot inside my ass with an assertive thrust. I came instantly.

"Ian," I managed as I rocked against his face, my bare ass squeaking on the surface of the car's hood.

Ian stood again just as the tremors were beginning to subside some, and I again heard the familiar sound of a zipper. My ankles were now on his shoulders as he towered over me, bound together by my pants, my white Nikes sticking up from behind his head presenting a comical, rabbit ears

effect. But again laughter eluded me as I felt his cock slip effortlessly inside me several inches. He pulled it completely out and then reinserted it, again going no more than three inches.

The shallow approach was something new to me and I was surprised by the sensation it caused. The slow rhythmic motion was hypnotic as he repeatedly pulled himself completely out of me and then came back in again, and I felt myself reaching that point again, triggered I supposed by the absolute uniqueness of it. As I began to writhe under him, my breaths now coming in moan-fueled throaty rasps, my hands clenched tightly against the rail underneath me. At this, Ian buried his cock inside me in one powerful thrust and I cried out.

"Fuck—yes—oh—fuck—yes!" I knew I wasn't allowed to say such bad words, but I couldn't help it. I was so taken by everything I couldn't think properly.

The wave crashed through me as my legs tightened against the sides of his head, my hands doing their best to hold their grip on the car. Ian began slow deliberate thrusts now, pulling back just shy of pulling completely out of me and then slamming it home again. With each thrust, I felt a new wave of vibrating pulses wash over my body. Not so much replacing the one before it as building on it, expanding it. The very outer edges of my existence seemed to expand to accommodate the growing sensation within me.

I had experienced multiple orgasms before on a couple of rare occasions, but never anything like this. It was one long, seemingly never-ending climax, building in intensity with each new wave, growing more powerful each time Ian slammed his cock inside me. I lost the ability to speak in any rational dialect, my words reduced to mere halfhearted syllables. I felt my mind struggling to register what was happening entirely as I drifted through levels of consciousness reserved for infants and Shamans. I had just enough time to realize I was holding my breath, and then I passed out.

It lasted only seconds, but it was enough time for Ian to remove the handcuffs and scoop me from the hood of his police car. I opened my eyes to see him waddling like a duck as he tried to get me into the back seat, his own pants at his ankles. I realized with immediate clarity that it had scared him, and he was planning to take me to the hospital. I started laughing. Ian stopped just as he was about to lower me into the car and stared at me, puzzled.

"I, are you okay?"

"Dear God, I'm fine," I laughed. "That was fucking incredible."

He still wasn't convinced, however, and kept looking at me with a very worried look on his face, and that only served to make me laugh harder. When I put my hands to my face to try and make myself stop laughing, I felt the wetness on my cheeks.

"Jesus, when was I crying?"

Now Ian was able to smile, and I was glad to see the color come back into his face. For a minute or two, I was beginning to think that he was the one who might need to go get checked out at the hospital. He was that pale. Even his beautiful dark brown eyes had begun to look white in the light of the near full moon. He carried me back to the front of the car and sat me on the hood. On the hood beside me was what remained of my panties. I had paid more than twenty dollars for that pair, hoping to someday show them to this very man, and he had torn them to shreds in a second. Guys had been in a hurry before—hell, most of them were in a hurry—but no one had ever done anything like that. He had been lost in his own lust for me and had just sex-hulked-out on me. It was fucking awesome.

"I always heard it was better to give than to receive," I said, tugging at his belt as I grinned.

"You don't have to do that," he said, but the look on his face said he'd appreciate it just the same if I did.

"After a fucking like that, there's no way you're getting out of here without a proper blowjob," I said, "now get 'em off, officer."

"If you insist," he said with a grin, already reaching for his belt.

He sat back on his hands as I took his shoes off and pulled his pants over his socks. Just for a grin, I had planned on ripping his underwear off of him as well, but I was surprised to see he wasn't wearing any.

"Going commando, I see," I said.

"Yeah, I love Tom Petty."

"What?"

"You know, from his song... Free Balling."

"Forget I asked," I said, taking his still semi-hard cock in one hand.

I knew there probably wasn't a male equivalent of what I had just experienced, but I intended to make this the best night I could for him. With my hand wrapped around the base of his shaft, I slowly began to lick the underside of his cock, my tongue circling around its tip each time I reached the top of it. In a matter of seconds, he was hard again.

I leaned forward and took it into my mouth, slowly sliding downward until I could feel it hitting the back of my throat. I heard him moan his approval immediately and slowly began bobbing up and down on him, allowing my tongue to trail along its underside as I went. From the corner of my eyes, I could see his hands moving restlessly beside him, clenching into fists and then straightening out flat onto the hood of the car. I sped up, tightening my grip around his cock as I went.

Now Ian was unable to keep both of his legs straight at the same time, raising one knee and then the other. I began stroking him with my hand as I worked it between my lips. I noticed that bending his knees was no longer an option at all, as his legs stiffened, sticking straight out past the edge of the car's hood. I could feel him tightening up and knew I had him on the brink.

Perhaps another time, I might slow down at this point and prolong the moment for him, but that would be another time. There was still plenty of darkness left in this night and I had every intention of having that big stiff cock inside me again before it was over.

Up until this point, I had been maintaining the same rhythm, with my hand and my mouth, but now I switched, causing my hand to meet my own lips and then separate again, causing a dual sensation that I knew he just wouldn't be ready for. I was right. Immediately, I felt his hand at the back of my head, gripping my hair, pushing himself deeper inside my mouth. I felt his legs as they began to shake and I knew he couldn't hold out much longer.

With my free hand, I reached between his legs and took a firm hold on his balls, and with a gentle squeeze, sent him over the edge. He rocked to the side on the car and his fingers clenched around my hair tighter as he shot the load into my mouth. I felt the hot stickiness hit the back of my throat, and I knew he was just as happy as I was. I stopped moving and let him finish. When he finally released his hold on the back of my head, I looked up at him and winked.

"Damn," he said, catching his breath, "thank you." He looked into my eyes. "Don't think I've forgotten about your swear words, young lady. You have a spanking coming."

Well, big girl time had ended and I could admit I was happy. I missed feeling so relaxed and comfortable with him. It was easier to be a little than a big girl sometimes. "Yes, daddy. I know. Let's go home…"

CHAPTER SIX

It had been a couple of days, and I was still stuck in my room since I was grounded from my stunt at the sleepover. Even though we'd had an amazing couple of days and connected as never before, Ian still made sure I knew what I did was bad and wanted me to stay inside.

Suddenly my phone buzzed. It was Kara.

Hey! You home?

I looked at the message and was confused. I knew Kara must know I was home. I was grounded. We both were. I texted back.

Is this a trick question?

I have to bring you something!

I wasn't sure what she could bring me. I didn't want to get in even more trouble. It didn't sound like a good idea to me.

Like a get-out-of-jail-free card?

Brody at work. Be over soon.

Oh, no. That didn't sound good. Kara wasn't supposed to leave the house. I quickly texted back.

Don't get in trouble!

I waited for a message back, but didn't get one. I jumped off my bed and ran to the window, looking outside for my friend. Eventually I saw her skipping toward my house, but I couldn't do anything about it. I knew Ian

was downstairs and if I went down before he called me down for pizza, then he would know something was up. I didn't want more trouble.

•••••••

I snuck downstairs and was sitting at the table in the other room, reading and watching through the other door while Ian answered the front door.

"Oh! I was just about to text you!"

"You were about to text me?" Ian crossed his arms over his chest.

"No… I… what I mean…" He sighed as Kara fumbled for the words. "I felt really bad about Bailey getting punished because it was all my idea. I made her favorite dessert. It took me all day!"

"Did you get permission to come here?" Ian's mouth turned up at the edges in a surprised smile. "I thought you were grounded."

"Of course I got permission. I baked Bailey cheesecake. It's got raspberries and white chocolate on top!"

Ian's smile widened as Kara's phone rang and judging by the look on her face, it was an unhappy Brody. "I'll get that for you." He narrowed his eyes and tugged it away from her and before she could protest, he had clicked 'answer.' "Kara's phone. Yes… uh-huh… really? Well, why don't I put you on speaker?"

"Go ahead. Say that last part again." Ian spoke to Brody and cocked his head to the side as he studied Kara.

"I came home early to surprise Kara, but I didn't find her at home. In fact, not only is she not here, but the door was unlocked. Anyone could have just waltzed in and taken whatever he wanted." Brody's irritated tone filtered through her phone. "I texted her without an answer, so I called thinking she was busy, but the last thing I expected was someone else to answer."

"I'm sorry, daddy!" Ian watched as Kara broke down and finally began to cry. "I felt terrible about what happened with Bailey and—"

"Kara, I don't really want to hear it right now," Brody firmly stated, then cleared his throat.

"Hey, Ian, keep her there, will you? I'll come get her in about five."

"Sure thing. Not a problem." Ian took the pie plate from Kara, then stepped back to allow her to go inside. "See you in a few." He clicked 'end' and handed the phone back to her. "Go sit in the kitchen. Hurry up. I don't like being lied to, and when your daddy hears that on top of what you did, I'm sure it will be very hard for you to sit down for quite a while."

•••••••

"I told you not to get in trouble!" I looked at my daddy. "I didn't tell her to come over!" *Yeah, that was smooth.*

293

"No, wait, I didn't say you did. I felt really terrible about blaming you at our sleepover. So, I, uh, made you cheesecake," Kara said.

I smiled weakly as Kara sat down next to me and kept talking.

"I lied to your daddy and mine. I'm in a lot of trouble."

Ian set the dessert down in front of me. "Next time make sure you ask for permission. It's easier than asking for forgiveness, not the other way around." A loud knock sounded on the front door and he went to go answer it.

"This looks delicious. And I do forgive you," I whispered into her ear. "But please don't get in any more trouble. Just be good so you can come over for real."

"I really am sorry."

Ian returned to the kitchen tailed by Brody, who approached the table. He took Kara's chin in his hand and titled it upwards to catch her eyes. "I thought something terrible happened to you! I was ready to call security because surely you couldn't have done something so irresponsible..."

"Well, I did. So can we just go now? I'm sure as hell not welcome back here anytime soon."

I gasped aloud. I could never talk to my daddy like that. I would be in big trouble.

"If Bailey spoke to me like that, after already being in hot water, she'd be sent to the corner for five minutes," Ian spoke up while looking at me. I lowered my eyes, unsure what to do. I knew it was true.

"Hmm? Do you have any corners around here?" Brody looked at Ian. "I mean, I hear they are the latest fad."

"You are in luck, my friend!" Ian grinned. "I happen to have four of them, in this room alone."

I rolled my eyes and luckily I wasn't caught. I hated corner time. I watched as Brody led Kara to a corner near the sink and asked her to turn around. My eyes widened as I watched Brody spank Kara four times for hesitating. I felt my cheeks turn red, but couldn't look away. I hadn't seen anyone else get punished before.

"I've got a paddle upstairs if you need one." Ian had a hint of amusement in his tone.

I slowly shook my head. I felt bad for Kara; I hated the paddle and hoped that Kara's daddy didn't use it on her. I couldn't watch anymore once Kara started to cry. I looked away from her and was happy when her daddy finally told her it was okay to leave the corner.

"I'm sorry I lied to you and I'm really sorry I came over without asking. I hope you like the cake."

I didn't know what to do, but I knew she was my friend and she was upset. I quickly pulled her into a hug. "I really do forgive you, and I'm sure it's awesome." I watched as Brody guided her to the door. "Thanks for letting

Kara borrow the corner. I should get some of those installed."

"No problem. Once these two get their privileges back, Kara is welcome to come over." Ian shot a look to Kara, who still had tears falling down her cheeks. "But not before then." Ian turned and looked at me once the door had shut.

• • • • • • •

He looked tired, like he always did now, but he kissed me hard, not just a peck on the cheek. A real kiss. I hugged him hard. It felt like I hadn't seen him in forever. I felt bad for what had happened. I know he had been working longer hours. He didn't need the added stress.

"You've been such a good girl lately, Bailey. I know it's been hard…"

"It's okay, daddy. Really. I know why, so it's okay."

He kissed my forehead as I spoke. "I just called for pizza before Kara came over. It should be here in about half an hour."

I looked up at him as he said "Then we have time." He brought a wrapped package out of his briefcase. "Let's go up to our room."

I squealed, grabbing for the box, but he held it out of my reach. "Not so fast. Upstairs."

I loved presents, and it had been ages since he'd bought me anything as a surprise. I danced alongside him down the hall to my room. He opened the door and stopped. It was a mess, as usual—clothes everywhere, DVDs and CDs piled on the floor. He turned around and gave me that look.

"I know, I know, it's a mess." I brushed a pile of clothes off the bed. "I'll clean it tomorrow."

There was a brief moment when I thought there would be a punishment, but Ian had really never stressed out over my room. We'd always thought of it as my space, my own private Idaho, where I could be myself. But even I could see it past the disaster stage and running into the toxic wasteland stage.

"Tomorrow. I promise." I crossed my heart, and he laughed.

Ian sat on the bed, the present in his hands. "Okay. Tomorrow. At least make a dent."

"Can I have it now?" I could hardly stand still, and I just barely managed not to jump up and down in front of him. He patted the bed, and I perched on the edge.

"For being so patient with me, with work and everything. I saw this and thought of you, thought you might like it." He handed me the box.

I reached up and kissed his cheek, then tore through the Hello Kitty wrapping paper. The box inside was blue, with a little gold sticker holding it shut. I slipped my finger beneath it, and the lid popped open. Inside was blue tissue paper. I pulled it back carefully, not really knowing what to expect.

It was a teddy bear, the old-fashioned kind with button eyes and a

stitched-on mouth and nose. Even without taking it out of the box, I knew it had arms and legs that moved and a tiny tab sewn into the back seam with the name of the company, and a tiny bear stitched on it in emerald green. My hands shook as I pulled the bear out of the box. I'd had the exact same bear as a child.

"Bailey? What is it?"

I couldn't stop it. Tears fell down my cheeks, landing on the bear's cinnamon-colored fur. He blurred, and I blinked back more tears.

"This is the bear my mom gave me. The exact same one. It was the last thing I had from her, before she... went away."

"Oh, Bailey. I'm so sorry." He wrapped an arm around my shoulders, pulling me against him. "I'm sorry. I didn't know. Do you want me to take it?" He reached for the bear, but I shook my head, holding it close to me.

"No. I love him. It's just..." I hugged the bear, tears starting up again. "I miss my mom. And I don't want... I don't want you to go away, because she did, right after she gave me the bear." My words came out in a rush, mixed with sobs. Ian rocked me against him, his voice soft, murmuring wordless sounds against my hair.

"I'm not going anywhere, Bailey. I'm not going to leave you. I'm fine. Your mom was sick..."

He knew the story. She'd had cancer. But I'd been too young then to understand. I knew now, in my mind, what had happened. But in my heart, when I was a kid—and now, sometimes—I still thought she'd left me, that she'd been mad at me.

We sat in each other's arms until the doorbell rang. Ian went down and took care of the pizza delivery. When he came back, I was still sitting on the bed. He sat beside me, and after a few minutes he picked up the hairbrush from the bedside table.

"Turn around."

I shifted so my back was to him. While I cradled the bear, he brushed my hair. My mom had done this, and when we were first married, on a day when I'd been in tears over something, he'd picked up the brush and brushed my hair. I don't know why it comforted me so much. Maybe it was how tight he clasped me, how he held me close. I felt safe.

We sat for a long time, until I was calm, until my tears and the fear of him leaving for no reason had passed. Finally he set the brush aside. I turned around, still holding the bear.

"Ian, make love to me. Please. I want to be loved."

"Where?"

I set the bear on my bed, kissing its nose gently and leaning him against my pillow. I looked at it for a minute, this small stuffed bear that had brought up such huge emotions. Then I looked at Ian, this amazing man, who loved me and understood me.

"In our bed."

He stood, holding out his hand. I took it, and he led me down the hall to our room.

It was dark, and we left the lights off, undressing each other slowly in the dark, feeling rather than seeing our way to bare skin, touching and kissing, each move slow and gentle.

When we were done, I curled against Ian, inhaling the scent of us together, running my fingers over the smooth skin of his chest. I felt the rumble of his voice beneath my fingers.

"Are you hungry? The pizza's cold, but it's there."

"No. I'm good." I was sleepy, content, and food wasn't on my mind. "But if you are, go ahead. I'm fine."

He slipped out of bed, and I pulled his pillow over, burying my face in it. It smelled of him, his scent, his aftershave. I nestled into the covers and closed my eyes, letting my mind wander, thinking about Ian, about our life together. And not for the first time, I thought about how lucky I was.

CHAPTER SEVEN

A couple of days later, Ian had made burgers on the grill, and we were eating outside, even though it was a cold Saturday. I could hear littles and adults splashing in the pool inside the community center down the street, and even though it was cold, I still wanted to go. It would be nice to relax in the water.

"I can read your mind, Bailey. If you want to go, we'll go."

"Really?" I leaned over and kissed him. "You're amazing. I'm going to get changed."

I dug out my favorite bikini. Ian came in, took one look at the skimpy little thing, and then chased me around the house, threatening to lock me in my room if I didn't wear a cover-up or something. I didn't think it was a big deal, but apparently a girl wasn't supposed to run down the street in a bikini. He'd finally caught me, wrestling me into some frumpy-looking thing. But the chase was fun, and I wasn't that upset. It really *was* cute, with the little white stars on the dark blue background. It looked like the night sky.

When we stepped inside the community center, I looked over the crowd. Kara wasn't there. I hoped she was having a good time with her daddy. There were other girls there, and a few guys, and I watched as they splashed and played, dunking each other, or climbing up on the guy's shoulders and getting tossed into the water. I dropped my bag on a chaise, and Ian pulled over another. He got settled and I got out of the horrid cover-up, heading to the edge of the pool.

There was one girl I knew, or knew of. Her name was Claire, and Kara had told me she was also a little, but a much younger role-player than either Kara or me. Because of that, we rarely saw her out without her daddy, and we'd never done more than just say hi.

Claire was sitting at the side of the pool, her blond hair in the usual pigtails. She seemed to be afraid of the water, and her daddy seemed to be trying to get her into the pool, but she refused, and he'd walked away. I was pretty sure his name was Jensen. I walked over to the girl. "Hi. I'm Bailey."

"I'm Claire. It's nice to meet you. I'm sorry that I didn't recognize you from before when our... when our husbands were talking."

She seemed to be uncomfortable, but I helped her out by smiling really big. She didn't have to be uncomfortable around me. "It's okay. Why aren't you in the water?"

"I... ummm... well, I need to wear these water wings because I don't know how to swim, but I don't want to. They're ugly and babyish."

"I know what will make your water wings awesome to wear! I've got these really cool stickers. If we put them on your wings, would you like to get in the pool and show them off? I think it'd be cool to show the other girls. Does that sound good?"

"Okay. I like stickers!"

Somewhere in my bag I had some stickers. I dug them out, and brought Claire over to where Ian and I sat.

I put the stickers on her wings while she watched, eyes wide, a big smile on her face. Her daddy came over, watching our progress, patting Claire on the head, and eventually he agreed to let her go in the water as long as I was with her and we stayed in the shallow end. That was fine with me.

I helped Claire back into her wings, and I held her hand as we walked to the pool. But she suddenly broke away, heading for the deep end.

"Claire, no. You're not supposed to..."

Before I could get to her, she jumped off the edge of the pool. I reached out to grab her, but she hit the water hard, and for a sickening moment she went below the surface, then came up sputtering.

I jumped into the pool and then pulled Claire to the edge. For a moment she looked petrified, but then she burst out laughing.

"I want to do that again." She started climbing out of the water, but before she could get out, her daddy reached down, pulling her out of the pool.

"You were told not to go into the deep end. You're in big trouble, Claire."

Ian walked over, and I pulled myself out of the water.

"But I want to do that again. That was fun." Her grin was from ear to ear, and she tugged on Jensen's hand, pulling him toward the pool.

"It's not her fault. I... I told her it was okay. I didn't stop her." Claire was just a littler version of me, and it really wasn't her fault. I should have been watching her. Ian's scowl deepened, and I thought I was really going to get it for lying to try to get Claire out of trouble. He gave me a look I didn't quite understand, and then turned to Jensen.

"Claire's having fun, and no one got hurt. I think if we agree to let me take care of Bailey when we get home, everyone can go back to enjoying the rest of the day." He took my hand, pulling me against him. "How does that sound?"

Jensen and Ian exchanged looks, then Jensen nodded. "If she promises to watch Claire, and stay with her, then it's okay."

I nodded. "No more deep end, Claire, unless your daddy's here with you. Okay?" She pouted, but nodded. Jensen and Claire drifted away, but Ian pulled me aside. "Bailey, I know what you did. Or didn't do. We'll talk about it later, okay?"

I nodded, wondering what my punishment for this was going to be. I hadn't done anything, but I'd lied, even if it was to protect Claire. And for Ian, that was usually the worst thing I could do.

CHAPTER EIGHT

The phone rang and I scooped it up. "Hello?"

"Bailey. I need your help. Can you come get me?" It was Kara.

"I'm grounded, Kara. You know that."

"From the thing at the pool with Claire? Still? My God. You barely did anything, and you got punished. And you're still grounded?"

I thought back to the whole weekend. "Yeah. It's complicated. What do you need?" I sat at the counter.

"I need a ride home. I'm… somewhere I'm not supposed to be, and I need to get home before Brody does."

"So you're in trouble, and you want me to get in trouble, so you stay out of trouble?"

"Yeah. You're my friend. What are friends for, if not to help? Besides, you have a car. It'll take just a minute and then you'll be home."

I sighed. "Where are you?"

"Oh, thanks. Third and Elm. At the coffee shop. I met… well, that's not important. Can you come? If you leave now…"

I looked at the clock. If I left now, I could get her, get her home, and have the car back in the garage in less than twenty minutes.

"Fine. I'll be there. Be outside, and I'm not really stopping, just slowing up enough for you to jump in the car."

And so I pulled out of the garage, drove like a crazy woman through town, and picked up Kara. I did a drive-by at her house, barely stopping to let her out. The clock in the car told me I'd been gone for almost half an hour. I drove back around the block, toward home. As I came around the corner, my heart took off at a double-time beat, and I thought I was going to be sick.

I could have sworn I'd left the garage door open. But it was down. I hit the remote, and the door rumbled up.

Parked in its spot was Ian's car. I was screwed.

CHAPTER NINE

"I don't know what the big deal is." I stood at the stove, spatula in hand, waiting to flip the pancakes. The first ones were always a bitch; they either burned or were raw in the middle. I was trying to perfect my technique when Ian had come barging in from the garage.

"The 'big deal' is I told you specifically not to take the car. But you took it anyway, didn't you?"

"I took it because…" The pancakes were all bubbly on the top. Maybe I'd finally gotten it right this time. I slid the spatula under the edge of the first pancake, lifted…

"Bailey!"

The spatula jerked in my hand, smushing the pancake against the side of the pan.

"I'm talking to you. The least you could do is pay attention!"

"And I'm trying to make dinner!" The pancake was a gloppy mess, quickly welding itself to the pan. I grabbed a potholder and took the pan from the burner, scraping the ruined pancake into the sink.

"Pancakes are not dinner, Bailey. Pancakes are for breakfast."

I turned around, pan in one hand, spatula in the other. "Pancakes are food. It doesn't matter when you eat them."

"You're still not listening to me, Bailey."

I set the pan on the burner, ladled up a scoop of batter and poured it in. It sizzled a little, then started to smoke. Shit, the pan was too hot. Maybe if I turned down the burner…

"Bailey! Would you at least pretend to pay attention?"

"It would really help if you'd stop yelling while I'm doing this, Ian."

I could practically hear the echo of his name in the air. I dropped the spatula, covering my mouth with my hand. "Oh, my God. I'm sorry, daddy. Really. It's… just…" I lost my voice in a hiccoughing sob. "It's just been a really crappy day."

He watched me from the other side of the island, eyes cold and hard. I'd

crossed a line, a big line. Not a tiny line somebody could easily miss. I'd taken a big giant step across a wide black line.

"Bailey... you're burning dinner."

I looked down. The pancake was a burning disk in the pan. In anger I grabbed the handle of the pan, minus the potholder. It was hot, and it burned my hand. I flung it into the sink. It hit the metal with a clang, knocking over a drinking glass, shattering it into a thousand shiny shards.

"Damn it. Fuck." I lunged for the faucet, dousing my hand in cold water.

"Bailey..." Ian was behind me. I wanted a hug, I wanted to be told it was okay, that burned pancakes and sneaking out didn't matter. I wanted him to tell me he loved me. But the tone of his voice gave his emotions away. There was no love in it all, just the sound of his disapproval.

"Fuck it. Just leave me alone." I pulled my hand out of the water, cramming my hurt fingers into my mouth. I tried to push past him, but he grabbed my arm.

"Let me go! Just ground me, send me to my room. Get it over with."

"You were grounded, you had been sent to your room. But you took the car, and now you're here, with a burned hand and no dinner. Doesn't that tell you something? Doesn't it tell you that maybe you should listen to me? That I know what's right for you?" He pulled me close, and I stared up at him, practically panting in frustration.

"Not all the time... not this time. And you won't even listen to me. I had a reason why..."

"I would have listened, if you'd act less like a spoiled brat. But you don't, Bailey. You just don't listen."

I wanted to tell him it was all a mistake, that at the time taking the car seemed more important than doing what he'd said. But everything inside me was tangled, and wrapped up in all the wrong emotions. I didn't want to argue or fight, but there didn't seem to be any other words that came out of my mouth.

"You're just mean, you know that? Just plain mean." I jerked my arm out of his hand, spinning against the kitchen cabinets. Everything inside rattled and it was pretty much the way I felt inside.

"I hate you!"

I fled the kitchen, hitting the door to the garage at a run, pushing it hard enough for it to slam into the wall. My keys were in my jeans pocket and I stopped for a heartbeat to pull them out. Behind me I heard Ian's fast step and it sent a sliver of adrenaline through me.

The car beeped as I hit the unlock button on the key ring. Jerking open the door, I fell more than climbed into the driver's seat. Ian was in the doorway and for a split second I saw his face and I hesitated. I should stop, go in, get out of role-playing and talk.

But the emotions raging through me didn't allow for rational thought. I

was caught up in something bigger than me, something verging on the extreme. Something almost out of my control.

Ian was beside the car now. I could hear his voice, hear him saying my name. I slammed the button for the electronic door locks, taking a perverse delight in watching as Ian tugged at the door. I wrenched the key in the ignition and the car roared to life. He said my name again and I hit the button on the CD player, Trent Reznor and Nine Inch Nails filling the car with throbbing industrial bass. Insanely, I remembered Ian's comment the last time he rode with me, that if I kept the bass turned up all the way, I was going to blow my speakers.

I met his eyes for just a moment, then jammed the car into reverse, turning away from him, turning around just in time to see the garage door was down.

"Shit..." I slammed on the brakes, my head bouncing against the headrest. I reached for the visor, smashing my thumb against the garage door remote. The door trundled slowly up and I started back up again. Ian was pounding on the driver's side window, his voice ragged above the pounding music. I caught his eyes again, seeing panic this time.

None of that seemed to make a difference in how I felt. I shot out of the garage, the door catching the roof of the car with a metallic shrieking. God, another insurance claim. I pushed that adult thought out of my mind. There was enough shit in my head without worrying about that. Let Ian handle it.

The car fishtailed wildly down the driveway, and I slung the wheel hard. The ass end rode up on the curb, taking out Mr. Fisher's garbage cans. I didn't care. The old fart always put his cans too close to our driveway. Everyone knew I sucked at backing up.

I hit the brakes, barely, and shifted the car into drive. Ian was in the driveway and it wasn't until I saw him lit by the garage light that I realized it was raining. I flicked on the wipers, hit the gas, and I was gone.

• • • • • • •

Old Highway 89 goes out of town to the east and has been replaced by a newer, straighter highway that cuts through about a dozen farmer's fields, but saves the residents a precious ten minutes getting to and from work. I drive the straight section to work, but take the old road home. It's a nice road, with cows and fields, and sometimes it calms me down to have to pay attention to the curves and dips, the blind corners, the cows by the side of the road.

Tonight the road was an inky black snake curving into the dark. The rain pelted the windshield and I reached for the control for the wipers, but they were already slamming back and forth as fast as they would go. I could barely see, but I knew this road. I didn't know where I was going, but right now I didn't give a fuck.

The car slipped on the first curve, skating over the yellow line, and my

heart chattered in my chest. I took my foot off the gas and pulled the car back in my lane. There was a straight section ahead and I pushed my foot down, watching the speedometer needle creep up, my heart thumping along in time with the music. It cleared me out, cleaned me out somehow—the hard bass, the gravelly sound of Reznor's voice, the darkness behind all that noise.

Suddenly I was in another turn, the car drifting again across the yellow line. I took my foot off the gas, turning the wheel like before, but the car kept going into the other lane. I jerked the wheel, but the car didn't respond.

There were headlights, and I couldn't see. The lights were too bright and I put up my arm, shielding my face. I wanted to turn right, to be in my lane, and I turned the wheel hard, hand over hand, bright lights all around me, the wheel slack in my hand. The music went all warble-y and strange, like I was underwater.

I looked out my window into the darkness, and wondered where the hell I was. The road had vanished, I seemed to be floating, the seatbelt pulling oddly against me. There was a moment where nothing felt right, but I couldn't tell what was wrong.

Then the car window slammed against my head, and I screamed in pain. Everything sped up, and I was upside down, arms over my head. I screamed again, or I thought I did.

I opened my eyes. Rain was hitting my face, and I wanted it to stop. I tried to roll up the window, but pain lanced through my arm, and I screamed again.

"Don't move. Just stay still."

I tried to see who was talking, but there was too much rain, and it was dark. There were odd lights coming from behind me, and in the distance I heard the thin wail of a siren.

"I want out... let me out." I reached for the seatbelt clasp. Another bolt of pain shot through me, and the world went away.

Someone was pulling me, gently, but it hurt. Then voices, some close, some far away. "She's awake, but..." "...hit her head..." "They got ahold of him..." "Her name's Bailey."

"Bailey. Can you open your eyes?"

"Yeah..." I looked up at the man talking to me. "Yeah... okay."

"Here. Can you tell me how many fingers I'm holding up?"

I looked at his gloved hand. Then I looked past his hand, at the bright white walls, the glass-fronted cabinets. Everything was so clean. I pulled my eyes back to the man and with a start, realized I must be in an ambulance.

"What happened? Wait... where's Ian?" There was something on my face, and I pulled at it. The man reached out, taking the strange thing out of my hand.

"This is an oxygen mask. You should keep this on." He pushed it back, but I batted it away, struggling to sit up. My arm hurt; a dull ache that burst

into full-on pain as I tried to move. But the arm refused to come with me, and I screamed.

"Bailey. Relax. You might have broken your arm. It's in a splint. And you hit your head. I need you to lie still." He pushed me back, gently, but forcefully. I lay back, watching him.

"Do you know where you are?"

I nodded. "Old 89. Somewhere... oh, God. I crashed the car." Fragments came back, the car sliding, the lights, the fall. "Oh, fuck. There was... another car? Are they... did I kill anyone?"

"No. No one else was hurt. Yes, you were in an accident. Your arm is bruised, at least, and you hit your head."

"Yeah... okay." If my arm hurt, it must still be attached to me. My head had started to throb, a dull ache somewhere behind my eyes.

"How many fingers am I holding up?"

"Two."

"Do you know what day it is?"

"The day I crashed the car..."

He smiled, shook his head. "I mean the day of the week."

"Oh... Friday."

There was a flurry of activity behind me, and over the sound of beeping vehicles and the rain, I heard Ian's voice.

"Where is she?"

"She's in this ambulance."

Then he was beside me and I was looking up into his eyes. "Oh, baby. I'm sorry..." He took my hand, winding his fingers through mine. "I'm so sorry."

"I crashed the car." Tears streamed across my cheeks, and I pulled the mask off my face again. The EMT guy sat back, filling out papers on a clipboard.

"It's okay. You're okay. The car is just... a car. I'll buy you a new one."

"I'm sorry, I should have listened... and I said I hate you. Ian, I never meant..."

"Shhh... I know. I know. Not now though. We'll talk about it later."

The EMT guy leaned over, talking to Ian. "You're her husband?" Ian nodded. "We're taking her to Mercy West. She's going to need x-rays, and maybe a CAT scan. She was unconscious when we found her. They'll want to check for a concussion."

"Okay." Ian turned back to me. "Listen, baby. I'm going to go. I'll be right behind the ambulance, okay?" He kissed my hand. I held on to him, not wanting to let go.

"I'll be right behind... I'll be there when you get there, okay?"

I nodded, letting go of his hand. It was the last thing I wanted, to let go of him.

• • • • • • •

The ambulance ride was chaotic, swirling lights and strange smells, a man who wasn't Ian telling me what to do, asking me questions I wasn't sure I knew the answers to. He said there'd be a little stick as he jammed a needle into my arm. There was a sharp metallic pain, and then he was doing something with plastic tubing, hanging a bag of liquid from a metal hook in the ceiling of the ambulance. Part of me—the little Bailey part—wanted to answer his questions, to tell the truth. To be a good girl. But that girl inside me was screaming in fear.

But this wasn't play, not anymore. In a detached part of my mind, the adult in me ran through what I'd done, in the space of less than a half hour. I'd told Ian I hated him, I ran out, I'd probably totaled the car, I'd done something bad to my arm, and my head… and I'd seen something in Ian's face I never thought I'd see.

He'd been scared. I'd seen Ian happy, angry—sometimes at me—and lost in whatever amazing things he felt when we made love. But I'd never seen him scared. And I'd made him look that way.

The sirens cut off abruptly, and the ambulance thumped to a halt. The backdoors were flung open and the EMT started unhooking the IV bag from its metal hook, laying it across my stomach.

"We're at the hospital. You're going to the emergency room now, and someone will look at you."

"Where's Ian? Where's my husband?"

"He's probably right behind us. Or they've got him in registration."

Someone grabbed the foot end of the stretcher, pulling me into the cool night air. It smelled of rain and exhaust, and then we were banging through a swinging door, and everything smelled like death and overcooked vegetables. The lights overhead were too bright and I closed my eyes.

"Bailey? Stay awake."

"I am awake…" Someone shook my arm. The stretcher bounced along, every jolt sending pain through my head.

"I'm awake, dammit. The lights hurt my eyes."

"We need you to stay awake." It was a woman this time, her voice nasal and very loud. "We're going to move you now."

I opened my eyes, looking for the owner of the voice. It turned out to be a tiny black-haired woman with a pinched face, a pair of glasses sliding down her nose. My dislike for her was instant and immense.

"I am awake." I was in a green-curtained square, voices and noises just on the other side of the thin fabric. My skinny stretcher was resting next to a slightly larger stretcher.

"Here, move over here." She patted the stretcher, and I sat up, inching

my bottom over the gap between the two. She seemed more concerned about the plastic tubing, admonishing me to be careful. She efficiently pulled the white sheet over my legs.

A man… the man from the ambulance… appeared and whisked away the narrow stretcher.

"We need to ask you a few questions…"

"It's the same day it was in the ambulance, we have the same president, and I know my birthday." I struggled to sit up, but the woman put a hand on my shoulder. For such a little woman, she seemed very strong. I lay back, glaring at her.

"We're not trying to be mean. You hit your head, so we need to monitor your mental status."

"Fine." I spat out the answers to her questions, and then started with my own. "Where's my husband? He was right behind me in the car."

"I don't know." She was busily writing on a clipboard. "He may be in registration…"

"I'm tired of hearing he's in registration. I want to see him."

Panic rose inside me, hot and sour. I wanted Ian. Things were out of control… I was losing control.

"I'm sure he'll be here shortly." She hung the clipboard over the end of the bed, glanced up at me, glasses sliding even further down her nose. There was a noise outside and the curtain was swept aside. I sat up, expecting to see Ian.

But it was a man in green scrubs, with a stethoscope around his neck. He grabbed my chart, flipping brusquely through the pages. I sank back onto the scratchy hospital linen.

"Headache?"

When I didn't answer he looked up at me, frowning. "Do you have a headache?"

"No. Yes… my head hurts, but it's not like a regular headache."

"Do you know what happened?"

"I lost control of the car. It was raining… I think I was going too fast."

"Good."

Good. It's good that I crashed my car?

"Is my husband here?"

He didn't look up this time. The nurse was back, holding out a gown. "I don't know. If he is, he'll find you sooner or later." The man dropped the clipboard on the foot of my stretcher and walked out.

"Here, we need to get you into this, and then someone will come take you for a CT scan, and an x-ray of your arm."

I sat up, she very efficiently pulled off my shoes and socks, and then eyed up my shirt. "We'll have to cut this…"

"No!" It was my favorite Tokio Hotel shirt. "You can't…"

She brandished a pair of scissors. "There's no way to get this over the IV tubing."

"Give me a minute…" I wormed my arm out of the tight sleeve of the shirt, pulling the tubing with me. "Just stuff that through here. I went through a lot to get this shirt."

She frowned at me, but she grabbed the bag of fluid and together we got my arm and the IV out of the shirt. My other arm was another story. The splint was big, inflexible, and my arm hurt. I struggled to get the shirt over the hard splint.

"I'm going to have to cut the shirt."

"No, please." I'd barely been able to hold back tears, waiting for Ian. This sent me over the edge. I grabbed for the scissors, flinging them across the room. "You're not fucking cutting my shirt."

"Bailey!" Ian was standing in a gap between the curtains. "What the hell?"

"Ian. Oh, my God. Where have you been?" I forgot about the splint and the t-shirt.

"I've been answering questions, getting you registered. What are you yelling for?"

"They want to cut my shirt… I got this at their concert."

"I know, Bailey. But…"

"My arm isn't broken. It just hurts…"

The woman was still waving the scissors near my shirt. Ian looked at my arm, then to me, then back to the nurse. He smiled at her, that charming smile that I knew would get him whatever he wanted.

"Can we just take off the splint for a minute? Enough to get the shirt off?"

The nurse glared at him a moment. But she dropped the scissors on the stretcher. "As long as you understand the risk…"

"We do."

She undid a complicated number of Velcro straps, and the splint came off. My forearm had a nasty purple bruise and it ached, but I didn't care how much it hurt. Ian gently pulled the t-shirt over my arm, carefully folding it, setting it aside. I sat in my bra, so grateful that Ian was here. The woman reattached the splint on my arm, giving the Velcro a vicious tug. I was pretty sure she did it on purpose.

"Bra comes off. Then jeans. You can leave your panties on."

The woman handed me a gown, and then left the room in a swish of green curtains. Ian turned to me, the smile fading. For a minute I thought he was going to yell at me, but instead he reached for my hand… the hand of the arm that wasn't in the splint.

"Bailey… what am I going to do with you?" He pulled me into a hug, a tentative hug, but still a hug.

We sat for a minute and then he pulled away. "We better get you into this

before the wicked witch comes back."

He helped me out of my jeans, then held the gown while I slipped out of my bra. He slid it up my arms, then tied it behind me.

"Back up on the stretcher."

I did as he said. There was a thin blanket at the end of the stretcher, and Ian pulled it over me. I really wanted to sit on his lap, have him stroke my hair, tell me everything was going to be okay. But he sat silently, just holding my hand.

A man in white scrubs pushed through the curtain and grabbed the foot of the stretcher, kicking the brake off the wheels.

"Where are you taking her?"

"CT scan."

Ian let go of my hand as the man maneuvered backward through the curtain.

"Come with me. Please. Ian…" I reached for him, but he was too far away.

The man pulling me out of the room glanced up. "Sorry. No can do. She'll be back in about fifteen minutes. You can wait here."

I couldn't read the expression on Ian's face and then he disappeared behind the green curtain. The man shifted to the head end of the cart, pushing me down the hall. I watched the lights overhead, blinking away tears that welled. I wanted Ian here with me, holding my hand. The fear that I'd be brought back to that horrible cubicle and he'd be gone was almost overwhelming.

The man banged the end of the stretcher through a battered metal door, then jimmied me through a series of narrow halls, finally pushing me into a small room, with a very large machine sitting silently in the middle. It had a narrow table, and a large circular piece that reached almost to the ceiling. It looked like some weird religious altar or something from outer space. The room was cold and I shivered beneath the thin blanket.

With a crash the man lowered the side of the stretcher. "Do you have any piercings? Earrings?" I shook my head. For a split second I silently thanked Ian for his adamant refusal to allow me to get anything pierced, besides the earlobe piercings I had.

"Is there any chance you're pregnant?"

I shook my head.

"Okay. I need you to get onto the table here. I'll help you down." He took my arm and I got myself off the stretcher and onto the narrow table of the machine. It was bone-chillingly cold, and my teeth started to chatter. He untangled the IV tubing, and hung the bag above my head on something I couldn't see. Something heavy went across my hips.

"This will just take a minute. The table will move, and you'll hear some noises. I need you to lie still, eyes open. Can you do that?"

I nodded, and he disappeared. For a moment nothing happened. Then I moved backward, my head sliding into the opening of the machine. With a jolt I stopped, my head and shoulders inside the circle. I looked up; there was a strip of a different colored material running around the inside. Other than that, it was a featureless beige circle.

There were thumps and bangs, and I jumped. The man's disembodied voice told me to lie still, and I gripped the edge of the table. There were more noises, and a strange clicking. Then there was a deep hum. The fillings in my teeth felt like they were tingling, and then everything went silent. The table went the other direction, and I came back out of the big doughnut.

No one came to get me or talked to me, and for a long time I thought I'd been forgotten. But the man came in with a wheelchair.

"I'm going to take you next door for an x-ray. Can you sit up long enough for that?"

I nodded and he helped me sit in the chair. For a minute the room spun, but it passed. I put my feet on the metal rests, and he pushed me through into another room.

He pushed me next to a flat table. With a lot more care than the nurse, he removed the splint. My arm had a big purple bruise. I flexed my fingers experimentally. Nothing hurt any worse than it did before.

The man fastened a lead apron over me, covering me from neck to knees. There was an x-ray plate on the table and he gently arranged my arm on it.

"Okay. Sit still." He disappeared. There was a humming, a moment of light, and then he was back. He changed the plates, moved my arm, and then disappeared. He came back once more, took the plate, and then I was alone. I thought I'd been forgotten, and wondered if I could find my way back to where Ian was waiting.

But then the man came back and helped me onto the stretcher. There was another twisty ride through the halls and then I was pushed through the green curtain.

Ian was still there, and despite trying hard to hold them back, I burst into tears. The man gave me a bemused look, then turned to Ian.

"Someone will look at the CT and x-ray, and come talk to you." And he was gone. We sat for a long time, not saying anything.

"Ian... talk to me."

"Not here, Bailey. Wait until we find out what's wrong with you, until we get home."

I wiped my eyes on the corner of the blanket. What he had to say must be so terrible he couldn't, or wouldn't, say it here. I'd failed him again, this time probably in a way that couldn't be fixed with a spanking. I'd crossed more than just a line; I'd walked out of the picture.

• • • • • • •

There were voices in the hall, and the curtain waved as someone walked past. Time stretched on, and I was dozing off when someone finally came to see me. It was a different doctor, holding a clipboard.

"I'm Dr. Marsh. Can you tell me your name?"

"Bailey."

"And do you know the date?"

I answered the same questions I'd been asked by everyone else. But this man seemed to be kind, and I bit back my impatience. Finally he flipped through the clipboard, making notes, eyes scanning the pages.

"The preliminary report on the CT shows nothing abnormal, no bleeds, no skull fracture. How's your headache?"

I shook my head. "It's pretty much gone."

He nodded. "Good. I think you may have a slight concussion. I want you to go home and get some rest. You can take something generic for the headache, if it gets bad. Your arm isn't broken, just badly bruised. I hesitate to prescribe anything for the pain, because of the sedating effect." He turned to Ian. "I'd like you to check on her, talk to her every couple of hours for the rest of the day."

Ian nodded. There was some paperwork to read and sign, and someone took the IV out of my arm. Then I was told to get dressed, and I was free to leave. I took off the hateful splint, tossing it on the stretcher.

"I want to go home."

• • • • • • •

And so I found myself in Ian's car, driving through the last bits of darkness. The sky was just turning gray along the horizon, and I was suddenly exhausted. But my mind refused to stop turning.

"Ian? Can we talk?"

"When we get home, Bailey." He reached across the console and took my hand. "It's okay. We're almost there."

He pulled the car into the garage, and then came around and opened my door for me. I stepped out into the space where my car should have been parked. I blinked at the empty space, and the tears I'd been holding back welled up again.

"Come on, Bailey. Let's get you into bed."

He led me by the hand to our bedroom and arranged the pillows, then set me on the edge of the bed. He undressed me with care, easing my t-shirt over my bruised arm.

"Do you want pajamas?"

I was sitting in my bra and panties. I shrugged. It seemed like such a monumental decision to make. Ian got up, rummaged through my dresser,

and came up with a cotton nightgown I never wore. He helped me into it and then got me under the blankets.

"Do you want anything to eat? Something to drink?" He was standing at the end of the bed, and I had the feeling all he wanted was to be anywhere other than with me.

"I want us to talk, Ian." I patted the bed. "You said we'd talk."

He came and sat beside me. I reached out and took his hand. "You're mad at me, aren't you?"

"I'm relieved you weren't seriously hurt." He wouldn't look at me, wouldn't meet my eyes. My heart was thumping in a painful way. *This must be what a broken heart feels like.*

"I was scared, Bailey. Really scared. All they'd tell me was you'd been in an accident. They didn't want me there, they kept telling me to go to the hospital. I finally got them to tell me where you were."

He looked up at me, and I choked back a sob. There were tears in his eyes, and he looked ten years older. "Bailey, I thought I'd lost you. And I didn't think I could stand it if that happened."

I reached for him and he climbed onto the bed next to me, and I wrapped my arms around him. For a long time we held each other, both of us crying. I'd never seen Ian cry.

Finally he sat back, wiping his eyes. "But you're fine. You're banged up, but you're okay. And you're here. That's all that I care about."

"But if I wasn't such a failure, then this all wouldn't have happened." I held out my arm, the bruise deep and bloody. "The car…"

"Bailey, I don't care about the car." His voice was rough, and he pulled away, looking at me with something like anger.

"I care about you, no matter what. I can't not care. Even if you fuck up so badly you crash the car. It was an accident. Granted, it was because you are impulsive, but it was an accident. You didn't do it on purpose, did you?"

I shook my head. "No, but… I keep messing up."

"I don't care, Bailey. I love you. Whether it's you, the adult, the woman I fell in love with and married, the one who is brilliant, successful, and competent. Or whether it's you when we're role-playing, the impulsive, intense, irrepressible, lovable Bailey that I discovered lived inside you, I love you."

I was crying again, big gulping sobs that shook my shoulders. He reached out, wiping away my tears.

"I love how complex you are, every part of you. But you've got to cut yourself some slack, Bailey. You're still learning, we both are. And it's okay."

"But… I can't… there's all the stuff you want that I can't give you."

"If you mean the bondage, I don't expect you to be into that at the same level I am. For me, it's something I've wanted for a long time, just like you wanted to role-play. But you're willing to try. You have tried…"

I stopped crying. "Tie me up now. Please."

"Bailey... your arm..."

"You can be careful. I'll be careful. Please. Let me try again."

He looked at me for a long time and I thought he was going to say no. But he opened the drawer beside the bed, and pulled out the red silk ties. He ran them through his hands, eyes never leaving mine.

"You don't have anything to prove, Bailey. If I never used these again, it wouldn't change how I feel about you."

"I know. But... I want this... need this. I don't think it's for you. I think it's for me." I took a deep breath. "It was scary last time, when you tied me up. But it was different the next time. I felt secure, and loved, and I want to feel that again, right now."

He leaned forward, kissing me hard. There was something almost desperate in his kiss, and I thought maybe the ties would be for him too.

I sat up and he pulled the nightgown over my head. I held out my arms, and he very gently wrapped the silk around my wrists.

"I don't want to hurt you..." He traced a finger over the bruising. "I'll just make a simple rope cuff."

I watched in amazement as he looped and wrapped the silk, creating a wide cuff around my wrist.

"Ian, it's beautiful." I held up my arm, looking at the knot, while he worked on the other. Then he took the ends and tied them together in front of me.

"It's not like before, Bailey. I'm not going to put any stress on you, or your arms. But..." He put one hand behind my neck, pulling me forward. "I want this, if you do. I love you, Bailey. I'll do anything for you."

"I love you too, Ian."

He pulled me forward, and caught my lips in a kiss. It was just this side of brutal, primal, and desire rose up in me, hot and insistent. I wanted to reach for him, but all I could do was run my fingers over his shirt, fumbling with the buttons.

Ian sat back, holding my hands, kissing my fingers. Then he stood up suddenly, pulling his shirt over his head, then swiftly undoing the zipper of his pants. It took him only moments and he was naked, standing at the edge of the bed. I let my eyes travel over him, over his flat stomach, over his erection.

I lay back, my arms in front of me, resting on my stomach. Ian looked down at me for a moment, then climbed up on the bed beside me. He leaned over, kissing me again, one hand caressing my breast, rolling my hardened nipple between his fingers. I arched against him, pulling against my ties. I couldn't reach Ian, or touch him, and it was mildly frustrating.

He rose over me, spreading my legs with his hands. I wiggled against his hands, stretching out my arms, but again I couldn't reach him. And to make

things more frustrating, he pulled away.

But there was a smile on his face, that cocky smile that I loved, the one that made me feel like he had a secret, and I was part of it.

"What do you want, Bailey?" His voice had lost the uncertain tone he'd had earlier, the fearful edge. He sounded confident again, the man who was in control, of his own needs, and now of me. It sent my arousal skyrocketing. The Ian I knew and loved. I lay back, smiling for the first time that day.

"I want you. I want you to touch me, anywhere you want, everywhere."

"You want to touch me though, don't you?" He knelt between my legs. "Say it, Bailey."

"I want to touch you... if I could. But I can't." I held up my hands. "I can't. You're too far away." I wiggled my fingers, inches away from his erection. "See?"

He grabbed my wrists, then stopped, a faint frown on his face. "Tell me if something hurts, okay? If this hurts your arm."

I nodded. "I'm fine. You can stop talking though." I grinned up at him.

The frown faded, and the cocky smile was back. He eased down on top of me, pushing my arms up over my head, easily holding my wrists with one hand. His cock rested against my inner thigh, and I slid my legs over his hips.

"I want you so badly, Bailey. No matter what you do, no matter who you want to be. I love you, and I don't want you to try to be anything other than who you are. Promise me that?"

I nodded, almost breathless between the feel of his body against me, and the anticipation of what was coming, and his words. He loved me, no matter what. No matter who I was.

He thrust into me slowly, exhaling, closing his eyes. After a moment he opened them, looking down at me. "But I love this best, being inside you, making love to you." He kissed me before I could answer, pulling slowly back, then thrusting forward.

I lost track of time, lost track of everything except the feel of Ian inside me, moving with him. I wanted to touch him, to run my hands over his back, reach down and cup his ass. But Ian still held my arms over my head, and with them tied together, it was far easier for him to control me. I strained against him, and I heard his soft laugh against my neck.

There was nothing complicated in what Ian did, nothing beyond what someone might call simple sex. But there was nothing simple about what he did to my emotions, to my body. It was what I wanted, to be close to him, to have him make love to me.

The heat inside me built, every movement Ian made fueling that fire. The feel of the silk on my wrists reminded me of the last time, the subtle pain the silk caused when it rubbed against my wrists. I twisted my arms, the silk warming my skin. I was in heaven, even if I'd crashed the car.

I let myself relax, let Ian hold my arms, restrain me, and work his magic

on my body. The heat built in me, and my body followed that familiar erotic path to a climax.

The climb was slow, my body moving beneath Ian, reacting, reaching the next level, the heat inside me building to a scorching inferno.

Just when I thought I couldn't take any more, everything split apart, and I arched hard against Ian. For a moment, a long moment, I held my breath, fingers outstretched, every muscle taut as fire raced through my body. I closed my eyes, letting it overtake me, falling into the flames.

My body wasn't my own, and I had no control over the way it moved, or the feelings inside me. Pleasure and pain, agony and ecstasy all crashed through me, from my fingers to my toes. I lost my sense of place, of up or down, of dark or light. I was pure feeling, pure sensation. And it was amazing.

I wanted to laugh, to sing, to cry... all at the same time. My body felt light, but I couldn't tell where I ended and the bed, or Ian, or anything else began. I wanted it to go on and on, but I wanted to tell Ian what was happening.

"Bailey? Hey..."

Ian was looking down into my face. I heard laughter, and blinked up at Ian. He looked worried, but I couldn't understand why. Everything was wonderful. I was telling him, but he wasn't listening.

"Bailey, slow down. Take a breath. It's okay."

"Of course it's okay." I realized I was speaking, but the words sounded garbled. I cleared my throat. "It's okay."

Ian's expression lost some of the unease that creased his forehead, and he managed a tentative smile. "You're back. You had me worried. I thought you were having a stroke or something bad from hitting your head."

I tried to reach for him, to touch his face, but I couldn't move. Then I remembered I was tied in a beautiful set of cuffs, made by Ian. I giggled again, and the unease returned to Ian's face.

"Bailey, are you alright?"

"I'm fine. Really. I know my name, and the date, and the name of the president. All that stuff. Listen to me though. I'm trying to tell you what just happened."

He shifted, turning onto his side, and I maneuvered my arms back between us. I snuggled against him, winding my legs through his. My body still hummed with the aftereffects of what had just happened and I felt jittery, high, excited. Ian wrapped his arms around me and I shivered against him.

"What did you call it before? Sub-something?"

"Subspace?" His eyes widened. "You went into subspace?"

"Yeah. It was... I can't even begin to describe how it felt. How it still feels. I want to... I can't even... there are no words."

He pulled me against his chest, and I felt the beat of his heart against my cheek.

"Bailey. You had me worried. You were laughing, and crying, talking but

not making any sense. I thought…" He pulled away, looking down at me. "I thought I lost you for a minute."

"You did, but in the best possible way." I held up my hands, the red silk flowing like a river between us. "I never want to take these off. They're magic."

Ian laughed, taking one end of the silk in his hand. "I can't leave you tied up in the bedroom forever." He kissed my forehead. "Even if I wanted to. You're not a captive, Bailey."

I thought about that. "I don't want to be captive. I want to feel like this all the time. Or remember how this feels."

Ian pulled the silk, and it fluttered away from my wrists. I watched them with a sense of loss, of regret.

"Bailey, everything that happened tonight happened because of what's between us, not because you had your wrists tied."

I swallowed, blinking back a film of tears. He was right; he was always right. And that's why I loved him.

THE END

DADDY KNOWS BEST

NORMANDIE ALLEMAN

CHAPTER ONE

"I still don't know why we have to move to the middle of nowhere-ville."

"It's a community of people with relationships like ours, princess. A place where we can be as kinky as we want to be, and no one will care." Neal Solomon reached over and tickled the spot between Tabitha's ribs, which drew a reaction every time.

She giggled, a result of reflex rather than mirth. "Stop it, daddy. This isn't funny."

With a sigh, he returned his hand to the steering wheel.

"I don't know that I want to be around kinky people all the time. What if they're weird?"

"Like us?" He laughed.

"Daddy... there's nothing weird about how I feel about you." Tabitha Gibson's mouth settled into a pout. Though she was twenty-six, she sometimes behaved much younger, which was something her thirty-year-old boyfriend and daddy dom Neal found charming.

"I agree."

She grimaced. "But Minnesota? It's freaking freezing here!"

"It wasn't warm in Chicago," he reminded her.

"I know," she admitted grudgingly. "But why couldn't you have found a place in Florida or something? I hear Atlanta is quite pleasant year round. I'm sure they have daddies and little girls there..."

"I promise I'll help you keep warm," he said, turning the car into the entrance of a gated community. The sign out front read 'Little Haven.' After Neal gave the man in the guard shack his name, he drove the car through the swinging wrought-iron gate and took a right, then a left onto Huron Ave. He drove slowly for two blocks and there stood their new home.

It was a two-story beige craftsman, with green shutters and rust-colored trim, the kind of home they'd never have been able to afford in Chicago. Opening the car door into a pile of snow, Tabitha gingerly placed a foot on the recently shoveled driveway. Someone had taken the time to at least clear

them a spot, and she appreciated that. She climbed out of the vehicle, pulled her faux shearling coat tightly around her, and gazed at her new home. "It looked bigger on the Internet."

Neal got out of the car and surveyed the property. "It'll do."

It was an understatement, of course, and Tabitha tried not to roll her eyes. Ever since she'd met Neal eighteen months ago when he'd been the mechanic who repaired her BMW, she'd known that he hated to argue. He avoided conflict as much as possible, while she thrived on it. The two had completely opposite ways of relating—she wanted to fight things out, while he wanted to smooth over their differences. When things got too contentious between them, he liked to throw her over his knee and show her who was boss. Not only did it distract her when he did that, but it made her swoon and forget all about what they'd disagreed over in the first place. Sometimes when she looked at him, her heart wanted to burst out of her chest, she was so overtaken with love for him.

But now as she looked around, Tabitha didn't want to be here. She didn't like the house, the new town, but what could she do? She'd agreed to it in order to keep the peace.

"I don't know why you dragged me to this Godforsaken place," she said irritably, looking around to make sure no one else was around to hear her. "With a bunch of outcasts." Immediately after saying the words she regretted them, but she was too stubborn to take them back.

Neal looked at her with piercing gray eyes. "That's it, Tabitha. I told you—you could complain all you want on the way here if it would help you get it out of your system, but you've done that. Now that's enough. Let's go inside."

She frowned, but followed him anyway. "What if I slip on this ice?" she whined.

With a half-smile he turned and offered her his hand chivalrously. "I'll help you."

She took his hand and gazed into his eyes, which twinkled like the sun sparkling in the blanket of snow covering the front yard. How lucky she was that Neal handled her moods so well.

They traipsed up the walk and to the front door, which he opened with the newest addition to his key ring. When they stepped inside, the whoosh of the heating system was a welcome contrast to the frigid temperature outside. With a shiver, Tabitha let go of Neal's hand and strode around the airy great room, admiring the two-story ceiling, impressive windows, and majestic view.

"This is actually pretty cool," she said.

Neal winked at her. "I'm glad you like it. Only the best for my little princess."

She rushed into his arms. "Thank you, daddy. I'm sure we'll like it here," she lied. Neal was so proud of himself for finding this place; he'd gotten

himself a job and this house all because he thought it would improve her health. He'd been determined to whisk her away from her high-pressure career and all the stress that came with it, and he'd won that battle. For the moment.

He held her tightly and kissed the top of her head. "How would you like a nice roaring fire?"

"Oh, that sounds lovely. What about the luggage?"

"I'll get that too." He headed out the front door.

That's what doormen are for, she thought, wistfully remembering Sam, the doorman at their building in Chicago. There were so many reasons to have a good doorman, what would she do without one? How would she ever find the best Chinese takeout or have her dry-cleaning sent out?

She sighed. With a sinking feeling, she suspected that she would be expected to take care of daily things like that. How could Neal possibly think moving here would be *less* stressful? Everything about this place seemed a lot more stressful to her.

While Neal brought in her four suitcases, his bag, and several stacks of firewood, Tabitha explored the house. The furniture the real estate company had used to promote their model home now occupied their new house. Little Haven had been kind enough to let them borrow the furniture until theirs arrived next week. Apparently the community had been in need of a maintenance man for a long time, and the board was so pleased when Neal applied for the position that they'd offered him several perks in addition to a great salary and a place to live.

The house was roomy yet cozy, with two upstairs bedrooms, an eat-in kitchen attached to the great room, and a separate library and formal dining room. The spacious master bedroom and bath were located on the ground floor. When she walked into the master bath, she did a double take. Not only was the room equipped with two sinks, it also boasted two separate toilet rooms. And one of them, obviously the women's version, sported a bidet! When she saw it, Tabitha clasped her hands together with glee. She'd always wanted one of those. Neal's sexual appetite for her often seemed insatiable, and she loved accommodating him. Having a place specially designed to clean herself afterwards would be a true luxury.

Glancing over at the oversized tub she pictured Neal giving her what he liked to call 'a sensual' bath. This would involve her sitting on his lap, his cock prodding at her backside, him sudsing up her breasts and delicately washing the intricate folds of skin between her legs. A warmth coursed through her, settling at her core, and she sighed. Okay, this place had definite possibilities.

Back in the main room, she found Neal placing logs in the fireplace. Even through his long-sleeved shirt she could see his muscles pulse, rippling as he worked. An old football injury had left Neal's nose too crooked for him to

be considered classically handsome, but his frame was as sinewy as a dancer's and as strong as a bodybuilder's. He hurled the last log onto the pile, lit a wad of old newspaper, and placed it underneath the bundle of wood.

Tabitha remained uncharacteristically silent as she watched him and waited for the fire to catch. The way Neal did things for her, 'manly' things, made her swoon. With a full heart, she tucked her complaints into the back of her mind and asked sweetly, "What shall we do for dinner, daddy?"

"Order a pizza?"

"Sounds good to me."

"Is my little princess hungry?" he asked, lifting a brow suggestively.

"Maybe," she responded, coyly chewing on a fingernail.

"Come here. We need to christen the place, don't you think?"

She glanced around and noticed that none of the windows in the room had any curtains, and that the front door was flanked by windows on each side, leaving them somewhat exposed.

"First, you need to get rid of those clothes." Firelight glinted against his blond, wavy locks as he shifted to give her his undivided attention.

She started to comply with his request, but an uncomfortable feeling in her gut stopped her. As she looked around the room, everything felt foreign, strange. With a frown, she turned to him and whined, "Daddy, how are we supposed to live here? We don't know anybody. All of my friends are in Chicago and there's nothing to do here. It looks terribly boring."

His face turned grim and he got to his feet. "Dammit, Tabitha, I put up with your griping for the last six hours." He closed his eyes wearily. "Now hush. You're going to have to suck it up and deal with it."

"But…"

He arched his eyebrows. "That's it. If you can't be quiet when I ask, I'll have to gag you."

She pursed her lips, but then gave him a triumphant smile. "Well, that's too bad because all the gags are packed and on a truck coming from Chicago." She shrugged daintily.

He placed a hand on the small of her back and pulled her into his arms, overtaking her mouth with his. His hands ran up under her sweater, and her skin reacted with a jolt of electricity. She melted against his chest and when he began undressing her, she didn't object.

Stepping back, he removed his cords and shirt so he stood before her in his boxer briefs. Every muscle in his torso appeared carefully outlined, its planes and valleys accentuated by sharp angles and the resulting shadows. His body was a work of art, and though she'd marveled at his beauty a thousand times, she couldn't suppress a silent gulp.

He pointed at the panties she still wore. "You gonna take those off?"

Wobbly with lust, she merely nodded and slid them down her legs.

"You haven't been a very good girl today, you know that?"

"Maybe, but…"

"How 'bout we talk about something else," he cut her off. "Hand me those panties."

Why did he want those? She picked up the scant wad of fabric off the rug and gave them to him.

"How wet is my baby girl?" he asked, a mischievous gleam in his eye.

"I don't know."

He shook his head at her. "Oh, darlin', you have gotten so far off track. Daddy needs to get things back to the way they need to be."

"What do you mean?" Standing there, naked, she was beginning to shiver. The fledgling fire wasn't doing much to heat the room yet, and she rubbed her upper arms trying to warm herself.

"All the whining and backtalk, being lazy about following daddy's instructions, not addressing me the right way, complaining constantly—the whole thing. I brought you here to help you, because I love you."

"That's great, daddy, but could you please get on with whatever you're going to do, because I'm freezing."

He shook his head again. "Open your mouth."

With suspicion she unhinged her jaw slightly.

"Wider."

She huffed, but opened more, and he shoved the wet panties in her mouth. A muffled protest gurgled from her throat, but he just smiled and said, "Hush and get on that coffee table on all fours."

She shot daggers at him with her eyes, but her pussy throbbed with need. The more he dominated her, the more aroused she became. Thank goodness the coffee table seemed sturdy as she climbed on. She'd hate for them to break the community's furniture their first day here.

He retrieved a wooden paddle from the side of the couch. He must have brought that with him in the car. She shouldn't have been surprised. Her daddy loved to spank her bottom. It was his favorite means of discipline, and sadly, she required a significant amount of it.

When they'd first gotten together, it had seemed odd that he wanted to spank her for her bratty, bad behavior, but she'd grown accustomed to it, and even sometimes craved his hand smacking her ass. He'd slowly introduced her to the daddy dom/little girl lifestyle and it turned out to suit their relationship well. Tabitha needed someone to keep her in line, and Neal needed someone to nurture and protect.

"This ought to heat you up quite nicely." The paddle landed on her upturned bottom with a smack. She moaned through her mouthful of panties and felt the blood rush to her lower region.

Thwack! Wood hit flesh, and the impact sent a rush of adrenaline zipping through her bloodstream. Another swat, then another. Her buttocks were singing now, the pain lighting them up like a holiday light display. She

groaned as the smacks started to sting more and more.

"And you thought I wouldn't gag you because you'd packed the gags." He laughed. "Silly girl. Daddy knows how to improvise."

The fabric felt soft and rough against her tongue at the same time. She preferred her pink sparkly ball gag, but having him fill her mouth with her own panties was deliciously humiliating. In the back of her mind, she was aware that she was testing his patience so that he would take charge and put her in her place—because she enjoyed submitting to him.

She was often torn between being her feisty, independent self and being his love slave. Deep down, she wanted to be both, and somehow Neal helped her achieve that. He loved her and accepted her totally, like no one else ever had, which was why she'd agreed to his harebrained plan to move here.

Another swat brought her back to the moment. Her ass burned now from his paddling, but she didn't feel cold anymore. Quite the contrary, she felt warm and energized, though her pussy still throbbed with need. She hoped he'd give her some relief soon.

To give him a hint, she shook her booty slightly at him and managed to purr sweetly through the gag, her practiced way of nonverbal begging.

She heard him set down the paddle. His large hands caressed her screaming globes, and she delighted in the luxurious sensation of his touch. Mmmm.

"Now that you've been punished, it looks like you're going to need a good fucking. Am I right?"

She swung her head in an enthusiastic nod and mumbled, "Yes, daddy," through the gag.

He kissed the small of her back as his hands roamed her body. He nipped the flesh along her spine until he buried his face in the nape of her neck. Brushing her long blond hair aside, he whispered, "I love how you need daddy so much. I need you too."

He tugged on her earlobe with his teeth before standing over her to inspect her naked body. "Open those knees wider."

She scooted her legs farther apart, adoring and loathing the inspection at the same time. It made her squirm with discomfort, but there was something so freeing about having her most intimate body parts on display that it gave her a thrill.

He patted her still-warm buttocks, then cupped her pussy in his hand. His hands acted like a magic wand on her and when he spread apart her petals to reach her core, she listed on the table, wobbly with lust. "You're glistening." He groaned with satisfaction. "So ready for me."

She flushed with happiness. Serving him with her body fulfilled her in ways she'd never dreamed. Using his index finger, he rubbed her clit, stroking it up and down, then switching to the exquisite little circles he knew would make her come.

But then he stopped.

"Daddy!" she squeaked.

He chuckled. "Don't worry. I'm going to let you come—on my cock. I want to feel you come all over me." His erection pressed hard against her pussy, then prodded at her entrance, poking, until he sheathed himself inside her.

Her walls enveloped him and she steeled herself for the onslaught of his lovemaking. Neal liked to fuck her hard, and she did her best to take whatever he gave her. Rough sex was the best kind, and having daddy pound her hard and deep was something she craved.

The pace was slow at first, as he was intent on extending the pleasure of each thrust. His hand reached under and toyed with her nipple. The feeling was so intense that she whimpered and fell to her elbows, resting her cheek against the hard wood surface of the table.

Suddenly he grabbed the majority of her mane and tugged her head backwards, lulling her out of her floaty state and giving her a slice of pain to go with the ecstasy his cock was bringing her. He held her head up by her hair as if the locks were reins and he was trying to break a wild mare. "You're so fucking hot, baby girl," he said, pushing deep inside her.

Letting go of her hair, he clutched her hips and impaled her with his rock-hard shaft. His strokes grew harder and faster, until she felt the tingling sensations of an orgasm fluttering in the distance. Just a few more… she bit her lip and focused. She wanted this climax, needed it after the day she'd had.

Brrring! Brrrring! Brrring!

"What the hell is that?" Tabitha rose onto her hands.

"I think it's the doorbell," Neal said and kept fucking her.

Her body chilled, and the potential orgasm vanished, as alarm bells chimed in Tabitha's head. She was buck naked on a table getting her brains fucked out with her panties shoved in her mouth right in front of an open window. With a whimper, she gathered herself and directed her attention to the front door.

Indeed, there was someone standing there, and just as Neal grunted and came inside her, Tabitha locked eyes with the stranger.

CHAPTER TWO

Tabitha yanked the wet panties out of her mouth and squealed, "Daddy!"

Neal seemed oblivious to the woman standing outside their front door peeking through the window, watching them fuck like bunnies with a bemused expression on her face. Tabitha, however, felt like the bottom of her stomach had dropped through a trap door. She scrambled off the table, cum dribbling down her leg as she tried to gather her clothes.

Angrily, she whirled around. "Neal! There's a woman at the door."

He shrugged and pulled on his pants.

"Handle it!" Tabitha snapped and scurried into the closest room, which happened to be the library. She shut the door behind her, but could hear Neal holler, "Coming!"

Tabitha placed her hand over her mouth, stifling a laugh. She doubted he meant the pun or even realized he'd said. The woman already knew he was coming—she'd watched the whole thing! What kind of person did that— stood in the doorway watching people screwing anyway?

When she went into the adjoining bathroom to get dressed, she found herself wishing she'd fled to the master bedroom. This would have been the perfect time to clean herself off with the bidet, but she had to clean herself up as best she could. Coming back into the library, she heard a woman's voice in the great room. What was happening? Neal had let the woman into their home? Tabitha opened the door just a crack so she could hear what was going on.

"Chicago, you say? My late husband had relatives from Illinois. I recollect they were from Champagne-Urbana. How are you liking Minnesota so far?"

"It's nice. We've only been here a few hours, but so far so good."

"I'll say," the woman's voice said with a snort.

Was this woman actually commenting on what she'd just seen them doing? How unbelievably rude! She had to put a stop to this right now, Tabitha thought, marching into the great room. After the embarrassment of being caught *in flagrante,* Tabitha hadn't intended on meeting this woman face

to face, but this was her house. Who did this woman think she was? She was the one who should have been embarrassed for interrupting her tryst with Neal, for intruding on their privacy, not the other way around!

Plastering a smile across her face, Tabitha glided into the great room where Neal and the woman stood talking and extended a hand to their unexpected guest. "Hi, I'm Tabitha."

"Agnes," the woman said while sizing up Tabitha from head to toe. This only made Tabitha smile harder as she returned the favor.

"Lovely to meet you," said Tabitha with an enthusiasm that came off as fake as a porn star's breasts.

"Likewise." The older woman crossed her arms over her chest.

Tabitha was nothing if not polite. The granddaughter of a senator, Tabitha had been raised with impeccable manners. "Please, have a seat. May I offer you something to drink?" As soon as the words tumbled out, she realized she and Neal probably didn't even have any glasses to serve the woman some water, much less the ability to brew a cup of tea.

When Agnes declined, Tabitha breathed a sigh of relief.

"I can't be staying. But I wanted to stop in and welcome you to the neighborhood, bring you a housewarming gift," she said, handing a stubby little green plant to Neal.

Neal took it and showed it to Tabitha before setting down on the coffee table where they had been screwing only minutes earlier. "That's mighty kind of you, Agnes," Neal said.

"Yes, it is, thank you," Tabitha echoed. An awkward silence clouded the room as all three of them stared at the coffee table, each of them clearly thinking of the activity that had taken place there only moments prior.

It was Agnes who broke the silence. "And I wanted to invite you," Agnes narrowed her eyes at Tabitha, then continued, "to a little knitting class I'll be having at my house on Tuesday."

"Knitting? How quaint." Tabitha hoped this time her enthusiasm sounded more convincing.

Neal moved next to Tabitha and slid an arm around her protectively. "My mother goes to a knitting group at her library every Friday. She loves it. That's a great way for you to get to know some people here, Tabs."

"Yes," Tabitha said, feigning interest. "Who all will be there?"

"Just some of the other girls who live here. Claire, Angela, Kara, and another girl who's new to the community—Bailey."

Neal elbowed Tabitha gently. "See, darlin', another girl who's new like you."

She wanted to elbow him back harder, but she refrained, and responded with a noncommittal, "Oooh."

"Well, I'll let you two get back to what you were doing," Agnes said and headed for the front door. Tabitha was glad she didn't have anything to drink.

She was afraid she might have spit it out all over the place—*what* they'd been doing was fucking in plain view of this woman. Why was she so nonplussed about what she'd walked in on? Maybe she was a voyeur. Damn, she'd been so close to orgasming too when the woman interrupted her concentration. She crossed her legs tight, hoping for some welcome friction as she realized she was still aroused.

Neal walked Agnes to the door, thanked her again for the gift, then bid her goodbye.

When he shut the door and turned to face Tabitha, she was all over him. "What is wrong with that woman?"

He frowned. "What do you mean?"

"She just watched you fuck me, then came in here like it was nothing. She didn't even apologize for watching us like a pervy peeping Tom or something. Or did I miss that when I was getting dressed, and she was ogling you?"

He scooped her into an embrace. "Nobody was ogling me." He laughed and kissed her neck.

"I'm sure she noticed how handsome you are." Tabitha scowled, refusing to be distracted by his nibbles. "She just stood there watching us. Doesn't that bother you?"

"It's not a big deal," he mumbled between kisses.

"Maybe not to you!" Neal was much more easygoing than she was. Whatever happened, he rolled with it—Mr. Flexible. Not her. Tabitha didn't like surprises, and she didn't like change. The way she'd been brought up, people behaved properly, and sex was private. A cold dread filled her gut. The people here were strange.

She wriggled out of his grasp and turned to him, eyes flashing. "What kind of hippie commune have you moved us to, Neal? I didn't sign on for this."

He sighed. "You're overreacting. Maybe she didn't see us."

"Oh, she saw us alright, our eyes met," Tabitha huffed.

"Fine. Maybe she's just an old lady who's lonely. Her husband died several years ago. Maybe that's the most action she's seen in a while."

"Ew," she said in a tight, clipped voice, "so we live next door to a dirty old lady."

"Better than a dirty old man. I think you need to give her a chance. She seemed perfectly harmless to me." He yawned, picked up his duffel bag and one of her suitcases and started for their bedroom.

"Where are you going?"

"To bed. It's been a long day."

"But, but…" She trailed after him.

In the bedroom he set down the suitcases and unbuttoned his pants. He lifted his shirt over his head and a flash of desire passed through her again. She took a ragged breath and whined, "I don't even know where my nightgown is."

He gave her a sexy grin. "You know you don't need a nightgown with me, princess."

She bit her lower lip and slowly took off her clothes, her gaze locked with his.

He stopped what he was doing to admire her, and as she finished her striptease she was rewarded to see the front of his underwear tented with an erection.

"I just realized what this mood of yours is all about," he said.

She raised a brow quizzically.

"When she interrupted us, you didn't finish, did you? That's why you're so pissed."

Clenching her teeth, she unzipped her suitcase and began rifling through it.

"That's it, isn't it?" He crowed over his detective skills.

"Well, she *did* interrupt us…" Tabitha didn't look at him. She removed several pairs of socks and underwear and placed them in the top drawer of the bureau.

He came over and placed his hands on her shoulders and she finally looked up at him. "I had to put my clothes back on with cum running all down my leg. Daddy, it was gross."

He hugged her to him and stroked her hair. "I'm sorry."

She relaxed in his arms. Snuggling with her daddy was the one thing that always brought her peace and helped her to calm down. Being in his arms made her feel safe and secure because she knew he loved her with all his heart and that he would protect her from harm.

"I know just how to fix this problem."

"You do?" she asked, expecting he meant to ravish her on their new bed.

"Sure. Go into the bathroom and I'll be right there."

The bathroom? "Yes, sir." She padded into the bathroom, unsure what he had in mind. A sensual bath? That actually sounded pretty amazing right about now. Daddy would draw her a bath, wash her, then bring her to orgasm in some clever way—maybe by fucking her, maybe with his talented fingers. Then there was his mouth…

Her reverie was interrupted when Neal came into the bathroom. He was unwrapping a small hotel-sized bar of soap.

"Go check out that bidet." He motioned toward the water closet that held the apparatus. Unsure of his plans, but curious about the bidet, she approached it.

"Turn it on." He handed her the soap. "Use this to wash your pussy. I want to watch you."

A flicker of discomfort twinged in her tummy, while a flicker of excitement flared between her legs. It would be humiliating for him to watch her clean her pussy, but the task was cloaked with an exquisite intimacy at

the same time.

Ignorant of how the contraption worked, she leaned over and turned one of the knobs, but nothing happened. Perhaps it wasn't hooked up. The house *had* been vacant before she and Neal arrived.

She inched her face closer to the three knobs to further inspect it. How did the silly thing work anyway? She turned the one on the right and a spray of ice-cold water shot up into her face. "Eeeek!" she squealed, and Neal erupted in a gale of laughter.

"Dammit, Neal!" she sputtered, frantically trying to turn the blasted thing off. Neal gently stepped to one side of her and calmly shut off the spray. He grabbed a towel hanging near the shower and handed it to her. She wiped her face, all the while glaring at him.

"The left one is for hot, the right one is for cold, the middle one is for on and off and controlling the spray. You must have turned the spray part up to high, then when you turned on the cold..." He laughed again. "I'm sorry, princess."

She started to soften. It was kinda funny..."Well, they're all round, not like I'm used to. How was I supposed to know?" She pouted.

"You weren't, but now you do." He gave her a quick peck on the lips. "Now, enough distractions. Sit down there and clean yourself. Let daddy see."

She finished drying off her face and sat gingerly on the bidet. "I'm going to let *you* turn it on," she told him, not certain she trusted herself with it yet.

"That's fine," he said and started messing with the controllers. "I'll turn it down low until we get the water to warm up." He patted her on the shoulder.

"Thanks, daddy."

A few moments later she felt a gush of deliciously warm water bubble up between her legs. "Mmm," she purred.

"Does baby like that?" He stroked her hair, handed her the soap, then went back into the bathroom and perched on the side of the tub where he could watch her.

She nodded.

"Open those legs and give daddy a good view."

Facing him, she spread her legs wide apart, leaving no room for modesty. Her cunt was on full display for him.

"Now, take the soap and lather up that little pussy." His words made her stomach dip like a rollercoaster ride. He continued, "Get all those girly parts nice and wet for daddy."

She doused the soap in the bowl beneath her and rubbed it between her hands. Taking it in her right hand, she slid it between her legs and ran the bar up and down her slit, furrowing it into her delicate folds and using it to suds up the tiny strip of hair that sat just atop her mound. A draft of cool air blew

into the room and her nipples puckered in the breeze.

"God, I wish I had some clothespins for those nipples right now." He'd never put clothespins on her before, but the thought only made her little buds tighten harder. She adored the mixture of pain and pleasure of having her nipples pinched, craved it.

"Are you getting everything nice and clean?"

"Yes, daddy."

"Good girl. Now rinse yourself with the water from the bidet. You can turn the knob in the back to the left and it will give you more water. Just be careful," he said with a grin.

"I will, daddy," she said with mock exasperation and twisted the knob slightly so the water rose higher against her bottom.

The water splashed up onto her pussy, rinsing the soapy residue away. She also washed the insides of her thighs where Neal's cum had smeared against her pants, and for a moment her audience was forgotten.

"Did you say that you weren't able to orgasm because of the interruption earlier?"

"Yes."

"That's alright. We'll take care of that now."

She glanced up to see what he had in mind, but he remained sitting upon the side of the bathtub.

"When you're finished cleaning yourself, I want you to touch yourself."

Warning bells clanged in her head. Cleaning herself in front of him was intimate enough, now he wanted her to masturbate in front of him? "I can't," she blurted out.

He chuckled. "What do you mean, you can't? Take your fingers, the ones that were just rubbing soap on your pussy, and rub them on your pussy again—just without soap this time." His voice slowed and he said thickly, "But do it slow, and keep your eyes on mine."

He'd tricked her. By having her clean herself he'd taken her slightly out of her comfort zone, but with this request he was pushing her even further and offering her little room for escape, since he was right—she had just touched herself in front of him.

Her boundaries, her upbringing, her fears—*everything* told her not to do it, but as she looked into his eyes, full of warmth and love tinged with lust, she wanted to please him. And that desire was stronger than everything else. So she closed her eyes and traced her outer lips with her index finger.

"Good girl, but you need to look at daddy." When she hesitated, he encouraged her. "You can do it, princess. It's just daddy, who loves you very much. If you do what I say, you will make daddy very happy."

Her eyelashes fluttered open and she stared directly into his eyes as she plunged her finger into her wet channel.

He nodded his reassurance. "Keep going."

She withdrew her finger, now moist with her juices and rubbed her clit. First she ran her finger over the ridge at the top, and began to make little circles on it. To her dismay, a little moan escaped her throat, and she felt herself flush.

"That's good. Now show me what you do when daddy's not around to help you come."

Furrowing her brows, she had to think. It had been ages since she'd masturbated by hand. "Daddy, I always use a vibrator."

"Then it sounds like it's time to get reacquainted with your body. Pinch those nipples with your other hand," he instructed.

She squeezed the tip of her breast between her index finger and her thumb, then pulled and twisted at the same time. Involuntarily, her body squirmed under her own touch and she closed her eyes, lost in the sensation. She quickly opened them before he could correct her. Keeping her eyes locked with his was a challenge. But it deepened the hunger palpable in the air between them, so she had to fight the urge to close him off and bask in her solo pleasure.

"That's it, pull on those titties. Roll that clit between your fingers. Knead it." She followed his instructions, and he licked his bottom lip and wrapped his fist around his inflating shaft. His hand moved up and down over his cock, flicking the head as he went.

She gyrated in her seat on the bidet, straining for him, wanting his hands on her, his body pressed against hers, his cock inside her. Watching him stroke himself inflamed her desire and she could see why it appealed to him to watch her do the same.

"Daddy..." she whined.

"Yes, princess?" He liked her to vocalize to her desires. It wasn't enough to simply call for him. He liked her to ask specifically for what she wanted, beg even.

"I need you. Please fuck me."

He stood up and approached her, his erection leading the way. "You've been difficult today, princess—very naughty. You're lucky I'm going to let you come at all today. You may suck my cock, but you'll have to make yourself come. Naughty girls don't get a good fucking, do you understand?"

"Yes, daddy," she said quickly and opened her mouth to him. She'd rather he fuck her, but she was so turned on right now that having any part of him inside her would help quell her desires. His cock poked her lips before inching inside her mouth. She enveloped him with her tongue and licked the underside of his shaft.

He pushed himself deeper down her throat, pressing until she gagged, and then he pulled back slightly. Eagerly, she pushed back, taking him deeper and deeper, then relaxed and let him fuck her face while she twiddled her clit between her fingers, rubbing, rubbing, pulling. She felt the fluttery sensation

of her climax approaching and groaned, the sound garbled because of her full mouth.

"That's it. Come for me, baby girl. Come for daddy." He thrust his cock between her lips again and reached down to grab her breasts. He fondled them, one in each hand before claiming her nipples and pulling on them until she whimpered. She slammed her eyes shut and focused on finishing herself off. She tweaked and massaged her clit until her hips bucked, her legs shook, and she grabbed the side of the bidet to steady herself as she flew over the edge of desire. Neal shot his seed down the back of her throat, then slipped out of her mouth and held her cheek close against his pelvis. The way he held her head in his big, strong hand while their breathing returned to normal was always one of her favorite parts.

He made her feel so loved, so cherished. She'd go anywhere with him if she knew things would always be like this between them. Even a community in the middle of nowhere in the frozen tundra of Minnesota…

CHAPTER THREE

The next day was spent meeting the movers, changing out the furniture, and unpacking. Tabitha and Neal collapsed in bed and fell asleep, legs and arms entwined, with *Monday Night Football* blaring on the TV. When she first opened her eyes the next morning, she could tell by the time and his empty spot in the bed that Neal had already reported to work.

Tabitha rolled over and slept for another two hours. When she finally climbed out of bed, she blearily plodded into the kitchen in her new fuzzy pink slippers and the heart pajamas she'd bought just for the move. She made a K-cup of coffee, settled at the kitchen table, and opened her laptop. She checked her email and was just about to see what was happening in the world of futures trading when she got a text from Neal.

Good morning. Don't forget the knitting lesson at Agnes' house this afternoon at 1 p.m.

She smacked her palm to her forehead. No, no, no. She wasn't going to do that. Just as she began texting him an excuse, another text came in from him.

I love you endlessly.

Damn. She let out a long, deep breath and texted him back.

I love you too. Have a good day.

She'd have to go to Agnes' knitting thing. There was really no excuse good enough to justify her absence. "I'm just feeling resentful and bitchy about moving" wasn't going to suffice.

She downed a handful of pills with the rest of her coffee. It had been a week since her last migraine. It wasn't clear whether the pills were working

or if taking a break from her job had done the trick. Neal would say it was the move, but then he had invested his whole life in that theory.

Normally, this time of day usually found her embroiled in heated battles on the futures trading floor. She loved the rush of adrenaline, the excitement, and she loved that she kicked ass at her job. With the best numbers in the firm's history for her age, she commanded a sizable salary for a twenty-six-year-old trader. Unfortunately, her job had taken its toll on her health.

The migraines had begun to plague her two years earlier, and the brain attacks had gotten progressively worse. These days they often involved significant neurological impairment even if only temporary. During some attacks Tabitha's right arm would become paralyzed, and often she lost the ability to speak. Once she wasn't able to dial a number on her phone. It had been a terrifying experience in which her brain knew she wasn't pressing the correct key with her fingers, but she couldn't make her finger press the right one. Finally, after her third hospitalization in a year, Neal proposed that they move to the Little Haven community. Life would be easier, he said, less stressful, and they could be around others who enjoyed the same kind of relationships they did.

At first Tabitha had balked. She loved her job and their life in Chicago, and she had no intention of leaving it. But Neal had seen enough of her suffering. He decreed that if she wouldn't take care of herself, if she wouldn't move away with him and let him take care of her, they couldn't be together. He set his foot down and gave her the ultimatum.

She peered at the photo of her and Neal that served as a screensaver on her laptop. Her love for him had potentially cost her the job she adored, but she knew her health was a consideration as well. It touched her heart that he loved her enough to make her well-being his top concern. As resistant as she was to change, she'd have to find a way to make a life here in this community. At least until she convinced him to go back to Chicago with her.

Neal had been under the impression for a while that she'd willingly given up her job to accompany him to Minnesota. In actuality, her boss had granted her a month-long sabbatical to deal with her health problems, and Tabitha intended to be back at her desk in Chicago in approximately four weeks. She rubbed her temples with her index fingers. It might take a month to convince Neal this place wasn't for them. Carefully setting those worries aside, she closed down the computer, and started tracking down the three huge wardrobe boxes that held most of her clothes. If she was going to play along with her new neighbor, the first thing she'd have to do was find something to wear.

• • • • • • •

When Agnes opened the front door, Tabitha realized she needn't have

taken so much care deciding what to wear.

The older woman greeted her wearing a bright red t-shirt that read 'I speak Gangsta' and a multi-colored shawl that Tabitha assumed she'd knitted herself. The shirt was an interesting and unexpected choice. Perhaps she'd underestimated the old broad. "Welcome, welcome. Come on in. I'm so glad you could make it," Agnes enthused in her gruff voice.

"I like your shirt," Tabitha said. You had to admire the chutzpah of an eighty-year-old rockin' a shirt like that.

"Thanks. My grandson got it for me."

"Okaaay…" Tabitha allowed herself to be spirited into Agnes' great room, which was not unlike hers and Neal's other than the southwestern décor that permeated the house. Clay pots, dream-catchers, Navaho-patterned blankets and rugs were all well represented in Agnes' décor.

"I see you're a fan of the Southwest," Tabitha noted.

"It's where I'm from. Lived near Taos for thirty years before I found my calling and moved here."

"Your calling?" Tabitha asked.

"Yes, I help little girls navigate their way, help them come to accept themselves. Some people have a hard time coming to grips with their true nature."

"I see." Suddenly the air seemed too thin and Tabitha felt trapped. She didn't want Agnes all up in her business and she certainly didn't need her prying into her 'true nature.' Tabitha frantically scanned the room for a seat. There were two girls already seated and a couple of others talking in the corner.

Agnes took Tabitha by the elbow and led her over to the girls who were sitting on a sofa in the middle of the room. "Tabitha, this is Angela…"

Angela smiled warmly. "Hi." She wore jeans and a sweater that matched her cool blue eyes.

"And this is Bailey. She's new to the community just like you are."

"Hi!" Bailey blew a bubble with her pink chewing gum.

"Hello," Tabitha said, taking a seat in the oversized chair next to Bailey. "How long have you lived here?" she asked Angela.

"About two years," Angela said. In Tabitha's mind, that made her an expert on this place.

"And how do you like it?" Tabitha inquired.

"Pretty well."

Tabitha nodded and turned to Bailey. "How about you? Where did you move from?"

"I've moved at least twenty-five times," Bailey answered. "How about you?"

"Oh, wow, that's a lot of moving! We came from Chicago."

Agnes tapped a wind chime and the room was filled with a tinkling song

that made Tabitha feel like they were in the desert rather than in frozen Minnesota. "Alright, girls, everyone is here. Let's go ahead and get started," Agnes said, and the other two girls came over and sat in the extra chairs Agnes had set out.

"Does anyone here have any knitting experience?" Agnes scanned the room.

Tabitha shyly lifted her hand, and in her periphery she saw Bailey raise hers halfway.

"Wonderful! You've been holding out on me, neighbor." Agnes smiled warmly at her and Tabitha started to relax ever so slightly.

"Not much. I knitted a pair of slippers in home economics class in middle school. I don't think I remember how," Tabitha explained.

"That's okay. It's the muscle memory that's important. It won't be hard to pick it up again," Agnes said. "Bailey, how about you?"

"My grandmother showed me when I was little. It's been several years since I knitted anything. I'm not very good."

"I'm sure you'll do just fine. It will come back to you in a flash," Agnes reassured Bailey, who was chewing her lip nervously. "Kara, help me pass out the yarn if you don't mind."

A pretty girl with multi-colored hair glanced nervously around at the rest of the girls before standing up. She wore a Hello Kitty jacket, a pair of jeans that hugged her curves beautifully, and aqua Converse kicks.

"Cute jacket," Tabitha said.

Kara smiled self-consciously. "Thanks," she said and gave each girl a different color ball of yarn.

"She has the cutest clothes," Angela said.

"Wonder where she shops," Bailey said.

"You girls can talk about clothes and shopping at the break," Agnes reprimanded. "Now, this is yarn you can take home, for you to practice with. Here are your needles," she said, giving each girl a set of metal knitting needles. "When you think you're ready, you can start a simple scarf with these needles from a similar kind of yarn. That way you can pick the color. You could all probably finish a scarf for your daddies by Valentine's Day. I'll be sending you each home with an information sheet that you can take to a store that sells yarn or you can buy it over the Internet."

The girls looked at each other, then back at Agnes. The scarf sounded great, especially since it was so blasted cold in Minnesota, and their daddies would be so proud of them. Tabitha would be back in Chicago by then, but Neal could still use a scarf. It was cold there too, but somehow the temperature there didn't seem as bad.

"The first step is to cast on…" Agnes went on to show the girls how to begin a new project. She had to show most of the girls how to hold the needles as well as how to wrap the yarn around itself and pull it through. At

first Tabitha was bewildered, but after a few tries, she got the hang of it and finished her first row. Agnes was right, some part of her subconscious brain seemed to remember how to do it, while her conscious brain didn't. But after a couple of rows she'd gotten the hang of it, only getting stuck a few times.

Seeing that Agnes was occupied helping the other girls, Tabitha nudged Bailey. "Hey, was this your idea? Coming to this class," she whispered. "Or your daddy's?"

Bailey made a face, and Tabitha noticed how dark her eyes were, like deep troubled wells. "Daddy's."

"Yeah, me too," Tabitha grimaced. "Moving to this whole place was his idea. I'm not so sure about it, though."

"I know what you mean. I was scared I might have to wear diapers." Bailey looked horrified.

Tabitha slapped her hand on Bailey's knee. "Me too!" she shrieked. The other girls looked up from their needles and yarn, and Agnes peered over her shoulder, her sharp chin pointing at them. "Alright, girls, it's nice for you to get to know each other, but let's stay on task, please."

Once Agnes turned back to helping Kara, Tabitha whispered to Bailey, "You know what my daddy said to convince me to come? That it was 'pacifier optional.'" Both girls fell into a gale of giggles.

"Am I going to have to separate you two?" Agnes asked, stern as an old schoolmarm.

"No, ma'am," Tabitha and Bailey chorused. They went back to their knitting and soon, Tabitha was helping Agnes teach the other girls what to do.

Angela and Kara sat next to each other, and each was hard at work trying to complete their first row of stitches. While Agnes was helping a girl on the end, Tabitha heard Agnes call the girl Claire. When Tabitha looked over, Agnes was pulling all Claire's stitches off her needles and starting her over again. Claire looked like she might cry, and Tabitha's heart went out to her. Knitting was difficult, especially until you had that 'aha' moment and you started to understand what you were doing.

Agnes went around the room checking the progress of all the girls. "Our daddies will love the scarves. Daddy loves when I have something special for him when he comes home from work," Angela said.

Tabitha giggled, then realized Angela may not have meant what she'd said in a dirty way, and she felt dumb for laughing. But she did see Bailey stifle a half-grin, which told her that her new friend knew what she'd been thinking.

"Much better than when they come home to a lot of complaining or bad behavior," Agnes said. "Am I right?"

The girls mumbled their agreement and this sewing circle was starting to feel more like a schoolroom. Tabitha wondered how long she had to stay. She'd already done her time in school, thank you very much.

"My husband used to call that 'the boo-boo report,' when he came home to a litany of everything bad that happened during the day. Nobody wants to be greeted at the door like that," Agnes said.

"That's true," Claire piped up and the other girls nodded their assent.

"So what do you gals do to greet daddy in a positive way when he comes home?"

"Give him a back-scratch."

"Ask him about his day,"

"Get naked?" Bailey snickered.

"Eeew. I don't know. Why do we have to talk about this?" Claire asked, and Tabitha echoed her last sentiment.

"Girls, I know some of you are resistant. I see that, but to make your transition here easier, you and your daddy are going to have to minimize the stress. Moving is one of the most stressful experiences a couple can encounter. Stress can either bring people together or it can tear them apart. Which would you prefer?" Agnes stared at Tabitha.

Squirming in her seat, Tabitha said, "Together." Maybe her nosy neighbor had a point. She and Neal had experienced some tense moments as of late, more than she was accustomed to.

The longer they knitted, the redder Claire's face grew. She'd had to unravel her project and start over again three times and when she glanced up from her work, unshed tears glistened in her eyelashes. "That's it! I'm done with this today," Claire spat, tossing her knitting to the floor, her ball of yarn unrolling slowly across the carpet.

The girls held their breath waiting to see how Agnes would handle the situation.

Agnes went and stood directly in front of Claire. "Young lady, you will pick that up and apologize to the group for your behavior."

Claire's bottom lip began to quiver and Tabitha felt sorry for the girl.

"I'm sorry, Agnes. I... I just got so frustrated. All I want is to make my daddy something nice, but I can't even do that! I'm horrible," Claire cried, wrapping her arms around herself.

Agnes let the poor girl cry out her frustrations. Once the crying stopped, Agnes cupped Claire's chin in her hand. "No, Claire. You are a wonderful girl. Sometimes it is your behavior that needs some work. Tantrums are not acceptable. Now, I realize that knitting can be a difficult skill to learn, but I'm sure that with practice, you will get it."

"Yes, ma'am," Claire whimpered.

"Now, pick up your needles and yarn or I'll have you stand in the corner." Claire dropped to her knees and began gathering up her supplies.

"Poor Claire," Tabitha whispered.

The girls near her all nodded. The knitting party broke up soon after that, with many of the girls exchanging phone numbers and Tabitha and Bailey

promising to go out for a hot chocolate in the near future.

Later when Tabitha thanked Agnes for the lesson and told her goodbye, the older woman touched her on the arm. "Tabitha, I know you have your doubts about this place. I did too when I first came here."

Tabitha gave Agnes a wry smile. "You did?"

Agnes nodded. "But if you need a friendly ear, I'm here."

"Thank you ever so much, but I'm sure I won't be needing..."

"Well, if you ever do... Also, if you have some time on your hands, I can always use some help at the daycare."

"Daycare?" The reference to a daycare confused Tabitha; she hadn't seen any children since she and Neal arrived.

"Yes, some of the littles come to daycare during the day while their daddies are at work."

"Wow, really? What do they do?"

"Color, draw, listen to music and stories."

"You read stories to them?"

"Yes. They like fairytales and sometimes books for older kids. We finished all the Harry Potter books last year."

"I'll think about it," Tabitha said and turned to leave.

But Agnes stopped her. "Thank you for coming. You'll get used to it here, find your place."

"Thanks for the lesson," Tabitha said, and strode back to her new house carrying a grocery sack filled with two knitting needles and a ball of yarn.

CHAPTER FOUR

The next day the sun came out and the snow began to thaw. Tabitha ventured out to the mailbox and got the mail. On her way back, she saw Agnes pull up to her house in a green golf cart. Agnes waved and Tabitha ambled toward her. "Hey! I thought of a question for you."

"Yep?" Agnes parked her vehicle in her garage, got out and came around to meet Tabitha on the side lawn that connected their two houses.

"How do you get any food around here?" Tabitha asked.

"Food, why, there's a grocery store about ten minutes south of here."

"I know, but I can hardly find any take-out restaurants, and surely those littles who need daycare don't cook for their daddies."

Agnes laughed. "That's the truth. One of the best things about being a really young little is not having to cook. Why? You don't cook?"

Tabitha huffed, "I know how to make," she paused for effect, "reservations."

Agnes shook her head. "Well, then, I can see why you're having a problem. Not many restaurants around here."

"I know. Neal has been bringing home pizza most nights, but that's getting old. I wish there were more places that delivered out here."

"Those big box stores will deliver anything."

"Yeah." Tabitha made a face. "Ingredients. I mean food someone cooked."

"Oh, yeah. You're supposed to do that yourself."

"Agnes! I'm supposed to be a little girl. How am I supposed to cook?" She pouted with great purpose. Getting out of doing domestic duties by regressing to a younger age might come in handy after all.

Agnes gave her an I-wasn't-born-yesterday look. "You can fix the basics, missy. Any twelve-year-old can."

Tabitha screwed up her mouth. She was about to argue when Agnes continued. "But I can get you Bridget's number."

"Bridget? Who's Bridget?" Tabitha asked.

"She's about to be your new best friend." Agnes strode toward her house and motioned for Tabitha to follow. "C'mon. I've got her number on the fridge. She's a little girl who loves to cook, and her daddy encouraged her to start a business cooking meals. You can purchase them, pop them in the freezer, then when you're ready you just thaw them, heat 'em up, and serve them. It's been really successful business for her; seems like all the girls buy her food. Hell, I might buy it if I didn't already cook for myself."

"Bridget sounds like a great resource, thanks."

Agnes gave Tabitha the once-over. "You know they say the way to a man's stomach is through his..."

"His cock, Agnes. It's his cock," Tabitha interrupted.

Agnes rolled her eyes and frowned. "I'm just sayin'. It wouldn't hurt you to feed the man."

Tabitha smiled to herself. She was beginning to enjoy Agnes' crusty banter. The old gal was growing on her. "Fine. That sounds like a good idea," Tabitha said, following Agnes inside to get the number.

· · · · · · ·

Tabitha wasn't sure how long she had been at Agnes' house when she heard someone banging on the front door.

"Hang on, let me get that," Agnes told Tabitha. They were sitting on the couch drinking an herbal tea that Agnes swore was good for warding off headaches.

When Agnes opened the door, Tabitha saw Neal standing there, running his hand through the waves of his sandy blond hair. "Agnes, have you seen Tab—?" He saw her then and relief filled his eyes. "Tabitha! I've been looking all over for you."

"I'm right here," she gulped. She'd left her phone in the house because she'd only planned on going to the mailbox and back. "Sorry. I didn't know I would be coming over here." She scooped up her stack of mail, crossed the room to Neal, and gave him a kiss on the cheek. "Hi, daddy."

"Thanks, Agnes. I appreciate the number, and the tea," Tabitha said, grabbing Neal by the arm and tugging him out the door onto the brick path outside.

"Anytime, dear. Anytime." Agnes smiled and closed the door behind them.

"What were you doing over there anyway? I thought you couldn't stand Agnes," Neal whispered loudly.

Tabitha shrugged. "She's not so bad once you get to know her."

"That's the way to start fitting in here, princess. I'm proud of you going out of your way to be friendly with the neighbors. Good for you."

Guilt welled up inside her, but she remained silent. All she'd done was ask

Agnes a question. It wasn't like she was hosting a block party for the whole community. She squeezed his hand, and he squeezed hers back.

"Daddy may have to give you a special surprise tonight for being such a good girl."

"Really?"

"Yes, but first I have to go to town and pick up a few supplies. Want to come with me?"

"Absolutely."

"We can pick up something to eat while we're out."

They went to the hardware store and Neal picked up some tools, a new headlamp, a roll of electrical tape, and Tabitha felt a shiver of excitement when she noticed him adding a coil of silky white rope to the cart. Afterwards they went to a little Italian bistro where they devoured large plates of spaghetti and meatballs.

When they got back to the house, Neal said, "Why don't you go inside and wait for me?"

The pasta had made her sleepy, but Tabitha perked up as she got out of the car and they walked inside. "Meet me in the bedroom," Neal growled in her ear, then gave her bottom a smack. "Lie on the bed. Naked," he specified.

Her breathing grew slightly more labored. "Yes, sir."

In anticipation of her daddy time, she'd painted her nails today and taken care of some hair removal.

She sauntered into the bedroom and heard him call from the kitchen, "I'll be there in a minute."

Tabitha checked her appearance in the mirror and removed her bulky sweater, jeans, and socks. Admiring her pretty pink bra and panties in the reflection, she thought what a waste it was for daddy not to see her in them. But daddy had said naked, so naked she would be. She slipped off her bra and pushed her panties down so they fell to the floor. Stepping out of them, she went and lay on her tummy on the fluffy down comforter that covered their bed.

A few moments later, Neal came in with a plastic bag from the hardware store.

She giggled. "Are you sure that trip to the hardware store was for *work*, Daddy?" she teased.

"Work, among other things." He winked.

"Mmm. Okay," she purred and he met her at the edge of the bed and bent to touch his lips to hers.

When he stood up, his thighs were even with her mouth, and her pussy tingled at the thought of his cock in her mouth. But apparently daddy had other ideas, since he retrieved a black implement from the bag.

Her pulse quickened. "What's that?"

"A toy I made. Two paint sticks wrapped together with electrical tape."

He tapped the ruler-shaped implement against his forearm. "Cheap, easy, and I have a feeling it will do the trick."

"What sort of trick?"

"Getting my girl to behave."

"Ouch."

"Let's test it out," he said with a gleam in his eye.

"Okay, daddy," she said, steeling herself for a spanking.

The stick met her rear end with a quick snap.

"Next time you go to someone's house, or you aren't going to be at home…"

The toy slashed against her skin.

"…you need to leave me a note. Or a text."

"Yes, sir," she bleated.

Another swat to her ass sent a mixed message of pleasure and pain to her brain.

"How do you like the toy?" he asked as he landed another strike to her butt cheeks.

With an exhale of breath she answered, "It's fine, daddy."

"Don't you think you deserve a spanking for making daddy worry?"

Thwack! Her bottom was beginning to warm now. "Yes, daddy, I'm sure I do."

"Good girl." He began swatting her ass with staccato little beats, as if she were a drum he was playing. The stick bounced off her bottom, leaving her skin feeling as if it were on fire. Yet each strike made her groan with desire.

"God, I love that ass. Love when I turn it cherry red."

Happiness bubbled up inside her. He did love to spank her so good, and being a source of his gratification was one of her greatest joys. "Thank you, daddy."

"You're welcome, princess." He grazed her steaming hot globes with his hand, providing a cooling sensation to her chafed skin. The way he soothed her after a spanking was probably her favorite part. She adored how tender his touch could be afterwards, such a stark contrast to the fiery swats he'd just inflicted.

Even though he was still dressed, he lay down beside her on the bed and embraced her, his tongue exploring her mouth and his hand still rubbing her aching backside. She wrapped a leg around him and drew him closer to her. Her hips ground against his pelvis and she felt his erection through his pants.

He groaned, disentangled himself, got up and started pulling off his clothes. She loved watching him undress, because each time was like her own personal show. No, he didn't gyrate and dance around sliding discarded articles of clothing back and forth between his legs or grinding his groin and wagging his junk in her face. That sort of over-the-top display wasn't necessary to get her juices flowing. All Neal had to do was remove his clothes

in the simplest of ways—unbuttoning his shirt and carefully tossing it aside, raising his arms overhead and yanking off his t-shirt in one swift, fluid movement, casually unfastening the top button on his jeans. It always made her mouth dry. Thirsty.

She licked her lips and thought for what seemed like the millionth time how lucky she was to have a man like him. Thoughtful, kind, loving—and with the stone-cut body of a Greek god with an eight-pack that would make angels weep. He had the grace of movement reserved for athletes and dancers, and he was completely oblivious to it. They had invented the phrase 'poetry in motion' for men like him. She sighed deeply and drank up all his naked glory.

When he pulled down his underwear, his rock-hard cock sprung back like it was made of metal. "Can I touch it, daddy?" she asked, and realized she'd been unconsciously sucking on the tip of her index finger.

"Yes, you can touch it, but then I have something else planned for you." His eyes were full of mischief. It had to be something good.

He came back to the bed and climbed on, one knee at a time, so that he knelt before her. Propped up on her left elbow, she reached out and wrapped her fingers around the base of his shaft and stroked the length of him. "May I please taste you, daddy?" she begged.

"You may," he said, inching closer to her. "Since you asked so nicely."

She tugged on his penis and brushed the tip of it against her lips. Her tongue darted out and licked the head with quick, teasing laps. He groaned at the torture and pushed further into the warmth of her mouth. She moaned a response as she opened her mouth and swallowed him deeper.

He fisted her hair in his hands and fucked her face, his hips rhythmically pushing back and forth, in and out, ravaging the open mouth she offered him. His cock banged the back of her throat, and she sputtered as her gag reflex kicked in. A shiver ran through her body and her nipples hardened. All of her senses kicked into high gear. She felt his pulse under her hand beating through his thigh and heard his breath catch as she licked the sensitive frenulum on the underside of his cock. The musky, male scent of him filled her nostrils as she dipped her tongue into the tiny hole at the tip of his cock and recognized the slightly salty taste of his pre-cum.

He thrust his cock into her mouth a few more times before stopping. When he withdrew, his actions were met with a disappointed whimper. "Don't worry. I have plenty more in store for you," he reassured her.

Tabitha smiled and tried to be patient, to not ask a lot of questions. It wasn't easy for her to give up control, but she was learning. Being a submissive didn't come naturally to her, but she found a great deal of satisfaction in it.

"Lie on your back," he said, and she did as he asked. "Now, open those legs for daddy like a good girl." Butterflies took flight in her stomach, but she

spread her legs—way too wide to hide anything or retain any modicum of modesty. She'd never been with a man as interested in her pussy as Neal was. Yes, she'd had men fuck her before, but she'd never had one 'inspect' her pussy or spend hours playing with it the way Neal did. The intensity of his interest made her both nervous and excited, and it always embarrassed her at first, and somehow that made her even hornier.

She loved how naughty he made her feel, and it was even more delicious that she did those things because daddy wanted her to. He wanted her all the time, and he made her feel like the most desirable woman on the planet, like she was the most special person in his world.

Suddenly a coil of white silky rope sat on the bed on either side of her legs, and Neal started circling one of her wrists with the soft material. "Such a good girl for daddy," he praised her as he began draping the rope around her thighs. "For now, you can rest your hands on your knees," he instructed, then proceeded to tie rope around her thighs and then her calves.

Tabitha loved rope; the slick sensuous feel of it sliding over her skin sent her into a dreamlike state and she felt her pussy grow wet as she thought about daddy rendering her helpless to do as he pleased to her. She bit her lip to keep herself from moaning. There would be plenty of time for wanton behavior later.

Once he'd bound both sides, her legs were frozen in an open position and her wrists were bound to her legs at the top of her thighs. He took the end of the rope and playfully lashed her breast with it. "Oooh!" she cried wantonly, unable to hold back. He drew it back and wielding it like a lasso, slashed at her other breast. She let out a lusty growl and he brought it down again, this time on the mound between her legs.

"Daddy!" she howled.

"Yes, princess?"

"Daddy." She swallowed and her mind seemed clouded somehow. It was difficult to articulate what she wanted. So she spoke the only word that came into her mind. "More."

CHAPTER FIVE

"You want more?" Neal asked.

She flung her head wildly. "Yes, daddy. More."

"That I can do."

He slapped her pussy lips—her right labia, then the left with his new, self-made toy. Her hips strained upward, begging for him to swat the core of her.

"Ah, ah, ah," he admonished. "Daddy knows when to touch you there." She could hear the desire in his voice as he teased her. There was nothing he liked better than making her thrash and whimper underneath him, and he liked to keep her in that state as long as possible, prolonging the enjoyment for them both.

"Close your eyes," he commanded, and she fluttered them shut, happy for the opportunity to lose herself in the sensations.

Swack! Another whack to her breast with the paint stick. Her nipple grew taut, hard under the stinging blow. He swatted the other one and she reveled in the bliss of his assault on her nipples.

His attentions moved south and she breathed deeply, focusing on the oddly cool feel of the stick as he trailed it down her abdomen.

Swack! The stick hit her inner thighs, first with several staccato swats to the left side, then an equal number to the opposing thigh. He teased her again with smacks to the sides of her pussy, then finally he landed that delicious blow she'd been craving. Needing.

"Ooooh!" She let out a howl, which seemed to encourage him to continue whaling at her plumped pussy.

The slaps were beginning to smart and with the tenth smack, she wiggled and whimpered in a way that must have told him she'd tired of the walloping and was ready for the next phase of his incursion. For soon she felt a thick, meaty finger dip into her well, pressing in and out, tickling the front wall of her wet, welcoming channel. He added another finger and curled one so that it nudged against her g-spot. He fucked her well and good with his hand, and the added pressure to her g-spot drove her closer to the edge.

His mouth closed on her breast and he took her nipple between his teeth, biting ever so slightly. The banging at her pussy, the stroking of that juicy button, combined with the exquisite torture of her nipples—it made her feel as if she would float away in a heavenly fog. Just then her body exploded in wave after wave of climax, sending her off the cliff, falling down, down, down, into his loving embrace.

When her body stopped shaking, he tenderly touched his lips to her temple. "Are you okay?"

"Better than okay," she murmured.

"Good," he said, repositioning himself. "Because daddy wants to fuck you now. Are you up for that?"

"Yes, daddy." She went to put her arms around him, but was halted by the ropes that attached them to her thighs.

He chuckled at her plight. "That's right. Daddy has you just where he wants you. Easily accessible." He ran a hand over her pussy. "Damn, you're so wet for daddy."

Her body felt as if it were on fire, and she itched and moaned for him to take her. "Daddy, please, daddy!"

"Please what?" he asked.

"Please fuck me!" she responded.

"Of course, baby."

He rubbed the head of his cock around her opening, dipped it inside and she jolted, lifting her hips, eager for him to fill her completely.

"Be still," he said firmly, then withdrew his cock and slid the tip of it lazily in a circle over her clit. The tension built to such a crescendo that she thought she would die if he did not help her climax soon. But she tried her best to control herself and lie still for him.

"That's better." He grabbed her thighs and slid his cock deep inside her. She lifted her hands, forgetting again that they were tied to her thighs. The way she was bound allowed him perfect access for taking her hard and fast. He picked up the pace and with each thrust she grew closer and closer to finding another release.

Rocking back, he pulled her onto him until he was sheathed entirely inside her. Then he pinched her nipples with both hands and pulled them until he elicited a cry of pain from her lips. He twisted them between his fingers, all the while fucking her pussy. He leaned down and kissed her deeply, invading her mouth with his tongue and sending her over the precipice. She kissed him back as she tumbled into a haze of ecstasy. Pleasure permeated her entire being and she slid down a rainbow into a cloud of billowy bliss.

"That's it, princess. Come for daddy. Come all over daddy's cock."

"Yes, daddy!" Her voice was shrill as she rode out the delightful tremors he'd inflicted upon her. After her climax wrung her out, she lay limp, grateful that her bonds held her in place. She wanted to please Neal, but she didn't

have much energy left. He continued fucking her with long steady strokes, and her head lolled from side to side as she enjoyed the sensation and basked in the afterglow of her climax. She heard a catch in his breathing, and with a few more surges, he came inside her.

"Oh, daddy, I'm so glad I can make you happy."

"You do make me happy. You're perfect for daddy, you know that?"

She nodded and he pulled out and started to untie her wrists and then her legs. He coiled the rope into neat little circles and set it aside. Then he climbed onto the bed next to her and held her for a while. After a long time, she got up to clean herself off in the bidet. Gosh, she loved that thing. And when she came back to the bed, Neal was almost asleep. She curled up in the crook of his arm and he said sleepily, "Love you, princess."

"I love you too, daddy," she said and snuggled even closer.

"I'm glad you're starting to adjust to living here," he said.

A slice of guilt ripped through her. She wasn't getting used to it, she was just biding her time until she could go back home. It made her feel bad that he thought she was really trying. She opened her mouth to say something, but a snore escaped his lips.

She was torn between her love for this wonderful man and her love for her work. With a sigh, she rolled over and stared at the wall, willing sleep to come.

CHAPTER SIX

The next week Tabitha awakened to the uncomfortable sensation that only occurred when her feet were sticking out from the covers at the end of the bed. Ugh! Her toes were frozen. She tucked them back up under the sheets and wished Neal were home. He always made sure her toes were nicely tucked under the covers, and that the sheets were tucked in at the bottom, just the way she liked them. But Neal had gone out of town on an overnight trip to pick up some exercise equipment that had been purchased for the gym in the community center, so he wasn't there to take care of her problem with the bedsheets.

She'd passed her time the previous evening unpacking until she'd grown totally bored with the task and started reading. She must have fallen asleep reading, and now she had another day of unpacking ahead of her. Coffee. Maybe that would help.

Slowly, she crawled out of bed and made herself a cup. Mindlessly, she turned on the television and watched a morning show out of the corner of her eye while she checked her email and procrastinated for another hour. Finally, she decided to get back to work. It wouldn't do to have Neal come home and see her lack of progress.

She was unpacking a box of toiletries in her pajamas when the doorbell rang. Abandoning the bottles of shaving cream, powder, deodorants, and Pepto, she hurried to the door, only to see Agnes through the glass. Ugh, she wasn't in the mood.

"Hi," Tabitha said as she opened the door and gestured for Agnes to come in.

"No time, but thanks. I was just heading over to the daycare center and I wondered if you'd like to join me. I see Neal's out of town." Man, but she was a busybody. How could Agnes have possibly known that? Neal had only left the night before. Agnes continued, "Gladys is sick today and she usually helps me out over there. I could use the help if you're not busy."

Tabitha thought Agnes was nuts, and she didn't care if the expression on

her face reflected it. "I don't understand why grown women need a daycare," she said, folding her arms across her chest.

"They don't *need* it, but it's a nice respite for them."

"From *what?*" Those women pretending to be little girls, sitting there finger-painting all day, they had no idea what stress was. Let them spend a day or two on the trading floor in Chicago like she had for years, make a few bad trades, lose a few hundreds of thousands of other people's money—in one day, then let them talk about needing a vacation.

"Well, that's okay. If you're too busy unpacking…" Agnes gave a half-shrug and turned to go.

Tabitha looked over at the mountain of boxes in the corner. Actually, *anything* would be better than unpacking all day. "Okay. Let me change my clothes and I'll come over and help."

"You know where it is?"

"Yes, Neal showed me. I'll be there in about an hour. I just have to wrap some things up first."

Agnes squeezed her arm. "I appreciate it, you'll have fun," she said before she left.

Fun? Tabitha wasn't so sure of that, but at least it was something Neal would approve of, and it wasn't unpacking. After she finished unloading the box she'd been working on, she changed clothes, then bundled up for the short walk over to the building where the daycare was housed.

The frigid air outside felt good and brisk against her face as she walked. The blue sky was a welcome sight and she noticed the sun beaming down and melting the snow. It was a beautiful day, too pretty to be cooped up indoors the whole time.

When she arrived at the daycare, she put her mittens in her coat pockets and hung the coat on a hook next to what looked like the classroom door. There was a row of similar hooks, reminiscent of a schoolroom environment, except all at adult height.

Tabitha stood in the doorway and surveyed the scene. A curly-haired brunette was sitting on the floor, legs crossed, working a large jigsaw puzzle. A blonde with a pixie haircut and a pink corduroy jumper was painting in the corner, and a redhead was reading a book alone in a corner sitting on a beanbag chair.

Agnes was in the center of the room helping one of the other girls with what looked to be needlepoint. Looking up, she waved for Tabitha to come over. Agnes introduced Tabitha to the women and they all said hi; most of them looked rather shy.

"What do you want me to do?" Tabitha asked nervously. She felt completely out of her comfort zone and considered fleeing. If she ran back to her house, she'd have time to catch her new favorite daytime talk show.

"In a minute you can help me get the juice and cookies for snack time,

then later maybe you can take some of the girls outside for play time."

Really? Tabitha thought, but nodded in agreement. Agnes showed her where the kitchenette was located and Tabitha prepared small paper cups of apple juice and piled a stack of oatmeal cookies on a paper plate. The situation has a surreal flavor to it, but in an attempt to embrace the experience, she added a stack of napkins and brought them back into the classroom.

"Snack time," Tabitha called cheerfully and was surprised at how quickly the women scampered over to get a cookie and a drink. Their enthusiasm was contagious and Tabitha found herself giggling along with them and enjoying a cookie at the table with the other girls.

"Agnes, these cookies are delicious. Did you make them?" Tabitha asked.

"No, actually Mary Jane brought them. Did you make them, Mary Jane?" Agnes asked the brunette.

Mary Jane nodded shyly.

"They're very good," Tabitha told her and the girl beamed at the compliment.

For the next fifteen minutes Tabitha watched the girls titter and tease each other good-naturedly. They talked about the blond girl's new pinafore and asked her where she got it. They gossiped about celebrities and discussed their favorite TV show, which was of the nighttime soap opera genre. Tabitha was surprised to find that they talked about the things most women talked about. Adult women things, but they were a lot more playful and less stressed than most of the women she knew.

Agnes prompted the girls to deposit their trash in the wastebasket, and Tabitha took everything else back to the kitchen area. When she returned, Agnes had everyone bundling up to go outside. "How about a game of foursquare?" she asked and the girls whooped their approval.

One by one they followed Agnes outside and Tabitha grabbed her coat and followed along.

A couple of the girls went to play on the swings, while the others handed Tabitha a red rubber ball and looked to her to start a game. It had been a long time since foursquare had meant anything other than a location app for social media, but slowly the game came back to her and she and the girls had a lovely time playing outdoors.

When they went back inside, Tabitha led the redhead and the brunette, Mary Jane, in a game of monopoly. After a while, she forgot she was playing with 'littles' and she found herself enjoying the game. The redhead, named Sue, continually forgot to collect $200 each time she passed go, and Mary Jane made hysterical faces every time she was forced to pay rent. Tabitha was more serious about the game, and soon she had a hotel on every yellow, green, and orange property, while the other girls were just acquiring their first monopolies.

"You're really good at this," Sue said.

Tabitha sighed. "My regular job is in finance," she said, trying to make an excuse for beating 'little girls' in a daycare. Though she wasn't sure if she should have let them win or not—they were pretty close to her age, even though they went to daycare. It was kind of confusing.

"Wow! That's cool. I used to work in a bakery," Mary Jane said.

"You don't anymore?" Tabitha asked, fearing she was being too nosy, but too curious not to ask.

"No. I had to get up way too early. It put me and my daddy on very different schedules. I like it better this way, and he does too." She smiled. "I can always bake for you guys, and daddy takes good care of me."

Mary Jane was content to go to a daycare all day and let her daddy take care of her. In some ways it boggled Tabitha's mind, but she was starting to see the appeal. She herself was too independent to rely solely on her daddy to take care of her, but she could see how fun this place was and why the girls liked coming here. It was like a mini vacation or a spa day.

Tabitha helped serve the girls' lunch, which consisted of loaded baked potato soup and a salad, which Tabitha thought was funny. She couldn't see real kiddies in daycare eating such a grownup meal, but she was grateful they weren't having chicken nuggets. When the little girls lay down on their mats for naptime, Agnes called her over and whispered, "You can go on home now if you like. I know you still have unpacking to do."

"I do. Thanks for letting me help today." Tabitha smiled but looked at the floor. She was ashamed at how she'd judged the girls and the daycare so harshly at first.

"No, thank *you!*" Agnes gave Tabitha's hand a squeeze.

"It was kinda fun," Tabitha admitted.

Agnes nodded. "Keeps me young, being around these girls. Helps me remember how to have a good time."

Tabitha nodded, then waved goodbye to the little girls. She left just as Agnes was putting on a sound recording of a rainstorm to help the girls drift off to sleep.

The rest of the afternoon she spent unpacking, and when she went to bed that night, Neal still wasn't home. When she got under the covers, her toes poked out the bottom again. Grumpily, she got up and tucked them in herself. She would certainly be glad when her daddy got home.

CHAPTER SEVEN

According to the note she found on the kitchen counter the next morning, Neal had gotten home late the night before and had left before she woke up.

You were sleeping so peacefully I didn't want to wake you.
Be home early tonight.
Miss you. Love,
Neal

Ugh! Why hadn't he woken her up? If he missed her... Tabitha hated being alone all day with nothing to do but unpack. She considered going to the daycare again, but decided to make a dent in the unpacking instead. She set her phone in her Beats speaker, turned on one of her playlists, and got to work.

When Neal got home from work, she didn't rush to the door to welcome him as was their usual custom. Instead she coldly offered him a cheek when he approached her. Apparently he noticed the frigid greeting, because he said with a sigh, "Had a bad day?" He walked around the couch and sat in the chair next to her, keeping a safe distance from the storm cloud that loomed directly over her head.

"Yes." She set down the magazine she'd been pretending to read. Before his car pulled up, she had been working on the scarf she was knitting for him, but since it was supposed to be a surprise, she'd stuffed it under the cushions when she heard him pull into the driveway and picked up a *Sports Illustrated* from the coffee table.

He sighed again. "What's the matter? I was expecting a little more enthusiastic greeting than that." His face seemed lined with more creases than before. Her usually upbeat daddy appeared almost haggard.

She frowned, considering whether or not she should confront the issue when he was clearly exhausted. Instinctively, she knew the timing was wrong, but something inside her burst and she couldn't contain herself. "I'm bored,

daddy. This place is boring, I have no friends, nothing to do but sit here all day and watch TV. I miss Chicago, I miss my job. There—I felt important. Here—I'm nobody."

He recoiled as if she had slapped him.

Unable to sit there and watch the hurt spread across his face, she got up and went into the kitchen. She hoisted herself up onto the counter at the breakfast bar; perching there made her feel less small.

"Do you mean that I make you feel like a nobody?" Concern filled his eyes, and she regretted her words even more.

"Just forget I said that. I didn't mean it. I'm just bored, you know. I guess it just got to me."

"No, you wouldn't have said it if you didn't mean it." He raked a hand through the waves of his sandy hair.

"Look, isn't moving supposed to be one of life's biggest stressors? It's an adjustment, that's all. But why are you working all these crazy hours? I didn't think it was going to be like this," she said, trying to change the subject.

"I know, I didn't either. Apparently they've been without help for so long in this community that the jobs have really piled up, and when you add the everyday emergencies that happen, well—there aren't enough hours in the day to get it all done."

"So you're saying it's not always going to be like this?" She gazed up at him, batting her lashes with purpose.

He favored her with a lopsided grin. "I hope not," he said, rising to his feet and walking toward her. "I'd like to be able to spend more time with you."

His close proximity made her heart beat faster and she started kicking her feet involuntarily, back and forth one at a time, swinging under the countertop. "Hmph! It doesn't seem like it. I can't believe that I quit my job and moved all this way for you to set me up in this house and leave me all alone. I feel like Rapunzel, all trapped at the top of a castle," she said dramatically. "What am I supposed to do all day?"

He raised an eyebrow and looked pointedly at a stack of boxes that held kitchen supplies.

She smacked her fists down on her thighs with a frustrated puff of air. "Besides that! Unpacking is so utterly boring, daddy. I've been at it for weeks and it seems like it will never get finished."

Taking her fists in his big hands, he said, "I know, princess. It is a big job, and I'll help you with it on my day off."

"You'll actually have a day off?" she said bitingly.

He smiled, clearly determined not to be drawn into a fight with her. "I think that somebody needs some of daddy's attention." He wrapped his arms around her and hugged her tightly. The embrace felt so good; he made all her stress melt away. Cupping the back of her head to him, he said, "I thought

this would be a chance for you to relax, get away from all your stress from work, and feel better. Have you made a doctor's appointment yet?"

She sighed. "Yes. I'm going tomorrow."

"But you haven't had any headaches since we've been here, have you?"

"Only little ones. Nothing too terrible."

"Well, that's good. I want you to relax and take it easy."

"That's fine, but I get bored. I miss my work." His concern meant the world to her, but how could she make him understand how important her work was to her? Best to plant little seeds along the way. She didn't want him to be totally blindsided when he discovered that she planned to go back to work in Chicago in a couple of weeks.

He let her go and walked over to the refrigerator. "Do you want anything?" he offered.

"No, thanks."

"Okay," he said and poured himself a large glass of orange juice. He drank the whole thing in a couple of gulps. As he set the glass down on the counter, the corners of his mouth slid up to his ears. "Do you know how pretty you are?"

She rolled her eyes to the side coquettishly, not ready to stop pouting entirely. "No."

"You are. The prettiest girl I know." He winked at her. "And you're so cute, sitting there on the counter swinging your legs like that."

"What?" She hadn't realized it until he said that, but his compliment not only made her blush, but now she was kicking her legs faster and faster, an indicator of her excitement.

He approached her and lifted the bottom of her sweater until he'd pulled it completely off over her head. She lifted her arms compliantly, making the task of undressing her easier for him. He unbuttoned the front of her shirt, and she marveled at how nimbly he could do that, considering the size of his fingers.

Since she wasn't wearing a bra, once her shirt was open in the front her bare chest was exposed. Her breasts were small enough she didn't really need one, and in weather like they'd been having, no one even noticed under all those layers of clothing.

He ran his hands over her torso, electrifying her skin, keeping her warm as the cooler air hit her skin. His mouth covered hers, and he explored her mouth with his tongue. She returned his passion with a swirl of her own. Her nipples turned to hard little peaks under his touch, and she yearned to feel his mouth on them.

"Lift up, put your arms and legs around daddy."

She did as he asked, wrapping herself around him like a firefighter preparing to slide down a pole. He raised her bottom a few inches off the counter and, reaching up under her short flouncy skirt, he yanked at her

tights, pulling them down over her ass. When he set her back down, he pulled them down the rest of the way until he tossed them on the floor, leaving her completely naked except for the skirt hiked up to her waist and the shirt that dangled on her shoulders, yet left her completely exposed for his pleasure. She knew he left it on because she tended to get a chill so easily in the winter. It melted her heart how he was always taking care of his girl, no matter the situation.

He took a step back, pulled his shirt over his head, and laid it on the counter next to her. "Stay right here," he said. When he walked over and bent to look inside a drawer on the other side of the kitchen, she watched the muscles on his back ripple slightly under the skin. She'd never seen anyone with a back like his, nipped in at the waist, then blooming into a broad expanse of muscles, and rounded out into two broad shoulders and arms as bulky as any action movie star. She had to swallow to keep herself from drooling and her pussy grew wet with desire.

"Here it is," he said, removing a roll of duct tape from the back of the drawer. "I knew I'd put it in there." He came back over to her. "Hands behind your back."

Unsure how the evening had gone from her trying to pick a fight to her being bound with duct tape, she obeyed. Reaching behind her, he wrapped the tape around her wrists a few times, binding her hands together so that she couldn't move them more than a few centimeters.

With an evil grin, he said, "You know... I'm tempted to put a piece over your mouth. You have been awfully bratty, little girl."

"Please don't, daddy. I'll be good," she promised.

"Alright, plus I do like to hear you scream when I fuck you, but no more complaining."

"Yes, sir. Sorry, daddy."

"It's okay. Now I'm gonna fuck my little girl. Hard."

His words sent a thrill dancing down her spine and her clit throbbed with need. As if reading her mind, he spread her legs wide and said, "What a pretty little pussy. Whose pussy is that, princess?"

He grabbed her by the back of the neck and bit her bottom lip, not hard enough to make it bleed, but hard enough to let her know he meant business.

"Yours! It's your pussy, daddy," she struggled to say while he had her lip between his teeth.

Obviously pleased with her answer, he released her. "Good girl." He began to lick her lips with his tongue and explore the slick folds of her pussy with his fingers. She wriggled under his attentions and pressed her chest against him.

"Baby girl is hungry for daddy, isn't she?" he cooed in her ear.

"Yes, daddy. Please take me, daddy," she pleaded, now controlled by her lust for him. She feared she might go insane if she didn't feel him inside her

soon.

"Oh, I'm going to take you." He pinched one of her nipples and a wave of pleasure zipped through her. "But not yet."

He walked back over to the same drawer, rummaged around and came back with two wooden clothespins. Her stomach lurched. Wouldn't those hurt terribly? Her mind went blank until she remembered—she did have a safeword.

"Daddy…" she started, her voice filled with trepidation, but she couldn't finish.

His facial expression changed from mischievous to serious. "If this hurts too much for you, tell daddy, and I'll take them off."

She stared at the torturous-looking devices and shivered.

"Just try it for daddy. That's all I ask."

She took a deep breath and nodded. "Yes, sir."

He held her close, her naked cunt pressed against his jeans. She felt his erection straining against his pants. She wanted to reach down and free him, take him in her hand and stroke him until he slipped inside her, but her hands were taped behind her back and all she could do was strain and allow him to control things.

He nuzzled her neck and slid a finger between her legs again, playing with her pussy. "So wet," he whispered in her ear, and it filled her with happiness knowing that her arousal pleased him. His fingers moved in and out of her, and she could hear her juices sluicing on his fingers.

As he toyed with her cunt, he bent his head and took a breast in his mouth. He flicked his tongue across her pebbled nipple, and she turned into a molten heap of lust on the kitchen counter. That delicious tongue darted over her other nipple and she reveled in the exquisite sensation when something sprung onto the tip of her other breast.

Yeow! Her eyes flew open. It felt like a mousetrap had been sprung on her tiny little titty. Ouch! Before she could protest, the same thing happened to her other nipple. Crap! Ouch. She looked down to see two clothespins, their wooden jaws angrily attached to her erect nipples.

"Breathe, baby. Breathe," Neal said.

Glancing up at him through a haze of agony and ecstasy, she gave him a foggy nod.

"Breathe through it and it will start to become more bearable."

He unzipped his pants, dropping them to the floor so that his cock pressed against her opening and he lifted her bottom and impaled her onto him. Her mind swam, overloaded with the biting sensation on both breasts and the feeling of him filling her completely. When he started to drive into her, it only took a few thrusts before she was calling out and shaking uncontrollably with an orgasm that rocked her to the core. She wanted to cling to him, but since her arms were pinned behind her back, she was at his

mercy. He held her close. "Shhh. There, there, baby girl. Hold still and it will all be over before you know it."

She shook her head wildly. "No!"

"What? You don't want it to be over?"

"Noooo, daddy," she eked out.

He pulled out and scooped her into his arms and carried her to the couch where he flipped her over face down. It felt awkward with her arms stuck behind herself so that she couldn't maneuver herself, couldn't break her fall or protect her face. Of course, daddy would do that for her, but it took her trusting him to be able to relax and not panic while he manhandled her.

He positioned her with her bum in the air, her shoulders and right cheek lying against the couch cushions, arms taped behind her back. Kneeling behind her, he lifted her skirt and spread her bottom cheeks.

"Daddy!" she squealed in protest. They'd tried anal sex once before and it had been a painful disaster. Ever since, she'd been hypersensitive to any attention he paid to her rear entry.

"Hush, princess. I'm simply doing an inspection. You know daddy isn't going to do anything you aren't comfortable with."

She took a deep breath and tried to relax as he spread her pussy lips wide. Being on display for him was humiliating and exciting at the same time. Having her most intimate parts inspected and being found desirable by the man she loved was an intoxicating feeling and her pussy throbbed from the forbidden nature of it.

Gathering a fistful of her hair, he buried his cock inside her cunt and tugged at her locks. Her head cocked back, the stinging of her roots gave her a jolt. As he fucked her, her clamped nipples brushed against the fabric of the couch, making them raw, which was uncomfortable and exquisitely sensual at the same time. She wasn't sure yet if she could admit it to Neal, but she liked the way it felt.

He barreled into her pussy over and over again, slamming his balls up against her clit. Writhing underneath him, the pressure began to build inside her again. The harder he pumped, the closer she came to careening into an explosive climax. He paused for a second, reached around and unclipped one of the clothespins.

Ouch! The renewed blood flow hit her poor nipple with a rush that stung worse than the clamping had. She groaned from deep in her belly; the pain was vicious, but somehow amped up her arousal.

Zip! There went the other clip, and her other nipple throbbed, providing her with double the delicious torture.

Grabbing her hips in his hands, Neal continued fucking her deep and hard. His efforts had pushed her head all the way to the end of the sofa, wedging it against the armrest on the end. Each time he plummeted into her, her body fought to push against his and not collapse completely. Her sore

nipples scraped against the fabric of the material and she teetered on the edge.

"I'm going to come, daddy!"

"Good girl. That's it. Come for daddy."

She relaxed and let the exquisite bliss roll through her body, seizing her every care and dismissing it, making everything in her world disappear except her orgasm at that instant. She couldn't have stopped herself from succumbing for anything in the world. Hot, electric currents roared into her extremities, and she shook with the pleasure of it.

He continued fucking her for several more minutes and she floated in a dreamlike state until he ejaculated with a satisfied growl and stayed inside her until he grew limp. Finally, he pulled out and ripped the tape off her wrists.

The sticky part zipping over her skin, yanking at her tiny arm hairs stung, bringing her back from la-la land.

"That didn't hurt too badly, did it?" he asked.

"No, daddy. It just stung a little, but it's fine."

He folded her into his arms on the couch and pulled a blanket off the back to cover them. Draping it over them, he curled his hips up behind hers. "How did you like that, princess? What did you think of the clothespins?"

This was the first time he'd used those on her, though secretly she'd always wondered how they would feel. "They hurt, but I actually liked it," she said, a shyness in her voice. It still made her uncomfortable to talk about sexual things, but Neal insisted that she do it and she was getting better at voicing her needs and opinions.

"Good. Daddy likes to make you feel good." He nuzzled her neck and nibbled playfully on her ear.

"How about you, daddy... did you like that?"

"Baby, I *always* love being with you. You make daddy so happy."

Her head resting on a pillow, she basked in the afterglow of his love. Soon he was snoring in her ear, and she considered getting up and turning on the television, but decided against it. His rasping breath comforted her and she tried to forget how much she missed her job in Chicago. She tried to simply focus on the wonderful big, sweet, bear of a man who loved her enough to move to the middle of nowhere with her to save her health and tried not to think of how she was going to break his heart when she told him she was going back.

CHAPTER EIGHT

The next morning Tabitha drove forty-five minutes away to see her new doctor. After what seemed like a super long wait, she finally met Dr. Tuck. The neurologist introduced himself and asked her about her medications. He was a short, balding man with keen, sharp black eyes like a hawk.

"I'm taking propranolol now as a preventative for my migraines," she said.

"Ah, good. Good. And I see you've made some lifestyle changes recently. Tell me about that." The balding doctor had a gentle bedside manner, and Tabitha liked him immediately.

"Well, I moved from Chicago with my boyfriend." She smiled despite herself when she mentioned Neal.

"Okay, and what about work?"

"Oh, I quit my job. At least for now."

"And has that helped the headaches? The move, quitting the job?"

"Well, I don't know what the difference is. It could be the meds. They seem to be working."

Dr. Tuck picked up her chart and flipped through it. "I see there's a note from your previous physician. He says he's concerned your emotions could be being expressed through your poor health." He peered at her with those dark eyes.

She nodded. "I know. I saw a psychologist a few times back in Chicago. She called it somaticizing."

He chuckled. "A big word, but it means that you tend to hold your stress inside and that can make you sick. How have you been managing your stress since you've moved here?"

Frowning, she said, "I don't know if I have. A lot of sex…" She broke off, wondering if she'd given him too much information, but she only saw him raise one corner of him mouth in an involuntary smile before he nodded at her to continue. "I have a treadmill I use when it's snowy out or too cold, but I run when I can. You know, I haven't been that stressed out here."

He set the chart on the counter and wrote something in it, then looked back up at her. "That's really the point, isn't it? The move? To give you a less stressful life. Well, it sounds like things are working. I'd like you to keep a journal for any headaches you do have. Let me know if you decide you want a referral for a psychologist in the area, and I want to see you back here in three months," he said and proffered her a hand. She shook his hand and thanked him, then went to the front desk to make an appointment.

As she drove home, Tabitha considered the doctor's questions. She was actually feeling better. She hadn't had a migraine since she'd come to Little Haven. Whether that could be attributed to her not working, her medication, or the new lifestyle, she wasn't sure. And she wasn't assured that her headaches wouldn't recur either, but it was nice to be feeling better.

When she got home, she checked her email and found a message from her boss asking about her return date. She smiled to herself. Knowing that she was missed made her feel good and she couldn't wait to get back to the excitement of the trading floor, but she wasn't ready to deal with that situation yet. Tonight she had something special planned for Neal.

One of their favorite play scenes involved her dressing up like a schoolgirl, so she threw a frozen lasagna in the oven and went into the bedroom to get ready. When Neal came home, she greeted him at the door wearing a plaid skirt and a white oxford-cloth shirt tied at the waist with several buttons undone.

His eyes lit up and he whisked her into his arms. "This is what I like to come home to," he said, planting a kiss on her forehead.

"Thank you, daddy. I also have dinner in the oven."

"You do?"

She nodded proudly.

"That's great, baby. You're so adorable, and I love when you wear your hair like this." He twirled one of her ponytails and gave it a playful tug. It filled her with happiness to please him. She held his arm tight as they walked to the kitchen together.

"It smells good," he said, setting down the mail.

She beamed.

As he sorted through the mail, he asked, "Did you go to your doctor's appointment today?"

"I did."

"And how was it?"

"Fine. Dr. Tuck seems nice, and I haven't really been sick since we've been here..."

He abandoned the mail. "See? I knew this would work. This is such a healthy environment for you to be in, baby. I'm so glad you haven't been sick."

She rolled her eyes to the ceiling. "We don't know if that has anything to

do with me being better. It could be the medication," she said with an exasperated sigh.

"You're kidding, right?" he asked, nostrils flaring.

"No, I'm not." She crossed her arms over her chest defiantly.

"You leave one of the most stressful jobs there is after being hospitalized three times in the last year, move to a remote, peaceful area, you're healthier, and you want to credit the medication? Weren't you on medication before?"

She shrugged. "A different one, and who knows? Maybe I'm learning to handle stress better."

"Ugh! You are so stubborn, you know that?" He ran a hand through his hair impatiently. "Tabitha, you've been on medication before and it never seemed to help then. Why the hell do you think the medication is helping now?"

"I don't know…"

"That was sarcasm, my dear. Because it's not the medication!" His face was red and she noticed a tiny vein along the side of his temple throbbing with every word he spoke.

Her heart sank. This wasn't how this evening was supposed to go. Maybe she could still turn this around. She sidled over to him and placed her palm on his chest. His heart was racing, and she wondered if perhaps it was *his* health they should be worried about, but she didn't dare vocalize that thought.

"I'm sorry, daddy. You're right."

He took a deep breath and exhaled loudly. "Alright, but you really know how to get me upset."

She giggled. "I probably deserve a spanking."

A lopsided grin spread slowly across his face. "You probably do. And maybe another visit to *this* doctor." He pointed at himself.

"Oooh! I hope I don't have to get a shot." She covered her mouth in feigned horror.

"A painful injection in your ass?" he teased and they both erupted in laughter. "No, I've got something else in mind. Keep those pigtails in your hair and let's go in the bedroom. I have a few things I need to examine."

With a little squeal of delight, she took off running. "Last one there is a rotten egg!" The sound of his feet bounding on the floor behind her told her he was chasing her, but as she anticipated, he let her win.

She stood at the edge of the bed and he bolted through the door.

"I want to watch you take that off. Do it slowly."

"Yes, sir." Slowly, she unbuttoned her shirt and dropped it to the floor. Then she unzipped her skirt and let it fall.

"Now the bra." He wiggled a finger at her.

Unhooking it in the back, she unwrapped her breasts like they were a gift, never allowing her gaze to waver from his. She slipped off her panties and

stood there, naked except for her white knee-socks. "Want me to take off my socks too, daddy?"

He shook his head with a grin. "Hell, no. I like the socks." She grinned back. It was so cute that her daddy had a sock fetish. "Now lie down on the bed and spread those legs for daddy."

She climbed onto the bed and lay back, legs splayed like he'd asked, and then she waited. He'd gone into the bathroom and he returned with a tube of sports cream, the kind that you used on sore muscles after a rigorous workout or an injury. "What's that for?"

Arching a brow devilishly, he said, "I thought we might warm things up a bit."

CHAPTER NINE

She felt her eyes widen. "What are you going to do with that?"

"You'll see," he said with a wink, slipping down his pants.

Grabbing her by the legs, he dragged her toward him so her bottom sat at the edge of the bed. He quickly stepped out of his boxer briefs and tossed his shirt to the floor. She hooked her legs around his neck and felt the press of his cock against her pussy. The feel of his skin against hers sent a bolt of electricity through her entire body, and she wanted him inside her, but she had an inkling he was going to make her wait.

He flipped back the top of the cream and squeezed some out onto his finger. With a wicked grin, he dabbed some on her right nipple, then the left. Watching her face intently for a reaction, he gently massaged the cream onto her areola, occasionally flicking the pebbled center of each bud.

"May I close my eyes, daddy?"

"For a minute. Then open them when you start to feel it warm up."

She allowed her lids to droop while she luxuriated in his touch. He traced the outside rim of her areolas one by one with a single finger, eliciting an exquisite sense of pleasure so delicate, yet so intense that her hips bucked against his pelvis involuntarily.

His shaft hardened against her pussy, and while he continued to stroke each tender nipple, he rubbed the head of his cock teasingly over her sex. Sliding it up and down her slit, wetting it with the telltale juices of her arousal.

Clutching the bedsheets with her fists, she groaned under his attentions, and she began to feel the burn. It came on slowly, insidiously. The fact that it was concentrated on the very tips of her breasts brought her entire focus to the warming buds. Her eyes flew open to see Neal's fingers tease her tight pink nipples.

Neal's eyes met hers. "How does it feel, princess? Is it hot?"

"It's getting that way."

He nodded his approval. "I want you to wait as long as you can, but when you can't stand it anymore, I want you to ask for what you want."

"Yes, sir."

He continued prodding her nipples, which were starting to heat into a slight stinging sensation. The feeling only made her more aware of her arousal, making the whole world shrink away to where the only thing on her mind was her drenched, needy pussy and her delightfully aching breasts. His eyes remained affixed to her face, reading her reactions—making sure she didn't have a bad reaction to the cream, but also because nothing seemed to please him more than making her squirm with desire. He loved turning her into his wanton little girl-whore.

"I've got one more exam to do on you," he teased, reaching for something beside the bed. Then he pulled a metal instrument the size of a fountain pen out of a felt pouch. He held it up to show her. "Did your doctor use one of these on you?" Light glinted off the silver object, which looked like a dental instrument except that it had a wheel with tiny tines on one end. It reminded her of a children's toy, a pinwheel or something one could use with Play-Doh.

"What is it?" she asked.

"It's called a Wartenberg wheel, and it's used by neurologists. I believe to measure their patients' sensitivity."

He rolled the tool across her nipple, taking the place of his fingers. "Ooh!" she exclaimed.

"How does that feel?"

"Interesting," was all she could manage. Between the heat and the sharp little tines running across her most sensitive parts, she felt like she might explode.

The tines rolled over the tips of her breasts, sowing seeds of arousal in their path. Her nipples ached, but it felt divine at the same time. He stroked and traced her nipples with the wheel and tweaked her burning mounds with his other hand until she couldn't stand it anymore. "Please, daddy! Please fuck me."

"Does my baby girl need her daddy inside her?"

"Yes, yes!" she whimpered. "Please take me!"

He sheathed his cock in her waiting opening, and she moaned as he filled her. The pressure inside her simmered to a boil and as he continued his unrelenting play with her breasts, she started to quake with the tremors of an earth-shattering climax. He tweaked and pulled her nipples until she howled and shook her head from side to side, clawing at the blankets trying to find purchase, but instead falling farther and farther down into a pit of bliss.

He pumped his cock into her pussy hard, finally releasing her breasts and taking hold of her hips, thrusting into her with long, sure strokes. Her titties still burned and she felt like all her nerve endings were on the outside of her body, she was so sensitive.

"Damn, baby, you are so hot. I love to see you like that, when you come

so hard and your eyelashes flutter like that." His breathing was labored and she felt a droplet of sweat fall onto her shoulder from his forehead.

"Oooh, daddy. The things you do to me," she purred.

"You love it?"

"Every minute of it." She threw her arms around his neck and pulled her to him, kissing him open-mouthed and roughly. His hips pressed into her one more time as he came inside her with a grunt.

She squeezed her muscles around him, milking him for every drop of cum. He let her legs fall to the sides and covered her body with his.

"Stay inside me all night, daddy."

Just then they heard a faint beep from the oven downstairs, and they laughed.

"Okay, maybe not. Don't want to burn dinner, but maybe later…"

"You bet," he said and stood up. Pulling his underwear on, he said, "I'll go get it. You stay here and get dressed."

"Aww, thanks, daddy," she said, padding to grab a robe out of the closet before heading for the bidet. How had she gotten along without that thing all these years?

"Just not too dressed," he called as he moved toward the kitchen.

She cleaned herself up and tiptoed on bare feet into the great room, where Neal was starting a fire.

"Can we watch a movie, daddy?"

"Sure, princess. Can you give daddy a backrub?"

"Sure."

They ate their lasagna in front of the fire, and he let her pick a movie. She chose *Brave*, which was her new favorite with the spunky little red-haired heroine. Neal liked it because it had a lot of action and humor. After she put the dishes in the dishwasher, she had Neal sit on the floor in front of her while she rubbed his shoulders, then scratched his back. He groaned with satisfaction as she squeezed his shoulder muscles, and it pleased her that she could make him feel so good after he'd satisfied her so completely in the bedroom.

Then Neal sat in his favorite chair, a perfect daddy recliner she'd gotten him for Christmas the year before, and he patted his lap for her to join him. They snuggled together, arms and legs entwined watching the movie, enjoying the roaring fire, and for a while she forgot all about the email from her boss.

CHAPTER TEN

The next afternoon, Tabitha received a text from Neal.

Have to work late again, sorry. Want to meet me at the community center later for a little fun?

Sure.

Great. Come by around 9 p.m.

Do I need to bring anything?

Just your sexy self.

She grinned, loving how he always made her feel so desirable. Overall, things had been so tense between them lately, with him working so much and her resistance to the move. It would be nice to spend some time together doing something fun.

That evening Tabitha fixed herself a quick frozen dinner and read a couple of chapters in her book before sprucing up her makeup and heading over to the community center.

It wasn't snowing, so she decided to walk. The stars shone bright overhead and her breath created wispy clouds in the cold night air. When she got to the community center, the door to the building was locked, so she walked around the side of the building and tried another door. Locked.

Ugh. It was too cold out to be stuck outside. She pulled out her phone and texted Neal.

Where are you? Doors are locked.

Sorry about that. Be right there.

She stood outside shivering, trying not to get too irritated. Within a couple of minutes, Neal opened the door to the main entrance. "Sorry, babe. I didn't know all those would be locked."

"It's okay," she said, giving him a hug. "What are you doing over here so late?"

"I've been fixing a broken pump. Got it working about twenty minutes ago."

"A pump? To what?"

"The hot tub." He raised an eyebrow mischievously.

"They have a hot tub here?"

"Yes," he answered gleefully. "And I just got it working again."

"So was this your master plan, daddy? To get me over here to get me in the hot tub with you?"

"How'd you guess?" He chuckled and held out a hand to her.

She took it and allowed him to lead her through the building to the area outside. About fifteen feet away from the pool, which was covered, was the hot tub. It looked beyond inviting with the swaths of steam rising up into the cold night air. "But you didn't tell me to bring my suit."

Neal dropped her hand and started stripping off his clothes. "Who needs a suit?"

Tabitha's eyes bulged. "Neal! You can't do that!"

"Why not?" he asked.

"Someone could see us!"

"Where? No one's here. The place is locked, as you saw."

"Did you lock it again?"

"Yes."

She looked around. There was a fence around the pool area that had a few visually open spaces in it. "If someone was walking by, they could see," she protested.

"No one's going to be walking by. It's a Monday night. People are inside, watching football."

"They might be walking their dog or something."

"Well, then they'll be watching their dog and not us. No one is expecting anyone to be over here so they won't be paying any attention." Stark naked, he stepped into the water. "Oh, baby, this feels good. You've got to get in here with me."

She frowned. It did look amazing, but she hated the idea of someone catching them naked in the hot tub.

"Don't leave me hanging, princess. Get out of those clothes and get your ass in here now!" His tone was playful and firm at the same time.

"Alright," she said reluctantly, "but if we get caught, you'll have to get me out of this." She took off her boots, her coat, then her pants and sweater. Finally she removed her underwear and bra and hugged herself tight. Damn, it was cold!

"It's a deal," he said and reached out a hand to help her in.

She hopped in quickly, and her ankles and calves thrilled to the water's heat, although she immediately wished she'd taken it slower. The difference in temperature shocked her system. Her nipples had been so erect from the cold that she'd thought they might fall right off if a brisk wind blew by. Now, as she immersed herself in the bath, everything felt so hot she almost swooned.

She eased herself onto the seat next to Neal, and he enveloped her in an embrace. "Ahhh!" she said, settling in and letting the warmth of the Jacuzzi course over her. "This was a good idea, daddy."

He positioned himself so that he was facing her, between her legs, and she wrapped her arms and legs around him, drawing him close. His body felt so good next to hers, the warm waters swirling around them, so she couldn't help but purr out loud. "Mmm."

"Oh, Tabitha, you feel so good. I need you so much." As if to echo his sentiments, his erection pushed against her opening.

"Now daddy," she said primly. "It's one thing to get caught skinny dipping in the community pool, but it's quite another to get caught doing *that*. They might kick us out of Little Haven for doing *that!*"

Ignoring her, he pushed his cock inside her. "Shhh! If you're quiet, no one will ever know."

He filled her then, and she felt more and more bliss with every inch he gave her. She wrapped her legs around his waist and encircled his neck with her arms. The buoyancy of the water made his movements more fluid since she felt light as a feather, and he seemed to be deeper inside her than usual.

His hands rested on her middle and he bobbed her up and down on his cock, while he simultaneously took possession of her mouth with his. The water felt slick against her skin and the steam only added to the decadent sensuality of the encounter. She loved the way it sluiced up against them with every thrust.

Holding him tight, she took his earlobe between her teeth and bit down lightly. "Oh, such a tiger! Has my baby been feeling neglected?" he asked.

She nodded. "Yes, daddy."

"I'm sorry. Really sorry, baby. Let daddy show you how much he's missed you."

She nibbled on his bottom lip and jutted her chest forward into his. Reading her signals, he dropped his head to her breasts and kissed and suckled them. She laid her head back onto the side of the hot tub and luxuriated in his attentions. "Daddy, you feel so good."

He continued fucking her and kissing her neck. "I'd spank you, but I'm afraid there'd be too much splashing."

She laughed. "You can spank me later. Just keep fucking me."

"You feel incredible," he said, driving into her again and again until finally their passion burst in the form of a simultaneous climax that left their bodies clinging to one another, neither wanting to let the other go. As they snuggled in each other's arms, Tabitha traced her finger over the stubble of his beard and giggled. "I hope nobody finds us and kicks us out."

"They are not going to kick us out," Neal said, squeezing her tight.

He was right. A man so dedicated to his job was difficult, if not impossible to find. The powers-that-be at Little Haven would find him almost impossible to replace. A feeling of guilt churned in her belly. She'd been putting off telling him, but she just couldn't continue the ruse anymore. The people of Little Haven had come to count on him. Hell, she was even starting to feel comfortable here. She couldn't keep lying to everyone.

Shifting in his arms so she could look at him, she blurted out, "Neal, I can't stay here."

He scrunched his brows quizzically. "You need to go back to the house? That's okay."

She shook her head. "No, I mean I have to go back to Chicago."

His eyelashes fluttered wildly as he blinked several times. "I don't understand. Why would you have to go back to Chicago?"

She closed her eyes and rubbed her face with her hands, wishing the whole situation would vanish. But when she opened her eyes again, her problems were still staring her in the face.

"Why, Tabitha? What are you saying?"

"Daddy, you know I never wanted to come here," she whined.

He stood up and she could see that vein throbbing on the side of his temple. "Then why did you?"

"Because I didn't want to lose you!"

"Well, it looks like that's going to happen anyway."

She felt as if she'd been kicked in the gut. "Daddy, please don't say that. We can just go back to Chicago together. My boss is holding my job for me."

"He's holding your job for you? So you never intended to live here with me... This whole time you've been lying to me."

This was what she'd been afraid of, that he'd find out that she'd been holding out on him. She wasn't sure what she expected, but nothing she'd imagined was as awful as the look of hurt in his eyes as he stood there now questioning her.

"I tried," she mumbled.

"You tried? What did you tell your old job—that you were just taking a vacation?"

"A leave of absence," she admitted miserably.

"A leave of absence," he repeated, nodding his head in irony. "I should have known. You agreed to come here way too easily. I should have known I'd never be as important to you as your job."

"But that's not true…" she pleaded.

"Oh, it is most definitely true. And it's sad. It's just a fucking job, Tabitha, and you're going to throw away all we have for a stupid job." He shook his head and climbed out of the hot tub.

"Wait! Where are you going?"

"Back to work."

"You're kidding."

"Nope."

"But you can't stay here. Plus it's freezing and you're wet."

"I'll find a towel in the clubhouse," he said dismissively and started putting on his clothes.

"But…" She started to get out of the hot tub. Bam! The cold air hit her like an uppercut to the circulatory system. "But, daddy, you'll go back to Chicago with me, won't you?"

He whirled on her. "You've got to be kidding me! Hell, no. I'm staying here. I've got a good job, a nice house, *a nice life*." He said that last part slowly as if he were speaking to a five-year-old.

As she stood there, naked and shivering, something inside her gave way. She hadn't considered it a real possibility that he would stay here. "Really?" she snapped. "You'd stay in a community for daddies and little girls without a little girl? That's absolutely ridiculous!" As soon as she heard the words come out of her mouth, she realized that she was the one who was being ridiculous. If Neal stayed there, it would take no time for him to find a replacement for her. She'd seen how some of the littles in the community looked at him. He'd be in their houses, fixing things, and before she knew it some little brat would have defected from her home team and joined team Neal.

"I feel at home here. This is where I belong, Tabitha. I wish you felt the same way."

"So what? You're just planning on replacing me with the next little girl with pigtails who comes along?" Her voice rose shrilly and she hugged herself, dripping icy droplets onto the concrete.

He handed her a pile of her clothes. "No, princess, it's you who I want. *You* are who makes me want to get up in the morning. You are who makes me want to be the best man I can be—*you*! Everything I do is for you—for us."

She stomped her foot. "But what about *me*? What about what I want?"

He shrugged, lost. "I don't know. I hoped you could be happy here."

She curled her lips into a snarl. "Well, I can't!" The goosebumps on her skin were starting to ache. She needed a towel in the worst way, but she was

too determined to make a stormy exit to stop and search for one. She threw her sweater over her head and pulled one leg then another of her pants on. Her teeth chattered as she scooped her undergarments and her boots off the pavement and marched toward the gate leading to the neighborhood street. Neal would follow her. He always did.

She crashed through the gate in a huff, and when she got to the street she leaned up against one of the cars parked near the clubhouse to put on her boots. Her soaking wet locks threatened to turn to icicles, while her soggy feet squished in her shoes, and her wet skin slid uncomfortably against her previously dry clothing. She cringed at how uncomfortable she was, and her pussy throbbed from the hard fucking Neal had just given her.

Hurry, Neal. Hurry.

But after a few minutes, the truth finally hit her.

He wasn't coming.

Maybe this time she'd truly lost him. She hugged herself tight in a futile attempt to ward off the cold, and with a whimper, she trudged back to their empty house.

CHAPTER ELEVEN

When Tabitha woke up the next morning, she looked over to find his side of the bed untouched. Maybe he slept on the couch. She got up and searched the house, but found no sign of Neal. He hadn't come home. A pit of dread formed in her stomach and she reached for her phone. With shaking fingers she texted Neal.

Where are you?

Then she waited with bated breath for him to respond.

Slept on the couch at the rec center.

What are you doing?

Working.

Unsure how to make things right, she texted back a sad face emoji. His response came only moments later.

We'll talk later. Gotta go.

For the rest of the day Tabitha sulked around the house trying to distract herself, but all she could think about was the rift between her and Neal.

The knot in her stomach tightened, and she decided to distract herself with some good, old-fashioned retail therapy. She called Bailey and they made a plan to go on a marathon shopping trip the next day. The biggest mall in America, maybe even the world, was only a few hours away, and they'd been dying to take a trip there.

Determined to do something productive, she sat down to do some online banking, and then realized she'd forgotten to bring in the mail the day before.

Their mail had been forwarded, but there hadn't been much yet, only a slow trickle of letters and bills had begun to arrive. They'd yet to receive a bill for their satellite TV service at their new address. She wondered if it had come the previous day, so she threw on some clothes and went to the mailbox.

Tabitha had been outside only a few seconds when Agnes' door opened. Tabitha looked up to find the older woman striding toward her. "Good morning," Agnes said enthusiastically.

"Good morning," Tabitha responded, waving the two small white envelopes she'd just retrieved from her mailbox in greeting, neither of which turned out to be the satellite bill.

"What are you up to this morning?" Agnes asked.

Tabitha shrugged. "Paying some bills. Maybe organizing a drawer or two, putting in some shelf paper..."

"Sounds fun," Agnes said sarcastically. "Hey, what about your job? Neal said you had a real high-powered job working for one of those big financial companies back in Chicago."

Tabitha nervously played with the hem of her shirt, rubbing it between her fingers. She wasn't about to get into the job conversation with Agnes, who seemed to have a pretty big mouth. "Uh, yeah. I don't know about high-powered, but it was high-stress for sure. That's one of the reasons we moved here."

"Yep, lots of people move here to get away from the stresses of fast-paced life in the big city." Agnes shook her head as if pitying those in possession of that foolish notion.

"What—you don't think it works, living here? It doesn't help your stress?" Tabitha was surprised at Agnes' reaction. Usually Agnes made it sound like Little Haven was the answer to everything.

"It is a great place to live if you want to reduce stress, but life is full of stressors no matter you live. Stress will always find you if you're not careful, that's all I'm saying. Are you gonna look for a job around here?"

Tabitha nodded. Another lie, she thought and hated herself for it.

"I don't know how I'd find a job myself if I didn't have the daycare. Everything is on computers these days. My grandson is even going to college online. Doesn't even have to report for class in person except for a few times a semester. Can you believe it?"

"Yeah," Tabitha responded absently. It felt her brain suddenly imploded. Why hadn't she thought of it before? She must have been too caught up in going back to Chicago to have considered it.

Computers! She could work from home if she had to. If she could find a job that used her skills but that she didn't have to be physically present for. There had to be something... and surely it would be less stressful than working on the trading floor.

She reached over and kissed Agnes on the cheek. "Thanks, Agnes. I've

got to go!"

Tabitha turned and ran back into her house, leaving Agnes behind saying, "You're welcome, but what did I do?"

Tabitha didn't bother to answer. She had a job search to do.

• • • • • • •

That night when Neal came home, Tabitha was glued to the computer screen.

"Hey," he said as he closed the front door behind him. His voice was tentative, like he was testing the waters.

"Hey," she called, keeping her eyes on the screen. She'd found several promising job leads, but she didn't want to tell Neal about them prematurely. "How was work?"

"Fine," he said with a clipped tone. "What's for dinner?" he asked, banging around in the kitchen. It was not a good idea to forget to feed Neal. Like a grizzly bear, he got grumpy when he was hungry, and that was the last thing she needed now.

"Oh." She glanced up. "I'm sorry. I haven't fixed anything. I've been busy…"

He opened the door to the freezer. "I'll find something."

She hated that she'd forgotten dinner, but she'd already blown it so she said, "Great! Think you could heat something up for me too?"

To her surprise, he said, "Sure" and gave her a tired smile.

She barely heard the sounds of him opening the boxes of frozen dinners, she was so focused on her research. There were tons of sites with great jobs online. The competition might be fierce, but she was optimistic as she scrolled down page after page of listings.

Ding! The microwave beeped, telling her that their food was ready. Reluctantly, she pulled herself away from the computer and went to sit down at the breakfast bar.

Placing a paper napkin in her lap, she said, "Thank you, daddy."

He dished their dinner onto a pair of paper plates. "No problem. Doesn't seem right you having to do all the cooking all the time. Sometimes, I like to take care of you." Setting her plate in front of her, he brushed the back of his index finger across her nose affectionately.

Something in her stomach settled, making her feel like things might turn out alright after all. "Let me get the silverware," she said, starting to get up.

"No, you just sit there. Let me serve you for a change." He opened a drawer and retrieved a knife and fork for each of them to eat their Salisbury steak dinners.

"If you say so, daddy." She smiled at him.

"I do." He sat next to her and they ate without saying much. Were they

going to talk about the night before or was it going to be the big elephant in the room they were going to ignore? So far, she was okay not discussing it.

After they finished eating, Neal stood up. "I'm beat. I'm going to go take a shower, then I want to talk to you about how you lied to me." There was a sad look in his eyes and Tabitha wanted to crawl under the table for having been dishonest with him. He walked out of the room without another word, and she tossed their paper plates in the trash and disposed of the extra wrappings.

Anxiety flowed through her veins, making her feel like she might just disappear into thin air at any minute. That, or collapse on the floor. She wanted to go curl up in a ball and shut out the world. When had things gotten so complicated?

With a gulp, she realized the moment that everything changed was the moment she fell in love with Neal. From that moment on, she needed to consider him in her decision-making. For every major decision—from what couch they bought to where they were going to live—she needed to think about how he would feel about it, and she hadn't been doing that. Instead, she'd been behaving like a selfish brat, and she felt crappy about it.

She walked into the bedroom just in time to see Neal stepping out of the shower. She was struck for the zillionth time at how heartbreakingly handsome he was. With his straw-colored hair and those piercing gray eyes, his face could have been chiseled from marble with the impressive bone structure he'd inherited. *Would our children have his cheekbones*, she wondered for the first time. Children had always been an abstract idea that was only mildly attractive, but suddenly the notion of growing a mini-Neal inside her seemed appealing.

He let the towel around his waist fall to the floor and to her surprise, he went over to his chest of drawers and pulled out a pair of flannel plaid pajama pants and put them on. Then he went over and sat down on the edge of the bed and patted the spot next to him.

She sat down next to him, and he cupped her chin in his hand. "It breaks my heart that you felt the need to lie to me about your plans to go back to Chicago. I hope you won't go because I love you very much, but right now we need to address your lying to me."

Tears welled up in her eyes. She really was a bad girl. Not just the kind they played like when he spanked her most of the time, but for real. She'd lied to her daddy. The man who loved her with his whole heart and cherished her more than anything.

"Come lie across my knee. I'm going to have to spank you. I don't want to do it, but you have to learn that you cannot treat me that way, Tabitha Jane."

Oh, dear. He'd never used her middle name before. She didn't even remember telling him she had a middle name. In an attempt to be helpful,

she gingerly pushed her sweatpants down over her rump, as she knew that would give him better access to spank her tushy.

He picked up a hairbrush she'd left lying on the bed, and she clutched his calf tightly, bracing herself for her punishment. Why had she left that damned thing on the bed?

Thud! He struck her with the hairbrush. The sensation was less stingy than when he used his hand, but it hurt nonetheless.

Smack! She was glad it was a plastic hairbrush. Something told her wood would hurt worse.

As he continued to spank her, she entwined her arms around his leg, shut her eyes, and thought about all the things she'd done wrong. She'd been a turbo brat—difficult and less than friendly to the people in this community, at least at first.

Thud! Her glute muscles clenched involuntarily.

"Relax," he reminded her, "and it will go easier."

"Yes, sir," she squeaked out.

His swats with the brush were starting to warm the skin on her bottom, but all she could think was that the whole mess was her fault. Neal had moved her here only because he thought it would be better for her health. Maybe he knew best.

Everything he did was to help others, especially her. And she had repaid him with selfishness. Tears fell from her eyes onto the carpet. "I'm sorry, daddy."

Another smack landed on her sit-spot. He was really making sure she'd have a hard time sitting at the computer now. She imagined her ass was plenty red now, as it ached and burned like crazy.

"One more," he said and landed a last blow to her fleshy cheeks.

Then without the caresses to which she was accustomed, he righted her and hugged her close. "Please, Tabitha, don't ever lie to me again. There are lots of things I can forgive, but lying—lying is a deal-breaker."

She felt like someone had removed a trapdoor underneath her and now she was falling, falling, falling. "But daddy, I'm sorry. I'll never do it again."

He kissed the top of her head. "I hope so. Now I've got to get some sleep. Have to be at work early."

With that, he got up and lay down in the bed, set his alarm, and rolled over with his back to her.

A flood of loneliness sank so deep into her, she wanted to wail at the top of her lungs. Instead, she curled up next to him. He didn't move or grab for her hand that was roaming over his chest. Determined for him not to leave her, even if for well-deserved sleep, she reached down between his legs.

He grabbed her by the wrist firmly and placed it back on her side of the bed. "No, princess. This isn't something you can fix with sex. Now let me get some sleep."

Stung, she turned over and cried herself to sleep.

CHAPTER TWELVE

The next morning Neal woke Tabitha up to kiss her good-bye. It didn't mean things were okay between them, but it was a start. Eager to be at the mall when it opened, she showered and dressed quickly. She was so glad Bailey was free. It would be good to catch up on some girl talk with another Little Haven resident.

It only took a few hours for the girls to drive to the mall. It was colossal, bigger than either of them had imagined. It was hard to know where to start, so they found a map and got started. They browsed in Burberry, window-shopped Williams Sonoma, and picked out some sexy surprises for their daddies at Victoria's Secret. By the time they purchased some must-have sweaters at H & M, they were starving.

They decided to treat themselves to the Rainforest Café, and as they ate their lunch amidst the lush foliage, tropical birds, and an Animatron gorilla, their conversation turned to their daddies.

Bailey had been having some problems with her daddy, who had punished her the day before for acting out. Tabitha could see when they sat down that her friend's bottom was sore.

"Is your rear end okay?" Tabitha asked.

Bailey giggled. "It was good enough for me to sit on it during the drive over here, so it will be fine. What's going on between you and Neal?"

"This move is hard. It's taking a toll on me. And this new job of Neal's, he's working all the time, and I'm bored at home."

"You can call me. I get bored too."

Tabitha touched Bailey's hand. "Thanks, I'll do that." It warmed her to know that someone else felt the same way she did, that someone else understood. She took a sip of her drink. "It will be nice to have someone to do things with, to talk to, but I miss my job. I'm used to working."

"Yeah, I can tell."

"I agreed to come here because Neal was worried about my health and he gave me an ultimatum. He said I had to quit my job and move here, or he

was going to walk away."

Bailey's eyes widened. "Really?"

"Yeah. He'd tried everything to get me to cut back. I'd tell him I would, but then it never happened. And last year I spent a couple of weeks in the hospital, which was scary."

Bailey nodded. "That's awful."

"But last night I told him I was going back to work. At my old job."

"You did *what?*"

"Yeah, I never wanted to quit for good. I just took a leave of absence."

Bailey's jaw dropped. "Did Neal know?"

"He does now. I just told him last night."

"No wonder he's so mad."

"Yeah."

"So what are you going to do? You can't leave," Bailey protested. "Just when I found a friend. And didn't you say you were starting to feel more at home in Little Haven?"

Tabitha sighed. "Yes…"

"Plus Neal seems like a super nice guy. It's not easy to find a man like that, especially one who will be a great daddy."

Uncertainty tugged at Tabitha's gut. Bailey was right. She pushed away her French fries.

Suddenly she'd lost her appetite.

• • • • • • •

The two girls didn't arrive home until late. After Tabitha dropped Bailey off at her house, her mind was consumed with her troubles with Neal. She was still lost in thought when she turned onto her street. When she got to the end of the street, she realized she'd missed her house. How had she done that?

She turned around in a neighbor's driveway, and when she did she realized why she'd missed her house—she hadn't recognized it. The house she was used to coming home to every day was now covered from top to bottom with tiny, twinkling holiday lights. Slowly, she drove to the beckoning dwelling and parked in the driveway. As she got out and headed up the walk to the front door, she wondered if she was dreaming.

The house sparkled like something out of a Disney movie. The roofline was outlined along with each of the corners and windows, and mini-icicles hung above her head. Who had done this, she wondered as she fumbled for her keys. Neal had been working nonstop, so he certainly hadn't had time to do it. For a split second she pondered if Little Haven might employ a few spunky elves to make Christmas magic when no one was looking, then she dismissed the notion as ridiculous.

Just as she stuck her key in the door, it opened. She practically fell inside, but Neal caught her by the shoulders. He looked more handsome than ever, wearing a cream-colored fisherman's sweater, one she'd given him for Valentine's Day the year before. It suited him, enhancing his rugged good looks and setting off his blond hair and ruddy complexion.

"Come in, sweetheart. Let's get you warm by the fire." He wrapped an arm around her protectively and led her to the sofa. A roaring fire crackled in the fireplace, and she sat down with a shiver as her body acclimated from the wicked cold outside to the toasty temperature of the room.

"Where are your bags?" he asked. "Surely you didn't go shopping all day only to come home empty-handed."

She laughed. "You're right. The bags are still in the car. I forgot all about them when I saw the lights. Daddy, who did that?"

He looked surprised. "I did."

"But, when? You've been working…" Her voice trailed off.

"True. But today the work I did was for you," he said with the sweep of his hand indicating the front door. "Do you like it?"

The look on his face made her heart lurch. That big, strong, handsome man had worked all day decorating their house just to please her, and now, his need for her to approve was so touching, so raw, that it almost meant more to her than everything he'd done. More than anything in the world, her daddy wanted to please her.

She took his face in her hands, kissed him on the lips, and said, "I love it, daddy. Those are the prettiest lights I've ever seen!"

He chuckled. "Well, I don't know about that, but I'm glad you like it." He pulled her to him and hugged her tight.

She squeezed him back. "When did you get the lights? How did you find time to do it?"

"I've been buying up lights and extension cords ever since we got here. Every time I went to the store I bought some more. I hid them in the garage, since you hardly ever go in there. And I told them I needed a day off, and I took one."

"You haven't been called away on an emergency?" she asked. "No burst pipes or ceilings caving in?"

He shook his head. "Not yet."

"That's a miracle."

"I know. Let me go get your bags for you."

"Okay. Thanks, daddy." He responded by kissing her forehead. Then he took her keys and went out to the car.

Tabitha got up and went into the kitchen to put the teakettle on. She stood there processing the events of the past few days and waited for the water to boil. Moments later, Neal returned with shopping bags hooked over each arm and a few more bags in his arms.

"Now, this is more of what I was expecting."

They laughed. "They had every store imaginable there," she explained.

He winked at her. "I know my girl loves to shop. I'm just glad I didn't have to go."

"What?" she teased. "You'd rather be here, climbing up ladders, risking life and limb to make a pretty light display than go shopping?"

"Uh, yeah!"

"You didn't go on the roof, did you?" She clapped a hand over her mouth. The fact that what he'd been doing might have been dangerous was only now occurring to her.

"Yeah, but it's okay. I went next door and told Agnes if she heard a big thud to come check on me."

Tabitha giggled. "What did she say?"

"She said she would."

The teakettle whistled and Tabitha removed it from the burner and retrieved two mugs from the cupboard. "Want some tea?"

"Sure, thanks, baby girl."

She grinned. He was being so nice to her. Maybe he wasn't angry anymore. Dunking a couple of teabags in their mugs, she filled them with the hot water to steep. "Are you still mad at me?"

He cocked his head. "Baby, I was never mad at you. I just want you to want to be here. With me."

Her face fell. "Daddy, I love you so much. It's not that I don't want to be with you. I do…" She broke off.

He reached out a hand to her. "Come here. There's something else I want you to see."

CHAPTER THIRTEEN

Tabitha placed her hand in Neal's and allowed him to lead her upstairs. "Where are we going?" she asked, glad for the distraction.

"It's a surprise," he said.

At the top of the stairs, the guestroom was to the right, the extra room to the left. Neal placed a hand on the door handle of the room on the left. "Close your eyes and don't open them until I say so."

She shut her eyes, curiosity growing inside her. The door opened with a slight creak and Neal whispered, "Open your eyes."

At first, she wasn't sure what she was seeing. The last time she'd seen this room it was filled with boxes. But now... now it looked like a dream.

In the middle of the room, suspended from the ceiling, a hoop of pink flowers supported a wisp of fine green netting cascading to the floor. On the floor beneath it was a heap of fluffy white comforters interspersed with lavender blankets and pale pink pillows embroidered with gold threads.

The whole room had been strewn with the same tiny lights that flickered outside. Feeling like she'd just crossed over into a fairyland, she turned to Neal. "Daddy, it's amazing! How did you do this? What?"

Neal brightened, and it was clear he wasn't able to contain his excitement. "I've been wanting to do something special for you, Tabitha. You've been such a good sport moving here with me, even when I know you didn't want to. I wanted to show you that it could be nice here, that I would spend as much time as I could making you feel special. I love you so much."

Tabitha jumped up and down and threw her arms around his neck. "This does make me feel so special. Like a fairy princess. It's like a pillow fort, the kind I used to build as a kid, but much, much prettier!"

He laughed. "So you approve." Then he sat down on the floor and pulled her into his lap. She took his top lip between hers and tugged playfully, sucking it into her mouth. He responded by running his tongue along her bottom lip, slipping a hand under her shirt. "I wanted to show you that this, what we have here—us being together—it can be enough."

"Oh, daddy." She ran her hands across his rough, stubbly cheeks, and she inhaled his scent, a mixture of sweat and pine. Her man had been working so hard for her today. He massaged her back and shoulders with one hand and clutched her to him with the other. Their mouths remained locked together in a sensual dance, and she imagined they could stay like this, making out, for hours.

Finally, she pulled away and lifted her sweater over her head. She stared at the twinkling lights all around her, and had the very real sense that all her dreams could come true in this place. Somehow, she'd have to find a way to stay here, with this wonderful man who loved her with all his heart, for she loved him too. And nothing was as important as that love. She would find a new direction, one that incorporated him and their new life here in Little Haven. She was making friends, and how could she possibly think of leaving this place with this magical space he'd created for her? Imagine the slumber parties she could have with the other girls here...

Neal reached up and unfastened her bra, setting her small breasts free. He laid her back onto the comforter and covered her body with his, loving and caressing every inch of her. He removed her jeans and his own clothes so that they lay in the makeshift bed on the floor, naked except for her knee-socks. She hooked her legs behind his knees, urging him to enter her, but he moved up toward her head.

"Does my baby girl need something to suck on?"

She made her eyes big and fluttered her lashes as she nodded. "Yes, sir, daddy."

He stroked his cock and straddled her face, his knees in front of her shoulders. Dipping the head to her mouth, he murmured, "Take this in your mouth."

She opened wide and took him between her lips. He pushed himself to the back of her throat. "That's it. Take care of daddy the way daddy takes care of you." She relaxed and let him fuck her face. He chose a slow and leisurely pace, so they could both relish the sensations. Tabitha had always loved taking him in her mouth.

Then he withdrew and wiped the end of his cock across her hungry lips, jerking himself a few times until thick ropes of cum spewed out the end of his cock onto her face. Then, like an artist, he aimed it at her breasts like it was a paintbrush and she was his canvas.

She moaned as he marked her as his, arching her back, weak with lust, happy to be his little toy.

"Whose little girl are you?" he asked.

"Yours, daddy. All yours."

He swiped a finger across her chest, scooping up a ribbon of semen. "Let's clean you up," he said, offering the shiny white liquid on his finger up to her mouth. She sucked his finger sensuously, licking away the sticky

substance and swallowing it.

Wiping a finger across her cheek, he captured the rest of his cum, and she sucked it from his finger. "All clean, daddy?"

"Yes, you did a good job, baby girl." He picked up his underwear off the floor and wiped her down with it.

"Thank you," she beamed.

"I love these socks on you," he said, indicating her Neapolitan socks with the pink, white, and brown stripes on them. "They remind me of ice cream. They make me want to eat you all up." He knelt between her knees. "Open," was all he had to say and she parted her legs, then he bent his head to kiss the insides of her thighs.

He teased her with his mouth, giving her shivers of anticipation as he nipped and nuzzled the tender skin of her inner thighs and her mound. Making a point with the end of his tongue, he traced the outer bands of her labia, making her strain and ache for him to touch it to her core. Finally, he gave in, providing her a delicious reprieve from his teasing tongue. Delightfully experienced, he made it flat when he lapped at the length of her, then made a point when he reached her apex, perfect for torturing the little head of her sex. He swirled circles around it, dragging his nose across it. She'd long since slammed her eyes shut and now she thrashed her head from side to side, screaming, "Daddy! Yes, daddy!"

Coming up for air, he ordered, "Tell me what you want." It made her uncomfortable to verbalize her desire for sex, and he knew it, but he'd explained that his purpose in having her do it was two-fold. Good communication was key in helping him be able to satisfy her sexually. He needed her to use her words to tell him what she liked, what was working. There was also the humiliation factor. Making her admit aloud her sexual needs made her feel slightly embarrassed and that turned her on. On some level she felt reduced to an almost animalistic being discussing her most basic needs, but it never ceased to thrill her.

He licked her again with short little whips of the tongue, and she wriggled with pleasure underneath him. "Lick me like that, daddy. I want you to fuck me with your mouth. Please suck my little clit. Mmm," she exclaimed, her body revving up for an exquisite orgasm.

"Such a good girl for daddy," he murmured before returning to eat her pussy. She dug her heels into his back and tweaked her nipples, grinding her hips up against his chin.

"Damn, you taste so good, baby," he said, lapping up her juices.

"Thank you, daddy."

When he glanced up and saw her playing with her breasts, he pushed her hands aside. His fingers clamped down on her nipples and he increased the pressure of his tongue on her cunt.

He developed a rhythm with his mouth and once he added the twisting

and tweaking of her nipples, she felt the zinging of fireworks begin to go off in her extremities, a signal she was about to come.

Just a little bit more…

He continued to work his mouth and fingers on her until she drifted into a sea of orgasms, swell after swell of rapturous joy crashed over her, ebbing then flowing, the thrill so intense she thought she might pass out. And as soon as she thought it was over, he'd change the pace slightly and soon she'd find herself shaking with another round of bliss.

When she finally stopped shaking, he scooped her up and kissed her full on the mouth, allowing her to taste herself on him. Her juices covered his face and he looked so pleased with himself for making her come so hard and so many times.

"You really are good at that, daddy," she said. The act was so intimate, and it had taken her a long time to become comfortable with receiving it, but now she knew there was nothing quite as incredible as when he gave her multiple orgasms with his mouth. That came from love, and pure devotion.

He stretched out on the floor and she curled her body up around him, resting a leg on top of his. They lay in silence until their breathing returned to normal and she said, "You know what I just realized, daddy?"

"What, my darling princess?"

"We forgot our tea." She giggled, and he kissed her and pulled her to him again.

CHAPTER FOURTEEN

That night Tabitha couldn't sleep, so she went to the computer and started filling out online applications and sending out resumes. She was determined to find a job where she could work and live in Little Haven.

The next morning when Neal trudged down at five a.m., she was still at her computer.

"What are you doing up so early?" He yawned.

"Well, I'm applying for a job. Several actually." She popped up out of her chair and poured him a cup of coffee from her second pot.

"You're what? I thought you wanted to go back to Chicago." He scratched his head.

"I did, but I can't do that now, daddy. Not if I can find something to do here." She hooked her arms around his waist and burrowed her face in his neck, inhaling the sexy, woodsy way he smelled.

He wrapped her in his arms. "I'm glad you told me, baby. I was thinking about giving them my notice."

"Here?"

He nodded.

"But you love Little Haven! You said it yourself. It's like home to you."

A big sigh escaped his lips. "True, but I love you more, my little princess." He kissed the top of her head. "If you were to go back to Chicago, I would have to go with you, my love. Even if it meant holding the hand of my precious girl in the hospital half of the year."

She leaned back to stare him in the eyes. "I won't do that, daddy. I know how much you care about me, and I'm going to listen to you better from now on. I promise."

"That's a good girl," he said, patting her rear end. "Now, what are you never going to do again?"

"Lie to daddy," she said, making her eyes big so that he knew she understood the gravity of her words.

"Or to anyone. Lying is bad. It makes people feel like they can't trust

you," he said with a reproving stare.

"I know, daddy. I'm sorry." She hung her head, and he tilted her chin up so he could kiss her lips.

"Everyone makes mistakes, sweetheart. Let's just say—no more lying."

"Yes, sir, daddy."

He hugged her close, then let her go to take a sip of his coffee. "How much of this did you drink?"

"A lot," she said, her head bobbing enthusiastically.

"Okay, then you're probably going to crash later. Be sure you do get some rest."

"Alright, daddy. You know best," she said and kissed him on the cheek before returning to her posts at the computer.

• • • • • • •

Tabitha didn't fall asleep until 4 p.m. after she'd sent in sixteen resumes and set up one Skype job interview for the next day. When she finally woke up, she was on the couch with a blanket covering her.

It was 9:00 the next morning.

There was a note on the coffee table from Neal. It read simply: "*I love you.*"

Her heart fluttered, and she knew she was doing the right thing. She couldn't imagine feeling more loved and cherished than Neal made her feel. She should email her boss and tell him she wasn't coming back. He'd likely find that out if some of these potential job sites called him for a reference anyway.

Looking at the time, she realized she had to rush if she wanted to prepare for her Skype interview. She jumped into the shower and dressed in her favorite work-casual blouse and sat down at the computer ready for work.

It was a good feeling. One she realized she could get used to.

After checking her email, she set up another two interviews for later in the day. Then she took a deep breath, plastered a smile on her face, and answered the incoming Skype call.

CHAPTER FIFTEEN

That evening when Neal came home from work, she met him at the door with a bottle of champagne and two glasses.

The corners of his mouth stretched from ear to ear. "Does this mean what I think it means?"

She nodded, flashing him a grin of her own. "That your little girl got a big girl job today."

"You did?" He picked her up and twirled her around. "Tell me all about it."

Giggling, she squealed, "I will if you put me down." Secretly, she was thrilled with his enthusiasm.

"Okay, okay. I'll open up this bubbly, and you start talking. I want to hear everything." She handed him the bottle, and he started to remove the cork seal.

Pop! The cork flew across the room and they both laughed festively.

"It's a good job. You know how before I mostly traded in grain futures?"

"Yeah," he said, though a clueless mask covered his face, the way it always did when she talked about her job. Probably the same glazed look that came over her face when he started talking about carburetors and head gaskets.

"Well, anyway, in this job I will be buying and trading grain futures for a cereal company."

He poured them both a glass and handed one to her. "Get out."

"No, I'm serious. And the best part is—they have an office in Minneapolis. But I only have to go there a couple of times a month. Most of the work I can do from home."

"Baby, that's amazing. And it's less stress?"

"Well," she hedged. "Trading futures is kinda stressful, that's the nature of it. But it's not on the trading floor. That part will be less stressful." She flipped her hair behind her shoulder. "And I'll be here with you so you can make sure I'm not too stressed."

"Yeah, my workload should settle down after the holidays and then I can

spend more time keeping an eye on you."

The idea of staying here, making a home with Neal, had begun to grow on her. She took a sip of champagne and said, "I want to do something fun to celebrate!"

He raised an eyebrow at her suggestively. "That can be arranged."

But she waved him off with a hand. "Let's make snow angels!"

"In the dark?"

She shook her head. "It's not so dark anymore with all the lights you put out there."

"Hmm. I guess you're right. But it's going to be cold," he warned.

She gave him her sassiest over-the-shoulder look. "Then maybe you can run us a hot bath for when we're done."

His eyes lit up. "Be right back." He bolted toward the master bathroom.

Tabitha took another sip of the champagne, savoring how the bubbles tickled her throat as she swallowed. She started bundling herself in all her winter gear—hat, coat, boots, scarf, and mittens so that by the time Neal returned, she felt like the Michelin man.

Neal laughed. "I see you're all ready to go." He grabbed his coat and opened the door for her. "After you," he said. "And don't let me forget I've got that water running."

"Yes, sir," she said with a salute. The champagne made her feel silly, and tonight she felt like a weight had been lifted off her shoulders.

Taking a few steps away from the house in the front yard, she plopped to the ground and lay on her back. "Oooh! This is cold. I can feel it through my jacket."

Neal came and lay down beside her. "You're the one who wanted to do this…"

"I know." She splayed her legs out wide and thrashed her arms up and down, then clapped her legs together like closing a pair of scissors.

Neal did the same. "You know, this is fun. I haven't done this in years."

"Me either. It's fun!" She rolled onto her side to kiss him.

"You're going to mess up your snow angel," he warned.

"I don't care. I want to kiss you."

He pressed his lips to hers, and folded an arm around her, pulling her close. She tasted the champagne on his breath and luxuriated in his warm wet mouth, so hungry for her. But there were too many layers of clothes between them. She couldn't feel any of his sexy body through all those coats and sweaters.

"Let me take you inside and give you a sensual bath," he whispered in her ear.

"Yes, daddy. I'd like that." She bit her lip in anticipation and he stood up and offered her a hand. She took it and let him pull her to her feet. "Thanks for doing that with me," she said, looking back at their snow angels. They

were somewhat botched by them rolling together in the snow, but it looked like two angels kissing and that made it even better.

He shooed her inside and locked the front door behind them. "Go check on the water while I get us a fire started."

"Sounds good," she said and went to find the bathtub was about half full.

Returning to give him the water report, she saw Neal bending over a fledgling fire, and ran her tongue across her lips as she admired his divinely rounded butt cheeks. "Almost ready, daddy," she sang.

He turned to look at her. "My, my, but you are beautiful." Throwing another log on the fire, he set the screen back in front of it and crossed the room to her. "Go back there," he said, pointing. "I'm going to take those clothes off you."

She squealed with delight and ran back to the bedroom with him following close behind. He stopped her in the doorway between the bedroom and the bathroom and removed her coat, then he removed his clothes down to his underwear while she kicked off her boots and accessories. Lifting her sweater over her head, he planted kisses across her collarbone as he unbuttoned her pants and helped her wriggle out of them.

Finally, she stood in only her baby blue bra and panties. "Stay here," he commanded. Then he walked over the tub and added a few drops of silky pink liquid.

"Oooh! A bubble bath, yay! Daddy, I love bubble baths."

He arched a brow. "I know, and I want to give my little princess a good bath. Get her all clean, make her feel so good. Now take off the rest of those clothes and come here to daddy."

She unhooked her bra and tossed it aside, then slid her panties to the floor. She always felt self-conscious when she stood naked in front of Neal, but the way he looked at her with lust in his eyes made her feel so desired, so adored, that she became aroused herself.

When she took a step toward him, he stopped her with the palm of his hand. With a devilish grin, he said, "No, no. Daddy wants you to crawl."

Her breath caught in her throat. There was something so raw and primal about getting on all fours, especially naked. She felt a spike of desire in her pussy, and she knew his request was making her wet, ready for whatever else he had in mind.

"Yes, sir." Dropping to her knees, she placed one hand on the floor, then another and slowly started moving forward. His eyes remained fixed on hers as she crawled toward him. With each step the connection between them strengthened. The power differential was never more apparent than when he ordered her to her knees, and she complied. It was a demonstration of her submission and his dominance over her, and she gave herself over to him completely: body, heart, and soul.

"Good girl," he said. When she reached him, he helped her up and into

the bath. The bubbly water warmed her chilled skin. "Lie back and get comfortable," he said, getting up to fetch an armful of towels. He brought over a washrag and knelt down beside her on the outside of the tub. Propping his elbows on the side, he dipped the rag in the water, squirted soap onto it, and began to scrub her back.

"Mmm, daddy, that feels good," she purred.

"You like that?" he asked.

"Yes," she said, holding up her arms, subtly suggesting that he clean her front as well.

Picking up on the hint, he rubbed the washcloth over her underarms, then soaped up her chest with it. The texture of the rag combined with the slick feel of the suds made her nipples harden into pink little rosebuds jutting from her body in a show of arousal.

"Yes, that's what I like to see. Look at those pretty little breasts of yours, all clean and excited for daddy."

She bit her lip and nodded, proud that she could please him just by becoming aroused, a state she had no trouble attaining while he was present, and especially when he was playing with her.

"Let's see what else needs cleaning." He swiped the soapy rag over all the parts of her body that were above water, then dunked it under the water and started to wipe across her inner thighs. "Spread your legs for daddy," he growled in her ear. His words made her heart race and her legs fall open. How she wanted him then. Wanted him to jump into the tub and pierce her with his cock right then, but instead he teased her, putting his fingers to work sliding the bar of soap along her crotch, working it up and down her folds. Lifting her hips toward his fingers, she whimpered with need and he bent his head and suckled her nipple.

"Damn, you're irresistible," he said, setting the bar of soap on the side of the tub. "I think you're clean, but I have to be sure." He inserted two fingers in her quivering cunt and fucked her with them, fast enough to cause the water to ripple. She bucked her hips to meet his hand, until he said, "Hold still for daddy." Then she tried her best to remain still, but it was difficult to fight the urge to push back. She yearned for more. She wanted his cock inside her.

Ignoring her discomfort, or possibly enjoying it, he continued finger banging her, and when he added his thumb to the dance, flicking it over her clit, she convulsed with need. "Yes, daddy! Please don't stop."

"I won't," he whispered, and the sexy tone in his voice drove her over the edge. He toyed with her clit and kept fucking her through every tremor of her orgasm. Her arms flailed, reaching for him, and he caught her up with his free hand.

"Kiss me," she begged and he captured her mouth with his, invading it the way he had her pussy, hard and rough, a take-no-prisoners kiss from the

outset.

When her body calmed, he removed his fingers from her and brought them to her mouth. Shifting in the tub, she maneuvered herself onto her knees facing him, all the time sucking his fingers.

He took back his thumb and said, "If baby wants something to suck on, daddy's got a big, hard cock ready to go right down that pretty little throat of yours." He dropped his underwear to the floor, revealing a rock-hard erection protruding, right at her eye-level.

Still dazed in the afterglow of her climax, Tabitha nodded dreamily and parted her lips for him. He entered her mouth slowly, inch by inch, pulling back then thrusting forward, allowing her to wet him with her saliva bit by bit. He placed his hands on the sides of her head and pushed deep inside until he bumped the back of her throat. When she gurgled and gagged, he eased back a bit and pinched her nipples.

He withdrew, saying, "Get on your hands and knees and scoot to the front of the tub." Climbing in behind her, he fingered her wet little slit, then entered her swiftly, sheathing himself to the hilt with one stroke, making her cry out with the delight of being filled. "Daddy!"

"Yes, baby girl. Scream my name. I want to hear you." He pumped his cock into her, and she milked him with the muscles of her pussy walls.

"Please! Fuck me, daddy!" she begged, and he held onto her hips and gave her the fucking she asked for, the fucking she craved. He slapped her ass, slinging water all over the bathroom, but it didn't matter. She caught a glimpse of herself in the distorted reflection of the faucet, and it turned her on even more. He rocked her cunt hard, with his cock pounding and pummeling inside her.

After the onslaught of his hard fucking abated, Neal slipped out of her and lay back in the tub. "Straddle me," he ordered her.

Tired, but eager for more, Tabitha turned and shifted so that her body was atop his. She looked into his eyes and saw the love she felt for him reflected there.

"Fuck me," he said, his gaze never leaving hers. The intensity of their connection burned into her soul and his steel-gray eyes made her want to weep with the purity of passion and emotion she saw in them. She would never find any*thing* or any*one* she would love as much as she loved this man.

With a groan, she impaled herself onto his cock and rode him at a deliberate pace. She ground her hips against his, rolling herself onto him so that her clit rubbed against his pelvic bone, sending her into spasms again. He took one of her breasts between his lips and nibbled delicately on the sensitive tip while he jolted her from underneath with rapid-fire strokes, quick and powerful like a jackhammer. She fell to the side, but he caught her and held her up as he fucked her like a machine until he emptied himself inside her, and she collapsed into his arms.

For several long moments, he stroked her hair and held her close. "I love you, princess. I need you to be with me."

She looked up at him. "I love you too, daddy, and I will stay with you." She threaded her fingers in his, holding up their entwined hands. "Always."

He kissed her on the nose and echoed back, "Always."

THE END

63431372R00220

Made in the USA
Lexington, KY
06 May 2017